Broken Bones

ALSO BY TANIA CARVER

BRENNAN AND ESPOSITO
Book 1: Little Bones
Book 2: In Her Bones
Book 3: Cage of Bones
Book 4: Broken Bones

BROKEN BONES

TANIA
CARVER

JOFFE BOOKS

Revised edition 2025
Joffe Books, London
www.joffebooks.com

First published as Choked by *Sphere* in Great Britain in 2012

This paperback edition was first published
in Great Britian in 2025

Cover art by Nebojša Zorić

ISBN: 978-1-80573-228-0

PROLOGUE: THE PASSOVER LAMB

1

He opened his eyes. Stood up slowly. He hurt. Everything hurt.

He looked round. Took it all in. And knew what he needed.

A gun.

He knew where there was one. A double-barrelled shotgun, kept for bagging rabbits and clay pigeons.

But not today.

The locked cabinet where it was kept was simple to open. He held the gun in his hand, felt the weight, the heft of it, like he was balancing it against what it was capable of. Or had been capable of.

He took his eyes off the barrels and surveyed the room. The house had been wrecked. The furniture had always been carefully positioned, regularly cleaned. He could remember being told off for playing on it when he was younger. The antiques had been out of bounds. He was never to touch them, or else. The drumming-in of the consequences of such an act was one of his earliest memories of life in the house. He had grown up too terrified to do so. If one of his hands had accidentally brushed against a vase or a porcelain figurine, he had gone to bed that night in abject fear of some terrible but unspecified punishment.

But all that was now gone. Replaced by carnage.

The furniture was overturned, glass-fronted cabinets smashed, upholstery ripped open. The antiques lay shattered all around, giving each room a new, shard-sharp carpet.

Something caught his eye. A vase, upright, sitting on the plinth it had always occupied in the corner. The last remaining antique. He crossed to it, reached out and touched it softly. Caressed it, stroked it like it was the only remnant from the old days, his old life. But he'd forgotten the shotgun balanced in the crook of his other arm. He brought it round too quickly. It connected with the vase. Hard. And the vase fell, shattering on the parquet flooring, rippling out in thousands of tiny porcelain fractals, making his ears ring.

He backed away quickly. Felt fragments crunch under his feet; felt that childhood terror once more. Someone or something would get him for this. He would be punished in some way.

He turned, fled the room. Looking for peace, respite.

But it was the same in all the others. Same carnage, same destruction.

Same dead bodies.

That was what he had been avoiding. Too scared to look. Blanking them out. All of them. Because he knew who each of them was. Or had been. The man he had called his father. The girl he had called his sister. The boy he had called his brother. And his mother.

His mother . . .

Now they were nothing. Just leavings in a stinking abattoir. Their blood and insides smearing and decorating the walls, ceilings and floors. He could plot their pathways, the journeys from room to room to avoid the gun. Running. Shrieking. Grabbing at antiques — carefully collected and collated antiques, expensive antiques — throwing them, hearing them shatter. Pulling over sofas, chaises, hiding futilely behind them. Knowing that nothing they did, said or could do would stop the gun from firing. From tearing them apart.

From tearing apart the people he had come to call his family.

He felt tired, as if suddenly coming down from an adrenalin high. He yawned. The shotgun felt like an extra, heavy limb in his arms. Or a sleeping baby. He trudged round the house, eyes seeing yet not seeing.

His mother.

His mother . . .

Up and down stairs. In and out of every room. Over and over. Nothing changed. Nothing moved. Outside, it grew dark. The sun sank over the hedges. He didn't turn on any lights, didn't notice. Shadows accumulated. His feet, and what was under his feet, made the only sound. Eventually he came again to the main room. The drawing room, as the girl he had been told to call sister insisted on it being referred to. In here was worst. Even more so than he remembered it the first time.

This was where most of his family had ended up. Hunted down, the shotgun taking them out like rabbits in the field, clay discs in the sky.

His mother had made it to the fireplace. Twilight shadows falling from the huge side window turned her body into a misshapen sack, of offal and bone, cloth and hair. He felt even more tired, more numb inside. He knelt over her body, meaning to stroke her hair, move it away from her face, her sightless eyes. His fingers touched wet sponge. He pulled them back, looked at them. The darkness of the room rendered her blood black.

He wanted to cry, but he was beyond tears.

He moved away from her, pulled a small footstool to the wall, sat down on it. Took in the room once more. Everything wrecked. Lives. Futures. Including his.

He sighed. I should be pleased, he thought. Because this is all mine now. No more arguments, no more whispering behind hands, saying things about me behind my back. No more telling me what to do. Making me feel small. Hurting me. Making me do things I don't want to do. Telling me I can't touch things when the rest of them can. When the girl who's supposed to be my sister can. No more. No more.

He looked at the shotgun. Felt emotions build within him that he couldn't even name. He sat there, breathing hard, his skin prickling and hot as though he had developed some virus, the room dancing before his eyes like the prelude to a migraine.

The emotions swam within him, whirling round and round, faster and faster, engulfing him.

No more.

No more.

He moved the shotgun out of the crook of his arm. Felt the slow, painful release of his elbow muscles where he had held it for so long, a rusty gate being unlocked.

He stretched his arms out fully, the shotgun in his right hand. Head still swirling, he placed the barrel against the underside of his chin, felt the cold metal against his hot skin. Put the stock between his thighs. Brought them together. Wrapped both his thumbs round the triggers. Closed his eyes.

No more . . .

'Can I just suggest something?'

He stopped. Opened his eyes.

'If you're going to do it, at least do it properly.'

2

He jumped, startled at the sudden sound. He had believed himself alone in the house. The only one there. The only living one there, anyway.

'It's the wrong way round.' A finger pointed at the shotgun. 'You're holding it the wrong way round.'

He looked down at his own fingers. The trigger guard was pointing outwards, away from him. That was the easiest way, he had thought, to bring his two index fingers down on the triggers. A sure way of making certain he didn't miss.

'Like *Village of the Damned*.'

Puzzled, he didn't reply.

'*Village of the Damned*,' the intruder said again, voice edged with exasperation. 'The film. With the spooky blond kids. Old one. Black and white.'

He still said nothing.

'Oh, you must have seen it. Remember?'

He couldn't process fast enough, couldn't keep up. The house. The people he called his family. The intruder. And now the things the intruder was saying to him. Prattle. White noise in his head. His brain felt like it moved seconds after his head did.

'Anyway, there's this scene in the film. This farmer's done something to upset the kids. And they make him kill himself. Point his own shotgun at himself. He does it that way.' The intruder pointed at his hands. 'The way you're holding it.'

He looked down again. Took his fingers away, suddenly self-conscious.

'I mean, it's all right, as ways go. But there's too much margin for error. Too many things that can go wrong. Your finger could slip. You could miss. The shot could just take your jaw off, miss your brain completely. You'd still be alive, but you'd be a hell of a mess. Is that what you want?'

The intruder stared at him. Scrutinised him. He felt embarrassed, looked away.

Still saying nothing.

He looked down at the gun once more. He could pick it up, point it, pull the triggers . . . the intruder would be gone. Simple. Easy. One little finger twitch. One loud noise. One dead intruder.

And one hero.

The intruder turned back to him and smiled. He looked away, couldn't hold the gaze. It was like the other man could tell what he had been thinking.

'If you're going to do it, turn it round, stick it in your mouth. Right the way back and up. So you're choking on it, gagging. Then pull. That's the way.' Doing the actions all the while. 'Or didn't you really want to do it?'

He realised he was being asked a direct question. Felt it demanded an answer. An honest one.

'I . . . I don't . . . don't know . . .'

The intruder smiled, like that was the expected answer. 'Thought so. Never mind.' A sigh. '*Village of the Damned*. Interesting. Based on the John Wyndham novel, *The Midwich Cuckoos*. Ever read it?'

He said nothing.

'No. Didn't take you for much of a reader. Should give it a go. Very interesting.' The intruder laughed. It wasn't a pleasant sound. 'Especially for you. Cuckoos are a bit of a thing with you, aren't they?'

Again he said nothing.

The intruder looked away from him, surveying the damage. 'What a mess. What a real . . . blooming . . . mess.' He turned back. 'And no questions. You haven't even asked who I am or what I'm doing here. Not curious?'

He opened his mouth, but no words came out. His head, his heart had stopped functioning. He no longer knew what to think or feel.

The intruder laughed. 'I'm your Jiminy Cricket, of course.' Another laugh. 'The voice of your conscience. Your imaginary little friend. Like Pinocchio had. Remember him? Surely you can remember him. The little wooden boy who wanted to be real. Wanted to fit in. Sound familiar?'

He looked round the room. Saw bodies that were now just lumps in the darkness. Indistinguishable from the overturned, destroyed furniture.

'Thought so.'

The intruder sat down on the floor next to him.

'You can put the gun down now. You're not going to use it. Either on me or yourself.'

He did as he was told. Placed it carefully on the wooden floor.

'Good.' The intruder looked at it. Made no attempt to pick it up. Nodded. 'Good. So, what we going to do with you, eh?'

'What . . . what d'you mean?'

'Well, we can't just leave you sitting here like this, can we? Or can we?'

'I . . . I don't know. I . . . hadn't thought about it . . .'

'Of course you hadn't thought about it. That would call for forward planning. Thinking ahead. But that's not Pinocchio's job, that's Jiminy Cricket's, isn't it?'

He said nothing. Instead he saw a brief mental image of the two characters in the Disney film, walking down a road, singing and dancing. It was false, untrue, but they both looked happy. In fact it looked so false it seemed attainable. He smiled.

'That's it . . . you know what I'm talking about. Smart boy. Now this . . .' another expansive gesture, 'is a mess. A mess that needs sorting. And with me beside you, it will be sorted. If you want me to, that is.'

His head was still all over the place. He couldn't process, couldn't compute what had happened, what was there in front of him. He couldn't work out how from him walking in the door of the house — of his home — feeling angry and bullied, self-pitying and wronged, feeling like he wanted to say his piece, get things straightened out, get everything sorted . . . how everything had gone from that to . . . He looked round the room again. To . . . this.

'All right,' he said, turning once more to the intruder. 'Help me.'

'I think this is the beginning of a beautiful friendship. Know where that's from?' The intruder laughed.

It left a cold, ringing echo round the blood-black walls.

PART ONE: A BLOODY GOOD FRIDAY

3

It should have been the happiest time of her life. But it had turned into the worst.

Marina Esposito opened her eyes slowly. Shock flooded her system. She couldn't believe what she was seeing. She gradually pushed herself up on to her elbows, trying to blink away the images before her. Failing.

It was as if she had gone to sleep and woken up in some hellish post-apocalyptic landscape. The cottage, the garden behind it, the stretch of Suffolk coastline before it, had all gone. The comforting, safe rural environment replaced by ruins, flames.

She tried to pull herself into a sitting position, willed her mind to catch up with her body's movements, but felt nothing but blankness in her head. It was too much to process, like she had just woken up and dragged a nightmare with her into the day. But she felt the heat on her face, her skin, the dust in her eyes. The gravel of the pathway she was lying on painfully imprinted on her hands and arms, her face. And she knew, subconsciously, that it must be real.

She blinked again, trying to corral her mind into some kind of rational order, to remember what had happened, why she was there.

The cottage where they had all been staying. The . . .

She looked at the blazing ruin before her and realised that that was the cottage.

'Oh God . . .'

She dragged herself slowly to her feet, ignoring the painful gravel rash, the grazed skin, her head spinning. Adrenalin began to pump round her system. She felt her heart speeding up, tripping along faster than her chest could contain it. She stood on unsteady legs, swaying, looking at the burning cottage before her. Slowly, as though her legs were made from concrete, she made her way towards it, crunching on gravel and shingle, breathing heavily through her mouth, her mind racing to catch up with her body.

A few days away before returning to work. That was all it had been. After the wedding and the honeymoon. Just herself, Phil and his parents.

And their three-year-old daughter.

'No . . . oh no, oh fuck, no . . .'

She looked again at the burning ruin before her, walked quicker.

Spending Easter in Suffolk. Aldeburgh, on the coast. Snape Maltings music festival nearby, a large stretch of beach, pubs and restaurants. A way of saying thank you to Don and Eileen for looking after Josephina.

And now this.

Marina was almost running in her haste to get there. She looked at the cottage, tried to make out shapes, called for her family.

'Phil . . . Phil . . . oh God . . . Eileen, Don . . .'

Nothing. Her only reply the sound of the flames, intensifying as she got nearer.

Her heart was ready to break through her ribcage.

There was a blazing car in front of the cottage. Marina didn't recognise it. Not theirs. Not Don and Eileen's. She dismissed it from her mind, kept going, moving towards the cottage. She hadn't realised how far away she had been.

Part of her mind was asking the question: why was she not in the cottage? Why wasn't she with the rest of them? Another part of her mind dismissed it. More important things to do. More important questions to answer.

She heard voices behind her, becoming louder. She ignored them. Heard footsteps running towards her. Ignored them too. Staying focused on the cottage. Moving towards it. Her world narrowed down to that burning ruin. To saving her family.

She had almost reached the car when she was grabbed from behind.

'Get away from there! You mental?'

She shook the hands off her, kept going. They grabbed her again.

'It's not safe, you'll be killed. Come on . . .'

The hands pulled her back, stopped her from moving forward, separating her from her family.

She tried to shake them off again, but they gripped harder.

'Please, stay back . . . see sense . . .'

Desperation and adrenalin gave her strength. She turned, saw a man about her own age, concern and fear in his eyes, his hands grappling with her shoulders. She shook him off, broke free from his grasp.

As she reached the car, she felt the heat on her face and body. It was so bright it forced her eyes to close, so powerful it knocked her back like a physical presence. She squinted through the flames. Tried to make out anyone else. Reality rippled through the heat haze.

She heard the man's voice behind her once more.

'Get back! The car's going to . . .'

She felt hands on her body, the sensation of being pushed roughly to the ground. Then a sudden burst of searing heat, like she was being devoured by a miniature sun, accompanied by a sound so loud it must have shattered her eardrums.

Then nothing.

Just blackness.

4

They had given him his own curtains. That was something. Curtains and a window. But not a view. That was asking too much.

That didn't stop him staring out of it, though. Staring and thinking. Some days that was all he did, because he had nothing else to do. Just stare and think. There wasn't much to look at. Sometimes he counted the pigeons. Tried to identify them by their markings. Individualise them. Anthropomorphise them even, give them names, assign character traits. That was when he knew he had been staring too long. He would be dressing them up in little waistcoats next. So instead he would sit on the bed, turn his attention inwards rather than outwards.

He would think about things he had read in books, the pencilled notes he had made in the margins. The books now sat permanently on his shelf. He didn't take them down much any more. He had looked at them so often, he had memorised the bits he liked. The important bits.

One of the main things he thought about was time. It occupied his mind a lot, and he had read plenty of books on it, with all sorts of theories. How it wasn't a straight line.

How it twisted, stretched. How sometimes it seemed short but was actually long. How it would loop in on itself. How it could fool you into thinking it was one thing when it was really another.

He applied the things he had read to his own life, his own situation. The way it seemed short but was actually long. Although most days it was the opposite, seeming long but actually short. No, not most days: all days. And nights. The nights were worse than the days.

Because he kept having the same dream, over and over, night after night. For years, since he had first arrived. He would dream his own death. And it was always a slow death. Cancer, MS, Aids, something like that. Something he couldn't stop, couldn't cure. Parts of him would be taken away, bit by bit. His body would become a cage, with him trapped inside. Sometimes it took everything away and left only his voice. A small, weak voice screaming silently within. Ignored. Unheard.

When he woke up, the dream would still be with him, clinging, convincing him he was dead. He would have to force himself to believe he was alive. Then he would lie in the dark, hearing the groans and cries from beyond his door, and think about being dead. His body rotted, his mind dissipated. No longer existing. No thoughts, no life, no memories. Just nothing.

And then he would feel more alone than he had ever believed a human being could feel.

Eventually morning would come and another day would start: the same as the last one, the same as the next. Dragging a greater piece of the dream with him every time he woke, barely existing until he existed no more, until he eventually became nothing.

Now he was just a collection of memories. And memories, he knew, were as reliable as time. If you told someone a table was a chair and you told them long enough and loud enough, they would eventually believe you. And that was what had happened to his memories. They had told him what he had done. What had caused it. What had happened as a result. And even though he hadn't believed them and had fought against them, pitted his own memories against theirs, theirs had been stronger and theirs had won. It had taken years, but eventually he had accepted what they said as truth. That their memories were his. That he had done what they said he had done.

It had been easier once he had let them implant their events into his mind. They had started to be nicer to him, talked about letting him go. Time might even have speeded up. But it may have just been time playing tricks on him once again.

Or not. Because the day had come. And it was today. No more staring at the curtains. No more sitting in his room with his memorised books, dreaming of living death.

He would be out. He would be free.

They all told him it was a good thing. That it must be what he wanted. And he had agreed with them. Because that was what they wanted to hear. And if they were pleased, he was pleased.

He heard keys in the door. Stood up. Stared straight ahead, at the wall. The door opened and two of them entered. One of them smiling.

'Going home today, eh?' the smiling one said.

He wanted to say *I am home*, but knew better. Instead he nodded.

Smiler laughed. 'Won't know what to do with yourself.'

Knowing a response was expected, he returned the laugh. 'Bet I will.'

Smiler laughed again.

'Get your things, then, come on,' the other one said, yawning.

He knew their names and had even used them sometimes. But he would forget them as soon as he left. Because he wouldn't need them any more.

He gave one last look round his cell. His home. He took in the curtains, the memorised books and the toiletries. 'There's nothing I want here,' he said.

'Suit yourself, then.'

He followed them out.

The door clanged shut behind them.

He walked off the wing, down the corridor and towards the gate, trying to think of the future and not the past. Hoping time wouldn't play tricks any more and that a table would become a table again and not a chair.

Trying not to feel death in his every step.

5

Marina opened her eyes. She tried to focus, but there was too much light in the room, too much brightness. She closed her eyes to block it out, then opened them again, slowly this time.

She saw curtains. Thin, patterned in a style she couldn't identify. She looked round. She was in a small room. No, not a room, a cubicle. There was a beige wall with a small sink against it. She looked down and realised she was on a hospital stretcher. For a few seconds her consciousness floated adrift from her memory, then the two came crashing together. She jerked upright.

The cottage . . . the fire . . .

'Whoa, hey, it's OK . . .'

She felt hands on her shoulders. Firm, not harsh. Not forcing her down, just holding her in place.

'Where am I?'

'Ipswich General. A and E.'

The voice sounded familiar. Warm and friendly. Another thought hit her. 'Phil, where's Phil . . . ?'

'It's OK,' said the voice again.

Marina focused, managed to look at the face of the speaker. She made out dark skin and lightened hair, a denim jacket and a T-shirt. Her friend and work colleague, Detective Constable Anni Hepburn.

'Anni . . . what—'

'Just lie back, Marina. Lie back.'

Marina didn't want to do so, but she trusted her friend. She looked at Anni's face once more. Her features were taut, drawn. No trace of the usual good humour there.

'What's happened? Where's Phil? Josephina?'

'Just . . . just take a minute. Just . . . relax, yeah?' Anni didn't seem to know what to say.

Marina picked up on the unease and tried to sit up once more. Her bones ached and pain cranked through her body. She lay back down again.

'What's happened? Tell me . . .'

Anni sighed and looked round as if for support. Finding none, she turned back to Marina. 'You were picked up outside a cottage in Aldeburgh in Suffolk. Last night.'

Marina nodded, her head swimming. 'We went there for the weekend.'

Anni looked at her. 'It was in flames . . .'

The brightness of the room couldn't touch the darkness of Anni's words.

'Flames . . .' Parts of Marina's memory returned to her, like garishly coloured jigsaw pieces against a dark matt background. 'Flames.'

'You tried to run towards it,' Anni said. 'A guy passing by pulled you away. If he hadn't . . .'

Marina closed her eyes, the jigsaw pieces slotting slowly together. 'The . . . the rest of them?' Her breath caught. She tried to resist forming the words in her mouth, but knew they had to emerge sometime. Knew she would have to hear the answers to her questions. 'Are they . . . ?'

Anni sighed. Marina watched her.

'I know that look,' she said, apprehension and fear overriding tiredness, giving her a voice. 'Phil does it. The one you put on when you're delivering bad news. Telling someone their son or daughter's been killed. Doing the death knock. I know . . .' Her voice trailed away. 'Oh God.'

'It's . . . Are you ready for this, Marina? I mean, you've just—'

'I don't know, Anni. Am I? Am I ever going to be ready for this?' Her voice snapping, harsh. She sighed. 'Sorry. Just . . . just tell me.'

'Phil's . . . alive.'

Her initial reaction was a huge wave of relief, spreading over her. *Phil's alive.* But she stopped herself from being too relieved. The hesitation in Anni's voice . . .

'Alive?' she said.

Anni swallowed. 'Yes.' Another sigh.

'Can I see him?'

'Not at the moment. He's . . .'

'What?'

'Unconscious.'

'Oh God.'

'We're . . . still waiting for him to come round.'

Anni's words hit her like a wrecking ball. She tried to process what she'd heard, but her head was a cyclone, the words spinning round and round.

'And . . . and . . .' She couldn't bring herself to say the name. Josephina. Her daughter.

'Eileen's fine,' said Anni quickly. 'Not too badly damaged. She was lucky.' Her voice dropped. Knowing she had to say the words. Not wanting to even hear them herself. 'Don wasn't so lucky.'

The cyclone spun all the harder. 'What? Don . . .'

Anni looked straight into Marina's eyes. Held them. 'He's . . . he's dead, Marina.'

The cyclone peaked. Picked up Marina's thoughts, her emotions, spun them. She felt like her head would explode. It was too much to cope with. Too much to process all at once. But there was one question she needed the answer to. The one question she had avoided asking.

'Josephina . . .' Her voice small, fragile.

Another sigh from Anni. 'We . . . we couldn't find her.'

Marina stared at her friend.

'Honestly, she wasn't . . . There was no trace.'

6

The firefighters had all but finished and the cottage had burned itself down to charred, smoking remains. A charcoal-blackened skeleton with the life blazed out of it. Detective Sergeant Jessica James stared at it, hand over her eyes, squinting against the sun.

She had been briefed on the way from Ipswich. Holidaying copper and his family. Explosion. Fire. Probably a faulty gas supply, but maybe not.

'Proceed with caution,' her DCI had said. 'One of our own, remember. Even if they're not local.'

'Brothers under the skin and all that,' she had replied.

He had nodded. 'Just be thorough. That's all.'

And she would be. Probably nothing, just an unfortunate accident.

But . . .

A copper. Retribution? A villain nursing a bitter grudge against the guy who'd put him away, something like that? Fanciful, she would have said. The clichéd stuff of desperate TV cop dramas. That would never happen in real life. Not round here.

But then if she'd been asked a few years ago whether a sexually sadistic serial killer could terrorise Ipswich and get away with murdering five sex workers, she would have said the same. A clichéd TV cop show. Not in real life. Not round here. But it had happened. And she had no intention of being the one getting caught out if something like that happened again.

She ran her fingers through her hair, shook her head. Mentally blowing the cobwebs away. If she had known she was coming to work today, she wouldn't have gone out drinking with the girls last night. Because those couple of drinks had turned into a couple more. Then a couple more. Then a curry, a half-remembered, slurry phone call home to say she'd be late, don't wait up, then . . . what? Tiger Tiger? Dancing with some bloke? Flirting? Finally tumbling into bed at God knew what hour.

And now this. Called back in to work, her weekend off cancelled, and sent up to Aldeburgh. Knocking back mints, paracetamol and Evian all the way.

She crossed to a man giving orders to uniforms. Small, neatly dressed and holding a clipboard, he looked and acted like an *Apprentice* contestant focused on giving a hundred and ten per cent. More of a Sugary hopeful than a detective constable. But that was exactly what Deepak Shah was and it irritated her more than she let on.

'What have we got, Deepak?'

Hearing her voice, he turned. 'Early days, ma'am, but it looks like the fire started in the living room,' he said, pointing helpfully to the front of the cottage. 'We've got a couple of eyewitnesses say it was an explosion. Then it looks like the fire spread to the rest of the cottage.'

'Any survivors?'

He nodded. 'Only one dead. The father, it seems.' He checked his clipboard. 'He was in the room where the blast happened. Caught most of it. Died instantly. Two are critical. And there was one outside. She tried to get back in. That car stopped her.' He pointed to a burnt-out wreck parked outside the cottage. 'Explosion knocked her back. They've all been taken to the General in Ipswich.'

Jessica James nodded and tried not to let her irritation at Deepak's organisation show. 'Wasn't there something about a baby?'

Deepak turned to her. The usual fussiness and officiousness were absent from his eyes. In their place was the professionalism she expected from her team, and something else as well. A kind of compassionate determinism. And that, she realised, was why she put up with him.

He shook his head. 'Nothing,' he said. 'No sign.'

'But there was definitely a baby there?'

'Little girl,' he said. 'They booked a kid's bed from the letting agency, for a three-year-old. We found some stuff, couple of toys, clothes, not much though. Might be a baby buggy in there.' He pointed to the ruin once more. Three blue-suited people were making their way inside, stepping carefully. 'Firefighters and forensics are still looking it over.'

'Hope they're careful,' she said. 'Mind what they're standing on.'

Deepak didn't reply.

Jessica James's eye was drawn by an approaching car. It pulled up to the crime-scene tape that had been stretched across the gravel road that led down to the cottage. A uniform was standing there, stopping the car from going any further. It came to a halt and the driver emerged. Tall, burly, cropped head, dressed in a plaid shirt and jeans and seemingly uncomfortable in leisurewear, she noticed. He held something up and the uniform let him pass. He walked towards them. Jessica waited until he drew up next to her.

'And you are?' she said.

He held up his warrant card once more. 'Detective Sergeant Michael Philips,' he said.

'Detective Sergeant Jessica James.'

They shook hands.

'Major Incident Squad,' he said, 'Essex Police.'

Jessica raised her eyebrows. 'MIS? You're a bit off your patch, aren't you? Is this a major incident?'

He nodded. Sighed, and some of the stiffness of his manner left him. 'Yeah. I'm not here officially.' He pointed to the cottage. Grimaced. 'That was my boss in there.'

'Never mind the was, Detective . . . what did you say?'

'Philips,' he said. 'Mickey. And his missus. Marina. She's a psychologist. One of our team too.'

'Right. Mickey. Is your boss the younger one? There was a father and son.'

Mickey nodded.

'Then don't say *was*. He's still alive.'

Mickey nodded again, clearly unconvinced.

Jessica decided to change the subject. If he had come to help, he would be no good in this state. 'So why are you here?' she asked.

'I just thought . . .' He shrugged. 'Just wondered if you could do with some help. It's my day off.'

'Join the club,' she said, the ghost of a smile on her face.

'Well, anything I can do . . .'

She looked at him. He was a bull of a man. Muscular, physical. More like a rugby player or a boxer. But there was a softness to his eyes. An intelligence and compassion that Jessica found appealing. Very appealing.

'Well . . .' It was her turn to shrug. 'More the merrier, I suppose. You can fill us in on your boss. Phil Brennan?'

Mickey nodded.

She smiled. 'Welcome aboard.'

Mickey was introduced to Deepak Shah and shook hands, but any further conversation was cut short by the approach of a blue-suited forensic officer. Jessica turned to him.

'Well? Anything?'

'No kid,' he said. 'We'll look in more detail, of course, but there's nothing there to indicate that a child was in that blast. Unless, you know . . .'

'Unless it was right at the centre, I know,' said Jessica, swallowing hard. 'Well keep looking.'

'We will. It's early days, but we think we've identified the area in the cottage where the blast originated from.'

'Cooker? Fire?' asked Jessica.

The forensic officer shook his head. 'Neither, we don't think.'

A shiver ran through Jessica. 'You mean it was started deliberately?'

'Let's keep an open mind,' he said, and walked away.

Suddenly the desperate, clichéd plot of a TV cop drama didn't sound so ridiculous after all.

7

As Anni's words sank in, Marina felt even more numb than the painkillers had left her.

'What d'you mean, you couldn't find her?'

'I mean we couldn't find her,' said Anni, fidgeting uncomfortably in her seat, like her skin didn't fit right and was too itchy for her body. 'We looked everywhere, but no sign . . .'

'Everywhere. You looked everywhere . . .'

'Yes. We did. In the cottage, outside . . .' She moved about, unable to settle. 'We found some of her things. Clothes, toys. Or what was left of them. But no Josephina.'

'I've got to . . . I've got to go . . .' Marina tried to swing her body over the edge of the bed, put her legs down, her feet on the floor. Her breath caught in her throat. She pulled air in sharply and gasped. The movement sent more pain spasming round her body. She fell back, hard.

'Marina, you should stay there.'

'I've got . . . got to go . . . my baby, I have to find my baby . . .'

'But we've looked . . .'

Marina once again tried to get up. Failed. 'Then . . . Look again.'

'We—'

'I'll come with you. I should be there. You need me. Josie needs me.' Ignoring the pain, Marina eventually sat up. 'She's got to be there. She's . . . I don't know, maybe she crawled out, got away from the cottage. Maybe she—'

'We looked everywhere, Marina. Honestly.' Anni's voice low. Calm yet authoritative.

Marina felt a pain far worse than her physical injuries move through her body. A fear, like lead spreading in her veins, poisoning her, weighing her down. Removing her contact with the normal world. 'Maybe she . . . maybe someone's got her, seen her and taken her in, looking after her . . .' Marina reached out, gripped Anni's sleeve, twisted the fabric, pulled hard, her voice teetering on the edge of hysteria.

'We're looking into every possible lead.'

Marina dropped her hand away, felt herself getting angry. She had heard Phil speak the same way. 'Don't talk to me like that, Anni, save it for the punters.'

Anni recoiled, shocked.

Marina sat up. The room spun, but she ignored it and concentrated on the other woman. Locked eyes with her, made sure she understood what she was saying. 'Josephina, Josie . . . She must be there. Must be. Must be somewhere.'

'We've looked. Everywhere.'

'Then look again.'

Anni sighed. 'We have.'

'But somebody must know . . . If she's been there, if she's . . . if someone's got her, taken her in . . . if . . . someone must have seen, someone . . .' Marina fell back on the bed, exhausted. 'Oh God, oh God . . .' The pain subsided and the room slowed, stopped spinning. 'I know,' she said, her voice suddenly weak. 'I know. I'm sure everyone's doing their best . . .'

'Mickey's gone to join them,' Anni said. 'He's up there now with the local team.'

Mickey Philips. The detective sergeant in the Major Incident Squad they were all a part of.

'Oh God . . .' Another thought had struck Marina. 'She might be . . .' Her voice wavered, broke. 'The cottage — she might be . . .'

'Mickey's there,' said Anni, her voice dropping. 'If she's there, he'll find her. Wherever she is.'

Marina nodded. Kept nodding. She didn't notice the tears until she felt Anni's arm round her.

'Oh God . . .' The lead weight in her veins increased. Her heart, her whole body felt heavy, the fear paralysing her. 'Oh God . . .'

The two of them sat like that, a still life of grief, while time became a vacuum.

The mood was broken when the curtain at the front of the cubicle was pulled back. Marina looked up. A tired-looking female nurse entered.

'How you feeling?' said the nurse. Her voice sounded distracted, professional interest only, but her eyes held compassion, albeit with black circles beneath them.

Marina stared at her. She couldn't begin to answer the question.

'My husband . . . how . . . how is he? Where is he? Can I, can I see him?'

'He's still in surgery,' said the nurse. 'They're doing all they can.'

'Oh God . . .' The heaviness again, the weight pressing down on her.

'Any news? Anything you can tell us?' Anni spoke as one professional to another.

The nurse gave her a level look. 'They're hopeful.'

'What's wrong with him?'

'The fire set off an explosion,' said the nurse, checking Marina over. 'Luckily he wasn't too near it, otherwise he wouldn't be alive now, but he was hit by flying debris. Head injury. They're operating now.'

The nurse's words left Marina feeling cold and numb.

'His mother's doing well. She doesn't look as bad as they first thought.' The nurse paused. 'I'm sorry about his father, though. Apparently there was nothing the paramedics could do for him.'

Marina said nothing. Couldn't speak.

'You're in shock,' the nurse said. 'We're just waiting for a bed to become free and we'll move you to that. We'd like to keep you in overnight. Plus I'm sure you want to be near your husband.'

She looked between Marina and Anni. 'I'll pop back soon as I can.'

She left, closing the curtain behind her.

Anni said nothing. Marina stared ahead of her, the pattern on the curtain dancing and swaying before her eyes.

Anni's phone rang. She jumped. 'That might be Mickey,' she said. 'Give me a minute.' Looking relieved to have a break, she went outside the cubicle.

Marina didn't move, just stared. Straight ahead, unmoving. Her daughter's eyes, that was all she could see. Her eyes. Her smile. Her hair.

She felt a sudden urge to scream, to pound the walls, smash her head against them. Let it all out, try to express the inarticulate, raging emotions she was feeling. But she fought it. For now.

Anni stepped back inside and resumed her seat.

'Any news? Josephina? What's happening? What's . . .'

Anni shook her head. 'Nothing yet. I'm sorry . . .'

Marina sank back. 'No. No. She has to be there. No. She must be.'

'They're still searching. They . . .' Anni sighed. 'I know. But . . .'

Marina said nothing.

'Look, I've got to ask some questions, I'm afraid.'

'No.' Marina shook her head, closed her eyes.

'Please, Marina. I know it's difficult. But we're here as a favour. Because it's you and Phil and you're in the job. The local force have turned a blind eye. Look, you have to help us. If there's anything . . .'

'No. No.' Marina looked at Anni. Saw the other woman was not just doing her job, but also trying to help. 'Just . . .' She sighed. 'Give me a minute. Five minutes.'

'OK.' Anni nodded and stood up. 'D'you want anything? I'm going to get a drink. Bar of chocolate. Famished.'

Marina barely heard her.

'OK, then.' She left the cubicle.

Marina lay back and stared at the curtain once more. Heard music, recognised it. The old Joy Division song, 'Love Will Tear Us Apart'. Absently she wondered where it was coming from.

Then realised it was a phone.

She looked round. Anni's bag was on the floor beside the chair. She bent over the side of the bed, feeling her head spin, her sides ache as she did so. No. The sound wasn't coming from there.

She lay back down once more. The song kept playing. She looked round. Her own bag was on the other side of the bed. That was the source.

Frowning, she reached down, picked up her bag. Rummaged through it and brought out a phone. A cheap black smartphone that she had never seen before. Puzzled, she answered it, put it to her ear.

'Hello . . . ?' Her voice small, quizzical.

'Marina Esposito.' A voice she didn't recognise. Electronic, distorted. Neither male nor female. But audible.

'Yes . . .' She looked round quickly, as if someone was standing nearby, could hear her.

The voice made a sound that wasn't a word. Marina just knew the person was smiling. 'I believe I have something of yours.'

A shiver convulsed the whole of Marina's body. She couldn't answer.

'Something you've lost.'

'Wuh — what?'

'Something by the name of . . . Josephina.' The voice relishing the pronunciation of the name.

She gasped. Began to tremble. 'Where is she? I've got to . . . got to—'

'Shut up and listen.' The voice harsher now, colder. 'If you want to see your daughter alive again, then just shut up and listen.'

8

The gate closed behind him. He had imagined the scraping of metal against metal as the key was turned and the bolts drawn back. The old hinges would squeal in protest as another one was let go. Then the door would slam shut, hitting its rightful place in the frame and staying there, seemingly immovable. The noise of its closing would be heavy and final, echoing slowly away to a deafening emptiness.

But it wasn't like that at all.

The gate had just slid open, like in a garage or factory, and he had stepped through. Then it had slid closed behind him, the whirring electric motor stopping when it was in place.

Leaving him standing, staring at the street before him. Cars went past. Quicker than he remembered them, different shapes too, colours, all metallic. Futuristic but recognisable. People walked the pavements. Men, women, old, young. Some still wore suits, but some, mainly the women and the younger ones, wore things he found alien, different. Like clothes from a parallel dimension.

He stared as a couple of women went past pushing babies in chairs. No jackets, just light T-shirts, jeans. They were young, looking better than he remembered. Talking and laughing like the world was a joke.

He watched them go, saw the sway of their hips in their jeans, felt something stir within him. Deep and primal, long-suppressed. Something he had ignored for years. Something *else* he had told himself didn't exist. But watching those two women walk up the street, something within him connected.

He kept looking at them. And noticed something odd about their skin . . .

Tattoos. On their bare shoulders, their arms. The sight of them killed whatever was rising inside him. Loads of prisoners had tattoos. Done to kill boredom. Crudely formed and badly spelled. But these women's were different. Elaborate swirls. Pictures. Florid, curling writing. Deliberate marking. How much had the world changed that young women needed to mark themselves like that? They couldn't be as bored as those on the inside. Not with the whole of life around them.

He watched them walk on. Stayed where he was, reluctant to step away from the prison. Not knowing where to go.

Before he left, he had been given an address. A halfway house, a hostel. Somewhere to stay while he got on his feet again, they said. He had the address in his pocket, together with his discharge grant and his travel warrant. He had told them he would go there. He was expected to.

But now, standing there, he didn't know what to do. Where to go.

The world outside might not be silent and empty. But his head and his heart were. Time had slipped again, twisted. He could have stood there for a few seconds or a few years. He had no way of knowing.

He looked behind him once more. Sixteen years of his life that place had taken. That and others like it. The factory gate was back in position, like it had never moved. Someone else would take his cell, his books, his clothes and toiletries.

And he would be gone. Forgotten about. Like the ripples in a pond after a stone hits it. Dying away to nothing.

He shivered, despite the morning's warmth. The thought depressed him.

Dying away to nothing.

While he was trying to decide where to go, a car pulled up at the side of the road. Tooted its horn. The sudden noise made him jump, but he didn't move. The horn tooted again, accompanied by a hand waving from inside the car.

Puzzled, he looked behind him, wondering who they were waving at.

The hand beckoned towards the car. He realised the person was gesturing to him.

He took one step forward. The driver nodded in encouragement, beckoned him further. While he was thinking, another car honked its horn. Was that for him too? He looked at the driver. No. He was just frustrated that the first car had parked and that oncoming traffic had stopped his journey from continuing. A line of cars began to appear behind the first one. The driver kept beckoning, insistent now.

Not wanting to be responsible for a traffic jam or for any anger, he walked towards the car.

The driver leaned across, opened the passenger door. He got inside.

'Well close it, then.'

He did so. Looked at the driver. The driver laughed.

'Remember me?'

He said nothing.

'The recognition of friends is not always easy, Doctor . . .' Another laugh. Why had he spoken those words in a terrible Chinese accent?

'Know where that's from? Yeah? No. Course you don't. Never mind.' The driver looked him over. 'That all you got?'

He nodded. 'Yes.'

'Suit yourself.'

He put the car in gear, flicked a V sign at the driver behind, his eyes flashing angrily, and pulled away from the kerb.

'I know you. You're . . .' He struggled to find the name. 'Jiminy Cricket.'

Jiminy Cricket smiled. 'Guilty as charged.'

'Where are we going?'

He laughed. 'We got a lot to do. But let's get you sorted first. Don't worry. Today is the first day of the rest of your life.' Another laugh. 'Plenty more where that came from.'

9

Marina's head spun with more than pain. She listened to the voice, forced herself to understand what it was saying, let the words cut through the white noise in her mind.

'Josephina . . .' Her daughter's name gasped out. 'Where is she? Is she hurt? Where—'

'Be quiet and listen.' The voice was sharp, authoritative.

Marina said nothing. Listened. But all she could hear was the rushing of blood in her ears, her breath in her chest, like Niagara Falls had exploded inside her head, gushing and rushing.

'You have to do something for me. Then you'll get to see your daughter.'

Marina couldn't speak. She didn't trust herself with words.

'Understand?'

'Yuh-yes . . .'

'Good.'

'Why?'

Silence.

'Why . . . who—'

'I told you. Be quiet. Listen.'

She did so. Tried to scan the voice to see if she recognised it. She didn't. Couldn't. Didn't even know if it was male or female.

The voice continued. 'You've got to go somewhere, and do something when you get there. Understand?'

'Yes . . .'

'Good. In your bag is a book of maps.'

The voice stopped talking. Marina took that as her cue to look for it. She grabbed for the bag on the floor at her side. Rifled through it. There it was. An atlas of Essex.

'One of the pages is marked,' said the voice. 'Open it.'

The book was brand new. One deliberate crease down the spine. She picked it up and it fell open at the marked page. A circle had been drawn in one of the grids. Underneath, a name.

'Go there.'

'And . . . and do what?'

'Ask for . . .' There was a pause. 'Tyrell.'

'And then what? Will Josephina be there? Is she—'

'Do as you're told.' The voice had been neutral until now. But those words were edged with ugly emotion. A sick thrill of control.

'Where's my daughter? I want to hear my daughter . . .'

'Just do what you've been told.'

Marina searched for words but didn't know how to respond. She was a criminal psychologist, trained to deal with these kinds of people, an expert on what to say in such situations. But she had only ever dealt with this in an abstract sense, come at it from a position of professionalism. This was happening to her. It was real. Her emotional state was already fractured, her head like a junkyard. And all her training had dissipated like steam off a hotplate.

She had to get a grip, not give in to hysteria. Find a still point somewhere deep within her chaotic mind. Respond like a professional.

'Why are you doing this?' She tried to tamp down her emotions, speak in as rational a voice as she could find. 'To me. Why are you doing this to me?'

There was a pause on the line. Marina could hear the zing of electrostatic, of dead air. She thought the call had been ended and felt helplessness creep up on her once more.

'Punishment. For the guilty.'

She fought down the rising hysteria and listened. Here was something. Just a small phrase, but something to work with.

'Guilty? What am I guilty of?'

Nothing. She could hear the person breathing. The breath sounded angry. Much less controlled than the voice itself.

'Shut up.' The words hissed. 'Do as you're told. If you want to see your daughter alive again.'

'OK, but—'

'And tell no one where you're going, what you're doing. No one. Because I'm watching you. Even when you don't think I am, I'll be watching you. I'm watching you now.'

Marina spun round. So quickly it made her ribs ache, her head spin. She couldn't see anyone else. She moved to the front of the cubicle, pulled the curtains aside. A couple of nurses were walking past, no one else. Then at the far end of the corridor she saw Anni approaching, coffee in hand.

'Remember, don't say anything. Especially not to the policewoman coming towards you.'

Marina's heart skipped a beat. She couldn't articulate, couldn't speak.

She felt the voice smile. 'Good. Now we understand each other. You've got a job to do. Go and do it.'

Marina was left holding a dead phone in her hand.

She snapped herself out of her daze, quickly pocketed the phone and picked up her bag. Felt in her pockets, looked round once more. Car keys. She didn't have her car keys. She didn't even have her car. It would still be at Aldeburgh.

She looked round the cubicle. Anni's bag was still on the floor. Without stopping to think, she bent down and started going through it. Anni's car keys were near the top. She pulled them out as fast as she could, crossed the cubicle, flung the curtains aside. Anni stood before her, coffee in hand. She jumped back, surprised.

'Feeling better?' Then she caught the wild look in Marina's eyes, took in her tense body language.

Marina started to push past her. 'I've got to go . . .'

Anni jumped to the side, fearful of ending up wearing her coffee. 'Hey . . .'

'I've got to go.' Marina felt light-headed, like the whole world was spinning and she was in danger of falling off. Anni didn't move. 'I . . . I need the toilet . . .'

'I'll get the nurse to come and—'

'No.' Marina saw the look in Anni's eyes, realised she had been too abrupt. She tried a smile. 'No, it's . . . it's OK.'

'You sure? You don't look—'

'I can manage.'

'Well I can help—'

'I said I can manage.' She spat the words out.

Anni's head snapped back like she had been slapped. 'Fine. OK.'

'Thank you. Now, I've . . . I've got to go.'

She swept past Anni, moving as quickly as she could, trying hard not to break into a run.

The thought of leaving Phil behind ground into her stomach like broken glass.

But the thought of not trying to get her daughter back was even worse.

10

'Shouldn't we be doing this somewhere else?'

'Where did you have in mind?'

Stuart Milton shrugged. 'I don't know. The station? Somewhere like that?'

Jessica James sat in the back of her car. She had wanted to go somewhere private, away from the camera crews and reporters who were starting to gather, long lenses pushing over the flapping tape cordon.

'Here will do,' she said, and looked at the man sitting next to her.

Stuart Milton's face and hands still had gravel rash from where he had pulled Marina down to the ground and away from the exploding cottage. His suede jacket was more distressed on one side than the other. He looked, Jessie thought, like the typical middle-aged, middle-class tourist that Aldeburgh attracted. Bet he reads the *Guardian*, she thought. Bet he goes to Latitude as well.

'Just want to run through a few things, take a few details. That's all.' She had her notepad open, angled away from him so he couldn't read what she was writing. The action made her aware of the small space in the car, the enforced intimacy. She was also aware of the discarded paracetamol and mint wrappers on the passenger seat. She was sure he had seen them.

'Run me through it again. What happened.'

He sighed in exasperation. 'Do I need to do this? I just wanted to see how the woman was.'

'She's fine. Thanks to you. So. You were walking down the gravel path at the side of the cottage . . .'

'Yes. And then the explosion happened.' He stopped talking, put his head back.

She looked at his eyes, tried to see what he was seeing. Tried to ensure that what he was seeing was what had actually happened. Not that she didn't trust him personally; it was just a habit she had developed. She didn't trust any witness until their testimony had been independently corroborated.

'Which direction were you walking in?'

'The . . . seafront.'

'And where had you been?'

'I'd been towards the Maltings. For a walk. Stretching my legs.'

'Are you local?'

'I live . . .' He stopped, looked at her. Face reddening around his grazes. 'Am I a suspect here? What's going on?'

'Just standard questions, Mr Milton. Wouldn't be doing my job properly if I didn't ask them. *Are* you local?'

'Sort of. I have a weekend home here. I live in London the rest of the time.'

'And are you married?'

'Are you asking me out on a date, Detective Sergeant?'

It was Jessie's turn to redden. She felt his eyes on her. Dark, penetrating. 'Just wondering if you were here alone.' Her throat suddenly dry. 'That's all.'

'Right.' He nodded. 'No. I'm here with . . . friends. Work colleagues, mainly. For the music. But it can get a little too much. I needed some time on my own, so I went for a walk.'

'Right.' Her turn to nod. In those few words, she saw his life. Weekends in Suffolk, summers in France or Italy, probably. Nights out at the theatre. Not the kind of man she would usually meet. Not many of them in Tiger Tiger in Ipswich.

'And as you walked past the cottage, the explosion went off.'

'That's correct.'

'And then what?'

'Well . . . I was thrown to the ground. There was a . . . mighty wind, a huge noise, and the heat . . .' He trailed off. Jessie waited. 'Then I . . . pulled myself up, opened my eyes. I thought I was dead. That was my first thought. I thought I was dead.'

'But you weren't.'

'No. I got to my feet, checking to see if I was OK. And then this woman came running towards me.'

'Towards you?'

'Well, towards the cottage. There were flames coming out of the window by now. Black smoke. And it looked like she was trying to get in there.'

'So what did you do?'

'I . . . stopped her.'

'By pushing her to the ground?'

'Pulling her, really. She fought.' He mimed the action with his hands. 'Wanted to get in there. Badly. But I couldn't let her, obviously. So I . . . I held her. Until she . . . until she stopped screaming.'

Jessie nodded. Looked at Milton again. His head was lowered, eyes hooded. Reliving the moment, she presumed.

'Did you see anyone else in the area?'

'What d'you mean?'

'Anyone near the cottage at the time of the explosion? Apart from the woman you mentioned.'

Stuart Milton frowned, thinking. Eventually he shook his head. 'No . . . can't recall . . .'

'A young girl? About three years old?'

'No. Is there a girl missing?'

'We don't know.' Jessica thought she'd got everything she would be able to get from him. 'Well, thank you, Mr Milton, I—'

'There was something else.' Stuart Milton was chewing his thumb, worrying away at a tiny nub of skin. His face contorted, as if fighting against the words that wanted to come out.

Jessie waited.

'She . . .' He sighed. Pulled the skin away from his thumb. Looked at Jessie. 'When I caught hold of her, she said something.'

'What?'

He looked down at his thumb once more. A pinprick of blood had appeared where he had bitten it. He sucked on it, hard. 'Something like . . .' He looked up. '"I've got to get back in there. What have I done?" . . .' He nodded. 'Yes. "What have I done?" Something like that.'

Jessie's mouth was open, ready to make him elaborate, when there was a sharp rap on the window. She looked up. Mickey Philips was standing there, gesturing to her. Urgently.

'Excuse me,' she said, and got out of the car, closing the door behind her. Milton's eyes followed her.

She stood opposite Mickey, waited for him to speak. His face looked drawn, his features tense.

'I've just had a call,' he said. 'From a colleague at Ipswich General.'

'What's happened?' The look on his face told her it wasn't good news. His boss had died? His boss's mother? Both of them? What a day this was turning out to be.

'It's Marina,' he said. 'She's gone.'

'Gone? What d'you mean?'

'Taken off. Run away.'

Jessie let out a breath she hadn't been aware of holding. 'Thank God. I thought you meant she'd died.' She frowned. 'What happened?'

'She told my colleague she was off to the loo, nipped outside and was away. With my colleague's car.'

'Any idea where?'

'Nope.'

Jessie walked away from the car, arms folded round herself. She looked out to sea. The sun made the day feel like summer. The kind of day where you just wanted to relax and have fun. Pretend there was nothing wrong in the world.

She turned back to Mickey.

'The witness in the car says she was trying to get back into the cottage. And she said something. "What have I done?"'

Mickey frowned. 'What?'

'Sounds like she was blaming herself. D'you think she might be on her way back here? Trying to look for her daughter?'

He shrugged. 'Anything's possible. I'll look into it.'

'OK. I'll get the team to keep checking for the daughter. Get the uniforms combing the area. See if anyone's seen anything. We'll keep an eye out for the mother, too. Get the reg of the car she's taken sent to me.'

'Will do.'

'Keep in touch.'

Their eyes locked. For longer than she had intended. Then she broke contact, and he nodded, turned, walked away.

Jessie watched him go. She knew a good bloke when she saw one. She turned back to her car to tell Stuart Milton he was free to leave. But the back door was open and he was already gone.

11

Southend-on-Sea hadn't just seen better days. It had stood at the platform and waved them off, knowing they would never return.

At one time it had been a respectable enough holiday destination for London's post-war East End families enjoying the novelty of a train ride out to the end of the Thames estuary. The longest pier in the world, fishing for Dad, shopping for Mum, cafés to park the grandparents and a fairground and penny arcades for the kiddies. All knotted handkerchiefs and rolled-up trouser legs, deckchairs and donkeys, sand in the ice cream and stones on the beach.

But nobody came to Southend for a holiday any more. People only went there when they had nowhere else to go.

The pier was still there, stretching out towards a handful of dying souvenir shops at the far end, and beyond that a vista of Canvey Island and beyond that the oil refinery at Shellhaven. The shops were slightly shabbier versions of those found in any generic British high street. The seafront amusements were lit in a way that seemed simultaneously overly bright and depressing. The electronic bleeps and repetitive jingles bleated out like some demented, amphetamine-fuelled

Stockhausen symphony. Inside, dead-eyed, white-skinned arcade zombies gave their days and nights over to target practice, racking up high scores as video killers, while in the neon-thrown shadows, feral-featured predators lurked to trap the unwary and the curious.

The fairground had expanded with Alton Towers-like dreams of empire but had contracted under council health-and-safety legislation. Now, out-of-town families trying to enjoy themselves found the local kids scarier than the rides.

The cosy cafés were long gone, but seafront food outlets thrived, serving anything as long as it was fast, fried and fattening.

The tentative appearance of the Good Friday sun had drawn an influx of people to the amusement arcades and bars. Marina passed old, scarred wooden benches outside run-down pubs occupied by tattooed men in vests rolling fags and drinking lager. Laughing with bared teeth and making passes at their friends' women with a barely restrained undercurrent of violence like their barely restrained attack dogs lying under the tables.

Marina hurried on down the front. Walking fast, breathing heavily. On the surface, controlled.

After leaving the hospital, she had driven straight down the A12 then the A127, not stopping for anyone or anything. Speeding at first, but she had soon stopped that. If the police picked her up, she would be delayed at the very least. Stopped and returned at the worst.

And that would be the last she would see of Josephina.

So she had stayed just under the legal speed limit, heart racing faster than the car's engine as she drove.

She didn't know Southend well; had followed the signs for the seafront and parking spaces. She had been about to leap out of the car, but caught her reflection in the mirror. She was a mess. Dried blood and scratches on her face. Hair a dark, tangled mass of scribble. She had done what she could, quickly wiped her face, rearranged her hair; nowhere near what she ordinarily would have done to make herself presentable.

But that was the old her. Living her old life. She was someone new now. Someone different.

She got out of the car, walked along the front. Ignoring the people outside the bars, but feeling eyes on her all the time. Judging. Malicious. Unseen.

And she didn't want to mess up while those unseen eyes were watching. For her sake.

For her daughter's sake.

She walked round the corner, away from the front. She had memorised the route from the map she had been given. A grid reference that led to a street. And a name. Coasters.

She kept walking and soon found the street. Away from the front, but its sounds and smells still reached her. Snatches of arcade song and jingle, rollercoaster screaming, the smell of cheap, stale fat. All brought to her senses on the breeze, then just as quickly taken away as the wind veered off, changing direction, like the swooping, scavenging gulls in pursuit of scraps.

She ignored it all. Kept walking.

Coasters was in front of her.

Even among the dive-bar fraternity, she thought, Coasters would be way down the list. A row of single-storey breeze-block buildings faced a scrappy car park full of potholes, broken glass and cars left there purely so the owners could claim on the insurance when the inevitable vandalism happened. Most of the buildings were boarded up. The remaining ones all sported heavy metal bars and mesh on the paint-peeling, filthy windows and metal rollers over the doorways. They variously advertised themselves as a second-hand shop that Marina immediately knew was a fencing operation, a couple of bars, a beauty salon and a tattoo parlour where, if the sun-faded photos in the window were anything to go by, the tattooist had all the artistic skill and flair of a six-year-old child.

She reached the doorway of Coasters. The outside had been painted, none too expertly, a deep purple. White paint had been applied over the top of the rusting bars covering the window. The door was open. Inside, a poster took an inspired approach to spelling and grammar advertising an eighties night. A notice next to it explained that the pub was on two levels but that the seafront bar could only be accessed from the seafront. It was written in such a way that a veiled threat hung over the words for those who ignored the advice.

'Abandon all hope,' said Marina quietly to herself, trying to build up her courage to enter, and failing.

She looked at the threadbare, dirty carpet in the doorway. The unmistakable smell of stale alcohol and uncleaned rooms wafted out of the darkness. She could hear voices. Low, conspiratorial. Underneath them the bland, susurrating buzz of a TV announcer. She saw figures moving, shadows against shadows. She felt rather than saw heads turn towards her.

It was the last place on earth she wanted to enter. But Phil came into her mind, lying there unmoving, unreachable . . . The voice on the phone once more . . .

And Josephina's face.

She took a deep breath.

And stepped inside.

12

'Here we are, then. Home sweet home.'

He looked straight ahead to where a rusty caravan sat on a patch of weedy, barren grass next to a run-down house. There was nothing else around for miles. It didn't look like home to him.

'What d'you think?' Jiminy Cricket said, laughing, as if anticipating applause.

He frowned. 'I . . . I'm not supposed to be here. This isn't where I'm supposed to come to.'

'Yeah.' Jiminy Cricket looked irritated. It wasn't the response he had expected. 'Don't worry about that. It's taken care of.'

'I have to report. Probation, they said. Signing. Can't disappear. Can't just go off like this. On my own.' He spoke the words like a learned speech.

'I told you. Don't worry about it. Now . . .' He turned, made a fanfare gesture towards the caravan. Tried again. 'What d'you think of your new home?'

He had no idea where he was. The drive had been long. Or it had felt long, because he hadn't known where he was going. He had looked out of the window but had recognised nothing. There had been a big road, lots of fast-moving, snarling cars. He hadn't enjoyed that. It had scared him. Then the big road became a smaller one, round a town. He thought he recognised it but wasn't sure. It had been a long time ago, and he had been a different person then. Something about Romans. An Avenue of Remembrance. He didn't know what he was supposed to remember. Or forget. It all grew confused in his head.

They drove out of the town and the roads became smaller still. Tight, Jiminy Cricket described them. Closed in. He didn't think so. They weren't closed in compared to where he had just come from.

The buildings got further and further apart until they were mostly replaced by trees and fields. There were fewer cars, which should have made it more tranquil. But it didn't. The open spaces with the huge sky above made him panic. He wanted noise again, more of it.

Eventually they pulled off the road and down a track that was all loose, sharp rocks and holes. The car threw him from side to side as it went down the hill. At the bottom was the stone house. A cottage, he supposed, since he was in the country. It had once been white but now it looked like it wasn't sure what colour it was. The windows were dirty, paint peeling round them. The front door battered. There were no flowers. Nothing welcoming. An old silver car, long and boxy, was parked at the side.

'Here we are, then. Out you get.'

He got out. Looked round. The air smelled different here. Salt. Like the sea. He closed his eyes, listened. Heard water. They were near the sea. Or at least a large river. He could hear dogs. The kind that were left outside to bark at anything and everything. And he could hear something else, over the top, a jagged, grating sound carrying on the wind.

'What's that? Is that a child crying?'

Jiminy Cricket acted as if he hadn't heard him.

He tried again. 'Where are we?'

This time, by way of an answer, his companion smiled.

They had walked round the side of the house and stopped before the caravan. And that was when he was told it was his new home.

He stared at the caravan. The rusting sides, the flat tyres. Filthy windows with horrible, holey curtains that looked they had been chewed. It didn't look like freedom. It looked like another cell. Like he was still trapped, even under the huge, blue sky.

'I don't want to stay here,' he said, suppressed panic starting to bubble inside him. 'I need to go.'

He turned, started to walk away. A restraining hand was placed on his arm. 'You're not going anywhere.' A laugh, an American accent, trying to lighten the weight of the words. 'I need ya, Decks. I need the old blade runner. I need your magic.'

He didn't know what he was talking about, tried to walk away. 'Please. I don't want . . . to stay here. I want to go.'

The American accent dropped but the hand remained. 'To where? Some hostel or B and B? Spied on? Made to sign a form every two weeks? That's what you want, is it?'

He didn't answer.

'A hostel. With the paedos, and the murderers. Real murderers, mind, not like you. And the nutters and the psychos.'

'But . . . prison was like that.'

'Yes, it was. But there was a big metal door keeping them out. You think you'll have that at the hostel?'

He said nothing.

His companion took that for assent. 'Thought not. No, you're better off here. And besides, we had a deal.'

'What?'

'Remember? All those years ago?' His companion's smile widened. Teeth sharp and shark-like. 'I said that if you played things my way, then you would end up on top. I said that, didn't I?'

He couldn't remember. He might have done.

'I had a plan, didn't I? Well, it's just taken a while to put into practice, that's all. We've been playing the long game.'

'And what . . . what is this plan? What do I get?'

'A new life. And revenge. On the people who put you inside. The ones who took your life away. Got your attention now, haven't I?'

'But . . . but how?'

'You'll see.' He gestured to the caravan. 'Until then, just make yourself at home. Put your feet up.'

He blinked several times in quick succession. Something niggled.

'But . . . Probation. I have to sign on. They give me money to live on.'

'You'll have money soon. You'll have everything you need. And more. Millions.'

'But I . . . my name. I'll be . . . they'll be looking for me.'

'You've got a new one.'

He stopped blinking.

'Yes, a new name. You're going to be a new person. Completely different. A fresh start. How d'you like that?'

He thought. And in that thought, a smile started. He liked that. He liked that very much.

His companion laughed. 'Thought you would.'

'Who am I?'

'Tyrell. Malcolm Tyrell.'

'Tyrell . . .' Rolling the word round his mouth, seeing if it fitted. 'Malcolm Tyrell . . .'

Jiminy Cricket laughed again and gestured to the caravan. 'So, Mr Tyrell. Would you like to make yourself at home?'

The dogs kept barking. He could no longer hear the crying child.

He would like that very much.

13

Everyone stared when Marina entered the bar.

She looked round, eyes adapting to the sudden gloom after the brightness outside. The pub was rough and unadorned. It hadn't fallen on hard times; it had never seen good times. As shadows took substance, she realised that clientele and surroundings were perfectly matched. A handful of men, all watching her. Eyes hard, wary. Items were swiftly swiped from tabletops, hands quickly disappearing underneath. She had been sized up and immediately identified as an outsider. Someone official and unwelcome. Social services. Probation. Police. Or just some wild-haired madwoman wandered in.

She felt like a lone gunslinger entering a Western saloon. If there had been a piano, it would have stopped playing.

Swallowing down nervousness, hoping it wouldn't crystallise into fear, she walked up to the bar. Placed her hands on the counter. Found it sticky and took them away again.

The barman was big, middle-aged, like an ex-boxer turned to fat. His face was red and badly repaired, his head bald and sweating. He wore a faded Hawaiian shirt over supermarket jeans, and leaned against the till, arms crossed and unmoving. Waiting to see what she wanted and what his customers would do about it. His eyes were hard and flint-like, two sharp stones in a face of red mud. They never left her.

I have to front this, she thought. I have to do it. A mental image of Josephina's face flashed before her. I *can* do it. She looked directly at him.

'I'm looking for Tyrell.' Her voice came out stronger than expected. She wished the rest of her could match it, and forced her eyes to lock on to his.

The pub had been silent to start with. Now, if anything, it became even quieter. The only sound was the babbling of the Sky Sports presenter on an old, heavy black TV set, tucked away in the corner.

No one paid him any attention. All eyes were on Marina.

She tried again. 'Tyrell. Is he here?'

The barman's eyes focused away from her, on someone or something behind her. She turned. Had he been looking at one of the drinkers in the bar? If so, which one? All of them were affecting not to look at her.

She turned back to the barman. 'Tyrell.'

He found his voice. 'No one here by that name.' His voice matched his frame, big and ugly.

Marina felt desperation well within her. 'Please.' Her voice caught. 'Tyrell. Is Tyrell here? I must — please . . .'

He leaned on the bar and looked at her. She could see the sweat, feel the heat coming off him. 'And I said there's no one here by that name.'

'I don't believe you,' she said, the words out before she could stop them. The barman's eyebrows rose in surprise. 'You're lying to me.'

He stared at her, lost for words. Then a smile spread over his features. 'Am I, now?'

Marina felt suddenly embarrassed by her outburst. 'Look, I'm sorry. I was . . . I was sent to meet someone called Tyrell. He's supposed to be here. He . . .' She sighed. 'He must be here.'

'Listen, love. I know everyone in this bar, and there's no one called Tyrell here.'

She looked round the bar, scanned every face she saw, looking for truth, a human lie detector. No one was giving anything away. They were either watching the TV or finding their drinks fascinating. One, small and middle-aged, poorly dressed, was staring at Canvey Island through the bar's tiny, cell-like window like he had never seen it before. They were stuck between wanting to be seen to help a damsel in distress and not wanting to get involved with the madwoman having a meltdown in front of them. She turned back to the barman. 'Please, there must be . . .'

He shook his head. 'Sorry, love, can't help you.'

Marina looked round the bar once more. She had never felt so helpless. All her training, her professionalism had gone out of the window. She had squandered whatever advantage she had by her outburst. She ran a hand through her hair and wished Phil was with her. They wouldn't have lied, wouldn't have held out on him. They wouldn't have dared. She decided to give it one last shot. She had nothing to lose.

Her voice dropped so only the barman could hear. She swung her gaze back on him once more. 'Look. Tyrell is here. He must be here because I was told he was. I have to meet him. It's very important that I speak to him. *Very* important. So please let me know which one he is so I can talk to him. Then I'll not bother you any more. Please.'

'Listen, darlin', I would if I could. But I can't. There ain't no one here called Tyrell. I don't know no Tyrell.' He shrugged as if that was the end of the matter. 'So there you go.'

Marina felt impotent anger rise within her. The image of Josephina was fading away, hope of finding her going along with it. She made one last attempt. 'You're lying. You must be. It's important. I need to find Tyrell. Please. You have to help me.'

'I ain't got to do anythin', darlin'. 'Cept run this pub.' He gestured to the meagre display of optics behind him. 'Gin and tonic?'

She shook her head.

'Then I think you'd better leave.'

Marina didn't know where to look, what to think or feel. Or what to do next.

Love Will Tear Us Apart. Her phone. She took it out of her bag, answered it.

'Step outside,' the voice said.

Marina did so. The light, the sun and the warmth hit her immediately, causing her to squint. She had forgotten it was still daylight.

'Well, is Tyrell there?' the voice said. 'Have you met him?'

'No,' she said. 'The barman said there was no one there called Tyrell.'

The voice laughed. 'Quite right too. There isn't.'

Marina frowned. 'What?'

'It was a test. To see if you could follow instructions. Do as you're told, don't tell anyone and don't get tailed. And you can. Good girl.'

Emotions welled once more. Anger. Unease. Desperation. Swirling around, turning her head into a vortex. 'Where is she?'

No reply.

'Where is she?'

'You'll see her. When you've done what we need you to do.'

'But when will—'

'We'll be in touch,' the voice said.

'What?' Marina couldn't believe what she was hearing. If the phone went dead, she feared that all hope of seeing her daughter went with it. 'You can't do this. Please. I did what you asked for, please . . .'

'You've done well so far. Don't spoil it.'

The phone went silent in her hand. She looked round, up and down the street. Checked doorways, passers-by. No one else was about. No one was on the phone.

She was completely alone.

14

'You took a risk.'

'And it paid off. I found out what we needed to know.'

She shook her head. That wasn't what she had meant, and he knew it.

The man who had called himself Stuart Milton sat down beside her on the bed. She had been waiting for him, dressed up as he liked her. All seams, heels, spikes, straps and sheer black see-through. The bed had been prepared with restraints of leather and rope. Tight knots and heavy buckles. Blindfolds and toys. The house slave had been banished to her room. They had been planning a celebration, just the two of them. Now everything had been put on hold.

She knew he was looking at her. Out of the corner of his eye. Taking her in, running his glance up and down, his tongue at the side of his lips, subconsciously licking. She felt stirrings inside her. Despite everything that was going on, she still felt stirrings. And he would be too. Because he could never resist her. She made sure of it.

She didn't move, just concentrated on her breathing. Looked at herself in the strategically positioned full-length mirror. She still had it. Her hair was still dark, her face unlined. Her skin smooth, tanned to a rich shade of coffee. Her legs looked good, tits firm. She loved to look at herself. It affirmed who she was.

The affirmation and maintenance cost — and not just financially. But it was worth it. All of it.

Her nipples hardened slightly just at the sight of herself.

'I gave them a false name,' he said, also looking at her in the mirror.

'What?'

He paused. A smile curled the corners of his lips. 'Stuart Milton.'

'You idiot! What if they—'

'They won't. They can't trace me. Or make a connection. Don't worry. I acted.' The smile opened his mouth. It was all sharp teeth. 'You'd have been proud of me.'

She said nothing. Just kept looking at herself. If she ignored him, that might make him angry. She hoped so.

'They took her to the hospital,' he said, voice rising slightly. 'They haven't got her. I know that.'

She kept her eyes on the mirror. 'How do you know?'

'Because the police told me. They haven't got her.'

She turned her face towards his. Eyes on his, locked, unblinking. Mouth full and red, like a bruise waiting to flower. 'Really?'

'Yes. Really.' His cheeks were starting to redden. 'I grabbed her first. Stopped her from going back in. And then . . .' She watched him. Knew he was remembering the explosion. Could almost see the memory reflected on his irises. The flames, the heat . . . 'They took her away. Said I'd saved her life.'

'That wasn't the plan.'

'No,' he said, voice rising once again. 'I know. But the plan changed. It had to, because . . . you know. *They* were there. I had to improvise.' He placed his hand on her bare arm. Stroked his fingers towards the crook of her elbow. Goosebumps raised themselves where his touch passed. 'We have to be flexible. Stay with what's happening. Move with it. It's quite exciting, really.'

She made no attempt to stop him. Or encourage him. But then she didn't need to.

'You should have stuck to the plan.'

He took his hand away, angry now. Stood up, walked away from her. She watched him go, her breath catching in her throat.

'It's gone. Everything's gone. I even lost the car.'

'You lost—'

'It went up in the explosion. Don't worry, it's not traceable. But everyone else went up too. They must all be dead.'

'Apart from her.'

He nodded. Conceding a point. 'Yes. Apart from her.'

'And the child.'

He turned to her. 'Yes,' he said, voice rising once more. But not in anger this time. In triumph. 'Exactly. The child. And I know where she is.'

'No you don't.'

'Oh yes I do. You know who I saw there. Before the explosion.' It wasn't a question, just a statement of fact. 'And you know what they were doing. Now they've got the kid.'

'Well if they've got the kid,' she said, speaking slowly as though she was explaining a simple point to a particularly backward child, 'then the mother will have it back soon. And we'll be no further forward.'

'Wrong.' He stood over her. Placed his hand on her chin. Forced her face upwards, made her look up at him. She put up token resistance, but they both knew she would submit eventually. 'Wrong. Because I dissembled. I seeded.'

'Tell.' She licked her lips.

'I said I'd heard her. Saying it was her fault.'

Something flashed across her eyes. 'That was risky.'

'I know. But it worked. Because then I overheard the police talking. They took her to hospital, but she left. They think she's running.'

'So she's on her way to meet them. To get the child back.'

He smiled. 'D'you think it would be that simple? They've got a job for her.'

'So what do we do?'

'Obvious. Follow the police. They'll lead us to her.'

'And them? How do we take care of them?'

Another smile. All teeth and reflected, glinting, razor light. 'Send in the Golem.'

Her eyes widened as his words sank in. He took her lack of response as an answer in itself.

'Exactly. What d'you think of that?'

Her breathing grew heavier.

He continued. 'If we can't trace the kid and the police don't lead us to them through her, the Golem will. So it's one way or another. And then . . .' he squeezed her jaw in his hand, 'we've got them.'

She felt her stomach start to tighten. Her body temperature to rise. Especially in her groin. Like coiled electric eels, swimming and sparking, trying to find a way out. She kept her eyes on his, opened her mouth slightly. The bruise flowering. He looked down at her, smiled.

There was nothing of the *Guardian*-reading, middle class aesthete in his features now. The veneer of civility was falling away, leaving something feral, carnal in its place. A primal lust. He let her face drop roughly from his hand. Hurriedly took off his suede jacket. Pulled at the buttons of his shirt.

She lay back on the bed, propped up on her elbows, watching him, her legs slowly opening, breasts rising and falling with her breathing. Wanting him. Wanting what he could give her.

He was soon stripped off and joining her on the bed. She saw straight away how hard he was. She smiled. He moved right in next to her. Pushed against her. Towered over her. She could feel the heat coming off his body.

'Do you love me?' Her voice was low, urgent. 'Do you love me?'

'Yes . . .' The word was a hiss through clenched teeth.

Her eyes widened, voice dropped lower. 'Do you hate me?'

He gave a reply that was almost a growl. He grabbed her. Hard.

She needed to hear it. 'Do you hate me?'

'Yes . . .' His voice a snarl now.

She smiled. Good. 'Then show me. Show me. Show me what I mean to you . . .'

He straddled her, his thick, muscled legs either side of her, balancing his weight. He drew his right hand back and, eyes locked on eyes, let it go.

The slap caught her firmly on the side of her cheek. Her head whiplashed sharply to the right. She quickly recovered, looked back at him. A face full of pain, eyes full of lust.

'Again . . . hurt me . . .'

He hit her again. Her cheek reddened, began to swell.

'Again . . .'

He did it again.

And again. Rage and lust driving him on.

She loved him. Like she had never loved anyone or anything before.

He kept at her. Both hands now. Her face, then her body.

She closed her eyes. Lost in pain.

Lost in rapture.

Lost in a special, private love.

15

Marina moved slowly towards the car. A dead woman walking. Her heart was heavier than it had been in a long time; heavier, even, than it might have ever been before.

She opened the door, sat down in the driver's seat. Put her head against the rest. She heard herself sobbing before she felt the tears on her face. Like something coiled so tight within it could only leave her body in short, jagged bursts. Anger. Pain. Loss. Helplessness.

Josephina. Phil. Don and Eileen. Her life.

Coming in sharp, emotional sword thrusts, every blow a hit, stabbing and wounding.

She clenched her fists. Hammered them against the steering wheel, screaming. Pounding hard, pummelling. No words, just incoherent rage. On and on. On and on. Until there was nothing left within her to come out. Until she no longer had the energy to expel it. Until she was spent. Then she sat, head back, eyes closed, breathing like she had just run a marathon. Empty. Empty and down. Her emotions crashed, burnt out.

But she knew it wouldn't last for long. The feeling would only be temporary. She would fill up again. The emotions inside her would need another outlet. They had to. What had happened to her was so huge, such a seismic shift in her life, that there would be no alternative.

She just hoped she would be able to cope.

Love Will Tear Us Apart.

She scrambled for her bag, thrown carelessly on the passenger seat. Began pulling things out, littering the cramped interior. She found the phone, held it to her ear, answered the call.

'Hello . . . hello . . .' Her voice high, shrill. She swallowed hard, tried to cap the desperation rising inside her. 'Hello?'

'Good girl.' The voice again. That same voice.

Marina said nothing. Waited.

The voice said nothing either.

Marina had to break the silence. 'Where is she? Where's Josephina?'

'All in good time.'

'I want to talk to her. Hear her voice . . .'

'Not yet. You've still got . . . there's something you still have to do.'

Desperation welled. A wave of impotent rage swept her body, her legs and feet tingling, her toes curling. 'But . . . please, let me talk to my daughter.' Silence. 'Please . . .'

More silence. She heard a rustling in the background. Muted voices, hushed tones. Nothing she could make out. Then eventually: 'Not yet. You still have something to do for us.'

Marina felt the tears threaten once more. She didn't know if she had the energy to cope with them. 'What . . . Tell me and I'll do it.' Her voice defeated.

'Put this into your sat nav.' It was a postcode. 'Now go there. You'll be given instructions.'

She tried to reassemble her thoughts. Regain her training. 'Why are you doing this?' she asked. 'Look, let's talk. What's . . . what's your name?'

The voice gave a bitter laugh. 'Don't try all that psychological profiler bullshit on me. You can forget that.'

'But—'

'Just go.'

She no longer had the strength to argue.

'And the same rules apply. No police. No one else. No traces. You've done well so far. Don't spoil it now.'

'And then . . . and then can I see my daughter?'

'If you're a good girl and you do what we want.'

'Please, don't . . . don't hurt her. Don't hurt her. Please . . .'

The phone went silent.

Marina had never felt more alone in the world.

She placed the phone on the passenger seat, perched on the summit of the mountain of debris she had taken from her bag. Put the car in gear, left the car park.

Kept one eye on the phone all the time, just in case it rang. Willing it to ring while she drove.

It didn't.

16

It was another characterless corridor in another hospital. Mickey Philips should have been used to them by now, but he wasn't. And in a way he was quite thankful for that.

Over the years, from uniform to plain clothes, he had sat in countless plastic chairs drinking awful brown liquid, and staved off boredom by reading and rereading posters full of stern advice. Advice he forgot instantly in the relief of leaving the hospital. But now, sitting in another plastic chair, nursing another plastic cup of unspecified brown liquid, all those years came back to him.

Waiting for car crash victims to come round and see what parts of their anatomies, their minds, they had lost in the process. Having to tell them they were lucky to be alive. Seeing the look in their eyes saying they didn't share his opinion.

Waiting for women whose husbands had turned their homes into war zones and used them as punchbags and target practice to come through surgery. Seeing if the latest tactical round of tough love had made them brave, given them the courage to press charges and break away to a new start, end the war and win the peace. Or left them wilting and broken, giving their nominated murderer one more chance, because he really did love them.

Waiting while injured children were opened up and operated on, watching every single solid belief the parents had built up about the world and their place in it shown up for the lie they were. Their life's guarantee torn up and no one to complain to about it.

Mickey had sat there every time and hoped their heartache wouldn't infect him. But this time was different. This time he was the grieving friend, the anxious relative. Looking up every time a nurse or doctor walked past. Asking them what was happening, knowing he would only get an answer when there was one to give. Knowing he had to wait like everyone else.

And it was his boss. *His boss.* Getting in this state about his boss. He couldn't believe it. Then he thought about it, and could well believe it.

Phil Brennan was more than just a boss to Mickey. Where others in the force had seen only a bull-headed borderline fuck-up, Phil had seen something special and given him a chance. And Mickey hadn't let Phil — or himself — down. Or he had tried his best not to. Phil had encouraged him, nurtured him. Brought out things in him he didn't know were there. Made him the best DS he could be. And feeling valued, working as part of Phil's MIS team — the Major Incident Squad — for the first time in his career, his life, Mickey had felt like he truly belonged. So to Mickey, Phil was more than his boss. He was one of his own. Closer than family.

The double doors at the end of the corridor opened. In strode a stocky, compact man. Red hair, red face. Early forties. Wearing a weddings-and-funerals suit, but under duress and clearly uncomfortable in it. He looked like a retired rugby player but one who could still surprise with a quick burst of speed or a bout of aggression.

DCI Gary Franks. Phil's — and Mickey's — new boss.

He reached Mickey, stopped.

'So, what have we got, then?' His Welsh accent as vivid as his red hair. 'How's our boy?'

Mickey stood up, ditched his plastic cup in a nearby bin, grateful to be relieved of the pressure of drinking it. 'Still the same. In surgery.'

'Chances?'

Mickey shrugged. 'Pretty good, they say. If they can . . . you know.' His features darkened. 'Better than his father's.'

Franks nodded. 'Bloody waste. His father gone like that, his mother hanging on . . . Any word on the daughter?'

'Nothing.' The words seemed reluctant to leave Mickey's mouth. Forensics are on the scene. They're thinking if she was right near the blast, it could have . . .' He trailed off.

Franks nodded. 'But they're not sure.'

'They've got uniforms on door-to-door. She's prioritised. If anyone's seen her, they'll find out.'

'And Marina?'

Mickey had opened his mouth, about to tell him what had happened, when DC Anni Hepburn arrived. Out of breath, perspiring. Chest rising and falling rapidly, her dark skin covered by a thin sheen of sweat. Mickey, despite the situation, couldn't help stealing an admiring glance at her. Or several. She caught them. The sides of her mouth flicked up in response, then it was back to work.

Mickey and Anni had been dancing around each other for months. Both of them clearly attracted to the other, neither wanting to make the final push. In case something were to go wrong and a good friendship — not to mention a great working relationship — was lost. But the attraction was there. It crackled in the air between them like invisible static.

'Just the person,' said Mickey.

'Sorry, got here as quick as I could,' said Anni, taming her breathing.

Franks turned to her. 'Marina?'

Anni looked at Mickey, as if unsure whether to continue. Mickey returned the look. She had no choice.

'She's gone,' Anni said.

'What d'you mean?' said Franks. 'Gone where?'

'I don't know,' said Anni. Cautious.

MIS didn't have a good history with its recent DCIs. But Franks, blunt and straightforward, honest to the point of offensiveness, seemed different. He had been brought in to give stability, to ground the team. He hadn't been in place long, but they had all taken to him. Even started to respect him. And the respect was mutual.

Franks gave her a look that would have terrified the Pontypool front row.

'She's taken my car.'

Franks frowned. 'What happened?'

'She told me she was going to the loo, and off she went.'

'And you just let her go.'

'What could I do?'

He kept staring. Mickey could see Anni becoming uncomfortable. 'What state was she in?' he asked.

'How d'you think?'

Franks didn't respond.

'But she's one of the team,' Anni said. 'One of our own. Maybe she'll come back.'

'You think it's likely?' asked Franks.

'I'm going after her,' said Mickey. 'I just called in here to see if there was anything she'd left that I could pick up. But there isn't.'

'And she hasn't contacted either of you?'

They both shook their heads.

'There was one other thing,' said Mickey.

The other two waited.

'An eyewitness at Aldeburgh. The guy who stopped Marina going back inside the cottage. DS James from Suffolk said he told her that when Marina was trying to get back to the cottage, she started shouting, "What have I done?"'

Silence. Franks looked at him long and hard.

'"What have I done?" You sure of that?'

Mickey nodded.

'It could mean anything,' said Anni. 'Perhaps she blamed herself, thought she'd, I don't know, left the gas on or something.'

'Did she mention that to you?'

'No,' said Anni. 'Nothing like that.'

'"What have I done?" . . .' Franks was again lost in thought. He looked up, back at his two junior officers. 'You've both worked with her longer than me. What d'you think?'

'You mean you suspect her?' said Anni. 'You think she'd deliberately blow her own family up?'

Franks shrugged. 'Would she?'

'No,' she said. 'Definitely not.'

Mickey agreed.

Franks nodded. 'Running always means guilt.'

'Not always, sir, just usually,' said Mickey.

'Ninety-nine per cent of the time,' said Franks. 'In this case, it's the only thing we have to go on. And since she's not around, we can't ask her.' He looked up and down the hall. Mickey watched his eyes, his face. Got the impression that Franks shared his feelings about waiting in hospitals.

'Right. This is still Suffolk's call and we can't be seen to be treading on their toes. They're looking into what happened at the cottage, they're looking for the daughter. But . . .' Franks pointed at Mickey, 'I want you looking for Marina. And even though it pains us to admit it, with no one else in the picture and her doing a runner, it looks like she's got some serious questions to answer.' He turned to Anni. 'Stay here for now. See what you can get from Phil Brennan or his mother when they come round.'

The three of them fell silent. No one daring to substitute 'if' for 'when'.

'I'll call this . . . DS James?'

Mickey nodded.

'James, right. See if he can question the witness again. Find out anything else.'

'She,' said Mickey.

'What?' said Franks.

'She,' said Mickey again, swallowing. 'DS James is a woman.'

He was aware of Anni's eyes on him. He didn't dare look at her.

'She it is,' said Franks.

He looked off down the corridor, then back to them. 'Somewhere down there,' he said, his voice rumbling, 'is an operating theatre. And in that theatre, surgeons are trying to save the life of one of my best officers. I haven't been here long, but that doesn't mean I don't recognise good coppers when I see them. That's what you all are. Bloody good coppers. And I can't afford to lose any of you.'

Mickey and Anni said nothing.

'So get out there and find out who did this. That explosion was deliberate. We're looking for a murderer. And I'm going to make sure that whoever they are — and I mean whoever — is caught and punished. They made a mistake. They targeted one of our own.' He placed his hands on both of their shoulders. '*Our* own. And we're not going to stand for that.' He straightened up. Dropped his hands. 'Off you go.'

He didn't have to say any more.

They turned and went.

17

With its pitched roof, bland colour and rows and rows of tiny, barely opening windows, the hotel looked like a prison. All it needed was brick walls and razor-wire-topped fences surrounding it.

The female voice of the sat nav, calm, clear and unruffled, announced that Marina had reached her destination. She pulled the car into the car park, turned off the ignition. Waited.

While she was driving, she had started to entertain the hope that her journey would lead to something different. An end. Being reunited with her daughter. Going home once more. She knew this hope was forlorn, that there was no real chance of it happening. Whoever was doing this wouldn't let it happen yet. But once the idea had started to form, the rational part of her mind hadn't been able to stop it. It had grown and grown until, following instructions, she had pulled off the A120 into the car park of the anonymous chain hotel. And then realised that she wasn't going to be reunited with her daughter. Not now.

Not ever.

That thought struck her almost physically. Razor-sharp knives plunged right through her flesh, scraping bone. No.

She couldn't think that. Wouldn't allow herself to think that. If she did . . .

No. Don't.

And then there was Phil, lying unconscious in a hospital bed. She yearned to be near him. To hold him, hear his voice. Something else she might never do again.

She thought of phoning the hospital, finding out how he was. Her fingers even made it to the keypad. But she stopped herself. They might trace the call. And she would never see her daughter again. They might still be watching. And she would never see her daughter again. So she didn't do it.

She checked the sat nav. Hoped — that word again — that she had entered the postcode wrongly. Taken a wrong turn, made a mistake. No mistake. This was where she was supposed to be.

The hotel had been well chosen. At the intersection between the A120 linking Essex to Hertfordshire and the Braintree turnoff, it sat by itself, the surrounding area undeveloped. A beacon of blandness in a desert of nothing.

But, from the road above, easy to spy on. Easy to watch.

She looked out of the window, scanned the car park for anyone suspicious, anyone she could claim as her nemesis, her reason for her being there. It was virtually empty. The hotel was mainly used by business travellers stopping over. Tourists would never venture there. Especially not on a Good Friday evening.

Sodium lamps were coming on, giving the car park a hazy, crepuscular feel. The cars were dark, shiny blobs against the encroaching darkness, insects gathered together to sleep.

She sighed. Thought of her husband. Her daughter. Felt like her insides had been scooped out, burned hollow by acid.

Love Will Tear Us Apart.

She quickly grabbed the phone. 'Yes?'

'You got here all right? Traffic was good?'

In such a short space of time she had come to hate that voice. Mocking. Laughing. Toying with her. Her hand began to shake as she gripped the phone. 'Where is she? Where's my daughter?'

'She's safe. For now. As long as you do what I . . .' An intake of breath. A pause. '. . . what we tell you to.'

Anger rose once more in Marina. Impotent. Hot. 'What? What d'you want me to do? Tell me. I'll do it.'

'Get a good night's sleep first. You've got a big day tomorrow.'

'What?'

The voice sighed. Like it was explaining something really simple to someone even simpler. 'Rest. Sleep. We want you all bright-eyed and bushy-tailed for tomorrow.'

'How can I sleep? With all this going on, with what you've . . . you and my daughter . . .'

The fire went out of her. She felt suddenly tired. So tired, it was an effort to even hold the phone to her ear.

'Finished? Good. Go into the hotel, get a room. There'll be plenty free, it's Easter. People will be at home with their families, asking why everything has to close early and the telly's such shit just because Jesus found himself on the business end of a bit of botched DIY. And wait for the call.'

She said nothing.

'You still there?'

'I'm still here,' said Marina.

'That's the spirit. We'll all get on so much quicker if you toe the line.'

Marina felt as though lead weights were holding her down.

'Have dinner. Sleep. Breakfast. And a shower. I'd recommend a shower. Then tomorrow the work starts in earnest.'

Marina sighed. She could feel bars all round her. Everything was a cage.

'And Marina . . . don't think about escaping. Or phoning your cop friends for help. Or telling anyone in the hotel what's going on. We're watching you. All the time.'

The line went dead.

She threw the handset down on to the passenger seat. Not in anger, just resignation. Then picked it up again, put it in her bag.

She got out of the car, crossed to the hotel.

Ready for a sleepless night.

18

The gym was one of a dying breed. The men inside it too.

Its doorway was down an old, decaying street in Bethnal Green, east London. The surrounding streets had fallen to creeping gentrification, as moneyed next-generation trustafarian bohos and City workers alike made like urban explorers and bought up property. This street had staved off those advances, but crumbling brickwork and increasing rental costs meant that it too would soon be gone. And the gym, its bare brick walls running with condensation, its stripped wooden floors suffused with decades of sweat, would be gone too. An ad agency, perhaps. A marketing company. A coffee shop.

The boxing ring was still in use. Two lean-framed teenagers danced round each other in vests and shorts, heads and hands padded, concentration fixed. Their trainer shouting instructions from the sidelines. Along the side of the room, the free weights were being used, the bags being hit. Boys and men, their skins all shades from pasty white to rich dark brown, worked the room. No trouble. Just the camaraderie of contained aggression.

But not in the basement. The regulars, the punters, never got to go down there. Never had need to. Because there was a different kind of aggression going on below. Not contained, no rules. A room for hire. Soundproofed. Where payments could be made and scores settled. For a price.

Mike Dillman knew all about that. He'd known Lisa was a handful when he met her. That was why he had married her. She was fiery, loud. Quick to anger and ready to fight. He loved that about her. Because it also made her a fantastic fuck. But there was a down side. She got hugely jealous. He just had to look at another woman for her to kick off. And Mike had done more than just look. Often. Now, sitting on a chair in the centre of this room, he wished he'd kept his eyes and hands to himself.

He felt dead. His arms tied behind his back, his legs tied to the legs of the chair. His shirt open. He felt blood running down his face, pain all over, like his body had been wired into the mains.

And there was Lisa, standing in front of him, sweating hard. Bloodied heavy metal glistening on her fists. Chest heaving, eyes shining with a primal light. She looked beautiful. He would give her that.

Behind her, a bored man in a suit sitting on a chair with a porn magazine open on his lap looked at his watch.

'That it, then?' he said. 'You done?'

Lisa shook her head, checked the clock on the wall. 'Got another quarter of an hour yet. Paid for it. Got to use it.'

The bored man shrugged. 'Suit yourself.' Went back to studying his magazine.

Lisa looked down at Mike. The hatred in her eyes, the rage. Beautiful. When she got like this, the sex afterwards was always brilliant. He still wanted her, even after what she'd done to him.

'Learned your lesson?' she shouted. 'Still want to go fucking around with other women? Have you, Mike? Need reminding who you're married to?'

'Yeah,' he managed to gasp in a voice he didn't recognise as his own. 'I'm sorry. You've . . . you've made your point an' I won't do it again. Let's . . . let's go home . . .'

Lisa nodded, pulled her fist back, brought it quickly forward, connecting with his chin. His head went back, blood and spit flew. Jesus Christ, that hurt. Not as much as the last time, though, he noticed. She was getting tired. Her aggression running out like her time.

She stepped back. Head to one side, she studied him.

'That's it,' she said, not turning. 'I'm done.'

Mike looked up. 'I'm sorry . . . Let's . . . Get me up an' we'll . . . we'll say no more about it, yeah?'

Lisa walked away, ignoring him.

The suited man stood up, threw her a towel. 'Go get yourself cleaned up. We'll finish off in here.'

Mike Dillman watched her leave the room, puzzled. The man put his magazine on the chair, looked at the beaten man before him. 'Shouldn't mess around, should you?' he said. Not judgementally, just as a matter of fact. 'Look where it gets you.'

'Yeah,' said Mike. 'Won't do it again.' He tried to move his arms. They hurt. He looked at the man, tried to focus through swollen eyelids. 'You . . . you let me out now, yeah?'

'Just got the cleaning up to do,' said the suited man, crossing into the shadows. He gestured. A shadow detached itself from the back wall, stepped forward. Mike's ruined face managed to register surprise.

And fear.

The shadow moved forward. It was a huge man, hair cropped short, wearing a T-shirt and jeans tucked into boots. His size was impressive, but that wasn't what had drawn Mike's attention. It was his skin. He was the colour of smoke, of shadow. He was grey.

'Who's . . . who's that?'

'We call him the Golem,' said the suited man, his voice businesslike. 'You'll call him the last person you'll see on this earth.'

The man's words registered. Mike began to shake, his earlier pain gone, the need to get away, to live now his only thought. He heard screaming, shouting. Realised it was him. Did it some more.

'Sorry, mate,' said the suited man. 'Out of my hands. She paid for the works. She has a go at you first, then we get rid of you. No point screamin' either. This place is soundproofed. Take it like a man, eh?'

The Golem advanced. Mike screamed.

The Golem reached out. Then stopped as a ringing sound filled the air.

Oh thank God, thought Mike. Thank God . . .

The suited man frowned. The Golem reached into his jeans pocket.

'I have to take this,' he said, pulling out a phone and looking at the display. He spoke heavily accented English.

He put the phone to his ear, waited. Mike stared at him, mouth open, breath held.

'Now? . . . Where? . . . Fee? . . .' He nodded. 'Good.' Pocketed the phone.

'Don't want to hurry you, mate,' said the suited man, 'but we got another one in at seven.'

'No trouble,' said the Golem with his heavy accent. 'Take seconds.'

'No,' said Mike, 'no, no, no . . .'

The Golem reached out, wrapped a huge hand round his neck. Mike stared into his eyes, expecting to see . . . something. Anything. His life flash before him. He saw nothing. Just empty grey pools.

No, he thought, this isn't fair. I can't . . . no. This isn't the way my life ends. It can't be . . . I've—

A quick snap and it was done. Mike Dillman was gone. The Golem straightened up, turned away. 'You clean up,' he said as he passed the suited man. 'He has pissed and shit.'

The Golem disappeared into the shadows. The suited man watched him go. Then he crossed to the centre of the room, began to clean up.

As he reached for the broom, he noticed that his hands were shaking.

A lot.

19

DS Jessica James checked her notebook once more. Looked up. Back to the notes. This wasn't right, she thought.

She looked at the house in front of her, expecting it to match up to the one she had pictured in her head. It didn't. Old, she had thought, but well maintained. Perhaps wooden or clapboard, with charm and character. Idiosyncratic even, but speaking of money and taste. Probably in a stylishly understated manner. Blue and white pottery on the windowsill.

The house before her was nothing like that. It was old, yes, but poorly maintained. The wooden window frames were flaking paint, rotting round the glass. The once white front was now a mottled, mildewed green. The path to the door was broken concrete, weeds sprouting unchecked through the cracks.

Not the kind of house she had expected Stuart Milton to live in.

DCI Franks had phoned her while she was on her way here. She hadn't minded; in fact she had expected it. Would have done it herself if the positions had been reversed. He wasn't trying to tell her her job, he had said, and from the tone of his voice she had believed him. He just wanted to check how the investigation was proceeding and see if there was anything he could do to help.

'Like what?' she had asked.

There came a noise down the phone. She imagined him puffing out his cheeks and blowing air. This, along with the gruff Welsh roll of his voice, gave her the mental image of a bull. 'Anything really,' he had said. 'Background, stuff you want to run by me, support, you name it.'

'I already told—' She stopped herself. Unsure whether Mickey Philips had told his boss that he had come along to help. She suspected Franks knew, but she didn't want to be the one to tell him, just in case he didn't. She didn't want to get Mickey into trouble. 'I've got a team out looking for the missing girl. We'll be following up any leads. I think we've got everything covered,' she had said. 'But if I need anything, you'll be the first to know.'

'Appreciate it.' Franks sounded genuine enough. He paused. For all the gruffness, there was a quality in his voice that she found appealing. Eventually he spoke. 'Marina, Marina Esposito, she's gone. Left the hospital. Did you know?'

'I had heard.'

'Walked out. We need to find her. She's in a fragile state of mind.'

'I can imagine. I'm off to re-interview the eyewitness who was with her. Something he mentioned got me thinking. I'll see if he can add anything else.'

Stuart Milton's testimony hadn't quite rung true. Something niggled and she didn't know what. When she had run the conversation back in her mind, she could find nothing wrong with it. He had seemed like a perfectly credible witness. He had stopped Marina from re-entering the burning cottage, and had the grazes to prove it. But there was something not right about him. Copper's intuition, she had thought. The fact that he had disappeared from the car just confirmed it. Or at least deepened her suspicions of him.

'Good idea, DS James. Keep me posted.'

She said she would, and cut the call.

It was only afterwards that she realised Franks hadn't pressed her on what Stuart Milton had said. That meant he was either a bad copper, which she doubted, or he already knew. That was more likely. At least she didn't have to worry about keeping Mickey's involvement quiet.

Jessie looked round, up and down the terrace. She wouldn't have said Aldeburgh had any mean streets until she came here. She stepped up to the door, knocked on it. There was a bell, but she doubted it was working.

She waited. Was about to knock again when she heard someone making their way towards the door. Slowly, like they were dragging something.

The door opened. A man stood there. Definitely not Stuart Milton. He wore tracksuit bottoms and carpet slippers. An old fraying vest with ingrained stains; on top of that an open shirt with a faded print. His hair was greasy, and although he wasn't fat, his frame looked loose and flabby, like his body had lost a lot of weight but hadn't told his skin.

'Yeah?' He was breathing heavily, like he'd just finished a marathon.

Jessie held up her warrant card. 'DS James, Suffolk Police. I'm looking for Stuart Milton. Is he in?' She'd guessed the answer to the question before she had even asked it.

His eyes turned away from her, unreadable. 'Who?' Said in a rasping voice.

Jessie glanced behind the man into the hallway. It was dimly lit, which hid the poor state of the decor. A little. Against the gloom she made out the frame of a wheelchair, the outline of an oxygen bottle. She didn't need to be a detective to work out that the man had severe respiratory problems. Fatal, even, from the sound of him.

She persisted. 'Stuart Milton. I spoke to him earlier. This was the address he gave me.'

His eyes closed. Once more, she couldn't read them. 'There's . . . no one here . . . by that . . . name . . .' He began wheezing, gripped the door for support. The wheeze threatened to turn into a rumbling, racking cough.

Cancer, thought Jessie. Lung cancer.

He made to close the door. It was clearly an effort.

'Can I just describe him to you? I won't take up much of your time.'

He said nothing. She took that as an invitation and described Stuart Milton.

As she spoke, the man's expression changed slightly. Jessie thought she caught a flash of recognition flit across his eyes. He might even have smiled. She stopped talking. 'You know him?'

The man shook his head. 'No . . .'

'Sure?'

'I said no, didn't I?' There was anger behind his words. It threatened to bring on another coughing fit.

'I won't take up any more of your time, then. Mr . . . ?'

He just looked at her.

'I didn't get your name.'

'Didn't . . . give it . . .'

'Mr?' She waited.

He'd obviously realised he wouldn't get rid of her until she had his name. 'Hibbert. Jeff, Jeffrey . . . Hibbert.'

'Thank you, Mr Hibbert. I'll be on my way now.'

She turned and started back down the path. The door closed behind her. She heard the deferred bout of coughing start, even through the closed door. It sounded like he was trying to cough up his insides.

She walked away.

The evening was gathering, the sky darkening. She should be getting ready to hit the town with her girlfriends for their regular Friday night out. Easter or no Easter. But she didn't want to.

Stuart Milton, who doesn't exist. Jeff Hibbert, who says he doesn't know him but probably does.

This is getting interesting, she thought.

20

Tyrell couldn't relax.

He had tried sitting down. He had tried standing up. Then walking round. First one way, then the other. But nothing worked. Nothing made him feel at ease.

He thought the caravan might have helped. It reminded him of his cell. Small and cramped, it smelled bad, even with the windows open, like the ghosts of previous tenants were still lingering. Everything was worn, overused, and nothing was truly his; he was just using it until the next occupant replaced him.

But he couldn't settle, and he thought the caravan, far from helping, was actually working against him, sending his emotions in the opposite direction.

He had spent the hours alone since Jiminy Cricket had left him there. No one had talked to him or looked in on him. That was OK. He was used to spending time in his own head. He had spent years there. But this felt different. He had decided to try and work out why.

It wasn't the space. That much he knew. It wasn't the view. He had been able to look out of his cell window. And now it was dark, anyway. The lack of noise? Perhaps. There had been plenty of noise in prison. Men locked up behind thick, soundproofed metal doors should have been silent. But prisons weren't silent places. He had lost count of the nights he had lain awake on his bunk trying not to listen to men screaming and crying. Blubbering and bargaining. Then the other voices, weak but trying to be strong. Shouting at the screamers. Sing us a song. Tell us a joke. Give us a poem. A life story. Laughing, promising what would happen if they did. And what would happen if they didn't.

At first he had tried to match the voices with the faces the next morning. Pick them out. But he soon gave up on that. Because while he was doing it to them, they were doing it to him. And he didn't want anyone working out his daytime talking voice from his night-time crying one.

Sometimes he doubted he would be able to sleep without the noise. And there was hardly any noise here.

Apart from the child.

He had heard it when he arrived. Asked about it. Where was the child, why was it crying? No reply. And then it had stopped and he had stopped thinking about it. Began to doubt he had even heard it. Not outside, anyway. For real. Just inside his head. He could always hear things inside his head. And was always being told they weren't real.

So he had ignored it. Let it go. Kept his mind blank, which wasn't hard. They had given him medication to help in prison. Tablets that took his headaches away and made him forget. Traded a head full of needles for a head full of fog. But it wasn't always his head that hurt, he told them. Sometimes it was his heart. But he couldn't remember why. And that made it worse. Forgetting was better.

Prison. Even that was starting to slip away. How long had he been out? One day? More? Less? No. One day. He was sure. Because he hadn't slept in the caravan yet. He would have remembered waking up there.

Prison was a room like this. Prison was someone feeding him three meals a day. Prison was walking in a square. Prison was classrooms and workshops. Prison was books. Prison was living inside his own head. Prison wasn't this. Prison didn't have a door he could open.

And that was what unsettled him.

He could get up, cross the floor of the caravan and open the door. Step out any time he wanted. No one had to do it for him. He didn't have to wait for special times. He could just get up and do it himself.

But he didn't. Couldn't.

Hadn't.

He looked again at the door. The handle. Both thin metal. Easy to open. One turn. A push. And out.

He kept staring at the door. And felt himself rise to his feet. Like an unseen force was pulling him upright and moving him towards it. Like a horror film zombie in a voodoo trance.

He crossed the floor of the caravan. Reached the door. Put his hand out. Held it over the door handle. Not touching, but he could feel it, sense it. Waves of energy came off it towards his hand. Willed him to grasp it, turn it . . .

He took his hand away. Let it drop by his side. He couldn't do it. Not after all this time. Not after . . .

His hand reached out again. Again he felt that force around his fingers. And again he let his hand drop by his side.

He sighed. Turned. Crossed the caravan again. Was about to sit down when he heard something.

The child crying once more.

Tyrell stopped. Looked round. It was coming from outside. From the house beside the caravan. He hadn't imagined it. The crying was real.

He turned back towards the door. Held out his hand. Let it drop.

The child kept crying.

He felt something in his mind. Some trigger. Long ago and out of reach of his memory. Something in the fog. It was about a child. A small child. A night-time crying voice. In his head. His heart. Buried deep. Way deep. And every time he wanted to make it stop. Had to find a way to make it stop. To give it rest.

The child kept crying.

He reached out for the handle. His heart was hammering, his legs shaking.

He gripped the handle.

He could feel the blood pumping in his head. Hear it in his ears. It nearly blocked out the child. Nearly, but not quite.

He tightened his grip. Took a deep breath. Another.

Turned the handle.

And stepped outside.

21

Marina couldn't sleep. Out of all the things that had happened to her that day, this was the least surprising.

The hotel was recently built and virtually deserted. No Good Friday business overnights. Muzak echoed round beige hallways. Marina wondered how somewhere so new could feel so haunted.

She sat on the edge of the bed, perched, ready to jump, unable to relax. She pointed the TV remote, flicked round the channels, looking for news of her daughter, her husband. A comedy panel show she had previously found funny was now just irritating and arch. Flick. A big-budget Hollywood blockbuster with last-second stunt escapes from explosions. Flick. A contemporary musical retelling of Jesus's crucifixion with stage-school kids pretending to be urban. Flick. The news. She watched, flinching, like she was expecting a punch. Nothing.

She dropped the remote on the bed. Lay back and stared at the ceiling, despair eating her up from inside, and thought about her family.

Until she met Phil, until they had Josephina, she had believed family to be something to escape rather than embrace. The nuns who taught her at school had told her that it was the most important thing a person could have in their life. Marina had sat there, not daring to speak up for fear of being hit again, but thinking: *Really? You haven't met mine, then.*

Her father, a lying, bullying, cheating, alcoholic wife-beater who had walked out on the family when she was seven, returning occasionally to spread his particular brand of anguish and upset. Her mother, more punchbag than person. And her two brothers, who, when she had last seen them, seemed to be doing their best to emulate their father's life and work.

But the nuns, for all their fierce attempts to impart to her a love of Jesus Christ with whatever instrument of punishment the law would allow, physical or otherwise, had at least done one thing right. Spotted her intelligence.

A scholarship had taken her from secondary school in Balsall Heath, Birmingham, to Cambridge, where she studied psychology. Revenge on her father was how she regarded it at the time. Trying to understand why he was the way he was and did what he did. Marina had inherited his dark Italian looks and sometimes, she feared, his temper. At the back of her mind the course might have been a way for her to understand herself. Or how to not turn out like him.

Her mother had died of cancer before she could see her daughter graduate, something Marina always regretted. But she knew in her heart that her mother had been proud of her.

Her brothers less so. The last she had heard of the elder, Lanzo, he was doing time for a string of robberies on petrol stations in Walsall, with no imminent release date.

Her other brother, Alessandro, had contacted her recently. Now living in Jaywick, Essex, he had suggested they go out to dinner. She hadn't wanted to respond, but Phil, having no siblings of his own, insisted she make the effort.

They met for dinner in the Warehouse, a brasserie in Colchester. As soon as Alessandro entered, Marina knew it was a mistake. He had brought with him a woman who was dressed as if for the late shift in a seedier copy of Spearmint

Rhino, and as soon as he found out what Phil did for a living, he cursed him fluently in two languages.

The meal never reached dessert.

Alessandro had phoned a couple of days later and apologised. Said he was under a lot of stress, shouldn't have said what he did. Wanted her to know he was there for her, his little sister, whatever she needed. Wanted to try again.

Marina had never phoned him back.

Phil and Josephina. That was her family. And she had never felt a stronger need to see them than the one inside her now.

She got up off the bed, fighting back tears, screams. She could see them both in her mind's eye. Phil, tall, blond and good-looking; Josephina, with her dark curls and wide eyes, taking after her. She wished they were together, wished she could touch them, hold them, tell them what they meant to her. She felt her body start to slip into emotional meltdown once more, knew that wouldn't help. She fought it. Tried to do something positive, something that would help.

She looked down at her bag. The alien phone stared up at her. She picked it up. Gazed at it. It would be so easy . . .

No. They might be monitoring it. She looked round the room again. The phone on the bedside table. A beige plastic box. She saw the faces of Phil, of Josephina, and felt how her whole being was aching to see them again. She had to risk it.

She picked up the receiver, punched the button for an outside line. Directory Enquiries.

'Ipswich General, please.'

She was connected. It rang. Was answered.

'Yes,' said Marina, voice small and croaking, trembling. 'You've . . . Phil Brennan. You've got a patient called Phil Brennan. I'd . . . I'd like . . . How is he, please?'

She was asked for her name and relationship.

'I'm . . . I'm his wife.' No going back now.

She was asked to wait. Plunged into silence. Her heart hammered louder than the hold music. The nurse came back on.

'He's stable,' she said. 'Out of surgery and resting.'

'Oh, thank God . . .'

The nurse was about to say something more but seemed distracted by someone else on the end of the phone. 'Can I . . . can I just ask you to stay on the line, please?'

Marina slammed the phone down.

No one was going to trace that call.

She tried to sit back on the bed but was humming from the conversation, the contact. She replayed the words in her head. Stable. Out of surgery.

She felt that ache in her heart, that yearning. She desperately wanted to be with him. Needed to. She looked round the room. Crossed the floor, looked out of the window. It was dark outside. The car park was in shadowed pools from the orange sodium lights. Beyond that was the A120.

Marina looked at the phone lying on the bed. It hadn't rung. She had been told they wouldn't ring until the morning. She looked again at the window, the road.

They can't be watching all the time, she thought. Not round the clock. Her heart beating faster, she made up her mind. She picked up her car keys. Left the room.

The lobby was deserted. No one on the desk, no one in the hall. She made her way to the front door, moving as fast as possible, then stepped outside. She stopped, looked round. Checked every angle, every corner of the car park for an observer. Looked up to the road, checked there too.

Saw no one anywhere.

Trying not attract attention by running, she hurried to the car, got in. Turned the engine over and, giving one last look round, made her way out of the car park. Up the slip road, on to the A120. Heading eastwards. Towards Phil. Scanning behind her all the time, checking for other cars following her.

Traffic was light. No one came up the slip road after her. No one joined the A120 at the same point. She breathed a huge sigh of relief. Felt a smile crawl on to the corners of her mouth. Gave a giddy laugh.

She hadn't been followed. She knew she hadn't. *Felt* she hadn't. She approached the roundabout, ready to turn left and speed away.

Then she heard it.

Love Will Tear Us Apart.

Her heart turning to stone, she put the call on loudspeaker.

'Who's been a naughty girl, then?'

That voice again. That same fucking stupid voice.

'I . . . I don't know what you mean . . .'

'You were told to stay in the hotel. You're not there now, are you?'

'I . . . I . . .' Her hands began to shake on the steering wheel.

'Turn the car round, go back to the hotel, wait for instructions in the morning.'

The roundabout was ahead of her. She signalled. Went right round it. Back the way she had come.

'Good girl,' said the voice.

The hotel was in front of her once more. She signalled and turned off. Pulled up in the same slot in the car park.

'Just do as you're told, Marina. Then we'll all be happy.'

The phone went dead.

Marina sat there, numb.

Eventually she got out of the car and went back to the room.

To stare at the ceiling all night.

22

The night air hit hard, making Tyrell gasp. It was unexpectedly cold, especially when the April day had been so warm. But then night was something he had only watched from his prison window for years, never actually experienced.

He shivered. The shirt he was wearing was long-sleeved, but he wished he had put a sweatshirt over it. A timid voice told him to go back inside, ignore the crying child and stay where it was safe, and he struggled not to let it win. He looked round, took a couple of deep breaths that fizzed coldly into his lungs and moved forward, away from the caravan.

He smelt salt on the air. It reminded him of the prison on the Isle of Sheppey. He could only make out street lights and house lights far away in the distance. The lights were on in the house next to the caravan. And that was where the noise of the crying child came from.

He stepped away from the caravan, shivering, and moved towards the house. It was old and big, although it may only have seemed that way to Tyrell after being in such a small space for so long. It reminded him of somewhere else. Another house. Another time. A time when . . .

No. He closed his eyes. Screwed them tight shut. No. Don't think about that. Don't go back there.

He slowly opened his eyes. The house was still in front of him. But the other one, the old one, was gone. Good.

He walked unsurely, the ground rutted, holed and uneven. The dogs outside the house remained quiet. There were lights on in the downstairs rooms. The car he had arrived in was parked out front next to the old boxy silver one.

The he heard it again.

He stopped moving, tuning out the wind in his ears, concentrating on the child. It was a child, definitely. A little girl, it sounded like. Crying. Not happy at all. He moved closer until he was right beside the window. He managed to make out some words.

'Mummy . . . Daddy . . . Lady . . . please . . .'

And then another voice cut in, one he didn't recognise. An angry voice telling the child to shut up, which just provoked more crying.

A shiver ran through Tyrell from more than the cold. A memory swirled into his head of another child. Sad and lonely. Wanting reassurance and love. Getting only anger and pain. Pain that hurt right down inside.

He closed his eyes again, trying to force the memory to swim back down into the blackness. Force it, force it . . .

He opened his eyes. The memory was gone. But the child was still crying. Tyrell had to do something. Make the crying stop. Find a way to make the child happy.

He knelt down beneath the window, feeling something rise within him that he couldn't name because he didn't recognise it. Bravery?

He poked his head up very slowly, looked inside. A kitchen. On the table was a laptop and some other electronic equipment, a half-empty whisky bottle and a couple of glasses. A rough-looking woman sat at the table, looking at the laptop. On the floor beside her, a length of rope tying her wrist to the doorknob, was a little girl. Dark-haired and sad-eyed, her face red and wet. The woman at the table was trying to ignore her. Her face was red too, but Tyrell imagined that was probably from the whisky.

The woman turned to the girl, who pulled away from her, scooting back on the floor as far as the rope would let her. The crying stopped, replaced by fear. Another shiver ran through Tyrell. What had the woman done to the little girl to make her so scared?

'Fucking shut up,' she said. Her voice sounded weird. Like it wasn't tuned in properly. 'Told you before. You'll go home when your mother does what she's told.' She shook her head, looking back at the screen. 'Little twat. Should just feed you to the dogs . . .'

The words shocked Tyrell. He moved away from the window as if he had been struck. As he did so, he lost his footing and stumbled backwards. The dogs heard the noise and began to bark. He got quickly to his feet, flattened himself against the wall. Slowly stuck his head round the back of the house. The dogs were caged up by the back door, snouts at the mesh, barking and slavering. He pulled his head back in. Fast.

Tyrell looked back in the window. The woman at the kitchen table was swearing at the dogs, telling them to shut up. They ignored her. The little girl cried all the more. The woman got up, made her way angrily to the back door.

Tyrell was breathing heavily, as if he had done something strenuous. He saw a pile of firewood stacked against the wall of the house, near the front. He scurried under the window, picked out a heavy log; small enough to grasp firmly, long enough to swing, heavy enough to hurt. He tested it out a couple of times, got a good action going. Then went under the window back to where he had been. He breathed deeply. Once. Twice. Ready to move for the back door.

'Going somewhere, Malcolm?'

Tyrell jumped, nearly dropping his club. He turned. There was Jiminy Cricket, the happy, smiling voice of his conscience.

He wasn't smiling now.

'I said, are you going somewhere, Malcolm Tyrell?' The name said with hard emphasis, like he was pushing it into stone with his fist.

Tyrell swallowed, his throat suddenly dry, his legs shaking. Despite the open air, the night, this was just like being back inside, facing down some bully on his spur.

'I'm . . . I'm . . . There's a girl in there. A little girl. Crying.'

'She's no business of yours.'

'She's . . . she's crying . . .'

'She's fine.'

'The woman at the table, she said she would feed her to the dogs . . .'

Jiminy Cricket tried to laugh, put on an American accent once more, screeched, 'Now get back in there and don't come back until you've got a toddler!' The accent dropped. His eyes flared. 'Go back to the caravan.'

Tyrell's shaking increased. Not from fear this time, but anger. He felt the wood in his hand. This wasn't like facing down a bully. His weapon made the difference.

'You wanna piece o' me? That it?' The American accent returned, this time a ridiculous gangster parody. He spread his arms wide and smiled. 'Give it your best shot.'

Tyrell pulled his arm back, ready to swing it forward.

'But do that, and I'll fuckin' have you.' His voice, down and dark, told Tyrell he would. And he would enjoy it too.

Tyrell looked between the window and his companion. Looked at the log in his hand. Saw how his arm was shaking. Looked back to Jiminy Cricket. Who smiled. 'Drop it,' he said, like he was speaking to one of the backyard dogs.

Realising he had no alternative, Tyrell complied.

'Good. Now go back to your caravan. You've got a big day tomorrow.'

As though he was following an order from a wing officer, he did as he was told.

The caravan was slightly warmer than the night outside. He sat down on the bed. He saw the door being shut, heard the key being turned.

His first night of freedom, and he was locked up again.

23

Jeff Hibbert sat up in bed, staring at the ceiling, unable to sleep. He kept replaying the visit from that policewoman over and over in his mind, but that wasn't what was keeping him awake.

Sitting like this was the only way he could get any respite from the pain, the only position he could sleep in. Like the Elephant Man, his wife had said, shortly before she left him.

Helen Hibbert had been a bitch. He knew that. It was why he had married her. She would try to outdo all the other women they knew, flirt with their men, lead them on, even shag a couple. All with Jeff's blessing. Because it had turned him on. She'd even let him watch sometimes. The other wives had hated it. Hated them. Or feared them. And that had been the real thrill.

Jeff and Helen had had what they liked to think of as an unconventional, uninhibited marriage. Unique, different. And they didn't care who got in their way. It had been fun, but Helen had eventually tired of it. Then she had turned on Jeff, and that hadn't been so much fun.

The lung cancer had hit at the worst possible time. He had just lost his job and with it their lifestyle. He had plans how to get it back, oh yes, plans that would make them a shit-load of money. Because Jeff knew where the bodies were buried. And where bodies that should have been buried were still walking around. But the lung cancer stopped that and Helen got tired of waiting. Started flirting with other men again. Younger men. Fitter men. Men who didn't cough up blood. Who knew how to treat a woman. In front of her crippled husband, if necessary. And Jeff stopped finding it all so funny.

'I don't know what'll hurt you more,' Helen had said one morning after the latest pick-up had been dispatched. 'Me leaving or me staying.'

So she had moved in with the latest one, leaving Jeff alone to die.

And all those dirty, filthy secrets that were going to make him rich, he could do nothing with. They would benefit someone, though. His co-conspirators, ex-partners. And Jeff hated that. *Hated* it. In fact, it was the hate that would kill him. But not yet. Because for now, it was the only thing keeping him alive.

Still, he thought, at least they won't benefit Helen. That's something.

What a waste. All that planning, the hours he'd put into it. A waste. He reached out his hand, felt the edge of his laptop under the bed. It was all on there. What had been done, the cover-ups, the plans he had made to get even, to make him rich, everything. All there. Safe.

And all fucking useless to him now.

He pulled his hand back up, stared again at the ceiling. Chest wheezing as he breathed in and out, lungs like needle-laced bagpipes. That policewoman.

Stuart Milton. Very fucking clever. Or so they thought. But dangerous. Almost giving themselves away.

He knew why that name had been given. And his address. It was a warning. *We know where you live*. Couldn't have been clearer if they'd trailed the message from the back end of a plane in the air along the seafront. *And we can get you any time.*

Yeah, yeah. Whatever. If the cancer doesn't get me first.

He tried to sleep. His eyes had barely closed when he heard the noise from downstairs.

His eyes snapped open.

He heard the noise again. Someone was entering the house.

Jeff Hibbert's heart began to pound, adding to the pain in his chest.

They've come for me, he thought. That's it. They've come for me.

As he struggled painfully to rise and leave his bed, common sense kicked in. Helen. That was who it was. Brought some bloke back to gloat. Bitch. He relaxed back against the built-up pillows. He would ignore her. Pretend to be asleep. Not care what she did. That would show her.

Something smashed. Then something else.

That wasn't Helen.

Hibbert sat up again, ignoring the pain this time. He swung his legs out of bed as quickly as he could. His heart was pounding once more, fear driving adrenalin round his system. Numbing him slightly, temporarily, giving him the strength he needed to move. He reached out, made a grab for his dressing gown from the back of the door. Couldn't hold it, dropped it.

Footsteps on the stairs. Heavy, trying to be quiet. Definitely not Helen.

He knelt down to pick up the dressing gown, but couldn't get his fingers to work. They brushed the edge of the laptop. Pushed it further in. No one was getting that. No one.

The footsteps stopped outside his door. Hibbert held his breath. The door opened.

Hibbert's eyes travelled up the huge legs of the visitor, took in the muscled torso, the thick arms. The head, hair cropped, angled down at him. Eyes blank.

It was like Frankenstein's monster had arrived.

'Get out . . .' Hibbert didn't have the breath to make the words carry, the strength to make them mean anything.

The intruder looked at him.

'I know . . . who you are,' Hibbert said. 'I know . . . what you want . . .'

The intruder reached out an arm, picked Hibbert up off the bedroom floor. The pain was excruciating. Hibbert cried out, tried to grab the arm, get it to put him down. It was like arguing with a concrete post. And the same colour. He looked at the skin of the intruder. Grey. Like concrete. Like a dead man.

Hibbert knew who this was. And with that realisation came another: I'm going to die.

Now.

He laughed. It sounded as broken as the rest of him. 'You . . . you can't kill me. I'm . . . already dead . . .'

'Yes. But a dead man with something to tell me. To give me.' The voice matched his skin. Hard. Dead.

'I don't . . . don't . . .'

The Golem cut him off. 'Where is it?'

Hibbert tried to laugh, to stonewall, but his eyes betrayed him. They glanced down to the side of the bed. The Golem caught the look.

'Get it.'

He relaxed his grip, and Hibbert slid down on to the bed. With his shrunken frame in his filthy, sweaty pyjamas, he looked like a collection of old rags. He stared up at the Golem once more, eyes burning. A last act of defiance.

'Get it yourself.'

The Golem leant down, slid the laptop from under the bed. Looked at Hibbert once more. 'Password?'

Hibbert gave another broken laugh in reply.

Then the pain in his body went off the scale. The Golem had grabbed him, was pushing his fingers under his ribcage, trying to squeeze his infected lungs. He felt one rib snap. Two. The pressure increased.

Hibbert screamed like he had never screamed before.

'Password.' The dead voice once more.

'Helen . . .' Gasped out. The pain subsided to manageable levels.

Hibbert kept his head down. He had soiled his pyjamas. He knew this was the end. Anger welled up within him. For himself. For Helen. For his whole stinking, rotten, fucking awful life. He felt tears on his face.

'This . . . It wasn't supposed to . . . to . . . end like this . . . wasn't supposed to end . . . at all . . .' More sobbing. 'Helen . . . Helen, I'm . . . I'm sorry . . .'

The Golem, laptop under one arm, reached out his other hand. Hibbert looked up.

'You don't need to . . . I'm . . . I'm a dead . . . a dead man . . .'

The snap was small, almost delicate. Hibbert slumped to the bed. The Golem looked down at him.

'Now you are dead man.'

He turned and left.

The house was still. Dark. As though no one had ever been there.

24

Midnight. And Good Friday became Easter Saturday. And DC Anni Hepburn was still in the hospital.

'You should go home, Anni,' Franks had said to her. 'Get some rest. There's others can take over here.'

She had given a weak smile in response. 'I know, boss, but I'll only be back here tomorrow. And it'll save me coming up and down the A14 again.'

'The road to hell,' Franks said, smiling. 'Well, OK. Just remember we're not supposed to be working this case. If something comes up and I need you, you've to come down straight away. Leave it to Suffolk.'

She had agreed with him and he had left.

Phil Brennan was out of surgery and resting in a private room. He still hadn't regained consciousness and Anni hadn't been allowed in to see him. No need, the doctor had said. He won't be saying anything for a while.

'What're his chances of a full recovery?'

The doctor had shrugged. 'Depends what you mean. He's been burnt and may need some grafts, if it comes to that. But we're hoping it won't. His head injury wasn't as serious as we first thought. We've relieved the swelling and we'll keep him under observation in case there's any sign of embolism or thrombosis. But on the whole, I'm optimistic. We're keeping him sedated for now. We'll look at him again in the morning.'

She thanked him and went back to the fold-out bed they had provided for her. But she didn't get far. At the end of the corridor she heard the squeak of rubber tyres. A wheelchair came round the corner, the occupant pushing it slowly towards her.

It took a while, but Anni recognised who it was. Eileen Brennan.

The woman looked dreadful. All bandages and bruises. Pale skin and deep, dark eyes. She pushed the chair level with Anni.

'Where is he?' she said, looking round. 'They said he was down here.'

'Eileen? Eileen Brennan?'

Eileen looked up. Anni caught the wildness in her eyes. She wondered what was holding the woman together, what kind of spirit she had.

'Who are you?'

'Anni Hepburn. I work with Phil.'

'Oh.' Her head dropped as she processed the information. Then back up at her. 'Is he here?'

Anni gestured to the room, the closed door. 'He's in there. But we're not allowed to go in.'

'Why not?'

'They say he needs rest. That he'll get better without interruptions.'

'Interruptions.' Eileen nodded to herself, then looked up and down the corridor, disorientated, as if she had suddenly come round and was surprised to find herself in this place. Didn't know where she was.

Anni was used to dealing with people. She found a smile. 'Did they tell you to come down here? Did they give you the chair?'

Eileen looked at her.

'Bet they didn't.' Another smile. 'But good for you.'

Eileen made a noise that started out as a laugh but mutated into a strangled gasp. 'They said I could see him tomorrow. That I should get some rest. But he's my son . . .' Her voice became a shallow, brittle thing. Her hands gripped the arms of the chair, trembling. 'I had to see him. He's . . . all . . .' Her body began to shake as the tears welled up and out. Her head dropped as if she couldn't bear to be seen.

Anni knelt down next to her. 'Come on, Eileen, let's get you back to the ward.' She repeated what the doctor had told her. Eileen looked up, a desperate hope trying to shine through her wet and wounded eyes. 'You can see him tomorrow.'

'Really? They . . . they think he'll be . . .'

'They're hopeful. Come on, let's get you back.'

Eileen allowed herself to be pushed. They talked on the way. Anni felt the measure of Eileen's loss, her grief.

'Don's gone . . . *gone* . . . and I just . . . I don't know. I can't lose Phil as well . . .'

'I know. Well let's hope we won't. He's my boss. One of the few I've liked.'

Eileen wasn't listening. Her grief had overtaken her.

Anni left her at the ward, where a nurse took over, and went back to her own bed. Hoping she would sleep and that tomorrow would be better.

Somehow she doubted either.

PART TWO: SILENT SATURDAY

25

Marina woke up feeling terrible. She could never normally sleep the first night away from home in a strange bed and would find herself waking up every hour at every unfamiliar noise, constantly wondering where she was and why her room had been changed round. And this situation was far from normal. This was extreme.

She had lain there, staring at the wall, the ceiling. Wondering if someone or something was hiding in the shadows, waiting to attack her. Watching the blade of light under the locked door for anyone trying to enter the room. Or even slipping a message underneath. Seeing the faces of her husband, her daughter, every time she closed her eyes.

At some point her body had been too exhausted to stay awake any longer and she had slept. But even then she couldn't rest. Her dreams were shallow and anxious, her subconscious screaming at her not to relax or give in, and her body had responded, jolting itself awake throughout the night.

And the phone hadn't rung.

She had picked it up from the bedside table whenever her eyes were open, checking without hope to see whether there was a missed call, as if somehow the noise wouldn't have woken her up. A text, even. There were no missed calls. No texts.

Sometimes she had curled herself up foetally, given in and cried. Other times she had screamed and kicked, rage surging round her body like electricity, angry words spat from a spittle-flecked mouth. Or she had just lain there, trying not to think about herself or her family, not to feel anything. Willing herself to numbness.

In this way, the night had passed.

She dragged herself out of bed and hauled herself into the bathroom. The light was as harsh and unforgiving as a convention centre. She checked her body, found she was externalising what she felt internally. One side of her displayed bruises and gravel rash from the explosion and was sore to the touch. The face in the mirror belonged to a woman at least ten years older than the previous day's. Eyes haunted and dark-rimmed.

She splashed water on her face, tried to bring herself back to life. Then decided to have a shower. Before she did that, she went back into the bedroom, fetched the phone, checking for calls. None. She got into the shower, and immediately began to worry whether steam or water would render the phone useless and she would miss the call.

She closed her eyes. Tried not to think of anything. Felt the warm water on her skin. Caressing her, relaxing her. And immediately felt guilty for almost enjoying it.

Out of the shower, she checked the phone again. It still worked, but there had been no call or text. The action of checking, although nothing in itself, was becoming physically wearying.

She walked back into the bedroom, towelling herself off. Her heart sank even further as she looked at the pile of clothes on the floor. She wanted to never see them again, to burn them, forget them. They were dirty, torn from the explosion, sweaty from her exertions. But she had no other clothes, so she had to wear them.

Once she was dressed, her tangled curly hair finger-combed, she sat on the bed and waited. With nothing to do, she flicked on the TV. The news was on, local. Not much happening. A car accident on the A12. Cuts to public services in Braintree. A convicted murderer released on licence had failed to show up at his hostel. Marina, preoccupied, not listening, barely took it in.

And then the phone rang.

Love Will Tear Us Apart.

She grabbed for it, held it to her ear. Heart pounding.

'Yes . . . ?'

The voice was singing. 'This is the day-ay, your life will surely cha-ay-ange . . .' Then laughing. 'Good morning. Sleep well?'

'Where's my daughter? Is she safe?'

'All in good time. Today's the day! Do what we want, do it properly, the way we want it, and you'll get your daughter back. Unharmed. What a bargain.'

'No.' Marina swallowed down the rage, fear and panic in her voice. Trying to act professionally, she remained calm and reasonable. 'I want to help you. And I will help you. But before I do that, I want to hear her. I need to hear her. Put her on. Now.'

'Can't do that.'

Marina's heart was pounding so hard she could barely hear her own voice. Her hand was trembling. 'Then I'm sorry, but I won't be able to help you.'

A silence on the phone. 'Sorry you feel that way.'

'I do.' Marina was almost hyperventilating. All the words that had spun through her head during the night came spewing out. 'I do. You've got two choices. Let me speak to her, let me know she's alive and well, and I'll do what you want. Otherwise . . .'

'What?'

'I call the police. Right now. Tell them everything.'

A sharp intake of breath. 'I don't think so.' The voice was trying to be calm, but she clearly had it rattled.

'I do.' She wished her heart held the conviction her voice spoke with. 'And so do you. You know you have no choice. So put her on. Please.' Her voice caught on the final word. She hoped it hadn't been noticed.

Silence. No . . . they've gone, she thought. I'll never hear from them again. Josephina's dead for sure now. And it's all my fault. I was trying to be clever. It's all my—

'Mummy?'

'Jo? Josie darling, I'm here . . .'

'Mummy! Mummy! There's . . .' Her voice stopped, replaced by muffled sounds.

'Josie! Josie! Listen, I'm coming for you, I'm . . .'

The first voice was back on. She could hear her daughter's muffled cries in the background. 'There. Told you we've got her. Told you she's OK.'

'What have you done with her? What have you fucking done with her?' Screaming, not caring who heard.

'Nothing.' The voice shouted, struggling to be heard over Marina and her daughter's screaming. 'Nothing. She's well and unharmed. And she'll stay that way if you do as you're told.'

Marina tried to regain composure. 'And if I do that, I get her back and . . . and that's that?'

'That's that.'

Marina was breathing heavily. Adrenalin was pumping round her system. 'It had better be. Because if you're lying, or if you hurt her, if you so much as touch her, I will find you. And I will kill you.' As she spoke those words, Marina realised she had never in her life believed anything with as much conviction. She could feel her father's rage within her.

'Fine. OK. Whatever.' The voice was struggling to appear to be in control. 'Here's your postcode for the sat nav. Get on with it.'

The line went dead. A few seconds later, a text came through.

She left the room.

26

Dee Sloane watched as Michael Sloane lined Jeff Hibbert's laptop up with the corners of the desk.

'Right,' he said. 'Here we go . . .'

He typed in a password and sat back. The screen before them changed, the system allowing them entrance. He turned his face up to her, beamed. She smiled back in return. Winced as she did so.

Her face was still sore from where he had hit her. As was her whole body. But good sore. Sexy, tingly sore. She ran her tongue round the inside of her mouth. Found a loose tooth. Waggled it. Enjoyed the little charges of pain that shot through her jaw.

He was still looking at her. At first she thought he must be thinking the same thoughts she was. How good it had been yesterday. How he had almost broken her. How she couldn't wait for him to do it again. Then she caught the look in his eye. She knew that look. Knew what he was thinking. What it meant. Concentrate on what he was doing.

Her first instinct was to play up. A little thrill of defiance ran through her. She smiled, sending back her own message. He usually liked it when she did this. It was all part of the game they played together, how they had fun. But she had caught something else in that look. There was no trace of his assumed identity, kindly, *Guardian*-reading Stuart Milton.

Don't fuck me around, the look said. *This is serious.*

Do what he wants, she thought, or face the consequences later. Where a whole different kind of pain will be involved. She bowed her head submissively. Looked down at the laptop. 'Well done,' she said.

The correct response. He nodded. She smiled in return. They could always play their game later.

'It's on here,' he said. 'Everything we need. Somewhere. I've just got to . . .'

He began to hit buttons, scroll down menus. She watched over his shoulder. Trying to keep her mind on what he was saying. Interested but not excited. It was important, a matter of life and death, even. But the actual process was boring.

He became engrossed in columns of words and numbers. She looked round. Their living room had become a war room. Dee was used to it by now. Their business often demanded it. And she had always tolerated it, because business was important. It was their lives. She had allowed the expensive furniture to be moved, the table and chairs placed in the centre of the room. But she was always relieved when they went back to their proper places afterwards. When order was restored.

The house slave had been locked in her room. Not allowed to bear witness. There was just the two of them.

And the Golem.

He stood in the corner by the door. Still, silent. His body motionless, his face blank, his eyes hidden by shadow. Like an automaton waiting for a new instruction. Her eyes trailed over him. A very handsome, well-sculpted automaton. Even with the grey skin. In fact the grey skin made him even more interesting.

Michael was engrossed in the laptop. Dee moved away and left him to it. She walked slowly round the room, supposedly without purpose, eventually fetching up next to the

Golem. She looked at him closely. He was wearing a T-shirt and jeans, the fabric pulled tight over his honed torso. She felt that familiar ache, that tingling in her groin. The Golem didn't look at her, gave no acknowledgement that she was even there. That just intensified the ache.

When she felt this way — which was often — she had to be satisfied. There was nothing sophisticated about it, nothing civilised. It was just a physical craving, an animal lust that needed sating. Like a basic need, food to stave off hunger. Her mind would absent itself, her body would take over and she wouldn't stop until she had had enough. Usually Michael could satisfy it, but if he wasn't there, she had to find other methods. Other people.

And a grey-skinned killer would do just fine.

She licked her lips. Reached out a hand. Traced the line of his bicep with her finger. He turned to her as she did so. His eyes looking straight into hers. She felt her heart stepping up in her chest as she smiled in what she hoped was an inviting way. Anticipating what was to come.

She kept stroking, pressing harder.

He kept looking at her.

'Nice . . .' she said, her finger still moving. 'Strong . . .'

Eyes still locked, she bit her bruised lip hard, enjoying the pain. She worked her teeth round, drew blood. Bit down harder. Felt the taste of hot pennies in her mouth. Hot, wet pennies. She ran her tongue round her teeth, opened her lips, smiled, her red-stained teeth glistening.

He stared at her eyes, her teeth. Then, impassively, looked away.

His response was emotionless, but that made it all the more dismissive. She should have felt shamed, humiliated by it. She did. And that just made the tingling, the ache, stronger.

'You're a robot,' she said, her voice low, slushy with blood, 'a big human robot.' She giggled. 'You're all power. Scary.' Her breathing grew faster. 'Would you make me fear you? If I let you?' She moved in closer. 'Would you?'

He said nothing. Her fingers traced down the side of his body, down his hard torso.

'What if I begged—'

'Dee.'

She looked up. Michael had stopped work on the laptop and was staring at her. He didn't look happy. This wasn't part of the game.

Head down, she crossed the floor, stood beside him.

'What d'you say?'

'Sorry.' Her voice a small, breathy whisper.

He turned back to the laptop. Dee felt she should give it her attention too. She looked at the screen. And in that shiny surface she saw not what she was supposed to see, but her own reflection.

Not her usual reflection, the face she had now, but the old one. The way she once was. It had broken through. She felt her heart sink like a stone lost in a lake. The tingling stopped. Shame took over. She couldn't keep looking. She couldn't look away. So horrible.

'Dee.'

Michael's voice again. He knew what was happening.

'Look at me, Dee.'

She tore her eyes away from the screen, looked at him. He placed his hands on her arms. Gripped her tight.

'It's not real,' he said. 'It's not you.'

She heard his words but she didn't believe them. She never did. Not at first.

'What is it?' he said.

'It's not real. It's not me.' Her voice dry and dead.

'You're Dee Sloane. Who are you?'

'Dee. Sloane.'

'Good. Remember that.'

He let go of her. She stood silent, head down. As motionless as the Golem.

'It's hidden,' he said, pointing at the laptop. 'But it's here. Only a matter of time. Then we'll have them.'

She knew she was expected to say something here. 'Good.'
'That's the spirit.'
He went back to working on the laptop.
Dee just stood there, lost in her own world.

27

Tyrell had found sleep difficult to come by. The dogs had barked intermittently all night. He couldn't shake the image of them tearing apart the little girl in the house, and rose regularly to look out of the window and check they weren't doing that. There wasn't a full view of the dogs' enclosure from his window so he couldn't be entirely sure, but he thought if the girl had been there he would have heard her. Or he hoped he would. Since dawn broke, he had kept vigil from the window. It was fully light when Jiminy Cricket arrived.

'Hands off cocks and on with socks, as my mother used to say.' Jiminy Cricket laughed. Tyrell didn't join him.

'I've brought you breakfast.' Jiminy Cricket placed an old, cheap laminate tray down on the table. Tyrell looked at it. A mug of something brown. Some toast and a mound of scrambled egg that had hardened into a mini yellow Ayers Rock on the walk over.

Just like being in prison, Tyrell thought.

'Eat up,' Jiminy Cricket said.

Tyrell stayed standing. 'Where's the girl?'

'In the house. She's fine.'

Tyrell stared at him. Levelly, unblinkingly. The other man's eyes darted all about, zinged and ricocheted off surfaces like a speeding bullet in a metal bank vault. He finally brought them to rest on the scrambled eggs.

'Eat up. You'll need your strength. Big day.'

'Where's the girl?'

'She's all right.' Almost shouting, voice coming out of his body like steam erupting from a poorly closed pressure cooker. 'You . . . you don't need to concern yourself with her. She's fine. Just fine.'

'What about the dogs?'

'What about the dogs?' Tetchy, irritable.

'You were going to feed her to them.'

He sighed in exasperation. 'I wasn't going to feed her to them.'

'Yes you were. The woman in the kitchen said so. I heard her.'

'No one's feeding the girl to the dogs.'

'I don't want the little girl fed to the dogs.'

'She's not going to be fed to the dogs!'

'I won't help you if you do.'

Jiminy Cricket stopped talking then, stared. This time he did make eye contact. Moved up close, face to face. 'The girl is fine,' he said, struggling to keep his voice low, controlled. 'You don't need to worry about her.'

Tyrell stared.

'Look, last night I was . . . angry. But we're fine now, OK? Right?'

He wanted to be believed, but Tyrell wasn't sure he was ready to do that yet. He didn't think letting him know was the best thing to do, though, so he said nothing. His silence was taken for assent.

'Good. Right. Let's keep it that way.' Jiminy Cricket sighed, looked relieved to have headed off Tyrell's revolt, handled it so well. He smiled, pointed at the eggs.

'Eat up. Big day.'

'Why?'

Another sigh, a roll of the eyes, but hidden. Like he thought Tyrell was an idiot but didn't want him to know it.

'Like I said. This is the day all your questions are answered. Today's the day you find out who you are.'

'I know who I am. You told me. Tyrell.'

'Yes,' he said, moving close, putting his arm round Tyrell's shoulder like a friend or an overfamiliar used-car salesman. 'That's right. Tyrell. But that's just a name. Today you get your identity. Your legacy. Who you are, who you were, and most importantly, who you forever shall be.'

Tyrell said nothing. He was still thinking of the girl and the dogs.

'That's the spirit.' The other man laughed, squeezed Tyrell's shoulder, put on a cockney accent. 'Stick with me, mate, and this time next year we'll be millionaires.' He looked at his watch, laughed. 'This time tomorrow, even.'

Tyrell didn't know whether he wanted to go along with it. He wished he had gone straight to the hostel when he got out, not got into the car. He wished . . .

He wished he were back inside.

His friend took his arm away. Made for the door, pointed to the table. 'Eat your eggs.' And was gone. Locking the door behind him.

Tyrell looked at the plate of food, the rapidly cooling tea. He sat down at the table. Picked up the fork. He didn't want to do it, but he had no choice.

He ate. It tasted exactly as it looked.

28

Marina was just about to set foot in the hotel lobby when she realised something was wrong.

There were two uniformed police officers at the reception desk.

Usually she wouldn't have given that a second thought. After all, she was on the payroll as a police psychologist. But where she would once have seen officers as no threat, as allies even, she could no longer afford to think that way. Not when her daughter's life was at stake.

They're here for me, she thought. They know I'm here and they've come for me. It was the phone call last night, she thought, or my credit card when I checked in. They've traced me.

Her heart began to pound heavily. She had to get out. Get past them and into the car. Drive away. Do what was required of her and get her daughter back. Not get hauled in by the police.

Another thought struck her. They're not here for me. They're here about something completely unconnected. There's no way they could have found me yet. In that case, her reasoning continued, just keep going. Right past them. To the car and away.

But something stopped her from doing that. Paranoia. A sixth sense. A desire to not take unnecessary risks. Something like that.

Instead, she ducked back behind the corner, looking out to check they hadn't seen her. They hadn't. Good. She turned round, walked back the way she had come, glancing over her shoulder. She wished she hadn't. The receptionist was gesturing towards her, or at least towards the corridor she was in.

Heart rate increasing, she moved quickly towards the lift, punched the button. The lift was still there from her coming down in it. The doors opened. Slowly. Marina heard footsteps coming towards her.

She jumped inside, pressed the buttons for the first and top floors. The footsteps got louder, voices with them. The doors took millennia to close.

But eventually they did.

She was alone. The lift made its way slowly to the first floor. She jumped out, pressing the button to close the doors as she did so. The lift continued its ascent to the top floor.

Marina looked up and down the corridor. The maids' mobile cleaning unit was standing further along the hall, two maids working in unison, entering vacated rooms, removing bedding and towels.

She looked the other way. The stairs were through a set of heavy double doors on the left. She ran to them, opened them. Listened. Heard footsteps coming up. Voices.

The two officers.

An image of Josephina formed unbidden in her mind. Of Phil lying unconscious. She pushed them aside, concentrating. Her heart was hammering now, eyes darting everywhere. She closed the door to the stairs, went back into the corridor. Looked round.

No one about but the maids. She walked towards the cleaning unit.

Behind her, the door to the stairs opened.

Marina ran, not looking back.

Past the maids' trolley, eyes frantic left and right, desperate to find somewhere to duck into.

The cleaning supplies cupboard and service room was open. Without stopping to think, she jumped inside, pulled the door closed behind her.

Still holding the handle, she turned.

To find a cleaner staring at her.

The cleaner was young, foreign. Her initial amazement was quickly giving way to fear. She opened her mouth. To scream, speak, Marina didn't know. She couldn't take the chance and find out.

'Sorry,' said Marina in as loud a whisper as she dared. 'My husband.' She pointed to the door.

The cleaner kept staring.

'He's . . . I'm not supposed to be here.'

The cleaner still seemed unconvinced. Maybe she doesn't speak English, thought Marina. Maybe she just doesn't understand me. Here was a woman with wild hair and ripped, soiled clothing jumping into her room and closing the door. Holding her captive. Marina didn't blame her for being scared.

She could hear voices on the other side of the door, getting louder.

She turned back to the cleaner, who had heard them too. Her mouth was opening, making ready to shout.

Marina desperately thought of something that would convince her.

'My husband, he . . .' She took her hand off the handle, mimed punching herself in the face. Then she gestured to the door and the increasingly loud voices.

The cleaner nodded, understanding.

Marina thought she saw some spark of recognition in the young woman's eyes. Some shared commonality of experience. She felt a shudder of guilt at that, but smiled.

'Thank you,' she whispered.

The cleaner said nothing. Gave a small smile.

The footsteps, the voices receded.

Marina slowly turned the handle, risked a quick glance down the hall.

With another nod of thanks to the cleaner, she left the room, heading for the stairs.

She pulled open the double doors, taking the steps two at a time until she almost tripped and lost her footing. She took control of herself, paused momentarily. Continued the rest of the way as fast as she could.

She reached the ground floor. Panting for breath, she opened the double doors, looked down the corridor.

No one about.

She stepped into the hallway, then, taking a deep breath, walked towards the main doors.

As she reached the receptionist's desk, she kept her face averted. The receptionist had her head down. Marina was aware of her glancing up as she walked past.

'Oh.' Surprise in the receptionist's voice. 'Oh. The police . . . there's someone here to see you.'

Marina kept walking.

'Excuse me . . .'

'Just going to the car,' Marina shouted over her shoulder. 'Back in a mo.'

The doors opened. Marina was out into the fresh air.

She heard the receptionist calling behind her. Knew the girl would be deciding what to do next. Come out and chase her; go and find the police.

She couldn't risk either of those things happening.

She ran across the car park, found her car. Got in quickly, locked the doors. She checked that the phone was in her bag, started the car. She could enter the postcode into the sat nav when she was away from the hotel. She drove off.

As she passed the hotel entrance, the two uniforms were standing there, the receptionist with them. One of them, the male, moved into the path of her car, waving his arms about, trying to flag her down, stop her.

Marina speeded up.

He jumped out of the way.

She made for the exit and away.

She couldn't think about them, about what she had just done.

She just had to focus on where she was headed.

29

'Feels like we're paying our last respects in a funeral parlour,' said DS Jessica James. 'Should be playing organ music.'

The body lay straight on the bed, arms by its sides, legs together, head back, eyes closed. She leaned over it, scrutinising. Particularly the neck and the head. She straightened up, turned to DC Deepak Shah who was next to her. 'What d'you think? Are you fooled?'

He shook his head. 'As much as you are, ma'am.'

She nodded. 'If he was standing upright, his head would stay on his neck about as well as a bowling ball on a broomstick.'

The investigation was into its second day but hadn't made much progress. No one had reported seeing a child matching Josephina's description, either on her own or with anyone else. But they were still pursuing it, the uniforms out canvassing and the team searching the area.

With nothing else happening, Jessie had paid another call to Jeff Hibbert intending to ask him some more questions, and had received no answer. Thinking that it was unlikely he'd be out, she had gone round the back of the house and found the lock on the door frame hanging off, the frame splintered, the back door itself open.

She ran inside, calling his name with no response. Fearing the worst, she made her way upstairs. And that was how she found him. Laid out on the bed. Peaceful.

She wasn't fooled for a second.

And neither were the Forensic Scene Investigators. She had called it in straight away, keeping her hands off any surfaces, then carefully retracing the path she had taken into the house in reverse, stepping outside so as not to contaminate the scene further.

The pathologist and FSIs were finishing up their preliminary investigation and had allowed Jessie and Deepak in. They stood in the dull room, the drawn curtains lending it an ever-deeper atmosphere of depression.

Her own head was feeling a little like a bowling ball on a broomstick. Caning it two school nights in a row. Not good, but she couldn't help it. Just the one with a mate. That had been all. Or all she had intended. But it had spiralled and there hadn't been a happy reception when she had finally got home. She sighed, rubbed her eyes, pushed it all into a small corner of her mind. She could deal with that later. She had more pressing matters to attend to.

'What a horrible place to live in,' Deepak said, looking round.

'And die in,' said Jessie, turning away from the body and seeing what the rest of the room contained. 'Which he was doing. Lung cancer, I reckon.' She pointed to the oxygen cylinder at the side of the bed. 'He looked rough when I came to see him yesterday. Thought I'd better question him again as quickly as possible.'

Deepak frowned. 'Why?'

She told him about Stuart Milton and the address he had given. 'I got the feeling Hibbert knew more than he was letting on.' She turned back, looked at the bed. 'We'll never know now.'

Deepak nodded towards the FSIs. 'Unless they can tell us anything.'

'True.'

Jessie examined the room once more and noticed a couple of circular marks in the dust on the sideboard. She looked down at the floor. Two ugly figurines lay there, one with its head broken off. Knocked off in the fight, she thought. She knelt down beside them. Glanced under the bed. Saw something . . .

She got right down, nose almost to the carpet. From her position she could smell how unclean the fibres were. How infrequently it had been cleaned.

'Stinks down here . . .'

'I doubt housekeeping was top of his priorities, ma'am,' said Deepak, watching her.

Jessie took out her phone, switched on the flashlight, ran it over the carpet. She ignored the debris and accumulated dust as best she could, concentrated.

'Yes . . .'

She sat up. Felt the room lurch a little as she did so. Last night's alcohol making its presence felt again. Deepak watched her.

She stood up. 'There was something under there.' She pointed. 'There's a rectangular mark where something's been taken.'

Deepak got down on the floor.

'What d'you think?' she said.

He shrugged. 'Laptop? Old family bible?'

Jessie nodded. 'It looks like — and I don't think we're jumping to conclusions here — someone broke in, tried to take his laptop, there was a struggle . . .' she pointed to the broken figurine, 'and poor old Mr Hibbert got his neck broken.'

'Then the burglar rearranged the body, hoping to make us think he'd gone peacefully,' finished Deepak.

'Exactly.' She nodded. Looked at the body again. 'Or . . .'

Deepak waited.

'This was done deliberately, the laying-out of the body. No burglar does that. It's almost like he's been left . . .'

'At peace,' finished Deepak.

'Right. So . . . why? Is this all coincidence? Stuart Milton, the fire yesterday, the missing girl, or just some opportunist targeting the house of a dying man?'

'We don't believe in coincidences, ma'am.'

'No, Deepak, we don't. But what—' Before she could go further, Jessie's phone rang. She checked the display before answering. Mickey Philips. She felt something flutter inside her as she put the phone to her ear. Probably last night's alcohol again.

'Good morning, DS James.'

'Good morning, Mickey. And don't be so formal. Call me Jessie.'

There was silence on the other end of the line. 'Jessie . . . James?'

'Yeah. Wondered when you'd make that connection. But don't bother, I've heard all the jokes. And before you say it, Suffolk Police are not a cowboy outfit.'

He laughed. She liked the sound of it. Deepak turned away.

'We're at the house of a murder victim,' she said, recovering quickly. 'Just wondering whether it ties in with yesterday's events.'

'And does it?'

'We don't know yet.' She told him of the connection.

'Never ignore a coincidence,' said Mickey. 'As my boss always says.'

'Your boss and I think the same. How is he?'

'Still under sedation. But they're hopeful, apparently.'

'Fingers crossed, then.'

'Yeah, fingers crossed. Got an update for you.' He told her about Marina.

'Well,' said Jessie after he'd finished, 'I think we can rule her out of Mr Hibbert's murder.'

Mickey didn't laugh. Jessie wasn't sure if she had meant it as a joke.

'OK. This is what we're doing this end,' she said. 'We're looking into Hibbert's death. We're going to look for the guy who called himself Stuart Milton, see if we can find him and also run the name, see what we get. We've got a team out searching for the missing girl and we're trying to trace that car that was parked outside the cottage when it went up. We're going house to house, door to door, giving it the full Hollywood.'

'Great. I'll keep looking for Marina, then.'

'Stay in touch.'

She hung up. Deepak was staring at her.

'What?'

'Nothing, ma'am.'

She knew what he was thinking. He had his disapproving face on again. She ignored it. She had enjoyed hearing Mickey's voice. He was a nice guy. But she shunted it off into a corner of her mind once more. She had work to do.

A murderer to find.

30

The Golem had moved rooms. He was still in the house and waiting for instructions, but claiming the time as his own.

It was something he had to do every day. Spend time alone to meditate. Recharge. Rediscover his past self, make peace with it and in doing so reveal his forward path. His employers all knew he did this. They accepted, understood and allowed him time, even building it into their schedules. He delivered a very specific service. He had to do it in his own way.

But there was another reason for wanting to be alone. He wanted to get away from the Sloanes. Or Dee Sloane in particular. He thought again of her bloodied teeth, her lithe body. Her need to be dominated, to be broken, and her desire for him to be the one to do it. It was something he could do easily. And enjoy it.

But he was working.

He shut the door behind him. It closed with a satisfyingly heavy click, shutting him off. He stood in the centre of the room. Slowed his breathing down. Took in his surroundings.

The room was virtually bare. A spare room that hadn't been filled with anything. Considering their wealth, the

Sloanes didn't seem to have accumulated much debris or clutter in their lives. The Golem interpreted that as them living in the present, not allowing the past to weigh them down. He approved of that.

He closed the blind, blocking out the day, removed his T-shirt and boots, sat down on the floor, straight-backed, and crossed his legs. He slowly inhaled through his nostrils, filtering out the smells around him, concentrating on only pure air. He brought up the image of the red spot like he had been taught. Focused on it, stared at it in his mind's eye. The day died away around him. He heard only the symphony playing within himself.

He felt his heart valves open, the unclean blood being taken in, the locks and chambers filling, emptying, filtering, the good, purified blood punching its way round his system, cleansing him, renewing him, healing him.

When he had counted enough heartbeats, when he was sure enough blood had been circulated, he allowed the ritual to begin.

How many since last time?

Two.

Lives ended, souls freed?

As you say. It is for others to allocate specific names for things.

Names?

No.

Did they suffer?

No. It was over as quickly as possible. I am not a sadist.

Did they have families?

I do not know.

Will they be missed?

I do not believe so. I do not wish to believe so.

Are you ready to remove them from your heart and let them go?

I am.

Silence.

They are gone. You are cleansed, you are renewed, you are healed. You are once more at peace.

Thank you.

He stayed where he was, his consciousness focused only within himself. He saw his mother's face and gave an involuntary gasp. His mother's screaming face.

His other life. When he had a name. Before he was just the Golem.

He was back in the room as it shook from falling bombs. He heard more screams, more empty, hopeless prayers. His childhood, a time when hope of independence and self-determination for Bosniaks like his family soon turned into hate. When Milosevic's Bosnian Serb army attacked them, turning neighbours to foes. Legitimising hatred. When being born in Srebenica was the worst thing that could have happened.

Ethnic cleansing. A simple, clean phrase that hid a horrific truth. Rape. Torture. Murder. It was what the Serbs and the Yugoslav People's Army had done to his family. The ones they hadn't killed were herded into camps. The ones who survived the camps were damaged beyond belief.

Like him.

His mother, his sisters had been raped and mutilated before they died. His father murdered. And he felt that he had died along with them. He no longer felt human; he burned with a righteous anger and a hunger for revenge.

The war had ended in 1995. But it would never end for him. He rebuilt himself. Turned himself into a killing machine. Kept focused on tracking down the Serbs responsible for his family's death. He popped pills, took vitamin supplements. Kept himself clean, fit. And as his body became bigger and harder, it also changed colour. He turned grey.

At first he hated it, couldn't bear to look in the mirror. But gradually he came to accept it. He felt dead inside, and grey was the right colour for a dead man. The nickname soon followed. Golem. Made of clay, the mythical saviour of the Warsaw ghetto. He liked that. Kept it.

Eventually he was primed and ready to kill. And he did so. He couldn't track down those responsible for his family's death, so he attacked anyone who had been in the war on the side of the Serbs. It was messy, violent. And it didn't bring him the peace he thought it would.

But it did bring him to the attention of people who could use his services. Drug barons. People-traffickers. Gangsters. At first he wanted nothing to do with them, but eventually he gave in. He was a killing machine with no one to kill. Why not get paid for it?

He didn't enjoy it, though. He didn't know if his victims deserved it or not. And it plagued him. So he sought help, and found it in meditation. And now he had reached a still point. A place within where he could do his job and absolve himself of guilt afterwards. A way for a dead man to live with himself.

There was a sound behind him. The door opened, closed again.

His mind tunnelled quickly back from the past, barrelled down towards the present. Refocused on the red spot . . . then out. Back in the world once more.

'Hello.'

He turned, his vision jarred by his enforced return to the present, and saw who it was. Dee Sloane, standing against the door. Unbuttoning her blouse.

'I've been looking for you everywhere.' She undid another button. Her eyes travelled down his body, roamed over his naked chest. 'You've started without me.' She moved nearer to him. Slowly, each spike heel hitting the floor with a deliberate crack, like a bolt from a predator's crossbow hitting the bullseye.

He remained where he was. Tried not to respond to her.

'I know what you wanted,' she said. 'I could see it in your eyes. You tried to hide it, but I always know when someone wants me.'

Her blouse fell to the floor beside him. He didn't move his head upwards.

'You do want me. I know you do.'

He stared ahead, aware of her hands clenching.

'I meant what I said. I want you to dominate me. I want you to *break* me.' The word hissed, whispered.

Her bra dropped to the floor beside her blouse. He still didn't look up.

'Don't worry. Michael's playing with the laptop. He'll be ages. And he won't mind. Anyway . . .' a finger traced its way along his naked shoulder, 'you're bigger than he is.' The pressure increased. 'Much bigger . . .'

Her nails dug into his skin.

Her voice was down by his ear now, making the skin on his neck tingle. 'I love not knowing what you'll do to me next . . . the fear . . . it's such a turn-on . . .'

He grabbed her hand. Hard. She gasped. He turned his head upwards, locked eyes with her.

'Leave.'

Confusion crossed her gaze. She blinked it away. Found a smile.

'I said leave.' His voice low and steady.

'It's OK. Michael is—'

'Leave.' A final command.

She dropped eye contact. Bent down, picked up her discarded clothes. He heard her heels clacking, the door opening and closing. Then silence once more.

He sighed. Looked down at his hands.

They were shaking.

31

The car bounced down the rutted track. Marina felt herself being thrown from side to side as she drove.

She pulled up at the bottom of the hill. The road stopped, turned into sand dunes. She switched off the engine, got out. It was a seaside scene, but even in the sun it looked bleak. Ancient beach huts, weathered, peeling and rotting, stood in front of the scrappy, sparsely sprouting dunes. The sand looked close-pressed, muddied. Damp and wet. She could imagine it sucking down unwary travellers. Dead and dying boats lay chained and marooned on the shore. Beyond, the river sluiced out to the North Sea.

She turned to her left, looked behind her. She knew there was a walled garden somewhere near with a rusting caravan behind it. She turned her head to the right. The farmhouse was derelict now, left for the elements to reclaim. It didn't matter if it fell down; Marina would carry its ghosts within her for the rest of her life.

'You bastard,' she said aloud, 'you fucking bastard . . .' Her voice was borne away on the wind.

It was here that she had almost died. It was here that she had been born.

Or reborn.

Three years ago a homicidal maniac had kidnapped her and hidden her in a basement underneath the caravan in the field, wanting her unborn baby, the child who would grow up to be Josephina. Phil, leading the hunt for the killer, had eventually traced him to this spot and come to rescue her. He had joined her in the cellar's labyrinthine tunnels, trying to capture the madman. But ultimately it was Marina who had stopped his murderous spree and protected their unborn child. It was Marina who had killed him.

And that was when she had been reborn.

After that, she had known who she was. How much she would stand. The lengths she would go to to protect her own. She had thought the voice on the phone didn't know that. Now, she had to concede, perhaps they did.

Then she heard it.

Love Will Tear Us Apart.

She grabbed the phone from her bag, put it to her ear.

'You arrived?' said the voice. 'No trouble getting here?'

'You bastard,' she said.

Silence. Then: 'What d'you mean?' The tone was harsh but inquisitive.

'You know what I mean. Bringing me here.'

Another silence. 'I thought you would remember this place.'

'Oh, you're damn right I do.'

The voice sounded confused but tried to appear to be in control, without much success. 'I'm . . . surprised it means that much to you.'

Anger was rising within Marina. 'Funny fucker.' Spat out.

'You're in Wrabness.'

'I *know* I'm in Wrabness.'

'And you've been here before.'

'Well done, Einstein. It was all over the papers.'

Another silence. Marina began to think the voice had been cut off. Eventually it replied.

'Just . . . You'll be getting an email in a moment. It'll tell you what to do next.'

'So that's all this is for, is it? A really unpleasant trip down memory lane?'

'Look . . .'

'No, you look.' The anger was welling in Marina, threatening to burst. 'You blow up my family, kidnap my daughter and then bring me out here. I've dealt with some sick bastards in my time, but you're . . .' She could no longer find the words.

'Now listen.' The voice was getting angry too. Marina listened. 'I don't know what you're on about. Yes, you've been here before. That's why you were chosen. That's why we wanted you. But . . .' A sigh. 'Read the email.'

The line went dead.

Marina held the phone in her shaking fist. Stared at it. She looked back at the crumbling farmhouse. Over to the broken wall, the rusting caravan. Then back to the river, the sand. Bleak, desolate. She shivered. Phil wouldn't be coming to save her this time.

She felt something harden with her. No more, she thought. No more. She had already discovered what she would do to protect her family once already on this spot. The revisit just confirmed it. Whoever was on the other end of the phone, it was time to stand up to them.

The phone pinged. She opened the email, began to read.

And, slowly, began to understand.

32

'Jeff? Dead? Well, it was to be expected, I suppose. He was a very sick man.'

'He was, Mrs Hibbert.'

'Call me Helen. I've never liked being called Mrs Hibbert. Makes me sound like his mother.' She took a deep breath, a mouthful of vodka and tonic. 'And God, that's one thing I never wanted to be like.' Helen Hibbert shuddered at the thought.

Jessie James couldn't see this woman as anyone's mother. She would hate the competition for attention. In the car on the way over to Jeff Hibbert's estranged wife's flat, Jessie had put forward her version of what Helen Hibbert would be like. It was a game she often played with Deepak, a way to get him not to rely on profiles and generics, make his own mind up, think laterally, outside the box. She sometimes tried to make it competitive, put a bit of money on it, see whose description was closest. Loser bought lunch. He hardly ever bit. It didn't stop Jessie from trying, though.

'I reckon she'll be like him,' Jessie had said. 'Middle-aged, dumpy. Short hair, cut like a bloke. Big lumpen face. Like a farmer's wife. Or a farmer. Kitted out in Barbour's finest.'

Deepak, driving, had surprised her by volunteering an opinion. 'Dead wrong,' he had said.

Jessie smiled, genuinely curious now. 'Makes you say that?'

'You're thinking in terms of generics,' he said. 'Letting prejudices get in the way.' He gave her a quick glance. 'Ma'am.'

'Oh, am I now? Well, what's your highly individual, non-prejudiced opinion, then?'

'Younger than him, definitely.'

'You reckon?'

'And blonde.'

'Why blonde?'

'You asked for my opinion, ma'am. I think blonde. But not necessarily naturally.'

'Obviously.'

'She'll be more outgoing, more flashy than him. He'll have had a hard time keeping up with her.'

'Really? And on what do you base these non-prejudicial assumptions, then?'

'Police work, ma'am. Their house has seen better days. So had their marriage. What ornaments there are in the place were quite expensive at one time. A woman's taste, not a man's.'

'Not my taste.'

'Or mine. But someone liked them enough to buy them. I think she's got big blonde hair, dresses flashily, spends a lot on make-up, beauty treatments, that kind of thing.'

'Because that's the kind of woman who would buy those ornaments?'

Deepak nodded. 'Are we betting lunch on this?' A small smile played on his lips.

I'm encouraging my junior officer, she thought. It's my job. 'Why not?'

Deepak had been spot on. The flat was along Common Quay, in the newly gentrified waterfront area of Ipswich. She had buzzed them up when they told her they were police officers and it concerned her husband, held their warrant cards up to the video entryphone to prove who they were.

In the lift, Jessie had smiled at Deepak. 'Doing well so far . . .'

Once inside, Jessie realised immediately that she owed Deepak lunch. Helen Hibbert had deliberately arranged herself for their visit. She sat in the corner of her flat, one tanned leg crossing the other, a view of the Ipswich waterfront behind her, as if she was, literally, above all that. She was perfectly made up, her nails just manicured. Jessie imagined her nails always looked just manicured. Her dress and shoes were designer, Jessie noted, and, as Deepak had said, she was blonde. Her face, like her body, was composed. Helen Hibbert had been younger than her husband but not by much. It was clear that, despite all the treatments she had received, her skin was loosening, the crow's feet were lengthening and it probably took her longer each day to keep looking as she did. Time was catching her up.

She had offered them drinks, gesturing to her own sparkling vodka tonic.

'I know you might think it's early, but really, it doesn't matter. It's cocktail hour somewhere in the world.'

Jessie had told her about her husband and how they had found him dead. And Helen Hibbert had performed a near note-perfect grieving widow act.

'Poor Jeff.' A sigh. 'Poor, poor Jeff . . .'

Poor is right, thought Jessie, thinking of the squalor he had lived and died in. Must have been some divorce settlement.

'There was something about his death,' said Jessie, as airily as possible.

Helen Hibbert's eyes narrowed. Became beady, shrewd. She stared at Jessie as if her words were about to make her lose money. 'What d'you mean? He had cancer.'

'Yes, he did,' said Jessie. 'But that didn't kill him. He was murdered.'

She watched the woman, registering, recording her reactions. Helen Hibbert seemed genuinely shocked. Appalled, even. Jessie tried to read all the conflicting emotions that ran across the woman's eyes. She couldn't find empathy.

'Did . . . What happened?'

'An intruder, as far as we can see,' said Deepak, leaning forward. 'Perhaps he didn't expect to find anyone in. Perhaps . . .' He shrugged. 'Perhaps they struggled. Jeff lost. We don't know. Yet.'

'Is there anything you can tell us, Mrs Hibbert?'

'Like what?'

'Did he have any enemies? Was he in debt? Did he owe money? Would someone have robbed him, killed him, over money?'

'He was robbed?'

Deepak again. 'We think robbery may have been the motive.'

'What did they take?'

'We're not sure,' said Jessie. 'Perhaps it would help if you could give us an inventory of his belongings.'

'I don't know what he had.'

'A laptop, for instance?'

Helen Hibbert's eyes narrowed once more. Something was going on there, but Jessie couldn't work out what.

'I don't know,' she said. 'I have no idea.'

Jessie and Deepak shared a look. Jessie tried again. 'Did he . . .' They heard a sound from another room. Jessie looked quizzically at Helen Hibbert. 'Someone else here?'

'A friend,' she said, eyes darting to the door. 'Been staying over.' She stood up. 'I think I've answered enough questions for one day. This has been very traumatic for me. Please leave now.'

Jessie tried to talk to her again, but the shutters had come down.

Outside on the pavement, with gulls wheeling about in the fresh spring air, Jessie stared up at the flat.

'I hate being lied to,' she said. 'And we *were* being lied to. Question is, about what, and why?'

Deepak nodded. 'That's two questions, technically.'

'Pedant.' She turned to him. 'Anyway, I owe you lunch. Well done.'

'Thank you, ma'am.'

'Non-prejudicial profiling. Works well.'

He walked towards the car, a smile emerging on his face. 'And I saw a photo of her in his wallet.'

'You bastard . . .' Jessie followed. Smiling.

33

Helen Hibbert stared out of the window, watching the two police officers walk away down the quay.

'Oh shit . . .'

She felt hands on her shoulders. Warm fingers circling, smoothing over her muscles.

'Fuck off, Glen.'

The movement stopped abruptly.

'Can't I soothe you? Make it all better?' asked a man's voice in what he probably assumed was a low, sexy growl but which actually sounded more like inflamed tonsils.

'Not now. I've got to . . . to think.'

She felt her bought-and-paid-for man stepping away from her. She kept her eyes on the two police officers as they reached their car and drove away.

So they got him, she thought. They actually did it. She knew what had happened. Jeff must have tried his blackmail scheme and it backfired. Terminally. She took another sip of her drink. Where did that leave her? She knew just as much as Jeff had about what the Sloanes had done. Would they come after her next? She took another drink. If they did, then that was it. She would end up just like Jeff. But if she pre-empted them . . . A plan began to form.

The two police officers had disappeared. Her glass was empty. Glen reappeared behind her. She turned. He really was good-looking, she'd give him that. Talented and endowed. But expendable. There were plenty more where he had come from.

'I've got to go out, darling. Wait for me.'

He would. As long as she was paying him.

34

Michael Sloane stared at the laptop's screen and willed its secrets to appear before him. He punched more keys. Waited. Nothing.

He stretched and looked round. Dee was silent, which wasn't unusual. He knew where she would be, who with and what she would be trying to do. And he had a good idea how far she would get, too.

He didn't mind her playing her games. Took part in them, even, encouraged them, like their psychiatrist had told him to do. It kept her grounded. Happy. And, if he was honest, he enjoyed them too.

Michael put it all out of his mind and concentrated on the laptop. His keyboard skills were good; usually his fingers just glided. But on this laptop, it wasn't easy. The keyboard was old, the letters kept sticking. He made mistakes. And when he made mistakes, he got angry with himself. And that wouldn't do at all.

So he controlled the anger, accepted that it wasn't his fault and kept working. It was on here somewhere. It had to be. Locations, intentions, plans. How they were going to attack, when and where. Everything. All he had to do was find where Hibbert had hidden it.

He hit another key. It stuck. Blocked him entry to where he had been going.

He sat back, about to shout at the screen, but caught himself. No. This wasn't working. He had to change his approach.

He closed his eyes.

What would I do, where would I hide something, if I was Jeff Hibbert?

He thought himself into Hibbert's head. What did he like? What were his interests? His ex-wife. Everyone knew that. He could bore for England talking about her.

He opened his eyes. Photos. That was it. He checked the hard drive. And there they were. He opened them. Smiled. Helen Hibbert in various stages of undress, sometimes on her own, sometimes with various partners, often more than one. Sloane laughed.

Dirty bastard . . .

He scrutinised the photos, checked the files they were in. Kept scrolling through.

And found the folder he was looking for.

He sat back, reading. Once he had finished, he smiled. How obvious . . .

He reached for his phone. It was easier to phone rather than shout. Dee answered.

'The Golem's with you.' A statement, not a question.

Dee said nothing.

'Tell him I've got a job for him.' He looked at the laptop. 'Tell him he's going hunting.'

35

Marina stood on the beach at Wrabness, reading the email. Now she knew why she had been sent here. And it wasn't the reason she had first thought.

Stuart Sloane. Somehow this was all connected to Stuart Sloane.

She walked upriver along the beach, putting the dilapidated farmhouse behind her. The trees were thickening, blocking out the sunlight as she went. The beach huts were set back from what passed for sand, up on stilts, accessible only by wooden steps. Most of them looked occupied, people there for Easter. Some seemed to have permanent occupants. Marina thought it a curious place for a holiday, and certainly to live. But then the place was forever tainted for her.

This is everything you need to know, the email had said. *Read it.*

As she walked, she worked through in her mind what she had just read.

> *Once upon a time, there was a little boy called Stuart Milton. Stuart was different. He was special. He had learning difficulties. He was socially awkward, missed the cues other kids didn't, was out of step with the other kids by at least one beat. But a good kid. A nice kid.*

A harmless kid.

He had never known his father, who had left when Stuart was very young. His mother, Maureen Milton, had taken any job that came along, anything to feed herself and her son. She ended up working for the Sloanes, a local land-owning family. They, as the brochure said, 'had farming concerns, and were the producers and harvesters of most of the seafood from the area, particularly cockles, mussels and oysters'. Maureen worked in their house, cleaning and serving. She did work hard, we'll give her that. And she made herself popular with most people. One in particular.

Jack Sloane was the head of the family. He had just lost his wife, so he was in a bit of an emotional state. He liked Maureen and asked her to move in. She brought her son with her. Now Jack Sloane liked Maureen a lot, and let her know it. For her part, she was happy to respond to his attentions. Jack proposed marriage and Maureen accepted. The wedding was arranged and Stuart was adopted. He was now officially a Sloane.

So far, so happy ever after, Marina thought. But then the tone of the email had changed, become angrier.

But not everyone shared Jack and Maureen's delight. Michael and Deanna, his son and daughter, for instance. Because they saw Maureen for what she really was, a common gold-digging bitch, and they thought her son was a thick, use-less mong. They told them so before the wedding. And how did Jack respond? Threatened them with disinheritance.

The next part of the email was a link to a local newspaper from sixteen years ago. Marina had opened it. It was head-lined: *Bloodbath in Wedding Day House of Horror.*

The article told how the Sloanes had enjoyed a perfect wedding day and couldn't have been happier. The following day, however, the police were called to the scene of one of the biggest and bloodiest massacres they had ever come across. The house had been destroyed. Every ornament smashed, every piece of furniture upended, gutted, broken. Phone lines ripped out. The family had been stalked through the house by a maniac with a shotgun. Jack Sloane and his new wife were both dead. The son and daughter, Michael and Dee, had been shot and left for dead. One of the family's workers, Graham Watts, had phoned the police to raise the alarm. There had been horror on finding who was discovered holding the shotgun: Stuart Sloane.

Marina could remember the rest. Stuart Sloane was arrested and charged. Although he was technically an adult, his defence lawyers claimed he was unfit to stand trial as he was not mentally competent. They brought in as many psychologists and psychiatrists as they could afford, to assess Stuart and back up this claim. To diminish his responsibility, to plead for him as mentally unfit.

It was damage limitation and the defence knew it. The evidence, although circumstantial, was too damning. They were in no doubt that he had done it. All they wanted was for him to avoid prison. Serve his time somewhere that could help him, not harm him.

And that was why Marina knew the story so well, even without the email, because it was one of the first cases she had been assigned after leaving college. She knew that newly qualified psychologists were rarely presented with opportunities like this, and if she didn't mess it up, there would be a lot more work coming her way. It was also an opportunity to show just what she could do. But she remembered it for another reason.

She hadn't believed Stuart Sloane was guilty.

She remembered him being led into the psychologist's office in HMP Chelmsford. Everyone referred to him as a man because he was eighteen, but when she finally met him, she thought he was just a boy. A small, confused boy, underweight, his growth stunted by a childhood of malnutrition, his educational progress hampered by the damaged hard-wiring in his brain.

She stopped walking, looked at the trees ahead of her. Tried to think of the questions she had asked him, the answers he had given her. She couldn't recall specifics, but she remembered his attitude, his demeanour. Lost. If she had to sum him up in one word, it would be that. A lost boy cast adrift in the big city after inadvertently letting go of his mother's hand. He didn't understand what was going on around him, or how serious his situation was.

He had been found with the shotgun in his hand, and the police had, with good reason, assumed his guilt from that. She had gone along with that assumption, as directed by the defence lawyers, and her questions had been weighted accordingly.

What was he doing at the house? Could he remember what had led up to that? How had he felt about his mother marrying Jack Sloane? Specific, focused questions.

But he was vague in his answers, unfocused when asked about those specifics.

He couldn't remember how he had felt, or what he was doing there. But he had been very happy for his mother. His mother was happy so he was happy too.

What about his mother now?

Now he was sad. Very sad. And Marina remembered him looking sad as he said it. Then his expression had changed, his face had lit up in a smile. But it was all going to be OK, because Jiminy Cricket had said so.

Marina had been intrigued. Asked him more. Who was Jiminy Cricket? Why was everything going to be OK?

He had looked at her beatifically. Jiminy Cricket was the voice of his conscience. Jiminy Cricket had said his mother was in heaven with the other angels. And Jiminy Cricket had a plan. Everything would work out OK. Just wait and see.

Afterwards, she had repeated the conversation to the lawyers. They weren't surprised. Other psychologists had experienced the same thing. They believed that Stuart had a split personality. His damaged mind had been unable to cope with the enormity of what he had done, and he had abnegated responsibility in that way.

Marina hadn't been convinced. She had read his records. Stuart had never displayed any prior symptoms of multiple personality or dissociative states. This Jiminy Cricket sounded like a real person, someone else in the room with him. Stuart seemed to have no knowledge of how the shootings had been carried out, or indeed how to use a gun at all. She wasn't convinced he was actually responsible for the killings. Yes, the lawyers had said, but it could also be argued that the trauma of his actions had brought on the multiple personalities, had given him the knowledge to use the gun, the courage to act on his impulses . . .

And that was what they had gone with.

Marina had flagged something else up too. She was sure she wasn't the only psychologist to notice, but it never appeared in the trial. When she asked Stuart about his step-brother and stepsister, he recoiled, his expression filled with dread. He became agitated, stuttering and stumbling over words, unable to sit still. Convinced there was something there, she had tried to press him. She wanted to question him further on his relationship with them, but had been politely but firmly reminded what her brief was. The brother and sister were not a part of it. They were the victims in this case. And they were also very rich, so the defence had to think carefully before making any investigations into them or allegations against them. Marina had reluctantly agreed.

The case continued to gnaw at her, but since she hadn't been called on to give evidence, there was nothing she could do. As her colleagues suggested, she banked the cheque and settled down with a nice big gin and tonic to put it out of her mind.

But she still followed the case on the news, in the papers, and was horrified at the level of reporting, the scale of tabloid vitriol directed against Stuart from people who had never met him. She saw his supposed multiple personalities defence ridiculed and heard no mention of his relationship with his step-siblings. When he was found guilty and sentenced, she wasn't the least surprised. But she had to let it go. It was no longer her problem.

Until now.

She looked round, trying to find a path back to the beach huts. Then noticed what was in front of her. A huge old house, backing on to the river, crumbling and overgrown, nature trying to reclaim it, pull it back into the earth. And she knew immediately what it was.

The old Sloane place.

That had been one of the stipulations after the trial, she remembered. The brother and sister moved away but wanted the house to be left to rot away on its own. They had refused every offer from developers and the council to buy the land or do something with the old property. They wanted it left as it was.

They had got their wish.

The phone rang. *Love Will Tear Us Apart*. She answered it and was asked if she had read the email. She said she had.

'You were the only one who believed him,' the voice said. 'The only one who thought he was innocent. We checked the records. You knew what was going on. That's why we chose you.'

Marina said nothing.

'Now do you understand why you've been brought here? What you've got to do?'

Marina, still staring at the house, remembered the last part of the email.

Stuart Sloane was not insane. Stuart Sloane did not have multiple personalities. Stuart Sloane is as sane as you or I. She doubted that part but had read on. *Stuart Sloane has been made a scapegoat and been defrauded out of millions by the Sloanes that should rightfully have been his. Stuart Sloane needs to get even.*

Stuart Sloane needs your help to do that.

'Yes.' Marina sighed. 'I suppose I do.'

'Congratulations, Dr Esposito. You've got a new client.'

36

Tyrell saw the woman from the kitchen walking towards the caravan and felt immediately angry. He didn't want her anywhere near him. But he also knew that he didn't have a choice.

The door was unlocked, opened and she stepped inside. He had only seen her through the kitchen window. She had been angry-looking, red-faced. Now, up close, she looked different. The red had drained from her features, leaving her pale and blotchy. She had applied make-up, but it was uneven, poorly done. Tyrell had read somewhere that faces could be described as sculpted. This woman's had been chiselled. Her hair was messy, uncombed, and seemed to be at an angle to her head. Her clothes — leggings, trainers, fleece — were shabby and dull, as if they had been washed too many times.

'Come on,' she said. 'It's time.'

He stood up, stared at her. Didn't move. She wasn't meeting his gaze.

'I don't like you,' he said.

She sighed, looked at her watch. 'Which breaks my heart.'

'You were horrible to that little girl. Really horrible.'

She said nothing.

'You shouldn't have talked to her like that.'

'None of your business.'

He could feel something welling inside him but wasn't sure what. 'You scared her. You shouldn't have scared her.' Anger? Sadness? 'You should never scare children. Never . . .' He felt the hot pinprick of tears at the corners of his eyes as he kept staring at her. She looked away from him. Was she embarrassed in some way?

Tyrell moved in towards her. She flinched, moved back slightly. 'You threatened her.' He scrutinised her closely. 'What kind of person threatens a little girl?'

'Look, just . . . get ready. Come on.'

'Get ready for what?'

She sighed, spoke almost to herself. 'For this to be over.'

'Over? Today?'

'Yes, today. He's told you already.' Her voice was exasperated, like she was explaining something to an exceptionally slow child. 'Now stop being thick. Get ready.'

'That's not a nice thing to say. That's a really hurtful thing to say. Really hurtful.' He sat down on the bed again, upset by her words. He thought. Hard. Came to some conclusions. 'I don't like you. I'm not going to do what you say.' He nodded. 'No. I'm not.'

She put her hand on the sink, shook her head. 'Jesus . . .' She looked up. 'Just . . . just come on. We've got to get going.'

He didn't move or give any indication of having heard her.

She sighed once more. 'You're going to meet the woman who's going to help you.'

'To do what?' Said without looking at her, straight at the wall.

'To . . . make you feel better. Well.'

'Am I ill? I'm not ill.'

'No, no, you're not ill. But she's going to help you feel . . . happier. And make you rich.'

'Rich?'

'Yes. And . . . and make up for all the things that have happened to you.'

'How?'

'She just will. But you have to come and meet her. And we have to go now.'

He gave her words some thought. Rich. He couldn't imagine what rich was like. He remembered a time when he was supposed to have been rich, but that was a long time ago. Before prison. Before he was Malcolm Tyrell. He couldn't remember it clearly. All he knew was that it had been a happy time. Before . . .

Before everything went wrong.

But rich meant happy. He knew that much. He had been told. And happy, he knew, was good.

He stood up. 'All right, then.'

'Thank Christ for that. Just—'

'But there's one more thing.'

Another sigh. He could tell she was trying hard not to get angry. Not to get all red-faced again. She wasn't doing a good job of it.

'What?' She looked at her watch. 'Come on, we haven't got time for this.'

'I want to see the little girl.'

'Oh, Jesus . . .'

'I want to make sure she's all right.'

'She's fine. She's OK. Come on . . .'

He sat down on the bed once more, unmoving.

Another exasperated sigh from the woman. She looked like she wanted to hit him. He didn't look at her. She waited. Nothing happened.

'Right. Fine. I'll go and get her.'

'Thank you.'

'And then we'll go.'

She stormed out of the caravan. He heard her stomping angrily back to the house. He sat on the bed looking through the window, watching her go.

I'll see that the little girl is all right, he thought, then I'll go with them. He thought again. Go where? And who was this woman they wanted him to meet?

Although the caravan wasn't cold, he found himself shivering.

I wish I was back in prison, he thought.

I wish things could be easy again.

37

'You took your time.' Anni was waiting in front of Ipswich General. Franks had called her, said that since Suffolk were doing all they could to track down Josephina, she should join Mickey in hunting for Marina.

Mickey pulled up and she got in. He drove off, heading down the A14, on to the A12.

'Sorry,' he said. 'Been doing proper police work. How's the boss?'

She thought of the figure she had seen lying in the hospital bed, bandaged, wired and tubed. His eyes were taped up; his body was battered, misshapen and damaged. The dressings hid the areas that had been shaved and stitched, cut open and rejoined. They both defined and exaggerated the shape of him.

'Well as can be expected,' she said. She told Mickey that Phil hadn't been near the centre of the explosion but had been caught in the blast. The flames had seared his arms, his torso. Flying debris — most likely a part of the wall — had hit him on the head. That was what was giving most cause for concern. He had been operated on, the pressure relieved, and now left to recover.

Mickey winced. 'Fingers crossed, then.' For a long time he said nothing, then Anni became aware of him looking at her.

'What?'

He looked back to the road. 'What d'you mean?'

'You were staring at me.'

'Sorry.' He felt himself blushing. 'I just . . . You don't look like you've been roughing it all night, that's all. You look fresh. Alert. You look . . . good.' Eyes facing front all the time he spoke.

A smile crept around the corners of Anni's mouth. 'Thank you.'

He shrugged, mumbled, 'Welcome.'

'The things you can do with concealer.'

Mickey said nothing more. Put the radio on. Anni settled down into the seat, smiling to herself.

It took them the best part of an hour to reach the hotel near Braintree that Marina had last been spotted at. The two uniforms were waiting for them. Mickey parked up. He and Anni went into reception.

'She just ran,' said the first constable, Alison Irwin. 'We tried to stop her, talk to her, but . . .' A shrug. 'Tom tried to flag the car down.' She indicated her partner, who nodded.

'She just drove round me,' Tom Crown, the other uniform, said.

Anni crossed to the receptionist. Questioned her too. She had nothing much to add.

'Apparently she hid from us in a supply cupboard,' said Tom Crown. 'Told the maid she was hiding from an abusive husband.'

'Inventive,' said Anni.

They went to the car park, traced the path Marina had taken. They went up to her room to see if she had left a clue behind, anything to show where she was going, what she was doing. Nothing.

'We've put the registration number of her car out as a general alert,' said Alison Irwin, 'but we've had nothing back yet.'

They thanked the uniforms for their help, went back to the car.

'Where to now?' asked Anni.

'Maybe we should head back to base,' said Mickey. 'See if there's been any more sightings of her car.'

'You mean *my* car.'

'Sorry. Your car.'

They drove away from the hotel. Anni looked at Mickey this time.

'So I'm still looking good, am I?'

Mickey glanced at her, frowned, shifted his eyes back to the road. 'Yeah. Why?' Suspicion in his tone.

'Just wondered. I heard that this DS from Suffolk's been giving you the glad eye, that's all.'

'What, you mean Jessie?'

'Oh, it's Jessie, is it?'

'Yeah, Jessie James.' Mickey smiled. 'And she says she's heard all the jokes before.'

'What, even the one about the Suffolk force being a bunch of cowboys?'

'Apparently. But I don't know if she's been giving me the glad eye or not.'

'OK. Just checking.'

'Why, you jealous?'

She shrugged. 'You know me. Not the jealous type.'

Mickey and Anni had been involved in a tentative on-and-off relationship for the last few months. They had been out a few times, dinner, cinema, drinks, but neither had wanted to be the one to push it further. They were good friends, excellent work colleagues. And they were worried they could lose all that.

Anni's phone rang. Relieved at the break, she answered it. Milhouse, the unit's resident computer expert. Milhouse wasn't his real name, but with his thick glasses and studious demeanour, he bore such a strong resemblance to the character in *The Simpsons* that that was what everyone called him. Even his girlfriend, probably. If he had a girlfriend. Which Anni doubted.

'Got a lead for you,' he said.

Anni took out her notepad. 'When and where?'

'Shell garage in Marks Tey. Marina's debit card's been used.'

'We're on our way.'

'I'll phone ahead,' said Milhouse. 'Get them to line up any CCTV footage they've got.'

'Brilliant. Thanks, Milhouse.' She rang off.

'What's occurring?' said Mickey.

Anni told him.

'Let's go, then. Not far from here.'

The radio continued to spew out top-forty hits in between the DJ's banal inanities.

They drove on in silence.

38

The Golem enjoyed being in the car. The doors were locked and there was a metal and glass barrier between him and the rest of the world. And he was going forward. Heading towards something.

Even if that something involved someone else's death.

In the car, he could tune out everything else. Centre himself. Meditate while moving.

He drove a Prius. And took a small delight in the fact that it confounded expectations. It was not the car of an assassin, but that was what he liked about it. It was both anonymous and environmentally friendly. That was good, because when he died, he wanted to leave as little trace of himself behind as possible. Like a footprint in damp sand, washed away by the incoming tide. The way it should be.

That was what he tried to achieve with his victims. There one second, gone the next. Simple and clean, like switching off a light.

He knew that one day it would happen to him. And he was ready for it. Every day he prepared for death, either to give it or take it. And every day that he gave it and didn't take it he gave thanks.

But one day it would be him.

One day.

He was also pleased to get away from the Sloanes. They had been regular employers over the years. They paid what he asked and their assignments were not too taxing. They would have been good employers if not for the sister. She was getting to him. And he didn't allow that. Something would have to be done about her. One way or the other.

Jaywick was signposted left. He turned left.

He drove. He was centred, prepared.

He was ready.

39

Marina followed the sat nav, her foot hard down as far as she dared. On the way to Jaywick. On the way to meet her daughter.

She had insisted that that was part of the deal. The voice hadn't been too pleased. 'After you've seen . . .' it nearly said a name, 'your patient.'

'Look.' Marina kept her own voice as calm, as reasonable as she could. 'I've already told you I'll see *your patient*. I've agreed to that. But we're negotiating here. And I won't talk to him until I've seen my daughter and know that she's safe.'

'No,' said the voice. 'We're not negotiating. You're going to do what you've agreed to do and then you'll get her back.'

Marina wanted to scream, to rage. If they had been there in front of her, she would have attacked. But she swallowed that down, kept her voice calm, controlled. She knew she would only get somewhere if she behaved like a professional. 'No,' she said, in as measured and slow a tone as she could manage, 'this *is* a negotiation. You've told me what you want me to do. And I've agreed to do it. But that agreement comes with certain conditions attached. I want to see my daughter. If you won't do that, then I go to the police and tell them everything.'

'What'll happen to your daughter then?'

Again Marina had to control herself until she was sure she could speak without screaming. 'You'll let her go. Because there would no reason for you to keep her. You've explained your plan to me. And without my help, there will be no plan.'

There was silence on the line. Marina waited. She was suddenly aware that she was shaking. She wished she felt as strong as she had made herself sound. She wondered if she had gone too far. If they didn't go along with her proposal, she might never see Josephina again. She knew now what was at stake. She guessed that if they were desperate enough to kidnap her daughter to make this work, they wouldn't stop there.

'All right,' the voice said. Anger and defeat in its tone. 'You can see her. But then you do what we want. And you don't get her back until you've done it. Right?'

She felt a wave of relief wash over her. 'Thank you. Just make sure she's safe.'

'She's safe. Now get going.'

The phone went dead. The postcode was texted for the sat nav. She entered it and drove.

As she did so, she thought about the voice. In the time she had been talking to it, it had evolved. It was no longer intransigent, unyielding; it could be reasoned with. She knew that happened in negotiations; sometimes whole relationships developed. The way this person spoke led her to believe they were an amateur. A professional wouldn't have engaged with her on any level. If she had made demands, been obstinate or refused to play, a professional would have harmed her daughter, even executed her.

This person — or persons — was reachable, and Marina felt a glimmer of hope at that thought. Perhaps the initial intransigence was down to fear, she thought. Perhaps they didn't know what they were doing and had hidden behind a character.

She was glad now that she had left a clue. Just a small one, at the service station. She just hoped that someone had seen it, would be clever enough to work out what she had done, and follow her.

She kept driving. Hoping her daughter was all right. Wishing her husband was there with her.

Trying desperately to be brave, for their sake.

40

The Golem's sat nav told him he had reached his destination. He turned the engine off, took in his surroundings. Worked out logistics, made plans. Studied approaches, possible obstacles. The house was old, dilapidated. Detached. No neighbours to interfere. There was a caravan at the side, in as bad a state as the house. Two cars parked in front of the house.

He scanned once more, searching for other exits. To the back of the house were fields. To the side, fields also. To the front, the secluded road the Golem had parked on. If they wanted to leave, they would have to come past him.

Good.

He opened the glove box, took out a small telephoto lens. Looked through it. Scanned the front of the house for alarms, wires, anything that told of security. He knew the lengths people went to hide such devices, knew what to look for, what the giveaways were. A new wire on an old building, sometimes painted to blend in, the shade always slightly out. The raised outline of sensors on window frames, door catches. A rusted old alarm box mounted on the wall, seemingly not working, concealing a state-of-the-art security system. He had seen it all.

But this house seemed to be exactly what it said it was. He could detect nothing that wasn't meant to be there.

Another good sign. The omens were becoming auspicious for this job.

He turned the lens on the caravan, just in time to see a woman leave the house and walk towards it. Beside her was a small girl. She was holding her wrist, half dragging her along. The Golem studied the body language of the two. The girl looked like she was being held against her will and had been crying. The woman looked stressed, like she just wanted everything concluded as quickly as possible.

In another life, the Golem would have been upset about the little girl, shared some empathy for her situation. But not any more. Now it was just a job. He had his instructions: take the man and the woman out, any way he wanted. The other man should be brought to the Sloanes. The little girl . . . use his discretion.

He scanned the borders once more. If they saw him coming, all they could do was run. That would make his job more difficult, but not impossible. They wouldn't get far. Not with him blocking the entrance to the main road.

A line of trees fringed the road. He could use them for cover as he made his way down there. Good. He got out of the car, locked it. Started to walk, keeping in the shade of the trees, not allowing his own shadow to be cast in the open.

He looked once more at the house. Despite the sunshine, the place carried an air of depression. As if whoever lived here had reached the end.

How true, he thought.

As he walked, he saw movement in one of the ground-floor windows of the house. He stopped, took out the lens once more. A man was sitting at a table, laptop before him.

He would be the first target.

He put the lens away, walked on. Reached the house, rounded the corner.

Then the dogs started to bark.

41

'This is Josephina. Josephina, this is . . .' The woman thought for a few seconds. She seemed to have genuinely forgotten Tyrell's name.

'Malcolm,' said Tyrell, feeling strange saying the name out loud. As if it confirmed his new identity.

The little girl just stared at him.

He looked back at her. Her eyes were red-rimmed from crying, her nostrils encrusted with snot. She looked tired and terrified, like she had woken from a nightmare to find it was real. The woman still held her by the wrist. She looked like she should have been holding a soft toy in the other hand.

Tyrell, thinking he might be scaring her, sat down to be nearer her height.

He tried to smile at her. From the expression on her face, he must have failed.

'Hello, Josephina. How are you?'

She just stared at him.

'Have they hurt you?'

'Oh for God's sake . . .' The woman twisted Josephina's hand, trying to pull her away, back to the house.

'Stay where you are.'

She stared at Tyrell, surprised at the strength in his voice. At the stern words, Josephina looked like she was about to cry. He softened his voice again. Looked at the girl. Was careful not to touch her. He didn't want her to get the wrong impression about him. That was important to him.

'Sorry for shouting,' he said, his voice soft once more. 'But have they hurt you?'

Josephina risked a glance up at the woman, who was staring off out the window. She looked back at Tyrell, gave a slight shake of her head. No.

She's saying no, he thought, not because it's necessarily true, but because it's the answer she's expected to give.

'Good,' he said. 'I'm not going to hurt you either. You're safe when you're with me. When I'm here.'

Josephina looked like she didn't believe him. He wasn't sure he believed himself.

'I won't let them hurt you.'

A sigh from the woman. 'You finished? Yes? Happy? Good. Because we've got to get on.' She pulled Josephina's wrist, dragging her to the door.

But Tyrell wasn't ready to let her go just yet. 'It won't be long. They want me to meet your mother. They want her to do something for them. Then you and your mother can go home. Together.'

Another sigh from the woman.

'Mummy?' said Josephina. She looked around. 'Mummy?'

'We're going to meet her,' said Tyrell.

'Don't go telling the kid that, shit-for-brains,' said the woman. 'We'll never be able to manage her.'

Tyrell stared at her. Felt himself shake with anger at her words. 'You look after this child, or I won't do anything you want.'

The woman stared at him.

'And don't swear in front of her. It's not nice.'

Another sigh. Exasperation this time. 'Jesus . . .'

Then the dogs started barking.

The woman dropped Josephina's wrist, moved hurriedly to the window. 'Oh fuck.'

'What did I just say?' said Tyrell. 'No swearing in—'

She turned to him.

'This is bad,' she said. 'This is very fucking bad.'

42

DS Jessie James tried hard not to let her irritation show.

DC Deepak Shah had received a call on his mobile. Fair enough. But instead of just answering it or putting it on handsfree and loudspeaker, he had insisted on pulling the car over.

'Just take the call,' she had said, exasperatedly, not for the first time.

He had ignored her, followed his own procedure. She had shaken her head. Bet he demands an invoice every time he makes a cup of tea at home, she thought.

'No,' he had said. 'It's this one.' And had dug down into his trouser pocket, pulled out a second mobile. An old black clamshell.

Two phones. Jessie shook her head.

He listened, asked a couple of questions, and Jessie became curious, despite herself. Deepak took out his notepad, wrote something down. Jessie tried to see what it was, but he kept it angled away from her.

Sometimes she wanted to kill him.

He ended the call slowly, almost ritualistically, and pocketed the phone.

'Two phones?' she said.

He nodded.

'Why?'

'Because I can't be too careful,' he said. He patted his pocket, checked the notepad, entered something into the sat nav, put the car back in gear. When a space in the traffic appeared, he pulled out.

'Can't be too careful?' Jessie laughed. 'What, like the American cops that used to carry two guns? One a throwdown piece, for shootouts.'

He said nothing.

'That's you, is it? The British equivalent? What you going to do, call someone to death?'

'That was the station,' he said, ignoring her. 'They've traced the car.'

Jessie was suddenly all business. 'From outside the cottage? The one that was there when the cottage went up?'

He nodded.

'And?'

'It's registered to . . .' He glanced at his notepad. 'Michael Sloane.'

'Right. Good. We got an address?'

'On the pad. I've taken the liberty of keying it in. I presumed you would want to go there and question them.'

'Absolutely. No time like the present.'

They drove on.

'Sloane . . . Michael Sloane . . .' Jessie frowned. 'Why does that name mean something? I've heard it before.'

Deepak nodded. 'I agree. Can't remember where, though. Shall I pull over, ma'am? Make a few calls?'

'No, just keep going. We'll do it later.'

'You're the boss.' He kept driving.

Deepak annoyed the hell out of her. But she had to admit, he was a damned good copper. In fact there was no one she would rather have alongside her.

She smiled to herself. Well, perhaps Mickey Philips . . .

43

The Golem cursed and stopped walking. Such a simple mistake. An apprentice's error. Why would they need elaborate security systems when they could have attack dogs?

He looked round once more. Saw a curtain being dropped back into place in the caravan. Glanced at the house. Saw the person at the downstairs window look out, hurry away again. Saw activity. The laptop being closed up. Someone getting ready to leave in a hurry.

No change of plan. He made for the house. Quickly.

As he reached the corner, he heard something. The dogs' barking changed in tone. Lower, growling. Then he heard a gate opening. By the time the Golem realised what was happening, it was too late. The dogs were free and barrelling towards him.

He looked round. He wouldn't reach the car in time. There was no other shelter, no hiding place. They would catch him. He gave another glance round for a weapon, anything he could use to defend himself, fight them off. Found nothing.

He stood, braced, as the two slavering animals bore down on him, jaws apart, ready to pounce, to tear him to shreds.

He closed his eyes. Centred himself. There was nothing he could do about the physical contact, the pain. That was going to happen. The sooner he accepted it, embraced it, the sooner it would be over.

But he could do something about the noise. Most people, when faced with an attacking dog, were terrified. He knew that. And it wasn't just the open jaws and the anticipation of pain that terrified them; it was the noise too. The barking, growling, howling. That was what scared people. But the Golem wasn't people. He kept his eyes closed. Focused. Channelled. Blocked out the sound.

He opened his eyes once more. The dogs were still coming towards him, but he could no longer hear them. And if he couldn't hear them, then he could think. And if he could think, then he could strategise.

The first one, a slavering black and mustard Rottweiler, jumped up at him. It was huge, almost the same height as him at full stretch. But the Golem wasn't going to allow himself to feel scared or intimidated.

As the dog jumped, he pulled back his arm, brought it forward. Hard. Landed a punch on its neck. The dog's legs immediately went limp and it fell to the ground, dazed. The Golem kicked it in the head, hard as he could. His steel-reinforced boot connecting with the dog's skull, the bone splintering, crunching as it hit.

The dog lay twitching, spasming.

The Golem knew he would get no more trouble from that one.

He turned to the other dog. He had no opportunity to defend himself this time. Would just have to take the pain.

The second Rottweiler was on him. Its jaws opened, distended, clamped down on his left forearm. The pain coursed through him, hard and fast, like he'd grabbed an electric cable.

He tried to ignore it. Couldn't. Screamed.

Hearing that, the dog bit down harder. Tried to wrestle him to the ground, rip his arm off in the process.

The Golem resisted, pulled the opposite way. He could feel flesh and muscle, skin and sinew tear away from his bone as he did so. The blood pumped out, soaking his shirt, filling the dog's face, its eyes. The dog tasted it, got high on the bloodlust, bit down all the harder. Pulled more ferociously.

The Golem saw the figure from the window move outside. The target was getting away.

He brought his right arm over, bunched his fingers into a fist, brought it down hard on the dog's snout. The dog roared, either in pain or anger, he couldn't tell, but didn't let go. He hit it again. The jaws loosened slightly. Pursuing the advantage, he forced the dog to the ground. It struggled, tried to get away. He pinned it down with his legs.

He managed to get his fingers into the dog's mouth, pushing back against its teeth. The dog squirmed, tried to wriggle away. The Golem wouldn't let it. Despite the pain making him light-headed, he held on.

His fingers pushed against the dog's top jaw. He used his left arm to pull its lower jaw down. He could feel the teeth sinking further into his flesh the harder he pulled down. He focused, concentrated, tried to ignore the pain.

Kept his mind on his goal. His target.

The target must not escape.

He pushed further. Heard, felt something tear in the dog's face. Kept pushing. More blood, the dog's this time, as he prised its jaws apart.

He felt its grip on his arm loosening, heard a whimper from within its throat. He kept pushing.

The dog realised it was beaten, let go.

The Golem pulled his arm from its jaw, let the dog slump to the ground. It lay there, whimpering.

He looked over at the house. His target would be getting away. He glanced down again to the dogs. They were both in pain, dying. He couldn't leave a wounded animal in that state. He knelt down beside the first one, looked into its eyes. Snapped its neck. Did the same to the second.

Then stood up.

Target in his sights.

44

'There,' said Mickey, pointing at the screen. 'That's her.' Grainy CCTV footage showed Marina standing at the counter of the service station, looking around anxiously, handing over her card, getting out as quickly as possible, not even waiting for her receipt.

'She seemed to be in a hurry, I remember that about her.' The woman who had served her was speaking. She was big, heavyset. Anni thought she looked like a farmer's wife. Probably was.

'You sure that's all?' said Anni. 'Anything else you can tell us about her?'

The farmer's wife stared at the screen, trying to dredge up some memory that would help. Anni had found this a lot with witnesses. They wanted to feel involved, part of the investigation. They wanted to impart some knowledge that would be pivotal, that could crack the case. Something no one else had spotted, something unique. But the woman couldn't do it.

Probably because there wasn't anything more there.

'How did she seem to you?' asked Mickey.

'Just like she looks on there,' said the farmer's wife. 'Wanted to pay and get away, as quickly as possible.'

'Which way was she headed?' asked Anni. 'Towards Colchester or towards Braintree?'

The woman thought again. Trying hard to be helpful. Eventually shaking her head. 'Colchester, I think.'

'Can we see it again, please?' said Anni.

The farmer's wife rewound the tape. They watched Marina queue up, tapping one foot in impatience. They saw her look round, anxiety in her face. At one point she stared directly into the camera.

'Pause it,' said Mickey.

The woman did as he asked. Mickey and Anni both studied the blurred image.

'What's she doing?' said Anni. 'Is she . . . D'you think she knows she's being watched?'

'I think she does, yeah,' he said. 'She knows she's on CCTV.' He turned to the farmer's wife. 'Play it forward a few frames.'

She did so. They watched as Marina seemed to stare right into the lens. She looked apologetic, beaten. Then she paid.

'That's that, then,' said Mickey, sitting back.

'Keep watching,' said Anni. 'There's something . . .'

Marina had bought a pack of mints. They watched her take one, then, when the farmer's wife wasn't looking, screw the wrapper up and drop it on the floor.

'Nice,' said Anni.

Then she was out of the shop and on her way.

They both sat back. Looked at each other.

They fired a few more questions at the farmer's wife, but it was clear to both of them that the woman had told them everything she could. Mickey left his card with her in case anything else occurred to her. They thanked her for her time, drove off.

'Well, that was less than helpful,' said Mickey.

'What did you expect? She clearly doesn't want to be found. For whatever reason.'

They drove towards Colchester. Mickey checked his watch.

‘Nearly knocking-off time. We’ve got no more leads, no other jobs we should be doing. I reckon we should head for home.’

‘Reckon you’re right,’ said Anni. ‘We’re about to hit overtime. Franks wouldn’t like that.’

They drove on in silence. Anni eventually spoke. ‘So, you got any plans for tonight?’

‘Me? Nah. Nothing special.’

‘Really?’ There was a playful edge to Anni’s voice. ‘Not rushing off to Ipswich to see your cowgirl DS?’

‘Don’t be stupid.’

From the side, Anni could see that Mickey was reddening. His driving had speeded up too.

‘I told you,’ he said, feeling he ought to explain more, ‘there’s nothing in it. Not on my part, anyway.’

‘Good,’ said Anni. ‘Glad to hear it.’

‘Yeah?’ he said.

‘Yeah.’ Anni smiled. Moved towards him. ‘In that case, if you’ve got nothing special on tonight and you’re not after her, why not come back to mine?’

The expression on Mickey’s face, thought Anni, was priceless.

45

The pain was excruciating. The Golem sank to his knees, clutching his torn arm with his good hand. He wanted to black out. He wanted it to stop.

But he knew he could have neither.

Closing his eyes, focusing on finding a still point, removing the pain from his mind wasn't an option. If he closed his eyes, even for a second, his quarry might escape. And he couldn't allow that. So he had to give himself the mental and emotional equivalent of a field dressing. Attempt to block it out as much as possible and keep going.

He struggled to his feet, took a couple of deep breaths. Tried to stop his head from spinning. Concentrate on his task. He was a soldier. He was being paid to deliver a service.

So do it, he told himself.

The Golem resumed his walk towards the house. He saw the figure through the window, panicking, hurrying to disconnect a laptop and other electronic items. He watched as the figure gave up on the wires, bundling everything together and just making for the door, laptop under his arm.

The Golem would be ready for him.

He increased his speed, breathing heavily each time his booted feet thudded on the ground. Reached the door of the house. Tried it. Locked.

Of course.

Clutching his arm, he tried to move quickly round the side of the house, stop his target from leaving that way. He found him exiting by the dog kennels. The man stopped, stared at him. Face illuminated by fear.

'Look,' he said, 'you . . . you don't have to do this . . .'

The Golem said nothing. Just stood there waiting for the man to make a move.

The man had the laptop under one arm, gripping it hard, clutching it against his body. His other hand was hidden. He looked like he was torn between running and fighting.

Fight or flight. The Golem knew that feeling well. He had lost count of the times he had come up against someone, had to anticipate which way they would go. Had to be ready if they did either.

The Golem said nothing. Usually his silence unnerved opponents; this time it was out of necessity. He didn't have the energy to speak as well as move. Didn't trust his mouth not to scream if he opened it.

'I'm going to have money soon. Lots of money . . .' the man continued. 'I can give you . . . half. You want half?'

No response.

'Whatever, then. Whatever you want. As much as you want. Please . . . please don't . . .' The man edged forward slightly, eyes pleading. 'Don't kill me . . .'

The Golem stood his ground. The man, shoulders hunched, body imploring, moved towards him.

'Please . . .'

The Golem let him come. Made his job easier.

The man drew near. When he reached arm's length, his left hand appeared from behind his back. He was holding a huge kitchen knife. His eyes glittered and he brought it forward, straight towards the Golem's chest. He screamed as he lunged.

Last reserves of adrenalin kicking in, the Golem pivoted, moving his torso away from the blade. It struck him in the arm — his right arm — slicing along his bicep, sticking in. More pain.

His assailant quickly pulled it out, jabbed and slashed again. The Golem felt his arm being cut, sliced. His head swirled as the pain increased. He was staggering, about to black out.

His attacker sensed victory. The Golem could see it in his eyes. He couldn't allow that to happen. Wouldn't allow it to happen.

The man took another swing with the blade. It connected with the Golem's right side. He stuck the blade in hard. His eyes blazed. He couldn't believe he was winning.

The Golem had to do something. He had to turn the situation into an opportunity. He moved in close to his assailant, trying to ignore the feel of razor-sharp metal being pushed further into his body as he did so.

He reached out his right hand. Took his attacker by the throat.

His opponent knew immediately what was happening. What the Golem was doing to him. He tried to wriggle out of the grip, push his body away from the attack. Couldn't. Even though the Golem's grip was weaker than usual, it was still stronger than most people's.

Stronger than his assailant could break.

The knife dropped from the man's fingers. The laptop from his other hand. He brought both hands up to his throat, clawed at the Golem's fingers, tried desperately to prise them off.

The Golem felt pain running all over his body. Like he had been trussed up in electrified barbed wire. He tried to ignore it, concentrate on this one task, the job he had been paid for.

His assailant struggled. The Golem locked his fingers. Squeezed harder.

'I want more life, fucker . . .'

Attacker became victim. His face reddened, turned purple. His eyes bulged, looked ready to pop. His constricted throat made a rattling, gurgling sound. He stopped struggling.

The Golem felt the man's body begin to weaken, start to go limp. He gripped even harder, summoning his remaining strength to do so.

Eventually his victim's body lost the will to fight. The Golem's will was stronger.

He released his grip, watched as the body slumped to the ground, looked down at it.

'Time to die . . .'

His head felt light, his legs, arms trembled. His own body was going to give up soon. He knew that.

He heard a noise. Turned.

Saw his Prius rocking, moving, coming to a halt. The front left side crumpled, the light hanging out through smashed glass like a distended eyeball.

He saw the car that had knocked his out of the way driving off. Guessed that the occupants of the caravan had been in there.

Bending down and almost keeling over, he picked up the laptop and turned. Made his way slowly down the drive, past the corpses of the dogs, back to his car. His self-preservation instinct overrode everything else.

He got behind the wheel, put the car in gear, drove off.

He made it about half a mile down the road before pulling in to the entrance of a forest and passing out.

46

The day was winding down. The sun giving up the fight, falling out of the sky. Marina felt the same. She was tired and hungry, running only on adrenalin and hope.

She followed her sat nav. It told her she had reached her destination. She saw a house before her. Old, dilapidated. A caravan next to it in a similar state. A parked car.

No one about.

She got out of the car, locked it behind her. Walked slowly up the drive towards the house.

She couldn't help but notice that on her right were two black and brown lumps, the ground dark and glistening around them. Feeling a thud of trepidation in her heart, she crossed over to look at them. Her heart flipped at what she found there.

'Oh God . . . oh God . . .'

The two Rottweilers were dead. One was bloodied and torn; the other just looked broken.

Hurrying yet hesitant at the same time, she made her way up to the house.

Where she found the body of a man by the back door.

Marina turned, doubled over, retched.

Straightening up, she found her head spinning. She looked round, feeling like she was losing whatever tenuous control she had recently gained over her situation. She ran to the caravan, pulled open the door. No one there. But someone had been here, and quite recently.

Leaving the door swinging, she ran back to the house. Closing her eyes, she stepped over the corpse by the door, entered.

The house, despite the brightness outside, was in darkness. Someone had been living there and it looked like they had left in a hurry. On the kitchen table were the remains of a meal and some electronic equipment. It looked like someone had started to dismantle it then decided to leave. The food had been similarly abandoned.

Marina counted the dishes. Three. Two adult-size plates, one small one. Her heart lurched once more.

'Oh God . . . Josephina . . .'

Marina found her voice. She went through the rest of the house screaming at the top of her lungs.

'Josephina! Josie!'

Her only reply was an echoing stillness.

The house looked like it had been squatted in. Clothes, belongings, scattered all over the place. Sleeping bags lay on mattresses. There had been two people in one room. She spotted that.

But in the front room she found something else. A rope tied to the door handle. It stretched down to another mattress on the floor. A thin sheet covered it. At the side of the mattress was a small stuffed animal.

Marina felt her legs about to give way, her heart break. She fell to her knees. Picked up the toy.

'Lady . . .'

Josephina's toy dog. The one she thought was Lady from the Disney film. She never went anywhere without that. Slept with it clutched to her chest. Carried it round the house during the day. Talked to it at mealtimes.

Tears came then. But Marina didn't know whether she was crying from loss, helplessness or rage. Or all three.

Head swirling, she stood up, the toy clutched in her hand.

She made her way out of the house, back to the car. Got in. Drove away.

No idea where she was going.

Just as fast and as far away as she could.

PART THREE: CRUCIFIXION SUNDAY

47

Midnight. And Alessandro couldn't sleep.

He often felt like that before a fight. Tense. Agitated. Wired. His body just a machine of sinew and muscle, primed, fuelled and ready to be put to use. Coiled and unable to relax. His mind was focused on that one specific event, anticipating it, working towards it. Making and countering moves in his head, trying to out-think, outguess his opponent before the first punch had even been thrown. He planned and plotted. Tried to come up with an offensive strategy that would defeat his opponent while minimising the pain to himself. He had jabbed and weaved his way round the room all evening. And now he lay staring at the ceiling, the walls, unable to think of anything else.

Except Katrina. His girlfriend until two nights ago, when his anger, jealousy and fists had got the better of him. He knew that what he had done was wrong, but that still hadn't stopped him. The others had all been interchangeable, forgettable. But not her. She had got into his head, this one. And she still hadn't called. Not one word, one text. Nothing.

He had texted her. Repeatedly. Apologising. Saying he knew that he had done wrong, that it was all his fault. Asking for her forgiveness. Then, when there still no reply, begging for her forgiveness. He had checked his phone regularly. Too regularly.

And now he couldn't sleep. So he might as well stop pretending.

He sat up, threw the covers back. Swung himself over the edge of the bed, sat head in hands. He could feel the tension zinging round his body, his fingers static, his muscles humming like electric cabling. He stood up. Paced the room. Desperately, bouncing off the walls. It seemed smaller than usual, a zoo enclosure for a captured animal. He sat back down again. There was nothing he could do. He could find no outlet for his pent-up rage, his frustration. He had to wait until the fight. Let it all out then. Channel it. Make it count.

He looked round the room once more. It was run-down, cheaply furnished. Everything either rented, second hand or stolen. Nothing cared for, looked after. No value to anything. A mess. The room was his life.

He flexed and unflexed his fists. Tried to relax his jaw. He had been grinding his teeth unconsciously. Channel, he thought once more. Focus. Make it count.

He had to win this one. Had to. He couldn't keep living like this. Had to move on. That was why he had agreed to this fight. Make some money, let him and Katrina move somewhere else, somewhere decent. Have a good life together. A happy life.

And pay off his gambling debts. That was how he had got into this in the first place. Drinking, gambling, fighting. The unholy trinity, the nuns at school used to say. What he used to see at home. And that was him. The father and the son. The father *in* the son. Both imbued with the same unholy ghost. When he had become indebted to several people that he should have known better than to be indebted to, namely Mr Picking, it was suggested that he put his fists to good use. Start paying off some of that interest, said Mr Picking with a smile that had different meanings for both of them. Knowing what was waiting for him if he said no, Sandro realised he had no choice.

Before the first fight, he was terrified. He had fought before, won most of them. But they were scraps, clashes. Arguments settled. This was something different. He had stood there at the back of the barn, watching the crowd. Hearing them baying and cheering at the sight of blood. Watching them get turned on by two men hitting each other until they were unrecognisable. This wasn't the kind of fighting he was used to. This was gladiatorial combat.

And then it had been his turn. And he was scared. He saw the man he was supposed to face. A big guy, tough-looking, a traveller carrying his hardships on his body. And angry. A total stranger, angry at Sandro for no reason. Ready to make him hurt.

If Sandro didn't make him hurt first.

So Sandro went at him. Arms flailing, punching, jabbing. Wildly, desperately. No plan, no technique.

The bout didn't last long. Less than one round. Sandro took a smack to the ear, went down and stayed down. He was dragged out of the ring, face and body bruised and bleeding. His benefactor and debtor was waiting at the ringside.

'You were shit,' Mr Picking had said. Then, to his attendants, 'Patch him up and send him home. He'll get better.'

And he had. Once Sandro had recovered, he had been put in to another fight. And another. He had improved, until eventually he was like his first opponent, big and angry and wearing the hardships of his life on his body.

And yet he still hadn't settled enough of Mr Picking's debt to be free of him. But Sandro had been around long enough. He understood how it worked now. He knew what Mr Picking was like, how he operated. And he doubted he ever would be free.

But he had to do something if he wanted to get out. He had to bet on himself. He would wait until he got there, see what the odds were and then put plenty on himself to win. It was risky; it could lead people to think the fight was rigged. No. He had to be secretive about the bet, then go out there and fight to win.

No pressure, then.

He stood up once more, pacing the room. Maybe he should go back to bed. Try to get some sleep. But he couldn't. There was the fight, but there was Katrina too. He wondered where she was now. What she was doing.

And who she was doing it with.

Thinking that, his insides turned to acid.

And then he heard a knock at the door.

He stopped pacing, startled. Looked at it as if he could see through it, see who was calling. He checked his watch. Nearly half past midnight.

Another knock.

His heart jumped. He knew who it was.

Katrina . . .

The acid gone from his insides, he ran to the door, ready to pull it open. Ready for his lover to fall into his arms. Ready to do anything, say anything to start again.

Hand on the lock, he stopped. What if it wasn't Katrina? What if it was Mr Picking or one of his associates? Telling him to lose. Telling him what kind of punishment he had to take. It had happened before. If that was the case, his plans would all fall through.

Another knock.

His heart hammering, he knew he had no choice. He had to open the door.

He flung it wide open. And stared. Stunned.

Standing there was his sister, Marina.

She looked at him. 'Sandro . . .'

And collapsed on to the floor.

48

The needle was pushed into the Golem's ruined flesh. Poked through, pulled out again, leaving a visceral red trail. He watched, his eyes flat, his expression detached. His mind somewhere else altogether.

When he had woken up, the interior of his car looked like an abattoir. The thought was almost amusing. Because the only meat butchered in there had been his own.

Before he passed out, he had phoned Michael Sloane. Told him it hadn't gone to plan, that he was injured and needed picking up. He left the phone on so the GPS could track him down.

Sloane, clearly not wanting to be seen to be involved, sent two of his lieutenants. They hauled the Golem from his car, laying him in the back of a Transit van, and torched his car. That didn't upset him. He was never angry at the loss of possessions. Besides, he would invoice for the cost of a replacement.

He had lost consciousness again then, but he knew where they would be taking him. Dr Bracken. The Golem didn't know whether 'Doctor' was an honorary title or an actual one, or whether Bracken was currently a doctor or not, but it didn't matter. He had been treated by the man before. And no doubt he would be again. And he wasn't the only one.

Bracken was well known as the go-to guy for patching up people who didn't want to leave a paper trail or go through the system. He never asked questions.

The Golem knew where he must be. Down a secluded path off a roundabout between Romford and Ongar in the badlands of Essex. The road was quite picturesque at first, with overhanging branches and muntjac deer skipping about. There was even a large old country house at what seemed like the end of the road, nestling in amongst the trees. But take the unmade road at the side of the country house and travel down there until the branches were no longer overhanging but closing in claustrophobically and the deer dared not go because they might not make it out alive again, and there was the house of Dr Bracken. A huge, heavy metal gate sat at the far end of the unmade road, the kind that survivalists or a far-right group might hole up behind. All around the house was a high fence, electrified, topped with razor wire. Several signs, hand-painted and not always accurately spelled, had been erected to deter anyone not put off by the gate: *Keep Out, Private Propity, Strangers Not Wellcome.*

And that was where the Golem was being patched up.

He studied Bracken as the man worked on his arm. He was small, frail-looking, but his eyes burned with an intensity that often seemed to be the only thing animating his scrawny frame. Like he was lit and powered by an individual fire within. A fire that burned with a dark, ugly light.

Probably the same light that powered the soldiers who killed my mother, raped my family. Destroyed my village and homeland, the Golem thought. But it didn't matter at the moment. The doctor was helping him, patching him up, so he would call a truce.

Besides, he knew where he lived.

Bracken pushed the needle in again. The Golem smelled what he always did coming off the man. Alcohol, sweat. And something more. Fear and despair. Bracken didn't do this by choice. Perhaps this wasn't his place after all. Perhaps he was just a prisoner here. The Golem didn't care. As long as he patched him up, got him working again.

'Met you before,' Bracken slurred as he worked. 'Don't usually remember them, but you stick out. The skin.'

'I killed some people who killed my family. Then I was dead inside. My skin turned grey. Then I was dead outside.'

Bracken nodded. 'You take any colloidal silver?'

'Of course,' said the Golem. 'I take many things to keep me healthy and strong. Is good. Heals you. Keeps you fit. Stops Aids, they say.'

'And turns your skin grey.'

The Golem thought about that. 'No. It is because I am dead inside.'

'Whatever works for you, son,' said Bracken, and kept pushing the needle.

Bracken used big, looping strokes, like he was stitching leather or hide, and thick black thread. The local anaesthetic hadn't blocked out all the pain. The Golem had to rely on himself to do that.

His side had been done first. The easiest wound to clean, treat, stitch and bandage. Then the knife slashes to his arm. Again, relatively simple. But his left arm was proving problematic. It had been chewed to bits.

'You should probably have a skin graft on this,' Bracken had said. 'Reconstructive surgery. It's the only thing that'll save it. Make it good again.'

'I don't have time,' said the Golem. 'I am working. Put me together again, send me back out there.'

'You'll be going nowhere for the next few days, state you're in,' Bracken said.

'No,' said the Golem, not arguing but stating. 'Patch me up. Send me back. I am working. I have job to finish.'

Bracken waved his hand, shrugged. Not his problem. 'As you wish . . .'

He pulled the last length of thread through the Golem's arm, tied it, cut it. Stood back. 'There,' he said. 'Best I can do.'

The Golem stood up, looked at himself in the mirror.

'I wouldn't do that, you'll be unsteady on your feet . . .'

The Golem stood firm. Regarded his reflection.

More wounds to heal. More life markers on his body. More scars to carry. He could live with them. But Bracken was right. His left arm was a mess.

'Bandage me up,' he told Bracken.

'That arm needs more than bandage.'

'And it will get it. After I finish job.'

Shrugging once more, Bracken bandaged the Golem's arm. The Golem kept looking at himself.

'Now,' he said. 'Pills?'

'What?'

'Pills. You give me pills. You know the kind. You give before.'

'Oh, now look . . . that's not, that's not a good idea . . .'

'Pills now. You know. The kind to make me strong. To make me not give in. The kind that make me feel no pain.'

'I really don't think that's a good idea. You don't . . . They're dangerous. They could damage you when you take them. Hurt you.'

'If they do,' the Golem said, eyes hard and flat, 'then I won't feel it. Pills. Now.'

49

Mickey Philips had received the call over an hour ago. Murder in Jaywick. Get yourself there as quickly as possible.

Now he parked as near to the crime-scene tape as he could. Silenced the Fleet Foxes CD that had been playing and made his way to the barrier, warrant card at the ready.

Fleet Foxes, for God's sake. It was something Phil had burned for him and left in the car, insisting he listen to it. He had played it once, under sufferance, then relegated it to the bottom of the glove box, treating it with the contempt he reserved for most of his boss's music. At least he hadn't launched this one out of the window on the A12. The same couldn't be said for Neil Young's *Sleeps With Angels* album.

But today he had enjoyed it. Especially 'Your Protector'; that track had struck a chord with him. Played it three times. Even started singing along. And he knew why.

Anni. And the night they had just spent together.

As he walked, he thought back. They had sat together on the sofa in her living room. Glass of wine in her hand, beer in his. Budvar. Because she knew he liked it. He hadn't noticed at the time, but afterwards he realised that she must have got that in especially for him in case he ever called round. That made him smile.

Anni had been curled in one corner, legs beneath her, Mickey at the other end. Trying to relax but remaining upright and forward instead. She had put some music on. Fleet Foxes.

'Not usually my thing,' she had said. 'Phil downloaded it for me. It's really grown on me.'

Mickey nodded. Sipped his beer, listened to the harmonies. Something about coming down from the mountain, being gone too long. It wasn't bad.

'I think he did me a copy too,' he said. 'Never played it.'

'You should. You might like it.'

'Yeah,' he said, looking at her, 'I might.'

'After a hard day at work,' she said, 'glass of wine, this music, great way to unwind.'

'Yeah,' he said.

She placed her wine glass on a side table. Took a deep breath, let it out. Mickey watched her breasts rise and fall as she did so. He couldn't help it. He put the can to his lips, noticed his hand was shaking. Swallowed hard on the beer, put it down too. His body was burning with desire mixed with a fear of rejection. He looked along the sofa at Anni. She smiled at him.

'I can think of a better way to relax, though.'

She moved towards him. He thought of picking up his beer can again, draining it, just to take in some courage, but left it where it was. She had worked her way along until she was beside him. She placed her hand on his chest, ran her fingers down his shirt front. Her touch felt good.

She looked at him. Eyes locking with eyes. She smiled. Moved her head in towards him.

The first kiss. The first proper kiss between them. Her tongue was in his mouth, he met hers with his. Touching, exploring, mouth on mouth. Her lips so warm, so soft. Just like he had imagined. And he had imagined this a lot.

He pulled away. Looked at her. She smiled once more, eyes lit by an inner fire.

'D'you think . . .' he said.

'Yes . . .' Her voice breathy.

'D'you think we should be doing this? What with . . . y'know. Everything that's happened today.'

She sat back from him. 'Don't you want to?'

'Yes, but . . .' He sighed. 'The boss. Everything that's happened.'

She sat back from him. 'If you don't want to . . .'

'I do.'

'Come on, then.' She leaned forward. 'After today, I think this is just what we need.'

And she was back beside him, mouth on his, hands running over his clothed body, finding buttons, zips. Undoing them. Pulling his shirt off, breaking off from their kiss to slide her hands over his chest, smile.

He moved in to her neck, began kissing her there, hands slowly caressing her. Moving gently inside her T-shirt, down her chest . . .

She pushed herself against him. He kept caressing her. Her hands found the buttons of his jeans, began working them open. He kept his hands above her breasts.

Anni stopped what she was doing, looked at him.

'You OK?' she said, voice a near-whisper.

He nodded. 'Yeah.'

'You sure you want to do this?'

'Yeah . . .' He frowned. 'Why?'

'You just seem . . . I don't know. Like you're holding back.'

'Holding back? No, I'm . . . I'm not.'

'Good.'

And she bit his neck. He loved it. Felt an electrically sexual charge run through him. His hands moved down to her breasts. She groaned, pushed her body towards him again. His strokes became slightly more urgent. She stopped once more.

'Don't you fancy me?'

'What? Yeah, course . . .'

'Then show me. I won't break, you know.'

He sighed. 'I know, but . . .'

'What?'

'I'm just . . . I'm sorry. I just . . . you're someone special. To me. Very special. And you know . . . I respect you.'

'Good. So you should. And you can still respect me.' She smiled. 'In the morning. But tonight, I want some fun.'

'Permission granted,' he said, smiling.

And from then on, Mickey didn't have to be told twice.

50

After Mickey had left, Anni couldn't get back to sleep.

She lay there in bed, replaying the events of the previous night over and over in her head. And they were worth replaying. She and Mickey had just . . . fitted. Not at first, though. Mickey had seemed reticent. She had found it quite sweet. But since sweet wasn't the defining feature she looked for in a man — it wasn't even in the top ten — she had gently but firmly shown him that that wasn't what she wanted. And he had responded.

Oh yes, he had responded.

The night had been wonderful from then on. Filthy and tender by turns, thrillingly fast at times, achingly slow at others. Anticipation and fulfilment in equal measure.

But with Mickey gone, something else took hold of her mind. The CCTV footage of Marina in the garage from the day before. She kept replaying it over and over in her head. They had missed something, she was sure of it.

She ran through it once more, and . . . there it was.

Anni was up, showered and out of her flat in record time, calling ahead to tell the farmer's wife from the garage that she was coming back, asking her to have the CCTV footage ready to view again. And not to empty the bins.

Less than thirty minutes later, she was standing in the back room of the service station, looking at the TV screen. She saw Marina standing impatiently in line, waiting to be served. Watched as she looked up at the CCTV camera then moved forward in the queue, bought her mints. Took one, threw the wrapper on the floor.

'There it is,' said Anni. 'Stop it there.' She pointed at the screen. 'See?'

The farmer's wife paused the footage.

'She . . . throws the wrapper on the floor,' said the woman, a puzzled look on her face.

'Yes, she does. Have you swept up since then?'

'Yes, but . . .'

Anni pulled a pair of latex gloves from her pocket. 'Can you show me where the bins are, please?'

The farmer's wife took her outside to the back of the building, where black bags and flattened cardboard boxes were piled up. She told Anni which bag was the likeliest. Anni spread newspaper on the ground, split the bag, tipped the contents out. She talked as she sifted.

'I thought it was just rubbish,' she said. 'At first. Just her being untidy. But then . . .' her hands worked over the garbage, unfolding every piece of paper she could find, 'I thought of the way she found the CCTV camera, looked at it. It bugged me. And watching it back now . . .' she held up a piece of paper; discarded it, 'I knew I was right.'

The farmer's wife was standing beside her, watching. 'How d'you mean?'

'The look,' said Anni. 'At first I thought she was just checking where the camera was. Thinking about avoiding it. But no. She looks at the camera, then looks to the floor.'

'So?'

'Not just anywhere, but to a specific part of the floor. The identical same spot that she threw that bit of rubbish down at.'

'Oh,' said the farmer's wife, her voice becoming excited. 'You think she's left you a clue? From the wrapper on those mints?'

'Not the wrapper. She just wanted to make us think it was a wrapper. She was being subtle in case . . . I don't know. Someone else was watching? But she hoped one of us would see what she was doing.' She held up a piece of paper. Smiled. 'Here it is.'

As she unfolded the paper, the farmer's wife leaned in closer to see. 'It's a postcode,' she said. 'She sent you a message.'

'She certainly did.'

Anni thanked the woman, who said she would clear up, and that she was glad to help. Then she made her way to the pool car she had borrowed from the station, a Fiesta, buzzing like she had just speed-downed thirty espressos.

Thank God it's got sat nav, she thought, and keyed in the coordinates. She was ready to go.

She just had one phone call to make first.

51

'So who called it in?' Mickey Philips asked the uniform next to him, walking down the common approach path towards the crime scene. The morning was white, fogbound. The mist curled round him like a character in a Steve Ditko comic.

The circus had arrived before him. The house and grounds had been cordoned off behind black and yellow crime-scene tape, fluttering in the breeze like disgruntled wasps. Through the fog, the white-suited forensics team were treading carefully and warily, sticking to the square metal stepping stones of the CAP, not wanting to tread on the wrong thing, explode some hidden time bomb. They never failed to remind Mickey of a team of scientists in some Hollywood blockbuster, trying to halt the spread of a deadly virus or chemical spillage. The most visible symbol to observers that something in their ordered world had gone very wrong.

Ahead of them, two white plastic tents had been erected, both to preserve the crime scene and to obscure the view of any TV news crews. Mickey had noticed a couple getting into place as he pulled up. Finding good positions for their cameras and reporters. White mist, white tents, white-suited people. Wouldn't make for the most dynamic TV pictures.

Since Mickey was with the Major Incident Squad, he tried to avoid the crews. If they recognised him as he approached, they might think there was a story to be had, and that would make his job even more difficult.

The uniform by the inner cordon checked his notes, hurried to keep up with him. 'Someone out walking their dog. Proper angry old man. Saw a lump on the lawn.' He pointed to the first white tent. 'Thought it was someone asleep. A tramp, he said. Went to . . .' He checked his notes. 'Berate the person, as he said.'

'Berate? He used that word?'

The uniform nodded. 'His exact word.'

'Go on.'

'Right.' He looked down at his notes once more. 'He then realised they were dead dogs. Went up to the house to complain, found the body. And here we are.'

'Given a statement?'

'Yep. Got it. Very angry. Apparently there should be a law against killing dogs, he reckons.'

'Whereas doing it to people is fine. Thanks.'

The uniform went back to his duties.

Mickey reached the first white tent. He pulled on the offered white paper suit, shoe covers and gloves. He asked if it was OK to enter, was given an affirmative. The corpses of the two dogs took centre stage. Forensics had positioned a workbench at the side. The bodies had been marked, catalogued, inspected. The surrounding area cordoned off, subject to investigation. Mickey always regarded a crime scene as a spiral. Start at the edge, work inwards to the centre — the crime itself. And once that story was told, a conclusion could then be worked towards.

'What have we got?'

Jane Gosling, another MIS DS, turned to him. He knew her well. Pleasant temperament, passionate about amateur dramatics. He made a mental note: must get round to seeing her in something. Only polite.

'Two dead dogs,' she said, deliberately stating the obvious. She was a large woman, and although she filled out the white suit, she carried herself with a grace that belied her size.

'Great observation,' said Mickey, bending down. 'You'll go far.'

Jane joined him. 'This one here . . .' she pointed to the dog on the right, 'seems to have taken a punch to the neck. Then a boot to the head. Or something heavy.'

'And that's what killed it?'

'Not sure. The head's at an angle; looks like its neck's been snapped.'

'Jesus. And the other?' He indicated the second dog. 'Someone's had a right go at this one.'

'They have. Blood all over its face. What we think is that it attacked someone and they fought back.'

'Must have been a hell of a fighter. More than one of them?'

'Don't know. Yet. We're still examining the footprints around the area. We've only found one set so far.'

'One person did this? Jesus . . .'

'And look at the dog. What's been done to it. It looks like it attacked someone.' She gestured with the tip of her pen towards its mouth. 'See there? Bits of flesh on its fangs.'

'Should be able to get some good DNA off that.'

'Hopefully. All that blood can't be the dog's own.'

He felt himself staring at it, appalled but fascinated. 'But . . . what happened? It looks like its head's been ripped apart.'

'It has. Something very strong's been put in its jaw. And the jaw's been pulled apart.'

'And that's what killed it?'

'It's got a broken neck too. That seems the most likely. At this stage. But it would have died from the injuries anyway.'

Mickey shook his head. 'I don't get it. Why rip a dog apart, leave it for dead, then put it out of its misery?'

Jane stood up. 'Beats me. But if it's just one person who's done all this, we've got a maniac on the loose.'

'A very strong maniac.'

'Right.'

Mickey straightened up. 'Thanks, Jane. Carry on.'

He made to leave the tent. Jane placed a hand on his arm, stopped him. 'Any news?'

He knew what she was talking about. 'Phoned the hospital before I came here. Said he'd had a good night. He's stable. Wouldn't tell me anything more.'

Jane sighed. 'What they told me. We've been playing this game a long time. Don't know if that's a good sign or a bad one.'

'No,' said Mickey. 'Not so much fun being on the other side for once, is it?'

'No,' she said. 'Body's in the next tent. Good luck.'

Mickey stepped back into the fog. Not thinking about Phil or Anni. Just concentrating on the job in hand.

Going to inspect the body.

52

The two laptops lay side by side. Perfectly squared off. Different makes, models, but both holding secrets waiting to be uncovered.

Michael Sloane stared down at them. Smiled. He loved the precision of their placing, the symmetry they created. Two rectangular puzzle pieces just waiting to be unlocked. They held full specifics of the operation against him: intercepted and recorded conversations, dealings he didn't want made public, methods of permanently dealing with opponents. Not to mention all their plans of revenge in full detail.

'Beautiful,' he said. 'Worth dying for. Obviously.'

He turned. The Golem was standing behind him. To attention, face as impassive as ever, an automaton waiting for a command. But Sloane sensed there was something more to him. It seemed like his mind wasn't there. He moved towards him. 'Why are you standing there?'

The Golem's gaze seemed to be far away. At Sloane's words, his eyes returned to the world. Like a reconnaissance craft that had been charting the outer reaches of infinite space.

'You're back with us,' said Sloane. 'Good.'

'Sorry?' The Golem's voice was quiet, quizzical. Not, as Sloane had noted before, the expected voice of a killer.

'Why are you standing there? Here, in this room? You should be in bed. Hospitalised.'

'I . . .' the eyes were phasing out once more, 'am strong. Mind over matter. We feel pain . . . only if we allow ourselves to be hurt by it.'

'Right.' Drugs, thought Sloane. Has to be. 'You got the laptop. Good. And Watts is out of the way. But you let the rest of them escape.'

'I . . . yes. It is embarrassment to me.'

'It's more than that. It's dangerous. And not just for you. For me as well. You've left far too many loose ends.'

'I . . . apologise.'

'You'll have to do more than that. You'll have to make it right.' He looked the Golem up and down. His side, his arms were bandaged. He wore a loose shirt to cover them. He looked pale. Or rather, thought Sloane, a lighter shade of grey. 'Can you do that?'

'I can.'

'Good. But what happened yesterday could be very damaging to me. Permanently damaging, even. And I'm not prepared to allow that to happen. Not after everything I've done. So I need that damage limited. Stopped. And I have to know, are you capable of doing it? Today, now, in the state you're in?'

The Golem looked Sloane directly in the eyes. He was back, focused. No doubt about it. To look in the Golem's eyes was to stare death in the face. Sloane blinked. Swallowed hard.

'I can do it. Today. I am in perfect state.' He moved forward. Sloane took a step back. 'I feel no pain. I am . . . superman.'

'Good. Then let's . . . let's crack on.'

'Also . . .' The Golem moved, wouldn't let him get away.

Sloane waited.

'Also I need to redeem myself.'

'Redeem?'

'I am professional. I allowed . . . error of judgement. I considered all alarm systems except one. I did not consider dogs. It was sloppy. I need to redeem.'

'Good.'

'I *will* redeem.'

'Glad to hear it.'

'What must I do?'

Sloane returned his attention to the two laptops. 'We need to know where she's gone. And him, whatever he's calling himself now. And the kid. I can't see her getting rid of either of them. They're her insurance. She still thinks she can win with them. How wrong she is.'

He sat down at the desk. 'We need to find her. Hopefully one of these should give us a clue as to where they are. We also need to know if she's still in contact with the psychologist and what we can do about that.' He sighed. 'I should have got rid of her when I had the chance,' he said, more to himself than anyone else. 'Too soft, that's my trouble.'

Dee chose that moment to enter the room. Sloane looked round at her. She was dressed in a clinging black velour leisure suit, trainers. Hair tied back. No make-up. There was no trace of the provocatively sexual being of the previous day. She was all business now.

'Nice of you to drop by.'

'I've been working out.' She crossed the floor towards him. Didn't even give the Golem a second look.

Sloane smiled to himself. He never knew where he was with her. He couldn't predict how she would behave from one second to the next, what sort of mood she would be in, what would come out of her mouth or even what she would be wearing. Those capricious mood-swings had been very entertaining in the past. Exciting. And dangerous too. But he liked that about her. No. He *loved* that about her. His special switch bitch . . .

'I'm just briefing our friend, darling,' he said.

She stared at him.

'Damage limitation. Before it's too late.'

Her reply was cut off by the phone ringing. Neither of them made a move to answer it.

'Probably the police again,' said Sloane. 'They called round last night. We'll just pretend we're not in again.'

No response from Dee.

'I've briefed the house slave. They won't get through.'

Nothing.

Sloane looked between the Golem and Dee. Tried to work out which one was the more impassive. Couldn't decide.

The house slave entered clutching a handset, her hand over the mouthpiece. Sloane looked at her. 'You know we're not to be disturbed,' he said, voice low. 'I left you strict instructions. Do you enjoy your punishments?'

She trembled. Passed the phone over. 'I think . . . think you need to answer, sir.' Bowed her head. Stood there as if awaiting a blow.

He took the phone, quelled the anger rising within him. Spoke. 'Sloane.'

'Hello, Michael.'

It took him a few seconds before he recognised the voice. Then he understood why the house slave had been insistent. She had avoided her punishment. Unless she still wanted it, of course.

'Hello, Helen,' he said. 'A pleasant surprise.'

At the mention of the name, Dee's head swung round, eyes burning into him, as if she could see the woman on the other end of the phone. She knew who it was.

'Jeff's dead,' said Helen Hibbert.

'So I heard,' said Sloane. 'My condolences.'

'You know why I'm calling. I have to see you. I'm coming round.'

Sloane mustered a smile. 'Of course, Helen. Always a pleasure.'

The phone went dead. He handed it back to the house slave, who left the room. Dee was still staring at him.

'Let's hope,' he said, 'that it's not too late for all this damage limitation.'

The other two said nothing.

53

The fog was lifting. Not nearly enough for the sun to appear, but just enough for Mickey to make out the tall, cadaverous shape of pathologist Nick Lines standing ahead of him by the second tent. He looked like a ghost, or the Grim Reaper, ready to carry dead souls over to the afterlife. He beckoned to Mickey, entered the tent. Mickey couldn't shake the feeling that by following Lines, he was stepping out of one world and into another.

And in a sense he was. Phil Brennan, after a few too many beers, had once explained it to him.

'The ordinary world,' he had said, 'the normal, everyday world, the nine-to-five, alarm clock, *EastEnders* of an evening and dinner out on a Saturday world, is the one that most people inhabit. But that's not for us, Mickey. Not for us.'

Mickey had listened, thinking that if nothing else, he'd have a good story to tell the rest of the team the next morning about what the boss had come out with when he was drunk.

'We stand on the threshold,' Phil had continued. 'We're the gatekeepers to the other world. Where the dead live, the raped, the mutilated . . . the abandoned. The blind, the voiceless. The real world doesn't want to know, Mickey. They don't want to be reminded that it exists. Because if they knew, if they really, really knew what it was like . . . they wouldn't be able to get up the next morning.'

Mickey had listened. Nodded.

'And it's our job — you, me, Anni, the rest of the team . . . our job to make sure the two worlds never collide. Or hardly ever. And we do that . . . you know how we do that?'

Mickey had said he didn't.

'We do that by giving a voice to the voiceless. By speaking up for them. The murdered, the raped, the mutilated. The victims. We give them a voice. We find who did this to them.' He had taken another drink. Found his glass empty. 'MIS. Major Incidents. Doesn't begin to cover it. We're the gatekeepers, Mickey. All that stands between one world and the next. Never forget that, Mickey. Never forget that.'

And Mickey hadn't. He hadn't gone into work the next day and made jokes about what the boss had come out with when he was drunk. He had gone on his next case — a double murder of teenage twin girls — remembering Phil's words. Acting on them. When he finally amassed enough evidence against their killer — their father — and charged him, leading to a successful conviction, those words had come back to him. And there was nothing funny or ridiculous about them. Just an honest job description of what he did.

So when he stepped across the threshold of the white tent, he was prepared for what awaited him. Nick Lines was already there, staring down at the sight before him.

'There,' Lines said, accompanied by a quick wrist-flick gesture, in case Mickey was in any doubt as to what he was referring. 'Down there.'

Mickey looked. It had once been a man. And his death hadn't been easy. His face was swollen, dark. His eyes wide and staring, dotted and streaked with leaked blood from burst capillaries.

'Cerebral hypoxia,' said Nick Lines.

'You mean he was strangled. Choked.'

Lines didn't answer. He wasn't given to wasting time on unnecessary words. His dismissive manner and haughty attitude always made Mickey feel inferior. He was fairly sure it was a pose the pathologist had worked up, a mask he had initially worn to hide his own all-too-human reactions to his work. But like most masks worn for any length of time, instead of hiding the wearer, the wearer had grown into it.

Nick Lines was kneeling down, studying the corpse.

'Contusions to the neck . . . major bruising either side of the trachea . . . abrasions, scratches from fingernails . . .' He looked up at Mickey. 'I'd say you're looking for a very strong man with very large hands.'

'Large hands?'

'He was strangled with only one hand. With quite a wide span. He got both carotid arteries. If the lack of oxygen didn't kill our boy, the cardiac arrest would have.' He straightened up. 'So he's got at least one large hand. Although in my experience, I've found this sort generally carry two.'

'Not always.' If it wasn't Nick's erudition that made Mickey feel inferior, his attempts at humour always made him defensive.

'True. Although I think in this case we can assume that.' He glanced round at the ground covered by the tent. Forensics had made a thorough examination of it. 'There was a fight here. One on one. And by the way blows were traded, it's clear that both participants had two arms. Although . . .' He knelt down once more. Pointed to an area of earth that had been heavily sampled. 'Blood in the soil. Been taken for analysis. Shame. Nitrogen, calcium and phosphorous. Very good fertiliser. If they'd left it, they'd have lovely cauliflowers.'

Mickey said nothing. He could find no words with which to reply to that. Instead he said, 'Time of death?'

'Hard to say without a full post-mortem. But given the rate of lividity and the weather conditions, I'd say within twenty-four hours. Possibly less.'

'Thanks. Any idea who he was? Why he was here?'

Nick Lines didn't even look at him as he spoke. 'I just do the biology. Metaphysics is your job.'

'Thanks, Nick.'

'Any time.' Nick Lines straightened up, the remains of a playful smile fading from his lips. 'I will say one thing. It's the same chap who did those two dogs over there. No doubt about that. Same degree of strength, same area of the body attacked. The throat. The neck. Such a small, weak area for such an important job.'

'Does that tell us anything about him?'

Nick Lines shrugged. 'Well if you wanted me to do your job for you, I'd tell you that he had done this before. Or is probably a professional, given that he knew what to go for and where to target.'

'A hit man?'

Lines shook his head. 'Sorry. You've run out of questions. You'll have to find your answers elsewhere.'

Mickey prepared to leave. With his opinion of Nick Lines unchanged and relieved to be leaving the man behind.

Before he could go, Lines stopped him. He looked straight at Mickey. Addressed him directly. 'How is he?'

Mickey knew who he was talking about.

'No change, last I heard. I'm sure they'll let us know when there's some news.'

Nick Lines nodded. Sighed. 'Always difficult when it's one of our own, isn't it?'

'Yeah,' said Mickey. 'It is.'

It was the first time he had felt he was on the same side as Nick Lines.

54

Tyrell opened his eyes and found he wasn't where he had expected to be.

No grey walls, no barred windows. No thin sheet over the top of him. Nothing familiar, nothing safe. Just light all around. Cramp growing like plant roots within him.

He tried to uncoil himself, straighten, sit up. His back screamed out as he did so, fighting to stop him. He lay back down again. Looked round. Tried to orient himself. His neck hurt. He saw daylight through windows. Trees. Mist. Felt the fog in his bones, the cold, his muscles cramped and seized. Then he remembered.

The car. They had slept in the car.

If it could be called sleeping. He had passed out with a combination of anxiety and exhaustion and didn't feel rested. He began to remember why they had ended up where they were.

They had left the house and caravan, the woman driving, him in the passenger seat and the little girl in the back. She had been crying, screaming. He didn't blame her. They had watched as a huge grey giant of a man had appeared, fought off the dogs and killed them in as bloody a manner as possible.

Then moved on to the house, where he had strangled Jiminy Cricket.

They hadn't waited for him to get to them.

Jumping into the boxy silver car, they had driven away, as fast and as far as they could manage, until they ran out of adrenalin and road. He had tried to calm the little girl, tell her that everything was going to be all right and that she shouldn't get so upset. The woman had told him not to be so soft. Told him to shut up and stop telling the kid lies. He had felt like screaming and crying then.

He tried to sit up again. Slower this time, working with his back not fighting it. Managed to get himself into a sitting position. He looked into the back of the car. Josephina was sitting there, eyes wide in terror, too scared to move, her hands clamped hard between her legs.

'Are you all right?' he asked her.

'Wee . . . need wee-wee . . .'

He looked round again. The woman was sitting in the driving seat. Head back, eyes closed, mouth open. Asleep.

'Come on then . . .'

He opened the car door, began to uncurl his body. Josephina opened the back one, got out. Looked at him to see what she should do next.

'Go on, over there in those trees,' he said. 'Don't worry. I'll be waiting here for you.'

She did as he said, hurrying away.

'Aw, how sweet.'

He turned. The woman was out of the car and standing next to him. She looked terrible. Her make-up had rubbed away, leaving a face that looked like a patchwork quilt. Red and pitted in parts, smooth in others. It looked like it had been assembled from different pieces, none of which quite matched. The markings continued down her neck and on to her body, where they were hidden by her clothes. As he watched, she put her hand to her head, adjusted her hair. Tyrell noticed how shiny and plastic it was. Then he realised. She was wearing a wig.

'She's upset,' he said. 'She's had a bad shock. She shouldn't be here.'

The woman gave a contemptuous snort. Looked round. 'None of us should be here.'

He saw Josephina from the corner of his eye as she approached them. She spotted the woman and stopped walking, not wanting to come any further.

'Get her over here,' said the woman. 'Don't want her running off. That's all we need.'

Tyrell turned to the child, attempted a smile. 'Don't worry, Josephina,' he said, holding out his hand. 'I won't let anything happen to you. You're safe as long as you're with me.'

Wary, Josephina made her way forward. Tyrell kept his hand outstretched. She came towards him, took it. He held on to her.

'Lady . . .' said Josephina, looking round.

Tyrell glanced at the woman, then back to the child. 'I'll keep the lady away from you. Don't worry.'

The woman shook her head. 'Stop telling her it'll be OK. Stop lying to her.'

Tyrell felt anger rise within him once more. This woman seemed to be able to bring that out in him very easily. 'I'm not lying to her. I mean it. It's the truth.' He felt himself holding tight to Josephina. 'I won't let anyone hurt her.'

The woman gave another contemptuous snort. 'Yeah. Right. Whatever. You saw what happened back at the house. You saw what the Golem did to Graham.' Her mind slipped into a reverie. 'Graham, oh God, Graham . . .'

Tyrell was more interested in something else she'd said. 'The Golem?'

She looked at him, eyes red-rimmed and wild. Focus coming back, her words just a perfunctory explanation. 'Yeah. The Golem. That's his name.'

'But why is . . . why did he do that? Why is he after us? Who is he?'

She shook her head. 'Questions, questions . . . He wants to stop me. And you. And he's a killer. That's all you need to know.'

Tyrell couldn't believe what he was hearing. 'What about . . .' He gestured towards Josephina.

'And anyone who gets in his way.'

Tyrell's head was spinning. Hurting from more than the cramp and the sunlight. 'But . . . why? Who sent him?'

She looked at him. Straight. There was pity in the look. Tyrell didn't know if it was for him or herself. 'Ghosts,' she said. 'Ghosts from the past. They're after us. They're always after us . . .'

'Then . . . we'll go to the police. Tell them what's happened.'

Her eyes became slits, her mouth narrowed. 'Don't be stupid. We can't go to the police, can we? Remember? If we do, it'll be the end of everything. No money, no future.'

Tyrell said nothing.

'D'you want to go back inside? Is that it? Because that's what would happen. At the very least.' She shot Josephina a glance. The girl flinched. 'And God knows what would happen to *her* without you to protect her . . .'

Tyrell felt like crying. At that moment prison didn't sound too bad. But he wouldn't leave Josephina with this woman. Definitely not.

'So that's why you're doing this? Money for you, a future for me.'

'Got it in two,' she said.

A thought occurred to him. He had to voice it. 'No,' he said. 'You don't care about me. About giving me a future. Just so long as you get your money. That's right, isn't it?'

Her eyes flashed. It was like glimpsing a monster hidden behind a mask. 'Yes. The money. Because by Christ, I'm owed it.' She moved closer to him. He flinched, stepped backwards, taking Josephina with him. The woman's lips twisted into an ugly smile. 'Can't you remember? Why you went inside? Why you were put away?'

'No,' said Tyrell, eyes screwed tight shut. 'No. I don't remember. Don't want to remember. I never remember.'

'You mean you don't remember what happened? Any of it?'

'I . . .' Tyrell could feel his mind slipping back at her words. Could see the bodies before him. Feel the shotgun in his hands. 'No . . .' He shook his head. Tried to dislodge the memory, think about something else.

She watched him. 'What about me? Don't you even remember me?'

'No,' Tyrell said, shaking his head, not looking at her. 'I've never seen you before. Not before this, anyway.'

She smiled. Regained some control. Turned away. 'Good. Let's keep it that way. For now.'

Tyrell's heart was slowing. He was trying to think. He would have remembered meeting this woman before, he was sure. All he knew about her was that he didn't like her, didn't trust her and didn't want to be with her. And that made up his mind.

'I'm going,' he said.

She turned back to him. 'What?'

'I'm going. And I'm taking Josephina. You . . . you can do what you like.'

'Oh really?'

'Yeah. Yeah really.'

'I don't think so.'

Tyrell turned. The woman was holding a gun, pointing it at him.

'I really don't think so . . .'

55

'Thought I'd find you in here.'

'Love a gadget, me. You know that.'

Mickey had made his way into the kitchen. He found a pile of electronic equipment on the table, a mass of wires. And DS Adrian Wren.

Jane Gosling and Adrian Wren were often paired up together. The Birdies, as they had become affectionately known. But whereas Jane was large and gregarious, Adrian was the opposite. Everything about him was thin. His frame, his hair, his features. He was a marathon runner in his spare time, a subject on which he was obsessive to the point of exhausting. A conversation with Adrian and Mickey felt like he'd run a marathon himself. His other passion was electronics. Anything at a crime scene that needed a plug and an instruction manual and he was straight in.

'So what have we got here, then?' asked Mickey. 'Any ideas?'

Adrian looked down at the mess before them, rubbed his chin. 'Well, this here . . .' He pointed to a small black box. It had an illuminated screen, several buttons and lights, jacks for leads. 'I reckon that's a GPS tracker.'

'Right.'

'And I reckon it's been connected to . . .' he indicated the centre of the table, 'something here. Probably a laptop, from the space made. And given the tangle of wires and the way everything has been left, I'd say whoever was here took off in a hurry.'

'Probably when the dog murderer appeared.'

'That what we're calling him? The dog murderer?'

Mickey gave a grim smile. 'Press loves a nickname.'

'He killed a man, too.'

'Yeah. And you know what the media are like. Given the choice between reporting on the murder of a human and the death of a dog, you know which one they'll always go for.'

'Right. So dog murderer it is.'

Mickey straightened up, looked round the kitchen. The electronics, gleaming silver and black, were at odds with the surroundings. The sink and cupboards looked over forty years old, and any attempt at upkeep, or even cleaning, had long since been abandoned. The lino on the floor was cracked and stained, leaving huge threadbare gaps over the discoloured and dirty floorboards. The furniture was mismatched and well used. The windows were opaque with dirt, the walls a deep, greasy nicotine orange. Dishes at the side of the sink indicated that there had been three people here; two large plates, one small one, by Mickey's reckoning.

Lovely, he thought, and returned his gaze to the equipment on the table. 'So what was all this used for?'

'Well, if it is a GPS system, which I strongly suspect, then it's been used to track someone. Or to see if someone's tracking them. Either way.'

Mickey frowned. 'And there's no way of knowing who? Or why?'

'Not without that computer. But if — or should I say when — we find out who, then it shouldn't be too difficult to see why.'

'Ah,' said Mickey. 'Police work.'

'Right.' Adrian gave a grim smile. 'Find that laptop, Sergeant.'

'At once.'

Adrian opened his mouth to speak. Mickey knew what he was going to ask but didn't think he could talk about Phil again, so he thanked Adrian and turned towards the door leading to the rest of the house.

'Forensics done in here, are they?'

Adrian shrugged, already back examining the electronics. 'Don't know. They let me in, so it must be OK.'

Mickey moved out of the kitchen. The rest of the house was in a similar state. The place had been allowed to fall into serious neglect. He needed to find out who had lived there and what had happened to them.

He walked down the hallway — all peeling, faded floral paper, spreading triangles of mildew in the corners and everything coated in several layers of grease and dirt — and went up the stairs. Sleeping bags and mattresses on the floor. Clothes and belongings, litter and debris, from two people sharing the room. In the bathroom, more of the same. A few cosmetics, a fairly new bar of soap, the logo not yet washed off, the wrapper balled up on the floor, a half-used bottle of shampoo. Like someone had been camping indoors. Or squatting. Plenty of stuff for forensics to be going on with.

He went back downstairs and into the living room. Through the filthy windows he could see the team moving about like ghosts in the mist. He looked round the room. A portable TV had been hooked up in the corner, a cheap aerial on top of it. The settee was huge, horsehair stuffing falling out of it. An old blanket had been used as a throw. And on the door handle, a rope.

He crossed the room, looked at it. It hung down over a sheet-covered mattress. A small bowl at the side. This must be where the third one had been sleeping. He looked at the rope once more. Tied up? Against their will, a captive? Christ . . .

He hurried back into the kitchen. Adrian was still poring over the GPS system. 'Adrian, can you get the team together? Need to have a few words.'

It took a few minutes, but soon everyone was assembled outside the house, away from any TV cameras. They all stood there looking at him, expectant.

I've got to inspire them, Mickey thought. Say the kind of thing Phil would say if he was here. Send them off to do their jobs. Make them the best they can be. Searching for Marina would have to wait. This case would now take priority. That was how the system worked.

'Right, listen up,' he said, unconsciously echoing the words Phil always used to start a briefing. They were listening. 'The boss, as you all know, isn't here. And in his absence, it falls to me to take charge. So here's what we've got and here's what we'll do. First thing. Identification of the deceased. Jane, coordinate with uniforms. Get this area canvassed, door to door. I know neighbours are a bit thin on the ground round here, but someone saw the dogs so they may have seen something else. Hopefully something suspicious.'

'Like a murderer coming up the drive?' asked Jane.

'Exactly that. And Adrian, it looks like someone's either rented this place or was squatting here. Obviously rented would be best and easiest for us. Get on to that. Check rental agencies, find out who owns this place, who owns that caravan out there.'

Adrian nodded, making notes in his electronic notebook.

'And something else.' Mickey's phone rang. He ignored it. He tried to continue speaking, but the phone was insistent. 'Sorry,' he said. 'I'd better get that.' He took it from his pocket, checked the display. Anni. Not now, he thought. Later. I'm working here.

But then so is she . . .

He looked up, aware of everyone watching him. Knew he had no choice. Pressed the answer button. Turned away from them.

'Hi,' he said. 'Listen, I'm in the middle of—'

'Yeah, I know,' she said. 'And I wouldn't phone if it wasn't important.'

'Right.'

Just work colleagues again. No mention of the previous night.

'I've been back to see the farmer's wife at the service station, watched the CCTV footage again. I had an idea.'

Mickey waited.

'And Marina, she's sent us a message. That thrown-away wrapper. It had a postcode written on it.'

'Brilliant. If you can—'

'No, just listen. I put it into my sat nav, and guess where it came up with?'

'No idea, tell me.'

'Where you are now. After she left the garage, Marina was on her way to where you are . . .'

Mickey let the phone slip away from his face. His heart was hammering; he felt numb. He turned back to the group, saw them all staring at him. Thought of the mattress in the living room. The rope tied to the door handle.

'Shit . . .' he said. 'Listen up. There was someone kept here against their will. And I think I've worked out who it was. Josephina. Marina and Phil's kid . . .'

56

DS Jessie James threw her head back, dry-swallowed two paracetamol. This was becoming a habit.

Just one quick drink, she had told herself. Just one. Then back home for her regular Saturday night in with Terry. Takeaway, maybe a DVD. Then Sunday they had planned a day out. A run out to Audley End, maybe, make the most of Terry's National Trust membership. Dinner in some quaint country gastropub. She had told him she was on call, but neither of them thought she would be called in. But that was before she was handed this case.

So the previous night she had found herself dropping in to her neighbourhood pub on the way home. Just the one, she had said to herself. Just the one. A quick gin and tonic. Support the local economy, and all that. Maybe Terry would join her. They could make a night of it.

But of course he was at her house, DVD on the TV stand, takeaway menu in hand. Waiting for her. So she would just have the one. It went down so fast she barely noticed it. So she had another. And another. And when she arrived home, the house was dark, cold and empty.

So she had another drink.

She had noticed this pattern before when she was working on a case as big as this one. She would pull away from those closest to her, make excuses not to spend time with them. It was the only way she was capable of working. And it always involved alcohol. She was surprised Terry put up with it. She doubted he would for much longer.

DC Deepak Shah was looking out of the window. Away from the house, away from her. He had kept his eyes averted all the time she had sat there taking the tablets. He had made no comment, no judgement, but his lack of comment was judgement enough.

Jessie looked at him. He still had his eyes averted. 'What?'

He stayed where he was. 'I didn't say anything. Ma'am.'

'You didn't have to,' she said, running her tongue over her teeth. Feeling the bitter grit beneath. 'I think we've worked together long enough for me to know when I've disappointed you in some way.'

He turned, looked at her. Slowly. 'What you do in your free time has nothing to do with me. As long as you can still function when we're working together, that's fine. Ma'am.' He looked away again.

Jessie kept staring straight ahead at the big front door of the Sloane house. Willing it to open.

The two of them had visited the Sloanes as their last call on their way home the previous night. As soon as Deepak had taken the call concerning ownership of the car left parked outside the destroyed cottage in Aldeburgh, the Sloane residence had jumped to the top of their list for investigation. They had pulled up in the early evening, gasping audibly. The house, situated in Playford, between Ipswich and Woodbridge, was a huge, imposing sixteenth-century hall.

Jessie had stood at the front gates, spoken to the intercom. The voice on the other end had tried to fob her off, but she had been insistent. The gates had opened and they had both walked up the drive past the gatehouse, over the footbridge to the door of the main hall, trying to pretend they weren't over-awed. They flashed their warrant cards, asked to speak to Michael Sloane and were told by the housekeeper that he was out and wouldn't be back that night. They asked when he would return and were greeted with a shrug. They left a message asking him to call them and departed. The gates closed behind them.

That had been that.

And Jessie had spent the rest of the night hiding in a bottle.

Deepak, on the other hand, hadn't been idle.

He had called in at the station, run a check on Michael Sloane. Found out that he ran one of the biggest industrial farming operations in the east of England, with trade and shipping links to Europe. A very wealthy man, a very well-connected businessman. They would have to tread carefully when they spoke to him.

'Oh God, that's all we need,' Jessie had said, groaning. 'Involving one of the Chief Constable's golfing mates in this investigation. We'll have to be careful how we handle this, Deepak, me old mate. Or you and me'll be back in uniform working in Traffic.'

'We don't know that he knows the Chief Constable,' Deepak had replied.

'No, we don't. But until we learn otherwise, let's just assume.'

'There was something else,' Deepak said. 'A couple of things, actually.'

Jessie waited.

'I don't know if you remember, but the Sloanes were involved in a huge case a few years back. Their father remarried and their new stepbrother took a shotgun to the whole family.'

'Oh,' said Jessie. 'Those Sloanes.'

'Indeed. Michael and his sister survived but needed a lot of patching up. They took over the family business, extended into Europe and became recluses at the same time.'

‘A sister and brother? Holed up in that house together? Weird.’

‘And there’s something else. Get this. Jeff Hibbert, our dead man from yesterday, was one of the chief gangmasters for Sloane’s Farms.’

Despite the headache, something prickled at the back of Jessie’s neck. ‘Oh. Now that’s interesting. A mystery man gives Hibbert’s address at the scene of a crime and then disappears. Hibbert is then found murdered. And Michael Sloane’s car is found at the scene of the first crime. Interesting . . .’

They had cancelled their plans for Sunday and come to pay Michael Sloane another visit.

‘I’ve been thinking,’ said Jessie. ‘You know what was odd about last night?’

Deepak said he didn’t.

‘The housekeeper. She never asked why we were here. Two detectives rock up on your doorstep to speak to your boss. Never once did she ask what it was about. Don’t you think that’s strange?’

‘Maybe she didn’t think it was her place,’ Deepak said.

‘Or maybe we were expected,’ said Jessie.

They had resumed their vigil while they decided what to do.

Their minds were made up for them. As they watched, an Ipswich city cab pulled up. The passenger got out, paid the driver, watched the car pull away before turning to look at the gates.

‘Hey,’ said Jessie, ‘see who that is?’

Deepak nodded. He was looking towards the house now. ‘Helen Hibbert. Widow of the parish. Wonder what she wants?’

They watched as Helen Hibbert walked up to the gate, pressed the intercom, spoke. Waited.

‘No chance,’ said Jessie.

‘Shouldn’t have sent that cab away.’

Then the gate swung open and Helen Hibbert was admitted.

They looked at each other.

‘Someone’s home now,’ said Deepak. ‘Should we follow?’

Jessie thought for a few seconds. ‘Let’s just wait,’ she said. ‘See what happens. No hurry.’ She smiled. ‘Besides, we wouldn’t want to crash the party, would we?’

57

Even though Michael Sloane had agreed to see her, Helen Hibbert hadn't thought it would be this simple. Just walk up to the gate, announce herself, walk in. But as she approached the house, the gravel crunching beneath her heels, she began to remember that dealing with the Sloanes was never straightforward. Her previous experiences with them had been exhausting. Countering their lies, dodging their deceits had taken all her skill and concentration. Trying to get anything from them had been a nightmare.

But at least she was in and they were going to meet with her. That was the first step. Now all she had to do was make sure she didn't lose her nerve. Got what she came for.

No pressure, then.

She walked up to the front door, ready to ring the bell. Before she could, the door opened. The housekeeper stood there. Silent. Expectant.

Helen cleared her throat. 'I'm here to see Michael Sloane. He's expecting me.'

'Mr Sloane is unavailable at the moment.'

'You mean he's out?'

'He is unavailable.'

Helen felt anger rising with her. The Sloanes up to their old tricks. Messing her around again. 'No,' she said, speaking slowly so that this foreign woman could understand. 'I phoned him. He said he would be here. He is expecting me.'

'He is unavailable.' Her voice, her face flat, unreadable. 'Miss Dee is available to meet with you.'

Oh God, thought Helen. The weird sister. Brilliant.

She sighed. 'OK. She'll have to do.'

The housekeeper ushered her in, shut the door behind her. Once inside, Helen looked around. She had been in the house a couple of times before. Rare occasions, when Jeff — with Helen as his plus one — had been invited to the odd party. The Sloanes had tastes that overlapped somewhat with the Hibberts'. She had felt the place then to be cold and empty; even with all those people mingling, drinking and enjoying each other's intimacies, it hadn't seemed like a warm place. Now, with just echoing blank walls and the odd little piece of angular furniture, the interior of the house looked even more severe. Like a boutique hotel, to be admired rather than stayed in.

Helen was led into another room. It had two sofas facing each other. All black leather and chrome. A glass and metal table between them, the top polished and bare. And not much else. It was like a private doctor's waiting room. Or a very high-priced psychiatrist.

Helen had been in some posh places before. Plenty of them when she was still with Jeff and they used to make a habit of trying to enjoy themselves in the flashiest way possible, but there was something different about this house, this room. It wasn't flash and it wasn't posh. Although in its way it ended up being both of those things. It was designed to intimidate. Yes, it said, we're rich. Richer than you. But we're harsher than you. Colder than you. And because of that we could crush you. So don't you forget it. At least that was how it made Helen feel. And she was sure she wasn't the only one.

The housekeeper left the room quickly, as if she couldn't bear to be in it either. Helen wasn't alone for long. She glanced up and saw Dee Sloane standing in the doorway. She jumped.

'I didn't hear you come in.'

'I'm light on my feet.'

Dee Sloane walked into the centre of the room. She was right. Helen hardly heard her. She sat on the sofa opposite. Helen appraised her. Hair pulled back into a severe ponytail. No make-up. Her small, lithe body covered by a pink velour tracksuit. She curled her legs beneath her, stared at Helen.

'You wanted to see us.'

'I wanted to see your brother.'

'He's not available.' Eyes dark, unreadable.

Silence fell.

Helen felt uncomfortable. Dee looked perfectly composed. Anger started to resurface in Helen once more. She could feel her breathing speed up, her body vibrate.

'You wanted to see us,' Dee said again.

'Yes,' said Helen, controlling her temper, 'I did. And I'm sure you know why.'

Dee waited.

'Jeff's dead.'

Dee nodded. 'Very sad.'

'He was murdered,' said Helen, the words spat out. 'You know that.'

Dee frowned. 'Why should I know that?'

'Because you killed him.'

Dee's eyebrows raised themselves in surprise. 'Me?' Her face all innocent.

'No,' said Helen. 'Not you personally. You would never get involved. Never dirty your hands. Your style is to get someone to do it for you.'

Dee leaned forward slightly, as if genuinely interested, frown still in place. 'And why would I do that?'

Helen leaned forward too, opened her mouth to speak, but the words didn't come out. She sat back. Looked round. A thought had occurred to her. 'I'm not saying.'

'Why not?'

'Because you've probably got this room bugged. And you'll use my words against me in some way if you get the chance.' She leaned forward once more. 'But you know. So drop the Little Miss Innocent bullshit. Let's talk.'

Several emotions seemed to pass over Dee's face. Quick, fleeting and unreadable to Helen. Like coal-black crows flapping behind her eyes. Eventually she smiled. The effect was as though her body had suddenly become possessed by a human being.

'We can talk in here,' she said, head and shoulders dropping. 'It's safe.' A sigh escaped from her like a dying breath. 'It's . . . Michael.' She looked up at Helen, eye to eye. 'He did it. He killed Jeff.'

It was what Helen had wanted to hear, but now she was unsure of what to say next.

And that was when she saw the tear roll down Dee's cheek.

58

Jessie looked at her watch. Deepak stared out of the car window. Tension had ebbed away to boredom and Helen Hibbert was still in the house.

'Put the radio on if you like,' Jessie said.

'Thought you had a headache,' he replied, face still at the window.

She shrugged.

'It's fine,' he said. 'I can do without.'

Jessie's phone rang. She was grateful for the distraction. It was Mickey Philips, his voice breathless and urgent, as if he had run a long distance to deliver an important message.

'We've found where Josephina Brennan was being kept,' he said, ignoring niceties.

Jessie's boredom disappeared as he told her about the discovery at the house in Jaywick, the dead body, the dead dogs. The message Marina had left for them.

'It's your team investigating, so I thought you'd want the heads up.'

'Thanks. You got a name for the body yet?'

'There's a car at the scene registered to a Graham Watts. Looks like his driving licence photo, so we think it might be him. The name ring any bells?'

Jessie thought. 'Graham Watts? No. But I'll get it looked into.'

Deepak registered the name as she said it, took out his phone, started accessing the internet.

'Appreciate it,' said Mickey. 'You getting on it now?'

'I'll pass it on. We're following someone who may be able to lead us to Jeff Hibbert's killer and we can't break off from that. I'll get the DS dealing with Josephina to give you a call and liaise. Sort out whose patch is whose.'

'Cheers.' There was a pause. 'Well, speak soon.' He hung up.

Jessie did likewise, turned to Deepak. 'Got anything?'

He glanced up from his iPhone. 'Not yet. I'll keep looking.'

There was so much adrenalin coursing round Jessie's system she could barely sit still now. She called the station. Gave them Mickey's news. Then she turned her attention back to the gates. Deepak looked up.

'They must be getting on well in there,' he said. 'Wonder what they're talking about?'

'We'll find out soon enough,' she said.

59

Helen didn't know what to do. Of all the responses she had expected from Dee, this was definitely not among them.

'Yes,' Dee continued, 'I know all about it. Why wouldn't I?' She gave a bitter laugh. 'Why wouldn't I . . . ?'

Helen looked round quickly, checking the doors. 'Where is Michael? Is he here? Is he going to—'

'Don't worry.' Dee leaned forward over the glass table and touched Helen's hand. Pressed down firmly. Helen noticed that her hand was warm. Comforting. She had expected it to be cold. Something else surprising.

Dee gave Helen a shaky smile of reassurance, then sat back, dabbing at the corners of her eyes with a paper tissue she had produced from her sleeve. Helen stared.

Dee's head dropped once more. Soon her shoulders were shaking. Helen could tell even before the sobs came that she was crying. 'I . . . Oh, it's no good . . . Listen, I can't . . . It's Michael. He's . . .' Dee stood up. 'Look at this.' She unzipped her velour tracksuit top, pulled up her T-shirt. 'Look.'

Helen looked. She saw huge welts along the woman's stomach, yellowing bruises all joined together like a painful daisy chain. Dee pulled her T-shirt up further. More of the same.

'This is what he does to me,' Dee said, her lip trembling, tears still on her cheeks. 'This is what he does to me all the time . . .' She sat down again, head in hands, shoulders shaking uncontrollably. 'They're all over, all over . . . my, my body . . .'

'But if I remember, I thought you liked—'

'Playing's one thing,' said Dee through her tears. 'It's fun, it's consensual. But this . . .'

Helen stared at her. She had never liked Dee. Always found her creepy and strange, lacking any kind of human dimension, any kind of connectivity. When they had sat down to talk, she had expected her to try something. But she had never seen this coming. And now she understood. It explained everything. The way Dee was, her character, her manner . . . all because of this.

'I'm . . . I'm so sorry, Dee. It must be . . . horrible.'

Dee looked up, eyes red-rimmed. 'Oh, you have no idea.'

'And from your own *brother* . . .'

Dee nodded silently. 'Why . . . why did you come here, Helen? What did you want?'

'I . . .' Helen was thrown by the question. She had almost forgotten. 'It's about Jeff. I just wanted you to know that . . . that whatever he was up to, I had no part in it.'

Dee looked at her sharply. 'Do you know where they are now? What they're planning?'

'No.'

'Oh.' Her head went back down. The sobbing started up again. 'Did you . . .' It was hard to make out the words through the sobs. 'Did you want money — is that it? Money to say nothing about . . . anything?'

'Well, yes, I suppose I did.'

Dee nodded through her tears. 'Come here, get money, walk away and keep quiet.' She sighed. 'How easy.' Another sigh. 'How easy . . .'

'What d'you mean?'

'Take your money. Fine. I don't care. And walk away. You won't say anything. I know. You've seen what he did to Jeff. You don't want that to happen to you.'

'No. Definitely not. I won't say anything. You know me.' Helen couldn't believe how easy this was.

'I know, Helen. Money buys your loyalty.' Dee looked around the room, as if seeing it for the first time. 'Money can buy anyone's loyalty . . .'

'What d'you mean?'

Dee looked up, straight at Helen. 'I can talk to you. We used to be close, once.'

Helen couldn't remember that, but she kept listening.

'It's Michael. I want to . . . to leave.'

Helen shrugged. 'Then leave. There's nothing stopping you.'

'Oh but there is, Helen, there is. He's got all the money. I've got nothing. I have to beg him for anything I want.'

'But he's your brother, not your husband. I'd never stay with a man who did that to me."

'Doesn't matter what he is. The fact is I can't leave him.'

Helen sat back, thinking. A plan came to her. She leaned forward once more. 'Dee, that money you mentioned. To pay me off. Where were you going to get it from?'

'Michael's account. Or the company account.' She frowned as if the answer was obvious. 'Why?'

'How d'you get it?'

'Internet banking. Transfer it to my account.'

Helen smiled. 'Then why don't you just transfer a huge amount for yourself and leave him?'

Dee looked like the idea had never occurred to her. 'But . . . I couldn't . . .'

'Why not?'

'Because he'd find me . . . track me down and . . . like Jeff . . .'

Helen thought again. This was her area of expertise. Getting money out of men. 'Why not set up a new account and siphon funds off into that? Make it a shell company, some kind of subsidiary, a fake, and little by little take money from him until you've got enough to get away on?'

Dee thought about it, then shook her head. 'It's good, but . . .'

'But what?'

'I want to get away now.'

'What, right now? Today, you mean?'

Dee nodded. 'This thing with Jeff, it's . . . too much. Too far. I can't stay here any longer.' She leaned across the table, took Helen's hands. 'Help me. Please.'

'Right,' said Helen, her business head firmly on. 'How much can you get out of his account in cash, today?'

'Cash? I don't know . . . not much. But he does have a safe in the house.'

A shiver of anticipation ran through Helen. 'How much is in there?'

'He usually keeps about . . . seventy, a hundred thousand in cash . . .'

Helen could barely contain her excitement. 'Then go and get it.'

A cloud passed over Dee's face. 'I can't.'

'Why not?'

'He watches me all the time, never lets me out of his sight . . .' She fell silent. 'He's going out later.'

'What time?'

She chewed her lip thoughtfully. 'Seven. Tonight.'

'There's your window of opportunity, then,' said Helen, holding Dee's hand. 'Here's what we'll do. This afternoon you set up a fake account. Make it at a high street bank with a branch you can get to. At seven o'clock you clear out the safe. Then, with your bag packed, come and meet me and we'll take off and lie low somewhere. When a few days have passed and the new account has gone through, we walk into a branch of the bank and close the account, taking the money with us. How does that sound?'

Dee's eyes were wide. 'Can we do that?'

'Of course we can. Cut me in and I'll make sure it works.'

'The two of us together?' Dee laughed.

'The two of us together.'

'And you'll . . . you'll come with me?'

'Course I will. Make a new start together. Just the two of us.' Or just the three of us, thought Helen, including the money.

Dee was smiling. She had never looked more human. I've really misjudged her, thought Helen.

They arranged when and where to meet later that night, and Helen left the house elated. It couldn't have gone better if she had planned it.

60

'Well,' said Deepak, watching Helen Hibbert leave, 'she's looking pleased with herself.'

Helen Hibbert got into a taxi. She had almost skipped towards it, grinning.

'Doesn't she, though?' said Jessie. 'Wonder what all that was about.'

Deepak had his hand on the door handle. 'Let's find out, shall we?'

'Yes,' said Jessie, getting out the other side, 'let's.'

They walked up to the gate.

Jessie's headache, like the fog, had just about disappeared.

61

Marina opened her eyes to find herself in a strange bed in a strange room. She flung back the covers, began to panic. Then remembered.

Her brother, Alessandro. Jaywick.

She sank back down again. Closed her eyes once more.

Jaywick. She had driven here the night before, straight after going to the house. She shivered. The house. Her stomach turned over at the memory. She felt something in her hand, looked down. Lady, Josephina's toy dog, clutched tight. Her knuckles were white, fingers locked stiff. She closed her eyes, blocking out the light. She had turned up on his doorstep and collapsed from exhaustion.

She remembered the drive. Jaywick never got any better. Just south of Clacton, it was originally a small town of 1930s prefab holiday chalets for Londoners to vacation in. Many of them had decided to move there permanently. The intervening years hadn't been kind. Like a promising young starlet overtaken by career excesses, the original dimensions were still in place but the place was now a ruin. A very English shanty town, an Essex City of God. The chalets were all run-down, some derelict, their windows and doors smashed in and turned over to tramps and squatters. Crack dens thrived. Some owners had attempted imaginative home improvements — a caravan attached to the side of one house in place of an extension; a dormer window too heavy for the structure and forcing the lower floor to collapse. The streets were narrow, tarmac and concrete cracked open, decorated with massive, waterlogged potholes, choked with weeds and shrubs. The houses crammed together. Here and there were decent homes, well-maintained attempts to hold back the decay, but it was like a swimmer going against the tide.

Marina had last been to Jaywick for the opening of the Martello Tower art gallery a few years ago. From the clothes they wore and the way they spoke, she doubted everyone she met at the opening was local. And driving through the streets, seeing the boarded-up shops, cafés and pubs, she had wondered what sort of person would live there.

Now she knew. Her brother.

'You're awake.'

She opened her eyes once more. Alessandro was standing at the end of the bed. Mug of something hot in one hand. He sat down next to her. She felt the bed almost give under his weight. He handed her the mug.

'Drink this.'

She put it to her lips, sipped. It was awful.

'What is it?'

'Supposed to be tea.' He shrugged. 'Never was very good at the domestic stuff.' He looked down at the carpet. 'Don't drink it if you don't want to.'

She put it down beside her, sat up. Looked around. It was the main room of one of the chalet bungalows. She was lying on a fold-out sofa bed. The sheets and duvet were faded and worn thin, on the wrong side of clean. What other furniture there was seemed to have been either collected or gathered up rather than intentionally bought. Off in a galley to the right was something that looked more like an Al Qaeda biological weapons testing facility than a kitchen. The room smelt of damp and dirt and lonely, desperate male.

She caught Alessandro looking at her. Knew he was seeing the room through her eyes. And from his downcast expression, he was probably thinking something similar.

'So.' He looked up. 'What brings you here?' His eyes were sharp, his voice forming a hard, brittle shell around the words. 'Must be serious. Thought you'd lost my number.'

Marina didn't rise to his words, although she could feel herself gearing up for a fight. He was her brother. He knew which of her buttons to press. Just as she knew his. Instead she tried another sip of tea. Managed to swallow it. Not too bad when you get used to it, she thought, hoping she never had to get used to it.

She replaced the mug on the floor, ignoring the improbably breasted cartoon blonde on its side. Noticed that its interior was ringed brown like a centuries-old tree. Looked up at her brother and sighed. Awake but still tired. 'Where do I start?'

'The beginning.' He looked at his watch.

'Am I keeping you from something?'

'Got to be somewhere later. Tell me what's happened. Not every day my sister collapses on my doorstep.'

She told him. Hesitant at first, then with growing confidence as she became involved in the telling. Starting with the cottage, the planned Easter break. The fire, then . . . nothing. The hospital. The phone. *Love Will Tear Us Apart.* The calls.

'I tried to reason with them, find out what they wanted from me, talk to them like a human being, make them see me as one . . .' She sighed. 'I tried.'

She resumed her story. The chase with the police round the motel. Bet Sandro likes that, she thought. 'Then I called at a service station. And when I knew where I was going, I tried to leave a message for . . . for the police.'

He snorted. 'What for?'

'So they could help me out.'

'Thought they told you not to do that.'

'They did, but I thought I was on my way to where Josephina was being kept. If I could get word to the police, have them turn up while I was there, then they could get Josephina back for me.' She sighed. 'I thought they'd be able to help.'

'And they couldn't.'

She shook her head. 'No one could . . .' She moved on to the house on the way to Clacton. Turning up there, finding Josephina's toy. And the dead body. 'Then I came here. Didn't want to stick around there. Couldn't.'

Alessandro frowned. 'So why didn't you go to the police then? Much as I hate them, they would be the people to talk to.'

Marina sighed. 'Because . . . I couldn't. Someone still has Josie. Or at least I hope they do. Otherwise . . .' Her voice trailed off.

She felt tears form behind her eyes. Refused to give in to them. Not in front of Sandro. He waited while she composed herself, resumed her story.

'Anyway,' she said, wiping her tears, her nose on her sleeve, 'I couldn't call the police. They weren't there when I turned up so I don't think they got my message. Which might be a good thing. Because if the person who's got Josie knew I'd contacted them, they might hurt her.'

'And have they been in touch again?'

She sighed, shook her head.

'Maybe it was the dead body you found. Maybe that was him.'

Another sigh. 'Maybe. I don't know . . . I don't know . . .'

She felt herself unravelling again, managed to hold herself together.

Silence fell in the room. Eventually Sandro spoke.

'So,' he said, 'you came here.'

She nodded.

'Why? Haven't you got anywhere else to go?'

She gave a sad little laugh. 'Something like that.'

'What d'you want me to do?'

She looked at him again, eyes lit by a desperate light. 'Help me.'

He looked surprised. 'How can I do that?'

She leaned forward, imploring. 'You know people. People I don't. You've got connections I haven't got. Ways of contacting people.'

Sandro's voice was icing over. 'And why would I have all that?'

'Because . . . because that's the kind of circles you move in.'

'You mean I'm a criminal.'

'I didn't say that. I—'

'Yeah, you did. That's what you meant.'

She sighed. 'Please, Sandro. I need your help to find my daughter. Will you help me?'

He stared at her, thinking. Looked away. She watched his eyes rove over the walls, the furniture. He turned back to her.

'No,' he said.

62

Jessie smoothed her hair down, arranged her jacket. Cleared her throat. And pressed the buzzer for the intercom. She and Deepak stood outside the gates of the Sloanes' house, ready to go through the same ritual as the previous night.

The intercom was answered by the same non-English voice claiming that there was no one available to talk to the police and saying that they should call back later.

Time to be proactive, thought Jessie.

'We're investigating the death of Jeffrey Hibbert, who used to work for the Sloanes. We've just watched his widow leave, and since we believe she was here for the same reason as we are, we'd like to talk to whoever she talked to, please.'

There was another shared look between the two detectives. Then the gate swung open. Jessie gave Deepak a thumbs-up gesture. 'You're impressed by my silver tongue. Go on, admit it.'

Deepak shook his head. Managed a smile. 'At least you didn't lose your temper.'

'I'm saving that for when we get inside.'

They walked up the gravel drive and into the house.

They were shown into the living room, asked to sit on one of the two sofas and left alone, the door shut. They exchanged glances.

'Money in industrial farming,' said Deepak, looking round.

Jessie looked at the glass and metal table in front of her. 'Bet this table cost more than we both earn in a month,' she said.

Deepak looked at it, grimacing. 'Money doesn't buy you taste,' he said.

The door opened. In swept a woman; small, compact, dressed in a pink velour tracksuit and trainers that had never seen the outdoors or even the inside of a gym, hair pulled severely back from her face, no make-up. She walked briskly to the sofa opposite them, sat down, her back straight. Looked at them, her gaze businesslike.

'I'm Dee Sloane. You asked to see my brother, Michael. I'm afraid he's indisposed. And you are?'

Jessie and Deepak produced their warrant cards, gave their names.

'And this is in connection with the death of one of our ex-employees?'

'That's right,' said Jessie, taking the lead in the questioning. 'There are a few things we'd like to talk to you about.'

Dee Sloane frowned. 'Is this serious? Should I have a solicitor present?'

'That's up to you,' said Deepak, as breezily as possible.

Jessie managed a smile. 'Let's see how we go.'

Dee sat there, waiting. Her face expressionless, her body straight, alert, but in repose. Receptive. Giving the impression that she was relaxed, waiting, but Jessie wasn't fooled. She had learned how to interpret body language over the years, and she could see that Dee Sloane was seriously uncomfortable. On edge, even.

And there was something else. In the short space of time since Jessie had met the woman, she had taken an instant dislike to her. She tried not to do that, to pre-judge, especially in the course of her work. Sometimes she would feel it from a paedophile or rapist or wife-abuser, that creepily bad vibe, especially if they tried to be friendly and obsequious with her.

Then she would have to work through that feeling in order to do her job properly. And that was the vibe that Dee Sloane was giving off. It might have been a chemical thing or a personality thing, but there was something about her that was not right. Jessie glanced at Deepak, tried to see if he was experiencing the same thing. But her partner's gaze was impassive.

Right, thought Jessie. She had shaken off her hangover, banished all thoughts of the previous night. She was in the zone, ready to do her job.

63

Marina couldn't believe what she had just heard. Not from Sandro. Her own brother. She would have expected it from the other one, but not from him. He was always the more decent of the two. The more reachable. He must have changed.

'What? What . . . ?'

'I said no.'

'But . . . but . . . I told you what's happened . . . My baby, they've got my baby . . .'

'And they want you to do a psychological evaluation on some nutter, then they'll give her back?'

She nodded.

He shrugged. 'Then do it. What's the problem?'

'What did I just say? There's a dead body and Josephina's missing . . .'

'Why you anyway? And why go to all the trouble of snatching your kid to get you? Why not just phone you?'

'I don't know why. There must be something more to it, another reason.'

'And you think I can do something about it?'

'Yes! You know people. All right, maybe not the people who've done this, but . . . but they must have told somebody.

Someone else must know.' She leaned forward, grabbed his sleeve. 'Please . . . please help me. My daughter's gone, my husband's . . .' She shook her head, not wanting to think about it. 'Please . . . I've got no one.'

He looked at her, eyes locking, seeming to weaken. Then he pulled himself away from her, stood up. Began pacing the room, his back to her.

'That's a good one,' he said, laughing. It wasn't pleasant. 'I'm all you've got.' More walking. Nodding to himself as if two different conversations were going on in his head. 'All you've got . . .' He turned to her. Pointed. 'And where were you all these years? Eh? Where were you when I was on my own, when I was . . .' He shook his head angrily, as if trying to dislodge something. 'Yeah. I know where you were. With your copper boyfriend.' The words spat out. 'Your university friends. Yeah. Didn't want to know me then, did you? Didn't want to know any of us.' He turned away, began pacing once more.

'Works two ways, Sandro,' she said, getting out of bed, standing. 'Where were you in my life all this time?'

He turned back to her. His face angry, red, right in hers. 'You didn't want me. You didn't want any of us in your life. You made that perfectly clear. How we weren't good enough for you.'

'That's . . . that's not true . . .'

'Yes it fuckin' is. You were ashamed of us. You said so.'

Marina said nothing. Sandro stared at her. Took her silence for assent.

'Thought so.' He gave another mirthless laugh. 'Thought so . . .'

The hurt was disappearing, replaced by anger. She wasn't going to let him talk to her like that. 'Yeah? Well maybe I did think I was better than the rest of you. And you know what? Maybe I was. Because I wanted to make something of my life. Do something. Not just be stuck in the house with that sick bastard smacking us around.'

Sandro said nothing. Turned away from her once more.

She followed him, not letting him alone. She tried to drop her voice, sound reasonable. 'So now I'm here. And I'm asking for your help. Please.'

Another snort. 'Please? Begging now? So you need my help and I've got to fuckin' jump? Is that it? Click your fuckin' fingers and I come runnin'? Yeah? Fuck you.'

She stared him down, eye to eye. 'You sound just like Dad.'

He raised his arm, pulled it back. 'I should give you the flat of my hand . . .'

'And now you are him. Just like Dad.'

She looked at him with undisguised contempt.

Something cracked behind Sandro's eyes. 'No I'm not. I'm not . . .' His voice wavered, like he was trying to convince himself. 'I'm nothing like Dad . . .'

She moved right up close to him. Almost whispering. 'Then prove it. Prove you're not.'

'Shut up.' He looked at her. Eyes soft, wet, like broken eggs.

'Prove you're not by helping me find my daughter.'

He tried to meet her gaze. Couldn't. Turned away. 'Just leave,' he said. 'Get out.'

Marina stayed where she was.

'I said leave . . .' Sandro was almost snarling with anger.

'Fine,' she said, moving towards the door. 'I'll go. And you can stay here and live with yourself. Just like Dad and proud of it.'

'Shut up . . .'

She reached the door, turned. 'I'm just glad our mother isn't alive to see you do this.'

'What?' Sandro recoiled like he had been slapped.

'You heard.' She turned the handle.

Behind her, he sighed. It was like the last breath of a dying man. Or the first breath of a newborn. 'OK.'

She turned. 'Does that mean you'll help?'

His hands went to his eyes. He couldn't look at her.

'What d'you want me to do?'

64

Jessie was just starting to question Dee Sloane. Deepak was next to her.

'Do you drive a Fiat Punto?'

Dee Sloane's eyes widened at the question. She hesitated. 'No . . . What has this to do with the death of one of our ex-employees?'

Jessie ignored the question. 'Does your brother Michael drive a Fiat Punto?'

'No he doesn't.' She didn't ask a question this time, just waited.

Jessie nodded. 'Right.' She said nothing more, appeared to be thinking. In reality, she was waiting.

'Can I ask what this is about?' Dee Sloane was starting to look tense.

Jessie kept her voice, her movements as languid as possible. 'It's just that a Fiat Punto was found burned out at the scene of an arson attack in Aldeburgh a couple of days ago.'

'And you think . . . what? That Michael or myself was responsible for the attack? That's ridiculous.'

'Were you?' Jessie tried to keep the question light, even allowing a smile to play at the corners of her mouth.

Dee Sloane didn't answer. Just regarded Jessie with haughty contempt, as if the question was beneath her.

Jessie dropped the smile as she spoke. 'We checked, and the car is registered to your brother. Was your brother in Aldeburgh two days ago?'

'No. He wasn't.'

'Were you?'

'No.'

'Someone was,' said Deepak. 'And they were driving your brother's car.'

Dee Sloane said nothing.

'Was it stolen?' asked Jessie.

'No,' said Dee. 'We have a car for the staff to use. It may have been that one.'

'But registered in your brother's name.'

'Yes.'

'Not your company's.'

Dee Sloane hesitated. 'No.'

'Why?'

Dee moved around on the sofa as if she couldn't get comfortable. 'It's . . . something to do with tax. I think. Our accountant proposed it.'

'Right.' Jessie nodded as if that was cleared up. She saw Dee begin to relax. Keep going, she thought. 'D'you have many staff?' The question almost chatty.

'Two housekeepers. Two kitchen staff.'

Jessie sat back, eyes widening. 'Just like Downton. D'you watch that? I love it.'

Dee said nothing, but seemed to bask in Jessie's words.

'So which servant had the car?'

Dee looked thrown. 'What?'

'Which servant had the car? Who took it to Aldeburgh? When it got burnt out.'

'I . . . I'd have to check. I don't know.' Dee was back to finding the sofa uncomfortable again.

'And they never mentioned it?' asked Deepak.

'Something like that would be pretty major,' said Jessie. 'Losing a car. Especially when it's in your boss's name. Bet he wasn't happy about that.'

Dee was beginning to look trapped. Jessie smiled inwardly. Then stopped herself. Just because she'd taken an instant dislike to the woman didn't mean Dee was bad. Then she thought back to the others she had taken instant dislikes to and what they had been responsible for. No, she thought again. Trust your instincts.

'So you don't know who had the car?' she said.

'No.'

'And you don't know what they were doing in Aldeburgh?'

'No,' said Dee, clearly rattled. 'I don't know what they get up to on their days off.'

'So you don't know who it was or what they were doing but you know it was their day off. Could you find out for us, please?'

'Why?'

'We'd like to speak to whoever it was.'

'They were present at a crime scene,' said Deepak. 'Might be a witness.'

Dee leaned forward, fire in her eyes. 'I'm going to ask you to leave. You said you wanted to speak to me about the death of an ex-employee. And you haven't done. So please go.'

Jessie didn't respond, just nodded. 'Oh, what did Helen Hibbert want?' Again she made the question sound like a casual enquiry. She had no intention of leaving, not until she had asked the questions she wanted to ask. And she would use all of her tricks and techniques to make sure she did so.

'Sorry?' Again Dee looked rattled.

'She left just before we came in. What did she want?'

Dee looked between the two of them. Like a trapped animal, thought Jessie.

'She . . . wanted to talk about her husband.'

'Who used to work for you.'

'Yes.'

Dee seemed to think that was enough. Jessie said nothing, her silence encouraging the other woman to fill the void with words.

It worked. 'Her husband had been ill. Cancer.' Dee's voice took on a heavy, solemn tone. 'She wanted to let us know. About his death.'

'Doesn't she have a phone?' asked Deepak.

Jessie noticed rage behind Dee's eyes, quickly suppressed. Gotcha, she thought.

'She . . . she wanted to do it in person.'

'He meant that much to you?' said Jessie. 'As an ex-employee.'

'We were fond of Jeff. He was a . . . loyal employee.'

Her words were so hollow, thought Jessie, that she doubted even Dee believed them. 'You know, it's funny,' she said, in the kind of tone she would use if she was discussing an article she had just read in *Heat*, 'we only saw him two days ago.'

Dee said nothing.

'There was someone at the cottage when it went up. He saved a woman's life, stopped her going back in. Very brave. We asked him for an address. He gave us Jeff Hibbert's. Why d'you think that was?'

'How would I know?'

'He didn't give us Jeff Hibbert's name, though. Said he was called Stuart Milton.' She leaned closer. 'Name mean anything to you?'

'No.' Dee's voice was as flat and dead as her eyes were trying to be.

'And then Jeff Hibbert goes and gets murdered just after our visit.'

'Wasn't cancer,' said Deepak. 'He was murdered.'

Dee's mouth moved once more but no sound came out. 'He . . . his wife said.'

'And we can't find this Stuart Milton anywhere. Have you got any photos of your brother?' asked Jessie.

Dee, caught off guard once more, thrown by Jessie's sudden change of questioning, couldn't answer immediately. 'I . . . Not to hand. No.'

'None in the house?' Incredulity in her voice.

'We're not that kind of family.' Struggling to regain control.

Jessie smiled. 'We'll find one from somewhere, don't worry.'

'Why do you need one?' Dee's voice was rising, becoming shrill.

Jessie shrugged, smiled. 'In an inquiry like this, we can't rule anything out.'

Dee said nothing, but her eyes darted from one to the other, all round the room. Still rattled, thought Jessie, still uncomfortable. Good. Just where I want her.

'Did you know that Stuart Sloane was released from jail yesterday?'

Dee just stared straight ahead. Jessie watched her face, her eyes. The woman seemed to be auditioning answers, deciding which one to give, which one would be best received.

'I . . . we . . . heard something. No one informed us officially, though.' She leaned forward, suddenly on the offensive. 'I would have expected someone to have done that. Common courtesy if nothing else.'

Jessie shrugged. 'I'm sorry, Ms Sloane, but if we went round informing every victim of crime when a perpetrator was released, we'd have little time to do anything else.'

'Be that as it may, someone should have informed us. Given the seriousness of the crime.'

'Maybe you're right.' Jessie frowned, leaned forward too. 'How d'you feel about it?' Her voice light, genuinely enquiring.

'How do I feel about what?'

'Stuart Sloane being released. Aren't you worried he might come after you again? Try to finish what he started?'

Dee opened her mouth to answer, bit the response off. Instead she thought for a few seconds. 'We're not worried. No. We don't even know which part of the country he's in.'

'Although I'm sure you could find out if you wanted to.'

'What d'you mean?'

'Just that someone with your money and influence could find out where he was. If you wanted to.'

Dee Sloane didn't answer the question. 'I think it's time for you to leave.'

Once again Jessie ignored her. 'D'you think Stuart Sloane knew Jeff Hibbert?'

'I . . . don't know. Probably not.'

'D'you think Stuart Sloane killed Jeff Hibbert?'

'No. I don't. I don't know.' She stood up. 'Now please leave. If you have any more questions or accusations to make, you should do so through my solicitor.'

Jessie frowned, her voice dripping reason. 'Accusations, Ms Sloane? What have we accused you of?'

'Just . . .' Dee pointed to the door. 'Just . . . please leave. Now.'

Jessie and Deepak rose, made their way to the door. Once there, Jessie turned. 'Oh,' she said, 'one more thing. Do you or your brother know someone called Marina Esposito?'

Dee looked taken aback. 'No,' she said. 'I've never heard of her.'

Jessie and Deepak were shown out.

They waited until they were past the gates before they started talking.

'Very well handled, ma'am.'

'Thank you, Deepak. I told you, watch and learn.'

'Incisive,' he said. 'You'll get a job on *Loose Women* yet.'

'Thanks, smartarse.'

But Deepak wasn't finished. 'And "one more thing"? Are you channelling Columbo now?'

She smiled. 'Always worked for him.' They kept walking back to the car. 'So what did you think? Impressions.'

Deepak frowned. 'Didn't like her. Can't say why. Just . . . something about her I didn't like.'

'Strange. I felt the same way. Must be a chemical thing.'

'Or she's guilty of something.'

'There could be that.'

They reached the car. Before they got in, Deepak spoke to Jessie over the roof. 'That last question? The one about Marina Esposito?'

'What about it?'

'Only truthful answer she gave.'

Jessie smiled. 'My thoughts exactly.'

They got in the car, drove away.

65

Eileen Brennan looked at her son's face. They had removed the tape from his eyes. That was something, she thought. A gesture to be hopeful about.

She was holding his hand once more, clasping it with both hers, frightened it would be taken away from her. And talking. Incessantly. Telling him all the things she hadn't been able to say to him when he had been around, all the things she had kept inside, decided not to share, thinking there would be another time to do so, a later time, a better time. But the events of the last couple of days had changed her.

'And . . . and I'm telling you all this because . . .' A sigh. 'Because. Because I should say them to you. Before it's too late. There were things I wanted to say to Don, should have said to Don . . .' She drifted, her eyes watery glass. 'And now, now I never will . . .' Another sigh. 'So . . . there is no better time. There is no time. There's only now . . .'

She kept talking, kept clasping his hand. Telling him about her husband. His father. Don.

'I met him by chance, you know. And I didn't like him. Not at first. I didn't like policemen, see. I was a social worker then, properly political, militant you'd probably say now. We thought they were the enemy. And they could be at times. But not all the time. And not all of them. I thought he was at first. All cocky, Jack Regan, throwing his weight around.' She laughed, eyes no longer in the room. 'He said he was just doing it to impress me. Told me that years later. Thought it would be the kind of thing I'd go for. Didn't know me at all well . . .'

She drifted off. Lost in memories. Came back again.

'Kept asking me out. Eventually I said yes, just to shut him up. And he was different. To what he had been, to the others too. Softer, gentler. Talked about his work, about the things he'd seen. Some of the problem families he'd dealt with, the things he wished he'd been able to do but couldn't. To put things right. I liked him . . .'

She smiled at the memory, clung to it, instead of facing the present.

'And then we . . .'

Phil's eyes moved. Eileen missed it.

'We started to see each other regularly. And I knew. He was the one. The one for me . . .'

Phil's eyes moved again. Flickered back and forth beneath his eyelids.

This time Eileen noticed.

'No . . . no . . .'

She looked round to see if there was a nurse in sight. Not a seizure, an attack. She couldn't bear that.

His eyes kept moving. His body moved too. Shoulders lifting up, dropping, as if he didn't have the energy to move fully.

'Phil . . .' Eileen didn't know what to do. She held on to his hand. 'No, don't . . . don't go, I've got so much more to say to you . . .'

Then his eyes opened. Fully.

Eileen stared.

'Phil?'

She watched as they focused, flinched from the light in the room, closed again.

'Phil?'

And opened once more. Slowly this time, cautiously.

'Phil?'

He saw her now. Smiled.

'Phil . . .'

The tears sprang from Eileen's eyes, ran down her cheeks. A nearby nurse hurried in.

But Eileen didn't notice.

She had her son back.

66

'So you could handle them, could you? That's right, is it?'

Dee sat on the sofa. Unmoving. Stared as Michael paced the floor before her. Stared hard.

'Just police, you said. "Nothing to worry about. Wrap them round my little finger."' He waggled his own finger to emphasise the point. 'Well you couldn't. They outsmarted you. I told you to say nothing, let Nickoll handle it, get the solicitor to run interference, but you knew best. Now look at it . . .'

He walked away from her.

She stared after him, eyes like laser beams boring into him, pulling him back. 'I was trying to clear up your mess, Michael. That's all I was doing. The mess you made. The mess you *deliberately* made.'

He turned back, stood over her. Most people would have felt intimidated, would have backed down. But Dee wasn't most people. She stared up at him, unblinking. 'The mess you made. Leaving the car in front of the cottage. Letting it get burnt out.'

'Precisely. I didn't have time to move it, so I did the next best thing. Left it to burn.'

'But it didn't burn enough, did it? They traced it back here. They may even find some DNA in it.'

Michael shrugged, attempting nonchalance. Failed in his attempt. 'So? Of course there's my DNA in the car. I drive it. Yours'll be in there too, probably.' He tried to lighten his voice once more. 'Nickoll'll tie them up. We pay that fat fuck enough, let him earn his money for once. Keep them off our backs.' He stared at her. 'Like we should have done earlier today.'

Dee ignored his response, kept staring up at him. 'And the false name and address? Stuart Milton? At Hibbert's address? Couldn't you have just drawn them a map?' She fixed him with a cold, unblinking stare. 'They'll find you, Michael. They'll come for you. And then what?'

He opened his mouth, retort at the ready, but snapped his lips closed once more, biting it back. Instead he sat down on the sofa opposite. Leaned forward, hands clasped together.

'You know what you are, Michael?'

'Do tell, Dee.'

'You're like some celebrity who's got it all but still isn't satisfied, that's what you're like. You've got everything but it's too easy. And you're bored. Now you've got to mess it all up.'

He sighed, ran his hand through his hair.

'I'm not going to be part of your celebrity meltdown, Michael. You can go down if you want to. But you're not taking me with you. I've come too far and worked too hard for that.'

He sighed once more, let his hands drop. 'Look,' he said, voice full of reconciliation, 'we have to work together on this. Not fight each other. There's a way out. I'm sure of it.'

Dee didn't reply.

'Listen,' he said, 'I've spoken to some of our contacts on the force. Asked them about this DS James woman. And they all say we've got nothing to worry about.'

'Really.'

'Yes, really. She's an alky. Doesn't know if she's coming or going. Incompetent.'

'She didn't seem that incompetent a couple of hours ago.'

'It's her sidekick you've got to watch out for. He's the sharp one.' Michael put his head back, thinking. 'And he hasn't seen me.'

'So?'

'So there's only her word for what I look like. The man she spoke to. We can work with that. We can handle her.'

Dee was staring straight ahead. In the room but lost to her thoughts. She was thinking, plotting, strategising. She had done this for years. And she always came up with something. A way out, a way forward. Ever since . . .

Her eyes came back into focus. She looked at Michael. Calmly, levelly. Then she spoke.

'She has to go.'

Michael blinked. 'What?'

'She has to go.'

'Yeah, but . . . she's a police officer. We can't just . . . get rid of her.'

'Why not?' Her voice was light, inconsequential, as if she was discussing buying a new ornament or painting the room. 'We did it with Hibbert. Very cleverly. Very carefully. He won't be traced back to us.'

'Yeah, but . . . she's a *police officer* . . . They're untouchable.'

'No they're not. We just do it differently. Not be crude and obvious, like Hibbert. And not with the Golem. We have to be more subtle.'

'But . . .'

'We have to. And we will.'

Michael said nothing. Ran his hands through his hair once more.

Dee stood up. Crossed the room. Stood over him. He looked up to her as she spoke. 'This is damage limitation. It has to be done.'

'But—'

'And if you won't do it, I will.'

He stared up at her.

'An accident, I think,' said Dee. 'No. A disappearance. We could do this one together.' She climbed on top of him, one leg at either side. 'You'd like that, wouldn't you? Us both . . . getting our hands dirty . . . together . . .'

He felt his erection spring up as soon as her body rested on his. She always had this effect on him.

Always.

And he loved it.

'Helen Hibbert is already lined up. So what's the difference? We do another one at the same time . . .'

She unzipped her velour top, peeled it off. Michael watched as she did so. Then she took off her T-shirt, pulled it over her head. She stared down at him, eyes locked. Reached behind her, unclasped her bra. Let it fall.

'I'll do it without you,' she said.

He swallowed. Hard. 'No, I'll . . . I'll do it . . . with you . . .'

She smiled. 'Good.'

And pulled her hand back, let it go. Slapping his face. Hard.

He stared up at her, the pain setting off explosions all over his body, his erection straining for release.

'Are you with me?' She was breathing heavily.

'Yes . . . yes, I'm with you . . .'

'Good.'

She hit him again. Harder this time.

And he loved her for it.

67

Tyrell stared at the gun. It was a handgun, an automatic. He knew that much. Dull silver, heavy-looking. He stared right down the barrel, into that small round black hole that could kill him at any second. Fascinated but repelled.

Tyrell hated guns. Always had. But he knew how mesmerising they were.

He held Josephina close, clutched the little girl tight to his side. Looked at the woman holding the automatic. A thought crossed his mind.

'I don't know your name.'

She frowned, taken aback by the question. Tyrell said nothing, waited for her to speak, to move.

'Amy,' she said.

'Is that really your name?'

'It'll do.'

'You said I know you. I don't know anybody called Amy.'

'No. You don't. Now.' She looked directly into Tyrell's eyes, ignoring Josephina. 'We're in a situation here. A bad situation. And the only way out, the only way to get what we want, is to keep our nerve. Isn't it?'

Tyrell said nothing.

'It's not to go to the police, or do anything like that. Is it, Tyrell?'

He still didn't reply.

Amy swung the gun on to Josephina, stuck it in her face. The girl screamed. Tried to burrow into Tyrell's leg. He clutched her all the harder.

'I asked you a question.'

'No . . .' said Tyrell, not entirely sure what she had said but guessing what answer she wanted to hear.

'Good. That's better. Do what I tell you and you'll be fine. Both of you.'

Tyrell felt Josephina clinging to him. He looked down the barrel of the gun again. Knew what had to be done. Knew he couldn't live with himself if he didn't do the right thing.

'No,' he said.

Amy stared at him, eyes narrowing, darkening. 'What?'

'I said no. I'm not going to do what you say.' He looked down at Josephina. 'We're not going to do what you say.'

Amy moved forward, still holding the gun on him, her finger curling round the trigger.

Tyrell backed away, the little girl with him. 'Just let Josephina go,' he said, wishing he felt as confident as he was trying to sound. 'Let her go. Back to her mother.'

'We still want her mother.'

'No. No we don't. I've been thinking. Let her go.'

'We still need her . . .' Amy was starting to breathe heavily, her voice becoming more ragged, more angry.

'Just forget it,' Tyrell said. 'Forget everything. Let Josephina go. I'll say you didn't do any harm. You didn't mean it. That it was all an accident. A . . . a misunderstanding.'

'And what about you?' Amy's voice was now dangerously low, calm. 'What will you do?'

'I'll go back inside. I know that. And I'm prepared. I don't care. In fact I'd prefer it, really.'

Amy lunged at him. Tyrell never saw her coming, she moved so quickly. Josephina screamed, let go of his leg, ran away. Amy pushed the gun in his face. He felt the cold metal against his cheek, felt it knock painfully against his teeth as she pushed it into his flesh.

He looked into her eyes. Saw madness.

And something else.

He had seen those eyes before . . .

'The recognition of friends is not always easy, Doctor . . .' Tyrell managed to say against the barrel of the gun.

Amy pulled away from him, stared. Eyes wide, like she had just seen a ghost. 'What? What did you just say?'

'The recognition of friends is not always easy, Doctor.'

'Why did you say that? Why?' She waved the gun about in front of him. He thought she meant to aim it at him, but her hand was too unsteady. He was worried it could go off at any time, hit Josephina. He looked round tried to find the girl. Couldn't see her.

'Why?' Amy was almost shouting now.

'It's what . . . him. The dead man. Jiminy Cricket. He said it to me when he picked me up. I think he thought it should mean something. He said a few things like that.'

Amy seemed to relent. The hand holding the gun dropped a little. She seemed suddenly tired. 'Oh,' she said. 'Right.'

'What does it mean, then?' said Tyrell. 'Is it important?'

'It was something . . . something he always said. Graham loved his quotes.'

'Who's Graham?'

'Jiminy Cricket, who d'you think?'

'Oh.' Tyrell thought about the name. Decided he preferred Jiminy Cricket.

Amy continued. 'He was always quoting things. Old films and TV shows. That one's a Dr Who story. The Doctor meets someone he knew at a different point in his timeline. Someone he'd grown up with. And he doesn't recognise them.' She looked at him. Quickly. Then away. 'That's all.'

Tyrell said nothing. Just stared at her. Thought about her words. Thought about her eyes.

Eyes he'd seen before . . .

A different point in his timeline . . .

He looked round, suddenly remembering Josephina. Saw her cowering behind a tree. He tried to smile at her. She didn't return it. He didn't blame her.

He turned back to Amy. She had something else in her hand now.

'What . . . what are you doing?'

She put the phone to her ear. Her broken, patchwork face had a resigned look to it. She seemed tired.

'Phoning the kid's mother,' she said with a sigh. 'Getting this thing sorted once and for all . . .'

68

'I just don't know,' said Marina. 'Just don't know anything any more . . .'

Sandro was sitting opposite her, the sofa bed folded away. He was still wearing his workout gear and had made her a mug of instant coffee. Marina hated instant, never drank it. But she had thanked him and taken it gratefully. The mug sat on the floor, half drunk and ignored.

'Don't know what?' Sandro had forgone the coffee, was draining an energy drink can. He finished it, crushed it, threw it at the already overflowing rubbish bin in the galley kitchen. Missed. It clattered down the side to the floor but he didn't seem unduly worried by that. 'Sounds like this is enough to fuck anyone's head up.'

'Yeah, but I'm . . . usually stronger than this. I've had to be.' She looked up, directly at him. 'Some of the things I've done, situations I've been in . . .' She shook her head. 'You wouldn't believe.'

'Like what?'

She almost smiled. 'I'll tell you sometime.'

Sandro nodded, shrugged. 'Tell me now.'

Marina gave an almost-laugh to accompany the almost-smile. 'I used to think that a client wanting to kill me was the worst thing that could happen. That was before I was captured when I was pregnant and held in an underground cage where some maniac wanted to breed from me.'

'Jesus . . .'

'I know. That was after he'd put my old partner into a coma by smashing his head in with a hammer.'

Sandro stared.

'And then there was the time I tried to rescue a chained-up kid from a madman who wanted to sacrifice him. With sharpened gardening tools.'

Sandro's mouth was wide open.

'And almost got killed by a bent police officer in the process.'

'Ah, now that I can believe.'

She sighed. 'But now I just feel . . . I don't know. Weak? Helpless? I don't know . . .'

She sighed. Out of the corner of her eye she became aware of Sandro watching her. She looked up once more.

'What?'

'I had no idea.' He shook his head, trying to let what she had just told him settle in his mind. 'That you did . . . that you'd done . . . anythin' like that.'

She looked straight at him. 'Why would you? You don't know anything about my life.'

'I just thought, you know. You did your hours, sorted people's heads out, got well paid and . . .'

'Swanned off to some champagne bar?'

'I was goin' to say the theatre and some fancy restaurant. But yeah. Somethin' like that.'

Another almost-smile. Wistful, the kind given to a treasured memory or a fond fantasy. 'I wish it was that easy. But when I'm called in to a case, especially the kind that Phil works, the major incidents, then it's always something serious.'

'And after all this, you feel weak. Why?'

She looked directly at him. No smiles any more. 'Because my husband's gone. My daughter's gone. Maybe for ever. I've lost everything.' She stood up. 'This is not like me. Not like me at all.' She could feel the anger rising in her. Impotent, unchannelled rage.

'Like Dad,' said Sandro.

Marina wheeled round, turned on him. 'No I'm not. Don't ever say that.'

Sandro was taken aback by the vehemence of her words. 'I only meant that Dad had passed the fightin' gene down. That's all. Calm down.'

She stood over him. 'Don't tell me to calm down. And I'm not like Dad. Mum was the strong one.'

Sandro frowned. 'What? She did nothin'. Let him hit her. What's so strong about that? She was soft.'

'She was not soft, Sandro. She did what a mother's supposed to do. Protected her children.'

He still looked confused. 'How? He used to smack her as well.'

'She took the blows that were meant for us. As much as she could. She let him hit her rather than us. I'm not saying that was the best way to go about things, but she stood up to him in the only way she knew how. To go through that, to endure what he did to her, that's what made her strong.'

Sandro said nothing, thought for a while. 'Yeah,' he said eventually. 'Yeah. I see what you mean.'

'You'd know what I mean if you had kids.' She looked at him. 'Do you have kids?'

He looked taken aback at the question. 'Ah . . . don't think so.'

'But you'd know. Believe me.'

He didn't reply. Instead he stood up, went to the kitchen. Got himself another energy drink. Cracked it open.

'You're drinking a lot of those,' said Marina.

'Need the energy. Got a fight tonight.'

Marina's turn to frown. 'A fight.'

'Yeah. ''Swhat I do. One of the things.'

'What kind of fight?'

He looked away from her. 'Bare-knuckle.'

'What?'

'Ah look, don't start. I got in with these Irish travellers. Gypsies, y'know. They do it. Part of their culture, an' that.'

'Part of their culture? *All* of their culture. Sandro, they're bred to fight. They're born fighting.'

He locked his eyes on hers. 'And I wasn't?'

Marina couldn't find the words to reply. Her eyes slid away from his.

'Anyway,' said Sandro, 'I've always been handy with my fists. Just found a way to make a bit of money out of them, that's all.'

'And get yourself seriously injured in the process.'

'That never happens.'

'You mean it hasn't happened yet.'

He didn't reply.

'What . . . how did you get into this?'

He shrugged, tried to keep his explanation light and short on facts. 'Did a bit of sparrin' with them. Couple of bouts.' He shrugged again, like he was carrying something large and uncomfortable on his back. 'They're mates. Good mates. An' it's how they settle their grievances.'

'But you're doing it . . . what, professionally?'

'Ah, you know how it is, when there's big blokes hittin' each other, an' one wins and one loses, there's money to be made. Next thing you know, I'm in the ring.'

She looked round the room. 'I'm guessing you haven't seen much of it. This money.'

He looked away once more. 'Yeah, well . . .' He rubbed his face with his hand. 'Not all of us get to go to university, do we?'

'What d'you mean?'

'The rest of us just have to . . . do what we can.'

Marina looked at him. 'Are you in trouble, Sandro?'

He gave a bitter laugh. 'I'm always in trouble. According to you.'

'Do you owe money, is that it?'

He didn't seem to want to answer, but the words reluctantly left his mouth. 'Bit. But there's a bout tonight.' He raised the energy drink to his lips. 'That's what this is for. Win that an' I've paid more of it off.'

'Oh, Sandro . . .'

His features hardened. 'Don't give me pity. Like I said, we weren't all as lucky as you.'

'Sorry. I didn't mean . . .'

'I'll still help you. I said I would. But I have to do that first.'

Whatever Marina was going to say next remained unsaid.

Love Will Tear Us Apart.

She grabbed her bag, snatched the phone out, put it straight to her ear. Heard a woman's voice.

'Listen . . .'

69

Mickey and Anni had reached a dead end.

'And this was the last reported sighting?' said Anni.

Mickey turned round. 'Yeah. After this, she's . . . in the wind.'

They were following Marina's trail on DCI Franks's orders. After what they had discovered at the house, Mickey had expected to stay in charge of that, but Franks had different ideas.

'I want you two out looking for Marina,' he had said on the phone, directly after Mickey had received the call from Anni and they had realised who the child in the house had been. 'The Birdies can deal with everything there. They can look for the missing girl. They'll need to liaise with Suffolk since they're already working on it. It'll be a joint operation. I want you two trying to track down Marina. We find one of them, hopefully we find all of them.'

Mickey had tried to argue, saying that it wasn't a good idea — and in fact against police policy — to investigate someone in the same department.

'But you're not, are you?' Franks had replied. 'Investigating. You're just looking for her. Granted, you find her and everything else might fall into place, but at the moment you're just two colleagues tracking down a missing person who just happens to be known to you. Which should give you more insight into her whereabouts.'

Put like that, Mickey conceded, he could see the logic.

So he had waited for Anni to arrive, then they had both taken off in Mickey's car, following the last known sighting they had of Marina: a small yellow car on the way to Clacton, seen passing a housing development that seemed to reach a dead end on a cliff against the North Sea.

Mickey stood there hearing the waves below, feeling the cold air all around.

He also felt something else. Anni's arm snaking round his waist, her hand stroking his side. He looked round. She was right next to him.

'You OK?' she said.

'Yeah,' he replied, still staring past the houses to the sea. 'Just . . . trying to think where she could have gone.'

Her grip tightened. 'That wasn't what I meant.'

He turned to her. Eye to eye. She really was exceptionally beautiful, he thought. He turned his head away, wondering what she was thinking. Anni stayed where she was.

'I loved last night.'

Her voice sounded so small and warm against the cold air around him. He turned to her once more. Smiled.

'So did I,' he said. And laughed.

'What's the matter?' She looked concerned.

'It's just . . . Nothing.'

'No it's not. What's the matter?'

'Oh . . . just stupid stuff. Worried that I'd messed everything up. That's all.'

'And why would you have done that?'

'Because I have a tendency to. Everything that I want to go well, if I meet someone a bit special, it just . . . you know. You know what I mean.'

'You haven't messed everything up. Honestly.' Her grip tightened.

He responded. 'Good.'

She smiled. It gave way to a laugh. 'So I'm a bit special, am I?'

He reddened. 'I didn't mean it that way.'

'Not special needs, you mean?'

'Definitely not.'

His phone rang. He answered it. Milhouse.

'You working today, then?' Mickey asked.

'We're all on overtime for this one.'

'Justice never sleeps,' said Mickey. 'What can I do for you?'

'Got some information for you. Emailing it over. The dead man's been identified. Graham Watts.'

Mickey thought. 'The guy whose car it was. Anything on him?'

'Used to work for the Sloane family.'

'Now that rings a bell.'

'It should,' continued Milhouse. 'Stuart Sloane, the adopted boy who went mad with a shotgun and killed his family, was released from prison yesterday. And he's gone missing. Graham Watts used to work for the family. Didn't part on good terms, apparently.'

'Connection, you reckon?'

'The universe doesn't believe in coincidences,' said Milhouse. 'And neither do I. But I just provide the information; what you do with it's up to you.'

'Do my best.'

'You should have the email now. Happy hunting.'

He hung up.

'Milhouse?' asked Anni.

'Tell you in the car.'

They turned, made their way back to Mickey's car. Anni hadn't removed her hand.

Mickey hadn't removed his either.

70

'Your voice is different,' said Marina. 'I'm not talking to a Dalek any more.' There was no reply. 'And you're a woman.'

'Well done.' The voice was trying to sound flippant. And failing. It just sounded tired.

Marina felt there was a vacuum where the woman's control should have been, and decided to fill it. 'Look. It's all gone wrong for you.'

'Has it?'

'I went to the house. I saw the body.' No response, so she kept going. 'Why don't you give up, yeah? Just let me have my daughter back and we can leave it. It's all gone wrong. Let's salvage something. Give me my daughter and we can walk away. What d'you say?'

'What a coincidence,' said the woman's voice. 'I was just going to propose that myself.'

Marina said nothing. Just felt her heart rise at the possibility of the whole ordeal being over. Tried not to get too excited.

'But there's a condition.'

Her heart sank once more. She should have expected that. 'OK, then,' she said, as calm as she could manage. 'Tell me what the condition is.'

There was a pause on the other end of the line. Marina's first thought was that the woman had hung up. She was gone, and with her the last chance of seeing Josephina alive. But she came back. Thinking, thought Marina. Planning what to say next.

'You . . . you still have a job to do. I — we — want you to do the job still.'

Marina's mind whirled. She tried to think quickly, compartmentalise her maternal instincts, react once more not as a desperate mother but a trained psychologist. That last sentence had been rich in undisclosed meaning. Marina had to examine it, turn it round, use it against the speaker, make it a key to character, motivation. Force the woman to reveal herself.

Still have a job to do. She still wants me to diagnose Stuart Sloane, Marina thought. She couldn't let go of that idea. But the way she had said it, there had been no conviction in her voice. Like she knew the situation was reaching the end and she was preparing to salvage what she could out of it. A resignation, a sense of avoiding defeat.

But that doesn't mean she's defeated, thought Marina. It just means she wants to avoid defeat. At any cost? Depending how unhinged she is, there's no telling what she might do.

I — we . . . Self-correction. Gave too much of herself away with the first word. She's on her own. Her partner — in crime or whatever respect — is gone. Marina had seen the body. But the caller still wanted to give the impression that there was more than one of her. That she wasn't doing this alone. Was that because she wanted to seem more powerful? Or did she just miss him?

Want you to do the job still. Want you to do the job still . . . She ran the words in her head. The phrase seemed simple enough on first hearing, but again it was revealing of itself. The phrasing was haphazard, the sentence structure poor. Indicative of a disordered mind.

Marina tried to add everything up. She had a woman who was losing the stomach for her actions but who nevertheless wanted things to be finished the way she had planned. A woman who was missing her partner. A woman who wasn't stable to begin with and whose mind was now slipping into dangerous territory. Something to work with.

'Listen,' said Marina, in her professional, compassionate voice. 'We can end this now. *You* can end this now. Just give me Josephina back and that will be that.'

A sigh from the other end of the phone, then silence.

Marina pressed on. 'Look. I know you're finding this hard. Very hard. Especially on your own. Especially with what happened to . . . your partner. That must have been awful for you.' No response. She weighed something up in her mind. Yes. Kept going. 'I know what it's like to lose a partner. Like a part of your heart has been taken away. Part of yourself. And you feel . . . like you're never going to be whole again.' She tried to keep her voice even. Tried not to think of Phil.

She became aware of Sandro beside her, listening intently.

'But you also feel you have to keep going. Because if you don't, then . . . it's all been for nothing.' She waited, let the words sink in. 'It's a bad time. A hell of a bad time. But I can help you too. If you'd let me.'

'How?' The voice dead, monotone.

'Because that's what I do. That's my job.'

Silence returned to the other end of the line. In the background, Marina could make out a girl's voice.

'Is that Josephina? Is she there?'

'Yes,' said the woman, in a tone Marina couldn't read.

'Put her on. Let me talk to her.'

More silence.

'Please. I'm her mother. If you want this to end well, if you want me to help, put her on.'

There were sounds from the other end that Marina couldn't read. Scraping, movement. Then a small voice on the phone.

'Hello.'

Marina felt her defences begin to crumble. She tried to hold herself together. 'Hello, darling. It's Mummy. Are you OK?'

'Home . . . Home . . .'

'I'm coming to get you very soon, darling.' Marina forced back the sudden tears that sprang into her eyes. 'Very soon. It won't be long now.'

'Want Mummy. Daddy. Home.'

'I know, baby. Are you OK? They haven't . . . haven't hurt you?'

'Want Lady.'

Marina felt her heart break. 'You'll get Lady. Don't worry. I've got her.'

'When—'

The phone was snatched away from her.

'Josie? Josie?'

'You've said enough.' The woman was back. Her voice more together now. Less penetrable. 'You know I've still got her. And you know what you have to do to get her back.'

'And I'll do it. Then I'll get my daughter back and it'll all be over. OK?'

'Yes.'

Marina was about to speak again. She felt Sandro tugging at her sleeve. Her first instinct was to ignore him, but he was insistent. She turned. He was thrusting a piece of paper at her. She took it. Looked at it.

'Where the bout's on,' he said, keeping his voice low. 'Tonight. Arrange to meet her there.'

Marina was about to dismiss the idea out of hand, but stopped herself. It wasn't a bad idea. There would be plenty of people, the woman wouldn't be tempted to do anything rash in such a crowd, and Marina would have Sandro as backup. Not perfect, but the best that she could hope for.

'We'll meet tonight,' she said, voice as strong as she could make it. 'I've got a location.'

'I'll choose the location,' said the woman.

'Yeah. You haven't got a very good track record of this, have you? I'll choose. There won't be any police there, I promise.'

'How do I know?'

'Because when I tell you what it is and where it's at, you'll understand. There's a bare-knuckle boxing match going on tonight.' She read from the paper Sandro had given her. 'Leeson's Farm. Near Manningtree. On the Roman Road. I've got directions if you need them.'

'I'll find it.'

'Good.'

'This is your last chance. You got that? You try to mess me about, do anything other than what you've said you'll do, try to get out of what you've agreed, and you'll never see your daughter again. Got it?'

'Got it. And by the way,' said Marina. She felt the anger rising in her once more, but this time made no attempt to stop it. 'You do anything to my daughter, and I will kill you with my bare hands. As slowly as possible.'

The phone went dead.

Marina sat back. Drained. Sandro came and sat next to her. Smiled at her.

'Well done, girl,' he said. 'We'll make an Esposito out of you yet.'

71

Tyrell looked at Amy. She had changed since the phone call. And he didn't know if it was for the better.

She was standing on her own, looking down at the ground, the phone hanging loose in one hand, the gun in the other. Her mouth was moving, talking to someone who wasn't there. She began to move around, taking small steps as she spoke, completely unaware that the other two were there.

Tyrell thought this was his chance. He could run for it. Take Josephina and go. Leave Amy to whatever was in her head. He gathered the little girl next to him. Looked round for a way out. There was forest on all sides. He could just pick her up and run. Any direction, didn't matter. The woman was probably too far gone inside her own head to notice.

'Mummy . . .' Josephina was looking upset again. He hated to see her looking upset.

'Yes, Josephina. I'll take you to see your mummy.'

And he was ready to go.

But something stopped him. Something nagged at him about Amy. She had looked familiar when she got close up to him. He still didn't know who she was or how he knew her, but there was definitely something familiar about her.

The eyes. That was what did it. The eyes.

He knew them but he didn't. Couldn't explain why. Or how. Her eyes. And something else. When she had got mad with him before, got angry. That was familiar too.

He couldn't place it. The memory was just out of reach in his mind. When he tried to grab it, it slipped away like smoke.

He watched her some more. Tried to see her eyes, but her head was down.

It was like watching a ghost. He remembered a comic he used to read when he was little. An American comic that he wasn't supposed to have because it belonged to the boy he'd been told to call brother. Deadman. That was the name of the character. Deadman. He had a bald head, a white face, black eyes and a red acrobat's costume, and there was something about him that Tyrell had loved. Deadman was, as his name suggested, dead. But he could make his spirit live by putting it into other people's bodies. And then he would have adventures. When Tyrell looked at Amy now, that was what he saw. Deadman. A spirit living in someone else's body.

He just didn't know whose spirit it was.

He glanced at Josephina, looked back at Amy. This was it. Run for it.

But he couldn't.

He looked at Amy again. It wasn't just her being Deadman. She was troubled. She was behaving the way she was, doing the things she was doing because she was unhappy. Not right inside. And he couldn't just walk away and leave her. Not without trying to help her.

So instead of running away, he walked towards her.

'Amy . . .'

She didn't look up, didn't even acknowledge that she had heard him. Just kept walking round, talking to the invisible person she was having a conversation with.

Tyrell got nearer. 'Amy . . .'

She looked up then. Her eyes were wild, pinwheeling, struggling to focus on him, to recognise where she was.

'Are you . . . are you OK?'

She turned away from him. But before she did, he saw a flash of . . . something . . . in her eyes. More madness? Sadness? He didn't know what.

'Leave me alone.'

He stayed where he was. 'I just thought . . .' Then stopped. He didn't know what he just thought.

She turned back to him. There was no mistaking what was in her eyes now. Hatred. Pure, unmistakable hatred.

'I said leave me alone.' She was spitting, hissing at him. 'I wish . . . I wish I had never met you, wish you'd never come into my life . . . you freak, you retard . . . you . . . Everything that's wrong, everything that's been wrong, it's all because of you . . .'

He stared at her, didn't know what to say.

'You ruined everything. You ruined my life.'

Conflicting emotions ran through Tyrell. He didn't know what to say, what to do. He didn't know who she was, why she was saying these things. He knew he recognised her, or at least there was something familiar about her, but . . .

'I never . . .' he said.

'What.'

'I never ruined your life.'

She gave a bitter laugh. 'Really?'

'Yes. Really. I'd have remembered.'

And that was when she pulled the gun on him again.

He stared down the barrel once more, not knowing whether he was going to live or die. This time, though, it felt different. Like it was happening to someone else and not him. Like it didn't matter either way. Like he didn't care.

Amy screamed and turned away from him, lowering her shaking arm as she did so.

'No . . . you have to live . . . I hate it, but you have to live . . .'

He stared at her. Knowing she was too far gone, unreachable by anyone.

He glanced at Josephina, who was looking confused as to why he hadn't taken her to see her mummy.

He sighed.

Wished he had just taken the girl and run when he had the chance.

72

'So how are you feeling? Sorry. Bet you're sick of people asking you that.'

Phil Brennan smiled at the nurse. 'Not yet,' he said.

She smiled back. 'Good.'

The nurses and the consultant had been in and drips had been checked, monitors studied, tests carried out. Everything from near-forensic scrutiny of charts to fingers before his eyes and gauging reactions. The consultant eventually declared herself satisfied and left him alone. Phil had asked questions, but the only answer he had been given was to rest.

He had never been good at resting or at doing what he was told.

'Need to . . . get up . . .' He tried to sit up, put the weight of his body on his arms, pull himself upright. Pain tracked his every move. He slumped slowly back.

The nurse was checking his notes. 'I wouldn't try to move if I were you. Not yet.'

'Can't . . . lie here . . .' he said, trying again.

She turned her attention to him. 'No. You need to rest.'

He shook his head. It felt like his brain was in sloshing about in a bowl of water. 'Can't . . . I . . . What happened? Will somebody tell me . . . what happened?'

'I will.'

DCI Gary Franks was standing in the doorway. The nurse turned to him. 'I'm sorry, but Mr Brennan isn't allowed visitors until—'

He held up his warrant card. 'It's all right, love. It's work.'

The nurse reluctantly didn't argue any more. 'I'll leave you to it, then.' She left the room.

Franks took a seat next to the bed, pulled it up close to Phil. 'How you feeling?'

Phil tried to shrug. 'Felt better . . . I suppose. Just . . . hurt all over.'

'They giving you enough drugs?'

Phil managed the ghost of a smile. 'Can't . . . complain there.'

'Good.' Franks looked around, as though checking they were alone. His voice dropped. 'What have they told you? About what happened?'

'Nothing. No one says . . . anything. Where's . . . Marina?'

'We'll come to that in a minute. Just got to talk to you first.'

Phil frowned, trying to process Franks's words through his drug- and pain-fogged brain. 'What . . . ?'

'First of all, they say you're going to be OK. No brain damage. Well, no more than you had already.' Franks laughed at his own joke.

'Ha ha . . .' Phil moved his hand up to the side of his head, felt bandages. He noticed his hands were bandaged too. He felt his skin, found ridges, painful and swollen to the touch. 'What do I look like?'

'An oil painting,' said Franks. 'Something by Picasso.'

'You're full of them today.'

'Or Frankenstein.'

'How . . . long have I been asleep?'

'Just a day or so. Not too long.'

'A day or so . . . not too bad. Thought you were going to say . . . years. What happened?'

'What can you remember?'

'Nothing.'

'The cottage? Aldeburgh?'

Phil frowned. At Franks's words, he felt a part of his memory detach itself from the huge expanse of blackness in his subconscious and float slowly towards his conscious mind. 'Yes, the cottage . . . we went to Aldeburgh for the . . . the weekend.'

'That's right. Well . . .' All traces of humour fell away from Franks's face.

Phil scrutinised him. He recognised that look. All professional sympathy. It was the one police officers gave that transformed anxious relatives into grieving ones. 'What . . . what's happened . . . ?'

'The cottage . . . there was an explosion.'

Phil waited.

'Don was . . .' Franks sighed. 'Don died in it.'

Phil pulled the bedclothes back and tried to swing his legs round to the floor. The effort cost him, and he was soon out of breath.

'What you doing?'

'Getting . . . up . . .'

'No you're not.'

'Can't . . . can't lie here like . . . this . . .' He put one hand on the bedside cabinet, tried to pull himself out of bed. 'Got to . . . to . . .'

Franks placed a restraining hand, gentle but firm, on Phil's chest. 'You've got to stay where you are. Get well again.'

Phil shook his head, ignoring the swimming sensation. 'No. Don's dead . . . Got to—'

'No, Phil.' Franks used his most authoritative voice. 'You need to stay where you are.'

Phil, exhausted and riddled with pain, flopped back on the bed. He stared at Franks. 'Where's . . . Marina? I want to see . . . Marina . . .'

Franks paused. This was the bit he had been dreading.

73

Sandro stared at his sister. She had come off the phone on a high. Fired up, angry, ready to go and get Josephina there and then. But because there could be no immediate action, her emotion began to subside. And when the adrenalin dissipated away into her system, she hit a down.

'Can I . . . Is . . . You all right?' The words felt foreign on his tongue. He checked his watch. Not long to go now. He looked again at Marina. He couldn't leave her like this. 'Look, I've . . . Is there . . . ?'

She sighed. 'I want my family back.'

Sandro knew who she meant. He didn't think she had intended the words to hurt, and after all these years he wasn't sure they did. But she was still his sister.

'Why don't you . . . phone the hospital? See how Phil is?'

She looked up once more. 'You think I don't want to? You think I don't want to do that every second of the day? I tried it once before and look what happened.'

'Try it again. On that phone they call you on. What's the worst thing that can happen? Now?'

'You know what. I never see Josie again.'

'After the way the woman was in that last call? That won't happen. She wants this over as much as you now. Or you could do it from here.'

'Even more risky,' she said. 'They could trace it right back here.' She thought once more. 'I'll find a phone box. Call from there.'

'A workin' one? Round here? Good luck with that.'

'There must be one somewhere . . .'

'Can't think.'

She stood up. 'I'm going to go and look. See if I can find one.'

Sandro looked like he wanted to object but couldn't think of a reason. 'OK,' he said. 'You want me to come with you?'

'I'll be fine. The walk should take my mind off things, hopefully.'

She left the house before he could say anything more. It was cold outside, the sun seeming distant. She walked the broken, pitted roads looking for a phone box, or somewhere that would have a public phone. She came across the Broadway, a collection of shops, cafés and a pub that looked like it had given up fighting for life and accepted a slow, crumbling death.

And there she found a phone box.

She ran to it, willing it to be undamaged and working. To her amazement, it was. The cubicle stank of stale bodily fluids and the handset was greasy and filthy to the touch, but it had a dialling tone. Even the vandals have given up on this place, she thought.

She took out a piece of paper from her pocket with the hospital's number on it. Dialled it. Once connected, she took a deep breath, told them who she was and who she was calling for. And waited. A nurse eventually came back on the line, but not before she had heard a click. She knew someone was listening.

'Your husband's come round,' the nurse said. 'He's stable.'

Relief flooded her body, nearly took her legs away. 'Oh . . . oh. Can I . . . can I talk to him?'

'He's sleeping at the moment.'

'Is he OK? He's not . . .'

'He's shaky, but he's doing fine.' There was a pause. She heard someone talking in the background. 'If you can give me your number?'

'Just . . . just tell him . . .' She sighed. 'Oh, he knows.'

She hung up, leaned against the filthy wall of the box, unable to move for a few minutes.

He's alive, she thought. Phil's alive. Get Josie back and we're a family again. The euphoria she was experiencing soon subsided as she thought about her daughter.

She looked at the phone once more. The thought that Phil was well and alive gave her strength. She drew from it. And came to a decision. She picked up the receiver again, ignoring the rank smell coming off it, and placed it to her ear.

While she had been walking, she had come up with a plan. Call Anni, give her the address of the bare-knuckle fight. Tell her to get Mickey and the rest of the team there to pick up Josephina's kidnapper. Keep a low profile at the event, only move when given the nod. Sandro wouldn't mind, she was sure of that. Well, she hoped he wouldn't mind.

Right, she thought. Good. That sounds like a plan. Her finger was poised over the buttons when she realised she didn't have Anni's number. It was programmed into her phone and she usually called it from her contacts list. She had never bothered to learn it.

She put the receiver down once more, slamming it harder than she had meant to, angry that her plan couldn't go ahead. She stared at it, as if that would make it connect to Anni's phone, then turned her back, stared out along the desolate stretch of Jaywick seafront, her heart sinking.

Then she had an idea. She turned back to the phone, picked up the receiver, smiling to herself as she did so. DCI Franks. She knew his number.

'Easy to remember,' he had said to her when she had first met him and was programming it into her phone, 'Six, six,

six, three, three, three. A devil and a half of a number.' And he had laughed.

The quip had been rehearsed, but he was right, she had remembered.

She closed her eyes to recall the first five digits, then called the number. Her heart was hammering as she waited for him to answer.

'DCI Franks.'

She took a deep breath, another. 'It's Marina.' She didn't know what he would say next or how he would react, so she jumped in quickly. 'Listen. I haven't got long . . .'

74

Anni had always hated coming in to work on a Sunday. Easter Sunday even more so. The police station on Southway in Colchester was virtually empty. Just a minimum of officers and shift-working support staff keeping the building going over the weekend. The excesses of Saturday night had been mopped up, and with no football scheduled, those on call were making the most of not having to be there unless absolutely needed. Or working the murder in Jaywick, looking for Josephina.

She sat at her desk, booted up her computer. Mickey was beside her. After Milhouse's call, they had decided to go back to the station to check through records.

Walking into the building alongside Mickey, Anni had felt that those few people there were all staring at them. They know, she was thinking, they know what we've done. That we're now lovers. And they're judging us for it. Through the main door, down the corridor, into the MIS office. Feeling eyes, seen and unseen, staring at her. She had glanced at Mickey a few times, just to see if he was feeling the same thing. He was staring straight ahead, not looking at her.

Yep, she thought. He's feeling the same thing.

In the MIS office, at her desk, she had reverted to police officer mode. And now she was engrossed in what was appearing on her screen.

'Graham Watts,' she said.

Mickey scooted his chair across, sat next to her, looked at the screen. She was aware of his arm brushing against hers, his thigh. She could feel the heat from his body. More intoxicating than cannabis.

Mickey kept staring at the screen, not looking at her.

'Here,' she said. 'Worked for the Sloanes.' She peered closer. 'High up too. Very high. Trusted lieutenant, the works. Started as a gangmaster on the farm, worked his way up. When they diversified into industrial farming, he got promoted. And then . . . Oh. They let him go. Cut him off, apparently, just like that. That's when the law became involved.'

'How?' asked Mickey, turning to look at her.

'Cautioned for threatening behaviour. Says here they owed him money. Lots of it. Cut him off without a pension. He tried to talk to them about it, then said he was going to expose them. That was the word he used, expose. The Sloanes said he had nothing on them, that he threatened them, made up a lot of lies. Tried to attack them, got a bit handy.'

Mickey read the next few lines on her screen. 'They never pressed charges. Just let it go. And he never exposed anything.' He looked sideways at her. 'You know what that means.'

Anni nodded. 'He may not have got his pension, but they gave him enough to keep him quiet.'

'Exactly. Maybe they didn't pay him enough to keep him quiet for long.'

'You think that's what this is?' she asked, turning to him. 'Extortion? Blackmail gone wrong?'

'Could be. Maybe he ran out of money. Came back for more.'

'And you think, what, that the Sloanes had him killed?'

'Worth bearing in mind.'

They kept looking at each other. Anni saw a gleam in Mickey's eye, a slight upward pull at the sides of his mouth. He moved in closer to her.

'Stop it . . .'

'Haven't done anything.'

'And you're not going to. We've got work to do.'

They went back to the screen.

'The Sloanes,' said Mickey. 'Brother and sister. Bloodbath house of death, and all that.'

'That's them.'

He tapped some keys, brought up a different screen. 'Yeah. Thought so. They were left for dead when their adopted brother went mental with a shotgun. He killed the rest of the family, including his own mother. Stuart Sloane, that was his name.'

Anni frowned. 'Stuart Sloane . . .'

Mickey peered closer. 'And here's something else. Guess who the first person was to find Stuart Sloane with the shotgun?'

'No idea.'

'Graham Watts.'

Anni looked at him. 'Interesting. When was this?'

'Sixteen, seventeen years ago.'

She turned back to her screen. 'Stuart Sloane was released on Friday. He never made it to the hostel. Disappeared.'

'And now Graham Watts is dead.'

Anni shrugged. 'Coincidence?'

'Dunno.' Mickey sat back, thinking. 'There's something else. Wait . . . Didn't . . .' He frowned in concentration. 'Wasn't there some connection with them in that murder case Jessie James was looking into?'

Anni smiled. 'Just can't take her seriously with that name.'

'That guy she went to question. Turned up dead. He had some connection with the Sloanes, I think.'

Mickey's phone rang. He checked the display. 'Franks,' he said. He picked up.

Anni watched him as his eyes widened.

'Is she OK?'

She knew immediately who he was talking about, and gestured for him to put the phone on loudspeaker, but he was concentrating too intently on what Franks was saying. She moved closer and tried to follow the conversation, but it was too one-sided, so she settled for waiting until it had finished.

Eventually Mickey hung up. Anni looked at him expectantly. 'Well?'

'Marina called. She's alive and well. He's going to meet her tonight.'

Questions tumbled through Anni's mind, one fast on the heels of another.

'That's all I know,' Mickey said, pre-empting what she was about to say next. 'All he could tell me.'

'So are we on for tonight too, whatever it is?'

'No, we're not.' Mickey sounded disappointed. 'I told him we were turning up connections in the murder of Graham Watts and the Suffolk murder. He wants us to keep working that. Apparently our presence might cause a distraction.' Mickey's intonation made it clear what he thought about that.

'Is that so?'

'We're too closely associated with Marina.'

'So we're good enough to look for her but not good enough to bring her in.'

'Apparently.'

'So we just stay here. Keep on keeping on.'

'Yeah.' He thought for a few seconds. 'I'm glad she's OK, though.'

'Hope she's looked after my car.' Anni looked again at the screen. 'And we've got plenty to be going on with. We'll be here for a while, I think.'

'We will.'

She looked round. The office was empty apart from them. She turned back to him, a glint in her eye this time. 'You ever wanted to have me here, on my desk?'

Mickey's mouth dropped open. Words seem to form but failed to escape.

Anni giggled, pushed her leg nearer to his. 'Have I shocked you?'

Mickey swallowed, blinked. Twice. 'No,' he said eventually. 'Not shocked.'

'What then?'

The glint reappeared in his eye.

'Just amazed that you can read my mind . . .'

75

Marina had never experienced anything like it.

The barn was huge, modern and functional. Metal sheets clad to a concrete skeleton. Concrete floor. It had been cleared of its day-to-day use with bales of hay pushed to the walls alongside farming machinery, but it couldn't shake off the farm smell: animal waste, nitrates. Marina was sure it never would. That smell had permeated into the foundations. But it was about to be joined by other, more pungent smells. Sweat. Blood. Money.

She had returned to Sandro's house and told him the news about Phil. Sandro hugged her, somewhat awkwardly. She knew that wasn't the kind of thing he was comfortable with but was pleased he had done it. Because that gesture of affection made her, for the first time in her life, feel an abiding love for him. And she was sure he knew it.

And that in turn made her feel guilty about the phone call she had made to Franks. But she would deal with that later, as Sandro had to prepare for the fight and she had to ready herself too. She was going to get her daughter back. No matter what it took.

Sandro emerged from the bathroom, his gym bag over his shoulder, all tracked and hoodied up. She tried to talk to him but he barely responded. She checked his eyes. Her brother wasn't there any more. In his place was another person. Harder, colder, angrier. A fighter. Marina had flinched. She had looked in her brother's eyes and glimpsed their father.

They had taken Sandro's near-dead and rusted-out Mondeo, as she didn't want to be spotted in Anni's car. They had driven in near silence. Next to each other but inhabiting different worlds. Both focused on what they had to do in the next few hours.

Turning off the main road and driving up to the farm, Marina had been amazed. They had had to join a long queue of cars to get in. She had expected them all to be like Sandro's — junkers and clunkers, all tattered and falling apart. She couldn't have been more wrong. Although there were a fair few cars like that, there were also plenty top-of-the-range numbers, BMWs, Mercs, some Lexus models, dotted about.

There was also security on the gate. Stringent, serious. Big guys who looked like they could double for the night's entertainment took money and gave directions. Sandro didn't pay. He was just given a nod of recognition, directed to a field that had been turned into a car park. There, as in the queue to get in, status symbols rubbed bumpers with working Land Rovers, pristine 4x4s, Transits and rust buckets. It was, Marina was amazed to discover, one of the most truly democratic gatherings she had ever been to. All united in their wish to watch two people beat each other up.

Marina followed Sandro to the barn. When they reached the entrance, he stopped, turned to her.

'Time to part company for a bit, kid.'

Marina looked round. She didn't welcome the idea of being left alone in this environment. 'Where are you going?'

'Got to get ready.' He held up his fists. 'Got to prepare.'

'Right. Of course. Good luck.' She kissed him on the cheek.

He smiled. 'Jesus Christ, woman, you'll be gettin' me a reputation for being soft.'

She smiled in return, then quickly scanned the entering crowd.

'They'll be here. Don't worry,' he said. 'And you know where I'll be when you need me.' He walked away. Turned. 'I'm third on the card, remember.'

Marina watched as Sandro walked towards a group of men just inside the door. An older man stood in the centre of the gathering, the men around him bodyguards or acolytes. He was middle-aged, well dressed. His corpulent figure and red and pink features made him look like a huge, boiled pig. Marina recognised him. Milton Picking, one of the biggest gangsters in the region.

Is that who Sandro owes money to? she wondered. Is that who he's fighting for? Oh baby brother, what have you got yourself involved in?

Sandro was greeted by Picking, then taken away by his followers. Marina took a deep breath, another. Stepped inside.

76

Inside the barn, a fight was just about to start. The centre of the building had been cleared and straw strewn on the concrete floor. Marina was confused by that, thinking at first that straw wasn't sturdy or thick enough to absorb an impact and make for a sprung base on which to fight. Then she realised what it was for, and with that realisation came a small wave of nausea: it was there to mop up the blood.

A rope had been placed round the centre, marking out the ring. The bales of hay stacked on all sides almost to the ceiling acted as tiered seating. Wooden benches made up the first few rows. Trestle tables served as a bar. It was crowded.

She looked round at the crowd. Like the vehicles outside, it reflected the same patchwork make-up of different types. She recognised the travellers straight away. Jeans and polo shirts; they all looked like they could handle themselves and would be happy for a turn in the ring. There were also plenty of women with them, young, blonde and orange, dressed like sexualised Barbie dolls. And children, the boys mini-mes of their fathers. Dressed the same, running round shrieking, doing their own bare-knuckle sparring in the corners.

There were other types. Men with Marbella tans and expensively tasteless clothes, chunky gold jewellery and reset noses. On their arms Chigwell-opulent trophy wives and mistresses.

And everyone in between. The career gamblers and born losers. The nine-to-fivers seeking a thrill. The curious. Those claiming it as research. All there with one thing in common: they enjoyed watching other people get hurt.

Marina checked her phone. Nothing. The place was noisy, so she kept it in her hand. An announcement was made: the first fight was about to start. She sat down on one of the benches, looking round all the time, scanning the crowd for Josephina. She couldn't see her.

The first two fighters were brought out. They were teenagers, boys. Both had the hard bodies and wild eyes of travellers. They were led into the ring and she saw immediately that even if they weren't making money from it, they would still be doing it for fun.

All around, the crowd were on their feet, baying and calling, the excitement palpable, the air thick with sweat and bloodlust. She saw money change hands as odds were made and bets taken. She watched as the two boys squared up to each other, fists in front of their faces, ready.

The referee looked like he could have just walked in from the crowd. He spoke with the familiar Irish-Essex traveller twang, implored the two fighters to make it a good clean fight. They both nodded, eyes fixed on the other. He went on to remind them that one clean hit was worth ten dirty ones, but it was clear they weren't listening to him. They were both ready to hurt.

The bell went. They danced round each other as the crowd shouted encouragement. Marina was suddenly surrounded by baying red faces. The boys became braver, started fighting. Fists were flung, blows placed. Marina heard the flat slap of knuckle on skin, like a butcher tenderising a side of pork. Felt the blows as they landed.

The larger boy had the footwork. He seemed able to dance out of his opponent's way, deflect shots intended to damage one part of his anatomy to another, less painful one. This just infuriated the smaller one. He began to throw out shots faster, harder. Wilder. One connected with the bigger boy's ear and he fell to the ground, cracking his head on the concrete.

That was it, thought Marina, the fight would be stopped.

But it wasn't. The fallen boy put his hand to his ear, cried out in pain and anger. The referee was holding back the smaller boy, who was mad-eyed with rage, dancing about, trying to get at his opponent.

The bigger boy climbed back to his feet, blood trickling from his ear. Marina wasn't an expert, but she thought that could be dangerous. The referee thought differently, however, and, after consultation with the fighter, allowed the bout to proceed.

The smaller boy had seen his advantage. His own bloodlust was high. He pressed forward. The bigger one stood his ground, tried to fight off the blows, but Marina, and the rest of the crowd, could see it was just a matter of time. The smaller one kept hitting. One blow connected with his opponent's nose. Marina heard bone and cartilage shatter. She closed her eyes. The crowd cheered. The small boy jumped out of the way as blood fountained out. He skipped to the side, threw a punch against the damaged ear. The other boy went down. Didn't get back on his feet this time.

The fight was over, the smaller boy declared the winner. He was jumping up and down, dancing while still in the ring, face a mask of his own and his opponent's blood, looking like the fight was just a prelude, ready to take on anyone, everyone.

He was led away.

The crowd's bloodlust temporarily sated, the noise in the barn dampened down to an excited hubbub. More money changed hands as bets were called in and placed for the next bout. Marina, still sitting by herself, felt physically ill.

She checked the phone in her hand. No call.

She looked back at the ring, at the blood on the straw. Couldn't believe her own brother was going to be in there soon. Couldn't believe she was here to watch him.

Fresh straw was thrown over the bloodied straw. She looked round once more. Still no sigh of Josephina. She couldn't even see Sandro. She waited.

The next fight was announced and two more fighters were brought into the ring. The same procedure as before started. Marina wasn't sure she could watch it all again.

She didn't have to.

Love Will Tear Us Apart.

She grabbed the phone, put it straight to her ear. Turned away from the action.

'Where is she?' she shouted. 'Where's my daughter?'

The voice on the phone sucked in air. 'Well played.'

'What d'you mean?'

'You must think you're so clever. Arranging to meet here. Thinking that you'd be safe amongst all these people. That you'd be able to snatch your daughter and make a run for it. Not agree to your part of the arrangement. Am I right?'

'Where is she? Where's my daughter?' Marina was screaming now. No one could hear her above the baying crowd.

The voice gave no reply.

'Where is she?'

'Look.'

'Where?'

'At the back of the hall. Right at the back. Behind you.'

Marina turned. The crowd were on their collective feet, shouting and screaming and fist-pumping. Marina tried to look through them, look past them. The bales of hay had a gap between them, making a narrow passageway. It was in almost virtual darkness, but she concentrated, managed to separate the shadows. She made out a figure. A small figure. Her heart almost pounded its way out of her chest.

'Josephina . . .'

She started to run towards her, pushing, fighting her way through the crowd.

'Not just yet,' said the voice on the phone. 'Stay where you are.'

Confused and apprehensive, she stopped running.

'Look. Look again at your little girl. What else can you see?'

Marina looked. And saw a flash of light in the darkness, glinting from something metallic.

A gun.

Pointed at her daughter's head.

77

Helen Hibbert pulled her coat closer to her neck. She didn't think it would make much difference, but she felt like it was doing something positive to keep out the cold, damp and fog.

She had reached Harwich with plenty of time to spare, constantly checking her mirror in case those two coppers were following her. She hadn't seen them or noticed any car that gave any indication of following. Although since her knowledge of that came exclusively from Hollywood movies, she wasn't entirely sure.

And now she walked, the only person out, her heels clacking and crunching, echoing all around. Behind her were houses, flats. Both old and old-looking. In keeping with the local character. The land stopped the other side of her. She could make out shapes in the fog, lights over the water from the port. It looked like something from a science fiction film, a hulking, crash-landed mothership sitting ominous and indistinct in the mist.

She walked along the footpath towards the agreed spot. A lifeboat station was on her right, the runway positioned on the stony shingle beach. On the other side of her were landed wooden boats. Pulled in and piled up. The dark disguising the fact that most of them, holed and rotting, would never set sail again. Their final resting place. Their graveyard.

She kept walking, away from the houses and flats now, finding herself alone. The boats were now piled up on both sides. Her breath caught from something more than cold. The overhead street lights cast deep, dark shadows, providing perfect cover for muggers and rapists. She could see ahead to where the path was clear and open, where it rejoined the rest of the town and her assignation was to take place, but to get there she had to walk through this first.

She moved slowly, eyes darting, alert for any sudden movement, any attack, listening for changes in sound. She could hear only the white-noise drone of the waves breaking against the shingle beach. That and the beating of her own heart.

She tried to joke with herself, think of it as a final test to go through before starting her new life. Go into the darkness, come out in the light. Just her and the weird sister. How was that going to work? Would they get on? Have much in common? If Helen had been asked earlier, she would have said no. Definitely not. But now she wasn't so sure. There had seemed to be a connection when they talked. Kindred spirits, and all that. And there was the money, too. That was probably what would keep them together.

She clutched her coat more tightly about her, kept a firm grip on her suitcase. Despite telling herself there was nothing to worry about, she wished she had something else to hold, something she could use as a weapon if she needed to.

And then she heard something. Or someone.

She turned. The sound came from her left. Movement, someone coming towards her. Helen froze. Then heard a voice.

'Hello, Helen.'

She turned. It was Dee. Sliding out of the shadows.

Smiling.

78

'Well I wish we'd stopped. That's all I'm saying.' Jessie looked sulkily out of the car window.

Deepak sighed and shook his head. A reply felt unnecessary. She knew what he was thinking, what he would say. They were working, they might lose Helen Hibbert if they stopped now, the fish and chip shop would still be there once they had finished . . . all that. She knew what he would say because she had heard it all before. Many times.

'Look,' said Deepak, staring through the windscreen. 'If she goes any further down there, we're going to lose her.'

'Then we get out of the car and follow her.'

Deepak didn't look happy about that.

'What, now you don't want to follow her?'

He shrugged. 'It's cold. I didn't bring appropriate clothing.'

Jessie smiled, looked away.

After leaving the Sloane house, they had gone back to Helen Hibbert's flat to question her and found her leaving, pulling a suitcase behind her. They had followed her, trying to be as inconspicuous as possible. Deepak was very good, she had to give him that. All the way down the A14 to Harwich. Sometimes he had been one car behind her, sometimes two or three. At one point he was even in front. But he never once lost sight of her. And never let her know she was being tailed.

They had pulled back as she had negotiated the old narrow lanes of Harwich, waiting until she had parked and got out before bringing their car alongside her. They had watched as she set off walking, pulling her suitcase behind her.

'Looks like she's got a hot date,' said Jessie, then turned to Deepak. 'Sorry. Cold date.'

'Very funny,' he said, face straight.

They watched her walk towards the stacked old boats.

'Very brave,' said Deepak.

'Or stupid,' said Jessie.

'Maybe she's meeting someone there,' said Deepak.

'Let's hope it's who she wants to meet.'

Deepak leaned over to the glove compartment, took out a pair of miniature binoculars.

'You think of everything, don't you?' said Jessie. 'Apart from bringing warm clothing, of course.'

Deepak ignored her, watched Helen Hibbert.

'She's stopped,' he said.

'Let me see.' Jessie made a grab for the binoculars. Deepak held her off.

'Just a minute.' He kept watching. 'There's somebody with her.'

'Let me see.'

Again he stopped her. He smiled. 'Well, well, well . . .'

'What? What?' Jessie scowled. 'I hate it when you do this.'

He put the binoculars down, turned to his superior. 'This gets better.'

79

Right at this very second, Tyrell had never hated himself more. Never *could* hate himself more.

They had arrived there with no trouble. Once Amy saw what kind of venue it was and what was happening there, she had become angry. Striding up and down in the car park, swearing, ranting to herself that she had allowed herself to be duped, played. Josephina and Tyrell had just stood there, silent. She had then hurried them inside, pulled them to the back of the hall, hidden from the rest of the punters by the huge hay bales. And that was when she had handed him the gun, told him to hold it against Josephina's head. The little girl had just stared at him, her eyes brimming with tears, threatening to spill over.

'Tell her,' Amy had said, 'that if she doesn't stand still and do what she's told, she won't get to see her mother. Ever.'

Tyrell had stared at the gun in his hand, felt its cold heaviness, then looked at the girl and back to Amy. He had shaken his head. 'No. I won't.'

'Really?' Amy had smiled then. It wasn't pleasant. 'One of us has to do it. You want me to? Shall I? Do you trust me?' He didn't have to answer her. She knew what he was thinking. She smiled, seeing he had no choice. 'Thought so.'

He had looked between Amy and Josephina and reluctantly held on to the gun. 'I hate guns,' he said to Amy. 'And I really, really hate you.'

She shrugged. 'Not the first time you've told me that. Just do as you're told. And make sure she does what she's told. And don't get clever. Don't even think about using it on me.'

He hadn't. Not until she had said it. And by then it was too late.

'Just do it. We get this done, go back to the house, get sorted and it's all over.'

Tyrell's hand was shaking. He really did hate guns. The sound they made, the look of them, the heft of them. They were cold, hard. Dead to the touch.

And now he was standing there, holding the automatic on a child. A child he had made promises to, who trusted him. Now she couldn't look at him. She was shaking too. The threatened tears had never happened only because she was too frightened to cry.

'It's all right,' he said. 'I'm not . . . not going to hurt you. You know that . . .'

He didn't know if he was speaking to the child or to himself.

'I know . . . you won't believe me, but please . . . I want you to go back to your mother. I want you to go home.' He sighed. 'I want to go home too.'

All around were too many people making too much noise. Screaming and braying. Worse even than the worst nights in prison. At least then he was on his own, just listening to the noise. Here he was right among it. In the thick of it. He didn't know what to do, couldn't think.

So he just stood there, holding the gun. Hating himself. Josephina wouldn't even look at him. That really hurt. Knowing he had let her down, betrayed her trust. And he had done it by being weak. Making the wrong decisions, the wrong choices.

And that made him angry with himself.

He looked again at the gun. At the child. At Amy next to him, talking on the phone.

At the gun. Again.

Yes. He was hurt. Yes. He was angry.

It was time to do something about it.

80

'You bitch . . .' Marina started to move through the crowd.

'I've told you already. Stay where you are.'

Marina knew this wasn't the time to antagonise the woman, so she did as she was told and stopped moving. She kept the phone clamped to her ear.

'That's better,' said the woman. 'I just wanted you to see that she's still alive, that she's unhurt. That I haven't been lying to you.'

'I need to see her,' said Marina.

'You can see her from where you are. She's fine.'

Marina knew she should react as a psychologist would, but she couldn't help herself. 'Bitch . . .'

'Whatever. You get her back when you've completed your part of the deal. Not before. Do that and everything will be fine.'

Marina wanted to look round but didn't dare. Was Franks nearby? Could he see her or Josephina? Could he see the gun? It was hidden from most of the crowd, so she doubted it. But she hoped he was watching her and could read her reactions. She had to play for time, so she reined her emotions in. Tried to keep calm, focus. 'Right. I'm here. You want me to give a report on your patient. Shall we do this now?'

'I had hoped we could. But this venue isn't particularly conducive to conversation, is it?'

'Well, we could . . .' A wall of sound sprang up around Marina as she spoke. The fight was over. Most people were cheering, some booing, shouting out threats. Marina, her back to the ring, ignored it. She also missed seeing Sandro appear and stand at the ringside. He didn't see her either. He was focused, in the place he needed to be to fight.

Marina gave another surreptitious look round. Still no sign of Franks. 'We could go somewhere else,' she said.

'We could. In fact we have to, since we can't do anything here.'

'Where is he?' asked Marina. 'Stuart Sloane, where are you keeping him?'

'He's right here.'

Marina looked around. 'Right where?'

'Right in front of you.'

Marina realised who she meant. Her heart skipped a beat. 'That's him? The one holding a gun on my daughter?'

'Your new client. Don't sound so surprised. I'd ask him to wave, but he's busy.'

Marina felt her legs begin to tremble. 'And you want me to declare him sane.'

'Oh yes. He's sane, all right.'

Marina fought the urge to scream. 'Then why is he holding a gun on my daughter?'

'Because I told him to. He's protecting my investment, Dr Esposito. So don't do anything stupid, or it'll get very messy.'

The trembling in Marina's legs spread to her whole body. She wanted to rush over and grab her daughter, call the woman's bluff, take whatever came her way and run. She looked round once more, desperate for Franks's intervention.

'Who you looking for?'

'What?' Marina had been too blatant. 'I'm not . . . not looking for anyone.'

'You looked round like you were waiting for a bus.'

'I was just . . . No . . .' And then she saw him. Off to her left, trying to walk through the crowd as unobtrusively as possible. He had spotted her, was coming closer.

She had to signal, tell him to keep back. She caught his eye, shook her head.

'Who's that? What are you doing?'

'I'm . . . Nothing.' Franks picked up the signal. Stopped moving.

'Liar. You were . . .' There was a pause on the line, followed by a sharp intake of breath. 'Bitch.'

'Sorry?'

'You've set me up.'

Marina felt her stomach churn. 'No I haven't, I—'

'Don't lie to me. You've set me up, haven't you? That's why you wanted to meet here. Who is it? Who were you signalling to? Bitch . . .'

Marina was going to argue but couldn't think of anything to say that wouldn't incriminate her further. The woman would be able to tell that she was lying.

The woman gave a sigh that was almost a growl. She spoke quickly. 'Why couldn't you just have done what you were told, eh? Why? Why did you have to . . .' Another sigh, another growl. 'You've done it now, bitch. I'm not responsible for what happens next.'

The phone died in Marina's hand.

81

Mickey was relieved that he and Anni hadn't had sex in the office.

They had both been seriously tempted, but common sense had eventually prevailed. They had kept working on the task before them, just giving occasional suggestive hints, quick, surreptitious strokes of arms and thighs, tantalising little promises of what they could expect from each other later.

They had focused, gone to work. Pulled out everything they could find about Michael and Dee Sloane, their company and their lives.

'Right,' said Mickey, leaning back from the screen and rubbing his eyes, putting together what they had found out so far. 'Graham Watts . . .'

'The dead guy from the house in Jaywick,' said Anni, sitting on the edge of the desk, swinging her legs back and forth and eating a packet of vending machine crisps. 'First on the scene to find the bodies that Stuart Sloane was supposed to have killed.'

'Yep. Now. Jeffrey Hibbert.'

'The victim in the murder case Calamity Jane's working on.'

'Very funny. Hibbert and Watts used to work together. For the Sloanes.'

Anni kept listening. Mickey checked the screen, his notes on the desk. 'They were both high up,' he said. 'Started as workers, went on to be gangmasters on the farms, did their own recruitment, hiring and firing, all that.'

'Farms,' said Anni through a mouthful of crisps.

'What?'

'You said farms. Plural.'

Mickey leaned forward, helped himself to a crisp.

'Oi!'

'Thanks.' He continued. 'Salt and vinegar. Not my favourite.'

'I'll remember that in future. Always get them. Stop you from nicking them.'

'Anyway, yes. Farms plural. After the death of their parents, the Sloane siblings diversified the portfolio, you might say. It was like they were just waiting for their father's death to take over the family business and get it going. They started speculating. Bought up shares in the industrial farms that were emerging in Europe at the time. Worked those shares up to controlling interests in most cases.'

'Industrial farming? Lovely.'

Mickey nodded. 'Saw a documentary on it once. Horrible. Almost put me off eating meat.'

'Almost. Carry on.'

'Right. The Sloanes diversified. Import–export, taking control of the supply chain. The works. Eventually they sold their farm, set up an umbrella company, Sloane Holdings.'

'So where do Hibbert and Watts come into this?' asked Anni.

'Glad you asked. Apparently, according to the official version put out by the Sloanes, Graham Watts didn't like the direction the company was taking and voiced his displeasure. As a result, he was kicked out. And since Hibbert was a close friend, he got the chop too.' Mickey stole another crisp.

'Stop it!'

'Not bad, actually. Could get used to them. Anyway, they were both kicked out. But they made a fuss. Started mouthing off: they knew where the bodies were buried, were going to ruin the Sloanes, yada yada, blah blah.'

'The usual stuff.'

'Yep. But the thing was, their version contradicted the Sloanes'. Watts and Hibbert said it wasn't about the expansion of the business. They were more than happy with that, it made them more money.'

'What then?'

'The Sloanes themselves.'

'In what way?'

'Well . . .' Mickey looked at the screen once more. 'Michael Sloane made a full recovery after the shooting. His wounds weren't that serious. But Dee Sloane, the sister, wasn't so lucky. She had to keep going abroad for treatment. Expensive treatment. Word was she wasn't quite right in the head. Needed mental as well as physical treatment.'

'Not surprised after what she'd been through.'

'No. And apparently she was never the same afterwards. Had to live as a recluse. But I've found something else, too. Some kind of weird sex parties.'

Anni smiled. 'How weird?'

'Get your mind out of the gutter, Hepburn. I don't know. But Watts and Hibbert alluded to them. In fact they were supposed to have been part of them. Rumour was that Watts and Dee Sloane had something going and the brother didn't like it. Then something else happened. Remember that case a few years ago? Dead cockle pickers at Wrabness?'

'Yeah. Migrant workers. Left out when the tide came in. Big court case.'

'Yeah, huge. And it was the Sloanes. It could have broken them. But they got away with it.'

'How?'

'Witnesses retracted their stories, a couple even disappeared. No evidence of negligence. Death by misadventure.

The Sloanes got off as lightly as possible. They started to diversify their business interests shortly after that.'

Anni screwed up her crisp packet, threw it in the bin. 'Not people to mess with.'

'Nope. And apparently a few of their business rivals have disappeared after dealing with them too.'

'You mean gone out of business?'

'No. I mean disappeared. Without a trace. Investigations took place . . .' He shrugged. 'Nothing. Like they'd vanished off the face of the earth. Sloanes completely untouchable.'

'Jesus. So where does Stuart Sloane fit in? Is he after revenge too?'

'God knows.' Mickey took his phone out. 'I'll give Jessie a call. She might have discovered something. She's been working this case too.'

'Don't you think she would have contacted us if she had?'

'Maybe.' Mickey smiled. 'Maybe she's scared of you. Doesn't want to call in case you answer.'

'Maybe she fancies me,' said Anni.

'Maybe.'

'And you can take that look off your face as well, Philips,' she said, laughing.

Mickey dialled the number.

82

Tyrell watched as Amy ended the call and put the phone away in her jeans pocket. Her shoulders slumped, her eyes stayed downcast on the floor. She didn't look good.

The whole situation didn't look good.

Tyrell glanced at Josephina, back to Amy. The woman shook her head. 'We've been set up,' she said.

'What?'

'Little Josephina's mummy doesn't want her back as much as she said.'

Tyrell was confused. 'I don't . . .' He looked at Amy, searching her face for answers. He read familiar emotions in her eyes. Anger. Madness. But he saw something new, something he hadn't yet seen there. Despair. And somehow he found that more distressing.

The crowd on the bales were still looking in the other direction, still screaming. He stood behind them at the back wall, between two hay bale seating areas, feeling like the still point in a raging storm. The calm eye.

But he was anything but calm. His heart was racing, panic threatening to overwhelm him. He could see Josephina's mother beside the ring, a mass of people between them. She looked distraught. Josephina was straining, desperate, crying to be free, to go and see her. Her cries were lost in the screaming crowd. He looked again at Amy. She had gone back into herself, unmoving.

'What . . . what did she say?'

Amy didn't reply. Didn't even acknowledge that she had heard.

Must be the noise, thought Tyrell. He tried again, louder. 'What did she say? What's happening now?'

'She's betrayed us,' said Amy. It sounded like the voice of a dead person.

Tyrell shivered. 'What? What d'you mean?'

Amy turned to him. Her eyes too were like those of a dead person. 'She told someone else. And they're coming for us. They're going to take you away. And me.'

From the way she was speaking, Tyrell thought he was expected to feel shocked or angry. But all he felt was relief. They could take him away. Put him back in prison. And he could rest.

'But I'm not going to let her win. And I'm not going to let him win either . . .'

'What d'you mean? Who are you talking about?'

'The kid's no good to us now.'

'So we can let her go?'

Another sigh from Amy. She looked him straight in the eye. And what he saw there scared him. 'Don't be stupid. No. We kill her. Now.'

83

'Oh thank God,' said Helen, her heart rate slowing, hand clutching her chest. 'It's you.'

Dee smiled. 'Who else were you expecting?'

Helen managed a small, tight laugh. 'I don't know. It's just . . .' She looked round, gestured at the piled-up boats. 'You know. Scary. Never know who could be hanging around in there.'

Dee's smile didn't waver. 'You're right. You don't.'

Helen gave another laugh, stood there regaining her breath. 'So,' she said, 'are we off?'

'Have you got everything you need?'

Helen pointed to her suitcase. 'Everything in here. For now.'

'You didn't tell anyone that you were coming here, that you were meeting me?'

'No. I told you I wouldn't.'

'And you weren't followed?'

A mental image of the two police officers flashed briefly into her head. She discounted it. No. There had been no one following her. She had checked. 'No. Just me.'

'Good.'

'Have you got . . .' Helen paused, not wanting to appear mercenary, 'the money?'

'Everything's sorted,' Dee said. Then she nodded, as if deep in thought, as if reaching a conclusion about something. 'Yes. Everything's sorted.'

Helen smiled. 'Great. Let's go.'

Dee placed a hand on Helen's arm. There was power in the grip. Heavy restraint.

'Ow, that hurt. What are you . . . ?'

Helen's sentence remained unfinished. Behind Dee, from further in the piles of stacked boats, a shadow detached itself. A huge shadow. It came slowly towards Helen, appeared in the street light. It was a man, one of the biggest she had ever seen. Hulking, grey-skinned. Arms wrapped in dirty, bloodied bandages. His eyes caught the light. Glittered, dancing to a demented tune Helen hoped she would never hear.

He moved slowly towards her.

'You're right,' said Dee, cruel laughter undercutting her words. 'You never know who's hanging around in here . . .'

84

Jessie and Deepak were out of the car and making their way towards the piled-up fishing boats when they heard the scream.

'Come on,' said Jessie.

Deepak was already running. Across the grass, down the path. Keeping out of sight of the main walkway, making sure he couldn't be seen. He reached the side of the stacked boats. Began to edge his way cautiously and silently but quickly along to the lit path, keeping hidden as he went.

Jessie caught up with him, joined him. Together they reached the corner.

Another scream, muffled this time, forcibly restrained.

They shared a glance. Deepak nodded.

They were both poised, ready to rush forward.

Jessie returned Deepak's nod.

Ready to spring forward, surprise whoever was there.

Then her phone rang.

85

Tyrell looked down at Josephina. Saw her round, tear-filled eyes staring back up at him. No, he thought. I'm better than that. 'I'm not a killer,' he said aloud. 'I don't care what they say, I'm not a killer . . .'

His mind slipped back. He couldn't help it; he was so stressed, it just happened. He was back in the house, back in that room. On that day. With that shotgun cradled in his arm.

He remembered. It had been his mother's wedding day. And he was so happy for her. He had been out for a walk, round the grounds, away from the house, the family. Enjoying himself. Planning his future. And when he had come back, he had found . . .

He knew what he had found. Bodies everywhere. Blood. Mess. The man he was trying to call his father. Like something from a horror movie. And his mother. Oh God, his mother . . . lying next to him. He was holding her, as if he had tried to protect her. Both of them dead. Gone.

That was when he had retreated. Found somewhere in his head to hide, to stay. And he had been there ever since.

But there was something else, some other memory . . .

Jiminy Cricket. Appearing before him, telling him what to do. And he had done it. Done as he was told. So numb, so dead from what he had just seen, he had done it.

And another memory was there too . . .

He closed his eyes. Didn't want to bring it back, yet knew he had to. His mind was a fairground ride now. It might make him feel sick, it might scare him, it might make him wish he was dead. But he had to go through with it. He couldn't get off until it had ended.

Until it had shown him everything it had to show him.

The other room. His brother. His sister.

Or the two people his mother had wanted him to call brother and sister.

Both lying there. Blood everywhere. But not dead. Moving. Looking up at him. Pretending. Like it was all some game.

He looked across at Amy. And it was like he was suddenly struck by lightning. He knew. He knew exactly what was happening.

'I'm not a killer,' he said aloud once more. 'And I never have been . . .'

He stared at Amy.

'I know who you are.'

She smiled. 'Well done, Einstein. Now do what you're told.'

'I'm not a killer,' he said. 'I would never kill a child. Never.' He clutched Josephina tightly to him. 'And I won't let you hurt her either.'

'Just do it! Do as you're told. Then it's time to go.'

'I would never kill a child. Never.' He swung the gun round, pointed it at Amy. 'I know who you are.'

Amy was about to throw back a nasty, glib remark at him, but she saw the look in his eyes, stopped.

'I know who you are. And what you've done to me. And my life.'

She said nothing.

'You've taken my life . . .'

He squeezed the trigger.

86

The Golem stopped, his arm round the woman's throat, poised to snap. Dee Sloane had placed a restraining hand on his arm. They both looked towards the sound of the phone ringing.

The Golem didn't want to stop. It didn't matter who was there, he could take care of them too. Take care of all of them. There was nothing he couldn't do. Nothing . . .

Dee Sloane was gesturing silently to him. Nodding her head, moving her arm. The back of the boats. Take the woman to the back of the boats. Continue there.

He nodded and was about to move.

That was when the woman screamed again.

'Help me, oh God, help . . . help me . . .'

The Golem began dragging her, but it was too late. Her screaming had alerted the person on the phone. Or persons. Two of them. Both running towards him.

'Leave her,' shouted Dee. 'Deal with them.'

He dropped the woman, turned to the two newcomers. A man and a woman. The woman's mouth was open and she was shouting something, making an identification of herself, giving him an instruction. She might even have said police, but he wasn't listening. He was doing as he was told.

He moved forward, grabbed her round the throat. She dropped her phone but it kept ringing. He squeezed.

And stopped. Because he was aware of something on his back. He turned. The other one, the Indian man, had picked up an oar and was swinging it towards the Golem's back. And again.

The Golem felt only the slightest irritation, but the man's aim was good and strong and he started to lose his footing. The man was tiring a little but still going. The Golem took his hand away from the woman, turned to face this new challenge. Swung out a fist.

Missed.

The man was small, wiry. Reflexes sharp. He dodged, twisted.

The Golem swung again. The man ducked. The Golem's fist connected with one of the stacked boats. The pile tottered, but didn't fall. The Golem looked at his hand. His knuckles were skinned, splinters of wood sticking out of the exposed flesh like spikes, but he felt nothing. Dr Bracken's pills were wonderful.

Out of the corner of his eye, he was aware of the woman kneeling on the ground, scrabbling for the phone. That couldn't happen. As she reached for it, fingers almost there, he kicked her arm. Heard the bone snap. She screamed, collapsed.

'This is taking too long! Finish it!'

Dee's voice.

The Golem turned, acknowledging his instructions. Turned back to the pair before him.

She was right. Time to finish this.

87

Marina felt as though she had been paralysed and forced to watch her worst nightmare. She couldn't move for fear Stuart Sloane would shoot her daughter. She couldn't stay where she was because she had to do something. Josephina was staring at her. Eyes shining with tears, demanding answers. Why are you standing there? Why won't you help me, Mummy? Answers Marina couldn't give.

The man holding the gun clutched her tighter.

Time slowed down. The voices around her phased out, people began to move in slow motion.

Marina's brother screams, runs past her, heads towards the man with the gun. Moves slowly in Marina's mind, yet also swiftly.

The man swings his gun sideways, away from Josephina. Even from this distance, Marina can see his finger squeezing the trigger, can sense that he is about to fire. She opens her mouth to scream. A dull roar emerges.

Sandro reaches the gunman. And is on him. The gunman looks up, eyes wide with surprise, mouth attempting to speak, no words coming out.

Sandro's hand clamps round the gunman's hand, wrenches the gun away from him, throws it behind him.

The gunman tries to shout something. His words don't make it.

Sandro pulls back his arm, balls his fingers into a fist. Brings the fist down into the man's face.

Hard.

Marina sees the man let go of Josephina.

Her daughter is free.

Time starts again. And Marina is back in the present. She can move once more.

'Josephina!'

Her legs free, she began shoving her way through the crowd. Sandro's exit from the ring had attracted attention. People were beginning to look towards the back of the arena, trying to see what she was looking at, what she was running towards.

She pushed, shouted, tried to force her way through, to get to her daughter. All around her were screams, rushing bodies, crushing her, stopping her from progressing. She caught only glimpses of her brother, her daughter, the crowd pressing in, obscuring her view. She pushed hard, moving forward all the while.

Then stopped suddenly as a pair of big, heavy hands clamped themselves on her shoulders.

She tried to shake them off, couldn't. Turned to scream at them to let her go.

'Don't worry, love,' said a familiar Welsh voice. 'I'm here, I've got you. You're safe now.'

DCI Gary Franks.

She turned back to where she had been headed.

Her brother, her daughter were now completely lost to the crowd.

88

'Taking ages to answer,' said Mickey.

'Maybe she's got a hot date.' Anni was sitting on the desk once more, swinging her legs.

Mickey waited. 'Not going to voicemail, either. Strange.'

'Not really. It is Sunday night. Easter Sunday. Maybe she's at home. Not everyone's like us. Some people have social lives.'

The phone was answered. Mickey held up a hand, indicating this to Anni.

'Hi, Jessie?'

'Oh, so it's Jessie now, is it?' Anni was speaking just loud enough to be heard on the other end.

Mickey waved his hand at her, trying to shush her. 'Mickey Philips here. I'm just—'

He stopped dead. The voice on the other end of the phone spoke.

'You're too late, Mickey Philips. Whoever you are. Much too late . . .'

The line went dead.

Anni had a wisecrack planned. The expression on Mickey's face froze it in her mouth.

'Shit,' he said. 'We've got trouble.'

89

'No!' shouted Marina, throwing off Franks's hand. 'My daughter, my daughter's down there . . .' She wriggled free from him and ran forward. He followed.

All around was chaos. Franks and his team had identified themselves as police officers and the crowd were panicking, desperately clambering towards the exits. The fight was over. The fight to avoid arrest for taking part in an illegal activity had begun.

Marina pushed her way through with a new-found strength. She wished that strength had been in evidence a few minutes ago. Eventually the barn began to clear, and she could make her way through the crowd. She reached the spot where Josephina had been. Her brother and the gunman were being marched away by police officers, arms up behind their backs. The woman she had spoken to on the phone had gone too.

'He's my . . . my brother . . .' she called out, but no one heard her.

She looked round, scanned the faces in the barn. Checked behind the bales, on the seats. Nothing. She turned to Franks, panic rising.

'Where's my . . . where's my daughter?'

He answered, but she didn't hear him. She searched frantically. Pulled everything apart. But the woman was gone.

And so was Josephina.

PART FOUR: RESURRECTION MONDAY

90

Midnight. And Easter Sunday became Easter Monday.

Michael Sloane paced the floor of the hotel room. Or as much as he could, given the tiny space they were in. The Holiday Inn outside Colchester wasn't where they usually stayed, but that was the point. No one would look for them there, Michael had said. Having spent less than half an hour in the room, Dee agreed.

She found it small, anonymous and dull. That must match the kind of people who stayed here, she thought, then felt a shuddering memory. Her own origins were much lower than this. But she was a different person now, and she intended to stay that way.

She sat silently on the end of the bed, ankles crossed, arms behind her, watching Michael pace. She knew better than to approach him or speak to him when he was in this mood. This was no time for their intimate power-playing games. When she saw that look in his eyes, that stiffness in his back, she knew that if she even attempted to intervene or turn the situation into a game, he would hurt her. Normally she would enjoy it, give it back, even, if he was in the right mood. But not when he was like this. When the rage was on him, he could carve her up — or anyone who got in his way.

'What . . . the fuck . . . was he thinking . . . ?'

Dee said nothing. She had not been invited to speak.

'Picking her phone up . . . *speaking* to the caller . . . idiot . . .'

More pacing, more waiting from Dee. Eventually he stopped, turned to her. 'And have you seen him? What's he on? What's Bracken sorted him out with now? He's . . . unravelling. Becoming a danger to us.'

Dee took the direct look from Michael as her cue to talk. 'Let's get rid of him, then,' she said, her voice deferential, her eyes downcast.

'I will,' said Michael. 'When he's finished this job for us, he's gone.' He ran his hand through his hair. 'If he's capable of finishing this job for us.'

The pacing resumed. 'We've let things get out of control, gone too far this time . . . too far. It's time to leave.'

'Where? The country?'

He nodded, still pacing. 'The route's been in place for years in case we need it. Nickoll can stonewall for us until we're away.'

Dee nodded. She had expected something like this to happen sooner or later. It would be sad to go, to leave everything behind. But their lifestyle would continue. They had enough put aside to take care of that. And that was fine. Because the lifestyle would be what she couldn't live without.

'What about the three in the car?'

The two police officers and the Hibbert woman had been left in the 4x4. Parked at the back of the car park, covered by blankets, the Golem watching over them.

'Hibbert I don't care about. But we can't risk them finding the bodies of the police officers. They'll have to disappear.'

Dee nodded. It was what she had expected to hear.

Michael stopped pacing, stood in front of Dee. He grabbed her face, forced it upwards, made her look at him. 'And when they disappear . . . we're gone too.'

She looked into his eyes, tried to smile, as a shiver of fear ran through her.

91

Tyrell stared at the wall in front of him. No. It wasn't a wall; it was a mirror. And he saw himself looking right back. But he knew it wasn't just himself. The mirror was two-way. He couldn't see them, but he knew they were watching. He had been watched all his life. He knew when it was happening.

His hands were in his lap, under the table. His feet together, back relaxed. He felt calm and composed. At ease with himself. He felt the best he had been since he had come out of prison.

Prison. It didn't feel like it at the time, but when he looked back, he realised he had been safe there. Happy, almost. But safe, especially. The safest he had been since childhood. Proper childhood, when it was just him and his mother. Before they went to live in the big house. With the old man who said he wanted to be his father and tried to be kind to him. And the brother and sister who only pretended to be kind to him.

He shuddered. It was one of the memories he had tried to keep hidden because it hurt to think it. But they had all come back now. The good ones along with the bad. He thought of his pretend brother and his pretend sister. How they would smile at him when their father was around or his mother was there. And how they would hurt him when it was just the three of them.

He closed his eyes. Tried to block out the things they had done to him. Too late. He had thought the thought, it was there in his head and he had to see it. He had no choice.

How they would hurt parts of his body. Pull, twist. Hit. How he would scream out and they would make him stop. Threaten to send him away from his mother if anyone heard. He would stop crying, but they wouldn't stop hurting him. They just got worse. Sticks, tennis racquets, cricket bats. Anything was a weapon. And burning him. Tying him up, gagging him, putting lit cigarettes on his skin.

He wriggled in his seat, reliving the memory.

He could feel the rope against his skin, the knots tightening as he tried to pull away from it. He could hear the hiss and crackle of burning skin as the cigarette was applied. Smell again the nicotine smoke, the cooking flesh. His own flesh. Hear the screams and sobs in his head, the cries he couldn't let go, that died against the gag in his mouth.

And he felt sad once more, sad for his mother, sad for himself.

Too ashamed to show his mother the scars, hiding them for years.

Hiding. Hide and seek. He was always the one to hide. And he was always found. But the way they played it was different. If he was found, which he always was, he had to do a forfeit. And the forfeit was always the same. He had to be locked in the cellar.

He hated that cellar. Every time they mentioned hide and seek, he knew it would end up in the cellar. But he couldn't say no. He had tried it a couple of times. They had just hurt him.

The cellar was at the back of the house, right by the river. The water used to come up to the back of the property, and they had a boat moored there. His pretend brother and pretend sister would lift the trapdoor and make him walk down the wooden stairs. Then they would slam it shut and run off, sometimes leaving him there for hours. Even forgetting him completely on a couple of occasions. Inside, it was cold, dark and wet. There was no light, no electricity, no candles even. Just him and the rats. And the slow, swishing sound of the water.

Sometimes when he touched the wall his hand came away wet. His feet too. When the tide came in, the wooden walls would groan with the pressure, sometimes even seep. At first he had been terrified, thinking they would give way and the water would flood in, drown him. But gradually he came to accept it. Could even time how long he was down there by the tides. But he still hated it, it still made him cry.

He shook his head, tried to dislodge the other memories that were coming back. The times his pretend brother and pretend sister would strip him naked before tying him up. Tie him up with his legs apart. He would try to struggle, fight, get away. But it was no good. There were two of them, and they were both stronger than him. The pretend sister, she was stronger than she looked. And sometimes the more vicious of the two.

And then when he was tied up and naked, they would hurt him. It was a different kind of hurt to the cigarette burns. This kind made him scared to touch his own body afterwards. They would shove things inside him. Laugh when he begged or tried to scream. They just shoved harder.

Hurting him like that would excite them. They would strip off in front of him, do things to each other's bodies. Laugh at his pain. They would push parts of their bodies in his face, his mouth. Force him to . . .

He closed his eyes. No. No . . .

Prison. Think of prison. In the cell. Alone. In his head. By himself. His own space. His own time.

He opened his eyes. Looked round. He had forgotten that he was here. In this room. He sighed. Relieved. Even this room was better than where he had been, back in his own head. Anywhere was better than that.

He looked at the mirror once again. Knew they were there. He wondered what they could see. He wished they could see what was inside his head. What he had just seen. If they had, they might have been able to stop it.

He shook his head at the thought. That was just stupid. If they could do that, they would have done it years ago. No. Some things just happened. And no one could stop them. That was life. His life.

He tried to tell himself it didn't matter. Because even with that in his head, he knew who he was now. It had all come back to him. Even that.

His life had come back to him.

92

'He's getting agitated . . . No. That's better. He's calmer now.' Marina looked through the two-way glass, kept observing him. 'Looking at us again. Right there. Like he can see us.'

'Pulling a gun on a kid?' said Franks. 'I'll give him bloody agitated.'

Marina stood, arms folded round her body, staring at him. The observation room was small, usually managing to fit only two people at the most. Although sparsely furnished, it also served as a graveyard for deceased office furniture. The chair Franks was sitting on had seen better days back when John Major was in power. The desk he leaned on was scarred and pitted by the frustrations of a thousand investigations. The filing cabinet behind them a sixties period piece.

Franks took his eyes off Tyrell, glanced at Marina. She looked terrible. Her hair was unbrushed, her clothes dirty and torn. Huge dark rings under her eyes. He couldn't begin to guess what she had been through the past few days.

'Marina . . .'

She kept her attention firmly on Tyrell, nodded to show she had heard.

'Why don't you go home? Get some rest. I can handle things from here.'

'No.' Still staring at Tyrell.

'You shouldn't be here, Marina. You shouldn't have come back here. And you shouldn't be working.'

Marina ignored him.

The bare-knuckle fight had been too tempting to resist for Franks and his team. As an added bonus, it had yielded a pleasant crop of minor local villains engaged in illegal activity, who were currently overcrowding the interview rooms waiting for various solicitors and mouthpieces to arrive.

In the process, though, they had lost Josephina and the woman holding her. They had, however, managed to get Tyrell, and had brought him straight back to the station.

'Marina.' Franks's Welsh baritone was firm with authority. She turned to face him, reluctantly drawing her attention from Tyrell.

'It's after midnight. You haven't slept in God knows when, and you shouldn't be here.'

'But Gary, I—'

He held up his hand. 'Let me finish. If you are directly involved with an investigation, personally involved, then you have to withdraw. You know the rules. And no one's more involved in this than you.'

She said nothing.

'If we want a successful conviction, then we have to be seen to have followed correct procedure. And if I keep you here, then your role could be questioned. Am I right?'

'With all due respect, Gary, I don't care about that. I just want my daughter back.'

He sighed, shook his head. 'And that's exactly why—'

'All right then, look at it this way,' she said. 'It's just gone midnight, like you said.' She pointed to Tyrell. 'And he's sitting right there, probably able to tell us where my daughter is. And you're going to question him. Fine.' She leaned on the desk, stared straight at Franks. 'But look at the state he's in. Mentally. Emotionally. You're going to get nowhere. You're going to need a psychologist. One who's familiar and up to speed with what's going on. And where are you going to get one at this time of night?'

It was Franks's turn to say nothing.

'Right,' she said. 'Apart from the one standing next to you.'

Franks crossed his arms. Set his jaw. It made his features look even more bull-like.

'Besides,' said Marina, 'I couldn't go home and sleep. You know that.'

He sighed. 'Yes. All right. But on your own head be it.'

Marina managed a small, tight smile. 'Thank you.'

'And if this all comes back on us, I'll tell them it was your fault. That you talked me into it with your . . . psychologist's ways.'

Despite the situation, her smile widened. 'My psychologist's ways?'

Franks was reddening. 'You know what I mean. Twisting my words and all that.'

'Fine.' She went back to looking at Tyrell, but a new thought struck her. 'Oh. Another thing.'

'Oh God . . .'

'My brother. He's . . . God knows where. Somewhere in this building. Can we let him go?'

Franks shook his head. 'He was charged with taking part in an illegal activity . . .'

'He was helping me to catch the woman who had my daughter. And that's not why you were there in the first place.'

Another sigh from Franks. 'Fine. Right. Yes. He's an asset to the community and a boon to the force. Let him go. Right.'

'Thank you.'

They both looked once again at Tyrell. Marina took a deep breath. Another. She turned to Franks. 'Ready?'

He stood up. 'Let's go.'

93

Amy's head was pounding. The pain sharp, intense, almost blinding. But she wasn't going to stop. She couldn't stop. Not yet.

The child was screaming. Screaming . . . screaming . . . screaming . . .

'Shut up! Shut up, you little brat.'

Amy pulled the child along by her hair, legs kicking and flailing trying to keep up, trying to walk. Failing.

She looked round, wanting somewhere to put the kid, keep her quiet, shut her up for a while. Because there was still a chance for all this to work out. She just had to think bigger, be bolder, that was all.

The kid kept screaming, wanting its mother, trying to pull away.

Amy turned, twisted the kid by her hair. The kid screamed all the more.

'Oh God, I've had enough of you . . .'

She backhanded her across the face.

The kid's eyes widened in pain and surprise. Then the screaming started again, louder even than before.

This was no good. This had to stop. She needed peace and quiet. She needed to be able to think.

She looked round the house once more. It was falling apart, almost before her eyes. Just how they'd wanted it, just how they had left it. But it had taken longer than they thought it would. She didn't know how it made her feel being back inside. She had thought it would be strange, with ghosts haunting every room, behind every door. Triggers for memories everywhere.

But it wasn't like that. Probably because the house was so dilapidated, so ruined, she found it hard to associate it with the home she used to know. This could be any crumbling old mansion. Any falling-apart Scooby-Doo haunted house.

But still she walked through it, room by room, familiarising herself with the layout, checking everything was still the same, as she had done when she had last been there.

The house's footprint was the same. But things had started to rot, collapse. Curtain rails had fallen, the curtains on them now rotted away to near-cobwebs. Here and there the floorboards had given way. The green and black of damp and mildew clung to the walls, growing, consuming. She touched things that came away in her hand.

Other people had been living there. Tramps, judging by the old newspapers, empty bottles. And the smell. Like someone had died there. Or had lived there on their way to dying. And rats. She could hear them, scurrying about everywhere. Unhappy at having their habitat invaded.

And still the kid screamed.

Then Amy had an idea. She smiled. Perfect.

She dragged the screaming kid towards the back of the house. Found the right room. It was still there. The trapdoor. Not letting go of the kid's hair, she knelt down, pulled. The wood was warped and didn't want to give, but she kept at it. Eventually, with a huge cry and a pain that went all the way up her arm, the trapdoor opened. Still kneeling, she bent down, stared inside. The stairs looked rotten, about to give way. And she couldn't see the floor for water. She leaned further in. The wall was still there, only just holding. And the water was only ankle deep. Perfect.

'You want to play hide and seek?' she said to the kid, a cruel smile on her face. 'Do you?'

The kid didn't answer. Amy doubted she would know what answer to give.

'Doesn't really matter,' Amy said, and hauled the kid over the side into the cellar.

She kept screaming until the trapdoor came down.

Amy stood up. Turned, walked away.

The kid's screams had disappeared. Become just another one of the house's noises. Creaking and groaning and scuttling and scurrying.

The silent screaming from the past.

And the present.

94

Jessie opened her eyes, but it was still dark. She was on her back, a cold, hard floor beneath her. She tried to roll over, get up. Pain shot through her arm, stopping her. She flopped back, gasping for breath.

She remembered going to the aid of Helen Hibbert. Being attacked by . . . God knew who. Some huge grey mountain. He had hurt her arm. She was sure it was broken. And then . . . nothing. Blackness. Then here.

She felt around with her good arm. The floor was metallic. Heavy. She shivered. And became aware of movement. Someone — or something — on the floor also. Right next to her.

'Huh-hello . . . who's there?'

'Me, ma'am,' came a faint voice.

She let out the breath she had been unconsciously holding. 'Deepak . . . you OK?'

'I . . . I think so, ma'am. Just . . . headache. Nothing seems to be broken.'

'Lucky you . . .'

'What?'

'My arm . . .'

'Hello?' Another voice. Female. Scared.

'Helen Hibbert,' said Deepak. 'Is that you? Are you in here with us?'

'Yes . . . yes, it's me.' Her voice small, hesitant. Terrified.

'You OK?' asked Jessie.

'I . . . I think so . . .'

'Good.' Jessie tried to get up once more. Failed. Flopped back again, gasping in pain. She looked round, trying to get her eyes accustomed to the dark. See if she could differentiate, grade the greys. She couldn't.

'Either of you got any idea where we are?' asked Jessie.

'None, ma'am,' said Deepak. 'We were there, then . . . here. I remember the attack, then . . . nothing.'

'Right.' Silence. Jessie listened, tried to make out any sounds that could help. Nothing. They were sealed inside something, that much she knew. Something cold and metallic.

'Helen,' she said. 'Why have they done this? Where are we?'

'I . . . I don't know . . .' Helen Hibbert's voice was on the knife-edge of hysteria. Jessie could sense she was about to panic, to start screaming. She had to keep talking to her, calm her.

'Why did you want to see the Sloanes? I'm assuming they're behind this.'

'I . . . I knew they were responsible for Jeff's death. As soon as you told me.'

'How?'

'Because . . .' She sighed. 'That's what happens when thieves fall out.'

'How did they fall out, Helen?'

'They . . . It was Graham and Amy, as she's calling herself now. They were waiting for Stuart Sloane to be released from prison. Have him assessed, get him declared sane. Contest the will.'

'Will?' asked Deepak. 'Whose will?'

'Michael and Dee Sloane's father, Jack. He made another will when he married Stuart Sloane's mother, making Stuart a full heir. Michael and Dee weren't happy about that. Didn't want him taking their money.'

Jessie tried to ignore the pain, thought. 'So . . . what? They were angry?'

'Oh, very angry. Very, very angry.'

'Are you saying they killed their father?'

'And their stepmother.'

'And . . . what? Blamed Stuart Sloane? How could they have done that?'

Jessie heard a laugh in the darkness. 'They had help. Help that turned on them.'

'Why?'

'That was later . . .' Her voice was drifting.

Jessie was worried the woman would become hysterical. She tried to keep her talking, keep her focused. 'Who helped them, Helen?'

'Graham.'

'Graham Watts?'

'And Jeff. Because Jeff did anything Graham said. But Graham was the one. He arranged it with Michael. He was on hand after the shooting. His job was to give the shotgun to Stuart. Let the retard take the blame, that's what Michael said. Stuart wasn't all there. Suggestible. Graham won Stuart's trust, told Stuart he would help him. Then hung him out to dry.' She gave out a noise that could have been anything between a laugh and a sob in the darkness. 'But really Graham was making sure Stuart had the gun when the police arrived. And that was that. Or it should have been.'

'What happened?'

'With Jack out of the way, we all made a lot of money. The Sloanes, the Hibberts and Graham. Good times. Then it all went wrong.'

'How?'

'Because Michael had his own plans. And Graham didn't like them.'

'What does that mean?'

Helen Hibbert sighed. 'I'm tired . . .' Her voice was beginning to tremble.

Jessie kept questioning her but she would say no more. She tried to think of something positive she could do to head off Helen Hibbert's breakdown. She felt inside her jacket for her phone. Missing. Of course. 'They've taken my phone,' she said. 'Anyone else got one?'

Helen Hibbert just sobbed.

Then came a sudden light. Jessie saw Deepak's face illuminated in the darkness. Like a disembodied spectre, floating before her. She saw him smile.

'Still think I'm stupid for carrying two phones, ma'am?' he said.

Jessie smiled also. 'Did I say stupid? No, you heard me wrong. Brilliant. That's what I said, Deepak, brilliant.'

95

Marina stared at him, trying to read him. Couldn't. She didn't know if that was because of him or because of herself.

Franks had made the introductions, careful not to mention Marina's connection with Josephina, then read him his rights. He had nodded along as he did so, answered when asked to and refused a solicitor. The only stumbling point had been his name.

'Stuart Sloane?'

He had shaken his head. 'No. Not that. No.'

Franks and Marina had shared a look. 'What would you like us to call you, then?'

He put his head back, seemed to be thinking. 'They said I was going to be a new man. Have a new life with a new name. They gave me a new name.'

'And what is it?' Franks was almost smiling, being patient.

'Malcolm Tyrell.'

'Right. OK. Malcolm it is.'

'But I don't want to be called that.'

Franks struggled not to show exasperation. 'So how would you like us to address you?'

Marina picked up the undercurrent to his question. She was left in no doubt how Franks wanted to address him.

'Just . . . Stuart.'

'Stuart.'

'For now.'

Franks bit back his reply. 'Good. Then let's get going.' He gave a sideways glance towards Marina, raised an eyebrow slightly. She knew what it meant: did she want to start the questioning? She gave a slight shake of the head. Let Franks lead.

She could have done this through the two-way mirror. Watched from the observation room, guided Franks through an earpiece. That was how she usually worked with Phil. But this was different. She wanted to be in there, alongside Franks, working up close with him. It felt right, under the circumstances.

She stared, again trying to read Stuart. Again, she couldn't. He seemed to be pleased about something yet at the same time worried. And the two seemed bound together. She didn't yet know what that meant, so she thought it would be best if Franks started and she could make an assessment as they went.

'So, Stuart. Let's start with the most important question. Where's Josephina?'

Stuart's eyes clouded over, brow furrowed, mouth turned down at the edges. He seemed to go into himself.

'Stuart?' Franks leaned forward, keeping his face open, his features as neutral as possible. 'Where's Josephina?'

'I . . . I don't know.'

Marina sat back, trying not to let her frustration show. She wondered, again, whether she couldn't read him because of what was going on inside her own mind rather than his. She was trying to be as professional and detached as possible and finding it more difficult that she had expected. Perhaps Franks was right, she thought; perhaps she should have just gone home.

'Come on, Stuart, you can do better than that,' Franks said. 'Where's Josephina?'

'I . . . I don't know. Honest.' He looked like he was about to cry.

The other two waited.

Stuart spoke again. 'I was . . . was trying to protect her . . .'

'By holding a gun on her?' said Marina. 'Looked like it.'

Franks shot her a look, but she already knew she had said the wrong thing, allowed her emotions to get the better of her. She fell silent.

But Stuart didn't seem to have noticed. 'No, no . . .' he said. 'I was protecting her. All the time, I was protecting her. When . . . when Amy was . . .' his face twisted up, 'not nice to her, to me — I would protect her.' His eyes became downcast. 'And then when we got to the, the barn place . . .' He sighed, shook his head. 'She . . . she gave me the gun. Said, said . . . said she would hurt Josephina if I didn't do what I was told.'

'Hold the gun to her head?' said Franks.

Stuart nodded. 'So, yes. I did it . . . to protect her.'

Franks was about to ask another question, but Stuart keep talking.

'Amy made me. Amy. I hated her. She was . . . horrible. The other one, Jiminy Cricket . . .'

Marina's eyes widened at his words.

'. . . he was nice. I liked him. Or at first I liked him.'

'What happened?' asked Franks.

'He met me out of prison. Took me to the caravan. Told me I was going to have a new life. And he was all nice about it.' Stuart smiled. Then his face darkened once more. 'Then I saw Josephina. Tied up. And . . .' He shuddered. 'Amy wasn't being very nice to her.'

Marina's stomach was turning over. 'In what way, Stuart?' Her voice was calm, quiet, like an oncoming storm.

'She . . . had her tied to the door handle. Said, said if she didn't shut up, she would . . .' He shook his head.

'Go on,' said Marina.

'. . . said she would throw her to the dogs.'

Marina remembered the two dead dogs and was suddenly thankful for whoever had killed them.

'And I didn't like that. No.' Another shake of the head. 'No. So when we had to leave the house, when Jiminy got . . .'

'Killed,' said Franks.

Stuart nodded. '. . . we went . . . I don't know where we went. But then Amy went mad. Even madder. And I said, I said I wouldn't do anything unless she was kind to Josephina. Told her she mustn't harm her or I wouldn't help her. And she didn't. And I helped her.' He smiled.

'Good for you, Stuart,' said Marina. She was trying not to think that her daughter's well-being — her life, even — had been in the hands of a man such as this. That was for later. There were more pressing demands.

'Thank you,' said Stuart, beaming. 'And I told Amy, no more. My mind was made up then.'

'When?' asked Franks.

'At the barn place. When she gave me the gun. I wasn't going to hurt Josephina, even though Amy wanted me to.'

Marina's stomach flipped once more.

'But I was going to hurt Amy.' He smiled. 'I was going to kill her.'

Neither Franks nor Marina spoke.

'I know it's wrong, that you shouldn't do that. I know. But she was . . .' He sighed. 'I didn't know what else to do.' He nodded, as if confirming that his action would have been the correct one. 'But the police stopped me. And brought me here.'

'Yes . . .' said Franks.

'I knew who she was. It happened then. It all came back. All the good things, and the horrible things too.'

Franks shot Marina a glance: help me out here.

'What came back, Stuart?' asked Marina.

'The memories. Because of Amy. And that's why I was going to shoot her.'

'Why, Stuart?'

'Because I know who she is.'

Marina was about to ask another question, but Stuart kept talking.

He smiled. 'And I know who I am now.'

96

Amy sat on the floor of what used to be the living room. Head against the damp, rotting wall. She had taken back her earlier thoughts. The house she used to know was still there. Even in the short time she had been back, the layers had peeled away, like the blackening wallpaper behind her, and the house had begun to reveal itself to her as it once was. As she remembered it.

She swung her torch round, the light illuminating only in patches. She kept trying to make out what was in the shadows, the darkness. She thought she could see things moving in there, jumping out of the way of the beam, trying not to be caught by the light. But they didn't scare her. She welcomed them. Because she knew what they were.

Ghosts. Memories.

The ghosts were all around her. In the darkness, the shadows, when the light moved away from them. She could hear them, see them running from room to room. Feel the warmth from them. Almost touch them. The happiness. Like paradise before the fall.

Before it all went wrong. A dead mother. And a retarded boy.

Then the end of everything.

And this was the room where it had happened.

She looked to where she had once stood. And she saw the ghosts live again.

There was Michael standing in front of her, holding out the shotgun. Pointing it at her. He had already taken care of their father and his new wife. Now he just had to do her and Graham would do him and everything would be set.

'It's going to hurt,' he had said.

'Just do it. Get it over with.' She had closed her eyes. Opened them again just in time to see the look in Michael's eyes, the smile on his face. Just in time to realise that it was going to hurt a lot. That soon she would be as dead as her father.

She had tried to jump out of the way, but the shot still hit her. Michael had been right. It had hurt. And that was the last thing she remembered about that day.

She blinked, back in the present. Looked round again. Saw the house as it was now. Left to rot. To waste away. To decay. To die. Unloved and alone.

She knew just how it felt.

'No . . .' she screamed. The sound echoed and died around the walls. 'No . . .' Much softer, just for her ears alone.

No. It couldn't be the end. It couldn't. There was still one thing she could do. One more roll of the dice, as her father used to say.

Or two, actually.

She took her phone out. Dialled a number she wasn't supposed to know but could never forget.

Waited. For the end.

Or the beginning.

97

Michael Sloane threw the last of his things into the leather holdall on the bed. That would have to do, he thought. It was only stuff he was leaving behind. He could always buy more stuff to replace it later. He could buy more of anything.

Dee was in the bathroom making herself beautiful. He looked at her bag next to his on the bed. Matching. His and hers. Two parts of the same being. Completing each other. That was how he had always felt with her. But he had felt like that before.

His thoughts were interrupted. His phone was ringing.

He took it out, checked the display. Recognised the number. He knew he shouldn't answer. But knew he also had no choice. He put it to his ear.

'Yes.'

'Hello, Michael.'

The voice was ruined and ravaged, but still unmistakable.

Dee came out of the bathroom, looked at him, raised an eyebrow. Wanting to know who was on the phone. She saw the look in his eyes. Knew.

'What d'you want?'

'Is that any way to talk? To me?'

'I'm in no mood for games.'

A laugh. Harsh. Bitter. 'Then you've changed, Michael. You always used to have time for games. Didn't you?'

'What d'you want.' Not even a question, just a flat sentence.

She detected the change in his tone. Knew better than to toy with him any further. 'You,' she said.

'Goodbye.'

'No. Wait. I want to talk. Please. We . . . we have to talk.'

'Why does it have to be now?'

'You know why . . .' She paused, seemed to be gathering herself up, stopping herself from unravelling further. 'It has to be now. After everything that's happened. We have to talk.'

Michael looked at Dee. Mouthed the words: *she wants to talk*. A smile crept on to Dee's features. Her fingers clasped and unclasped. She nodded.

'OK, then,' said Michael. 'We can talk.'

A sigh from the end of the line. 'Good.'

'Where are you?'

'Guess.'

Irritation entered Michael's tone. 'I told you, no more games.'

'Not a game, Michael. Guess.'

He knew. 'The house.'

'The house. I'm there now.'

'See you soon.' He hung up. Turned to Dee. 'As I said. She wants to talk.'

Dee gave another smile. 'That's the last thing she'll want to do when I've finished with her.'

Michael smiled. 'I knew I could rely on you.'

'I'll go straight away.'

'Take the Golem. He should be finished making our unwelcome guests disappear by now. Get her dealt with once and for all. I'll finish up here. You know where to meet.'

She crossed to him, kissed him on the lips, biting down in the process. He pulled away. Smiled.

'Later,' he said. 'Go.'

She went.

He watched her leave, then looked back at the bags on the bed. Side by side. Identical. Completing each other. But he had felt like that before. He thought of where he was going. Thought: it's just stuff.

He could always buy more stuff to replace it later.

98

Mickey lay back and smiled. He couldn't see Anni next to him, but he was sure she was smiling also. Or fairly sure. He checked. Yep. She was smiling too.

'What?' she said.

'Nothing, just . . . nothing.'

She turned over, settled into him. He loved the feel of her warm naked body against his. Hoped he would never tire of it.

'Nothing?' she said. 'Thanks a lot.'

She was smiling as she said it. Or at least he hoped she was. He checked again. She was.

After the call Mickey had made to Jessie James was abruptly ended, he'd got straight on the phone to the force in Suffolk, informed them of what had happened. He didn't like leaving it and walking away, but he had no choice. He didn't know where Jessie had been when she had taken the call — if indeed she had taken the call; if it had been a prank after she had lost her phone, perhaps, or if it had been genuine. Mickey's gut feeling was that it had been genuine. The DI he had spoken to from Suffolk had agreed with him and assured him they would take it from there. Jessie and Deepak were their officers, after all.

Then, as they were finishing up looking through the files on the Sloanes at the station, Franks had called. A catch-up call. He asked them what they had discovered. Mickey told him about the call he had made to Jessie James, its abrupt end. Franks agreed that, procedurally, he had done the right thing.

'Doesn't make it any easier to cope with when you're sitting on your own, though, does it, DS Philips?' he had added.

Mickey had looked at Anni before answering. 'No, sir. Doesn't.'

Franks had then told them about the raid on the bare-knuckle fight. And about finding Marina.

'Thank God for that,' Mickey had said. 'Is she OK?'

'Shaken. We're still looking for the daughter, though.'

'Oh God . . .'

'We're working on it. It'll be a long night.'

'D'you want Anni and me to stay on, sir?' Mickey asked. 'Come and help?'

'Stand down, DS Philips,' Franks had said. 'You two have done enough unpaid overtime for one day. At least I assume it's unpaid.'

Mickey had agreed that it was.

'Then leave it at that. Go home. Go to bed. Get some sleep.'

Mickey — and Anni — had done two of those things.

'What are you looking at me for now?' asked Anni.

Mickey smiled. 'No reason. Just—'

His phone rang. Anni looked at him. 'We're off duty, remember?'

'After the last few days?' said Mickey. 'You think so?'

He answered it, identified himself.

'DI Adrian May. Suffolk Police. You phoned us earlier about DS James?'

'Yeah, that's right. What's happened?'

'We just wanted to let you know that we've heard from DC Shah.'

'Thank God. They OK?'

'The signal was very weak. He mentioned something about DS James being hurt and both of them being taken against their will.'

Mickey sat up. 'Right . . .'

'But we've tried to put a GPS trace on his phone.'

'Where is it?'

'Harwich, we think.'

'Harwich? Our patch.'

'Exactly.'

Mickey glanced at Anni. She was sitting upright too, the sheets having fallen away from her body. She was beautiful, but he didn't have time to register that. She was also looking concerned.

'Do you . . . need us as, I don't know, liaison or something?'

'If you don't mind.'

Mickey said he didn't, ended the call.

'What's happening?' asked Anni.

Mickey told her. They were dressed and out of Mickey's flat in record time.

99

'You're Stuart, yes?' asked Marina, bending forward, trying to keep the urgency from her voice. 'That's who you are.'

Stuart nodded. Looked relieved to have been recognised.

'Then who is Amy, Stuart? Who is she?'

Stuart leaned back, seemed to study the ceiling.

'Who is she, Stuart? Who's Amy? Who is she?'

Franks gently placed his hand on Marina's arm. She relented, sat back. Stuart looked at them, a hurt expression on his face.

'There's no need to get nasty. I'm going to tell you.'

Marina nodded, tried to slow her hammering heart. 'Good. That's good to hear, Stuart. So who is she?'

'She's . . . Amy wanted to be my sister. Or she said she did. But she was only pretending. She didn't really want to do that. She didn't really like me.' His voice dripped sadness. 'She only pretended when other people were around. So she could get to be near me. And when she was near me, she would hurt me . . .' He clasped his arms round his body. Began to rock slowly back and forward.

Marina knew she didn't have much time. If Stuart's mood changed, if he slipped into a fugue state or became uncommunicative, she knew the interview would be over. And if that ended, then perhaps her daughter's life would too.

It was clear that he was damaged and she had to tread carefully. She tried another approach. One that might not excite him as much. 'She wanted you to talk to me, Stuart, didn't she?'

He frowned. 'Are you the doctor?'

'I'm a psychologist, yes.'

'Are you Josephina's mother?'

Marina looked at Franks, who nodded. 'Yes,' she said, 'yes I am.'

'I looked after her for you.'

Marina put her hands on the table to stop them trembling. 'Thank you for that, Stuart. I'm very grateful.'

He accepted the thanks by nodding, then frowned. 'You're here to tell me whether I'm mad or not, aren't you?'

'Well, I'm . . . Yes. That's . . . Yes.'

'Yeah.' He nodded again. Stopped rocking. 'Yeah. I've seen a lot of doctors like you. Lots and lots. They always asked me questions. Always wanted to know things. Things in my head.'

'And did you tell them?'

He shook his head. 'No. Things in my head are private.'

'They certainly are, Stuart,' Marina said, and noticed a glimmer in his eyes. Please let that be some kind of connection, she thought. Please. For Josephina's sake. 'I won't ask you about the private things in your head.'

'Good.' He looked relieved once more.

'But I do want to know why Amy wanted you to talk to me. Can you tell me that?'

Another nod. 'So I could have a new life. So I could have a future.'

'Right. And how was this future going to happen?'

'You were going to talk to me and then you were going to tell them that I wasn't mad and then I was going to be given a lot of money.' He shrugged. 'And we were all going to be happy.'

Marina nodded. 'Right. So . . . was there a will, Stuart? Was that it? Did I have to declare you sane so you could inherit the Sloanes' money along with the brother and sister?'

Stuart shuddered at the mention of the brother and sister, but nodded.

'And how much money were you going to get, Stuart?' Franks's Welsh baritone cutting in.

Stuart smiled, put on a bad cockney accent. '"You stick with me, this time next year we'll be millionaires." That's what Jiminy said.'

'Right.' Franks nodded. 'And this was the Sloanes' money?'

Stuart said nothing.

Franks leaned forward. 'So they killed their father? Is that what you're saying? You didn't do it, they did?'

He frowned. 'I hate guns.'

'Good,' said Marina. 'That's good. And you wouldn't use one?'

He shook his head.

'Good. And then what? You were going to sue for wrongful imprisonment, something like that?'

Stuart looked at the ceiling once more. 'We were all going to be happy.'

Marina could tell his concentration was slipping, that she was losing him. She kept going. 'And Amy? What would she get out of this?'

'She would be rich as well. She wanted to spend the money with Jiminy, but he got killed. So she would spend it on her own.'

'And,' said Franks, clearing his throat, 'did she want to be your sister again?'

'Pretend,' said Stuart.

'Pretend to be your sister again?'

'I don't know. I didn't want her to.' He yawned. 'I'm Stuart.' He nodded once more. 'Stuart Milton.'

'Right,' said Marina. 'You are.'

'Stuart Milton.'

'Yes.'

'Not Sloane.'

'No. Not Sloane.' Marina leaned forward once more. 'Where is Amy now, Stuart? Where is she?'

'She went home.'

'Where's home, Stuart? Where would her home be?'

Stuart stretched, arms up in the air, then yanked down suddenly. 'I'm tired now. Want to sleep.'

He closed his eyes.

Marina wanted to scream.

100

Amy put the phone down, looked at it. One call made. One more to go.

The house was creaking and groaning; a noise made in one place would be answered by something in another. It was carrying on a conversation with itself that she couldn't be part of. And she wanted to be, like she used to be. When she was part of it. And it was part of her. She wanted her old life back. But she couldn't. She knew that.

But she could try.

She pulled the wig off, threw it on the floor. No point in hiding any more. Not here. Not in this house. She could never hide anything from this house. It was the place where she had always been most truthful. She rubbed at her face, wiping away what make-up was left. She wanted to be herself once more. For her own sake. For the house.

But it wasn't enough.

So, ignoring the cold, the shivering from her body, she began to remove her clothes. She would hide away no longer. She would face herself. Now. Truthfully. Not as she used to be, or as she wanted to be. But as she was. Now.

No more lies, no more hiding. It was the end of that. And the beginning of something else.

She kicked the pile of clothes away. Stood naked in what used to be the living room. Where the bodies had been blown apart by the shotgun blasts. Where a family had ended that day. Where a life had ended. Where it would now be born again.

She picked up the phone. One more call to make. Then everything would be ready.

A new life rising out of the old.

101

'Stuart? Stuart.'

Stuart Milton opened his eyes. He looked irritated at the intrusion. 'I'm tired,' he said, a note of petulance in his voice. 'I want to go to sleep.'

'Stuart, we know you're tired,' said Franks, 'and we don't want to keep you up past your bedtime.'

Marina raised her eyebrows at his choice of words.

Franks ignored her, continued. 'We'll let you go to sleep. But first you have to answer some more questions for us. Will you do that, please? We wouldn't ask if it wasn't important.'

'And then can I sleep?'

'You can sleep.'

'Can I go back to prison?'

Franks and Marina exchanged a look. 'If . . .' Franks shrugged. 'If you want to. I'm sure we could arrange it. Or something like it.'

Stuart, eyes closed again, nodded. Smiled. The right answer.

'But you have to answer our questions first.'

Stuart reluctantly opened his eyes. He didn't look happy. He was drifting. Marina knew they didn't have long.

'So Amy's gone home,' she said.

Stuart nodded, eyelids fluttering.

'Where's home, Stuart? Where's home for Amy?'

'The house,' he said, irritably. 'The house where she lives.'

'The house? Which house?'

'Her house.' Even more irritable. They were starting to lose him.

Marina reached across the table, took Stuart's hands in her own. His eyes shot open and he jumped as if he'd been given an electric shock.

'Come on, Stuart. Just a little bit more. Help us out here.'

'Oh . . . OK.'

'Amy's house, Stuart. Where is it?'

He looked uncomfortable, wriggled in his chair.

'Where is it, Stuart? Where can we find it?'

More wriggling.

'Can you draw me a map?'

He shook his head. 'No. I don't . . . don't want to go back there.'

'Go *back* there? You've been before?'

He nodded. Tried to pull his hands away from Marina. She wouldn't let him go.

'When were you there, Stuart? With Amy?'

He nodded.

'When?'

'When . . .' He shook his head again, closed his eyes. Not to sleep this time, more to dislodge the memories that were there. 'No . . .'

Marina held on to his hands. 'Please help me, Stuart. Try and think. It'll help Josephina.'

Stuart looked up at the name. Marina pressed on.

'When were you there, Stuart? When was Amy there?'

'When she . . . my mother . . .'

Marina said nothing, waited.

'When . . . when Amy was pretending to be my sister.'

'And when was that? Just recently?'

He shook his head. 'Time isn't like that,' he said. 'Time bends. It doesn't go in straight lines. It curves. Bends round back on itself.'

'It does, yes,' said Marina, not letting go, 'but when were you in the house with Amy?'

'When she . . . when she was pretending to be my . . . sister.'

Franks leaned forward. 'When she was pretending to be your sister,' he said, voice low and authoritative, 'was she called Amy?'

Stuart shook his head. 'No.'

Marina and Franks shared another look. 'What was she called, Stuart?' asked Marina. 'What was she called when she was pretending to be your sister?'

He looked at them both as if the answer was obvious.

'Dee, of course.'

102

Dee had switched the car's headlights off as she approached the house and drove slowly down the narrow, isolated lane. She wanted her arrival to be as inconspicuous as possible.

Not that it mattered. Her passenger gave her such a clear advantage in any situation that she could have turned up in an ice cream van with the chimes blaring. She turned to the Golem.

'You know what to do?'

He nodded. She studied him. His lips had been moving the whole journey, as if in silent dialogue with himself. And she recognised drug-addled eyes when she saw them.

'Are you up to this?'

He nodded again. Gave a smile as if someone had told a joke only he had heard.

'Then go. You know where to meet, what to do.'

'I know what to do,' he said.

'Go and do it, then.'

He slipped out of the car and was soon just one more shadow in the night.

She looked up at the house. It was desolate, haunted-looking. She couldn't imagine how anyone could grow up in it, or call it home. But then she thought of the place she had called home. Unhappy childhoods could happen anywhere.

She got out of the car, left it unlocked in case the beeping of the key alerted anyone to her presence. Anyone. She knew who she meant. The woman she had replaced. The real Dee Sloane.

She had met Michael Sloane in a hotel while she was working as an escort, back when she had another name. Not the one she had been given at birth, but the one she had chosen for herself when she had created her first new identity. She had left her family home in Oldham at the first opportunity, determined to make something of her life. She had got as far as Manchester city centre and an escort agency.

Sloane was away on business, staying in a hotel, and wanted a little excitement. His own kind of excitement. He had called the agency, been specific. What the girl should look like, how much damage he would do to her. How much extra he would pay for doing it. They turned him down. He offered them more. Much more. They set about finding a girl who would do what he wanted.

She volunteered. It wasn't anything she hadn't done before. Or had had done to her. Except this time she would be paid for it. Highly paid. The money would help cushion the blows.

So she turned up at his hotel room, dressed as he wanted, following the script. And something clicked. She knew it from the way he looked at her as soon as she entered the room. As soon as he touched her. She felt that thrill of electricity shoot through her. He did too. She knew it. She could tell.

She stayed the night. He did exactly what he had said he would do with her. And she loved it. She would have done it for nothing. She told him that.

'Never say that,' he said. 'Never sell yourself short.'

And that was the start of it. He always asked for her when he was in Manchester on business. And he seemed to be on business an awful lot. Sometimes he just came up to see her. They talked. Got to know each other. He was rich but unhappy. Lonely. His partner — that was how he always referred to her, his partner — was ill. Mentally and physically. And it was an enormous strain on him. He felt responsible for it, and in a way he was. He had everything he had always wanted. But it didn't seem to be enough.

She had heard similar things before. Rich businessmen who claimed to be unhappy with their wives and families. Who wanted the excitement of someone like her. She thought he was just another one of those.

She was wrong.

Because one day he made her a proposition.

'Are you happy as you are?'

'I'm fine,' she had said. This wasn't the first such request she had fielded away. She had the answers prepared. 'I make a good living. I have freedom. I'm independent.'

'No,' he said. 'That's not what I meant. Are you happy being the person you are? Or would you like to be someone else?'

And then he told her what he wanted. Live with him. Let him remake her in the image he desired. Answer to a different name. Get a different face. A new body. Become a different person.

'Why not get someone else? Someone who looks like that already?'

'Because it's you I want. You're perfect. On the inside. I just want the outside to match.'

That had made sense to her.

'And you'll still have your freedom,' he said. 'But it'll be the freedom to do what I tell you.'

She had smiled. And agreed.

And she had become Dee Sloane.

Slowly at first. Painstakingly so at times. But worth it in the long run. She had asked questions, naturally. Who was the real Dee? What had happened to her? And he had told her.

'She . . . was involved in an accident. A shooting accident. I did what I could for her, tried to rescue her, rebuild her . . . I did what I could.'

'And she's dead?'

'She's . . . no longer with us.'

She knew what he meant.

And the more she became what he wanted her to be, the more he told her. Dee had been his sister. Did she have anything to say about that? She didn't. In fact it just gave her an added frisson. The shooting wasn't accidental. It had been planned. She had guessed as much. And did she mind? Why would she mind?

'Perfect,' he said.

And they were.

Now she wasn't going to let anyone get in the way of their relationship. No matter what it took.

She stepped into the house. It stank of decay, neglect. Corruption. The air felt cold and damp. Things darted away out of the corners of her eyes. She moved forward to where Michael had told her to go. Into the main living room.

She would be there, he had said. After what had happened, she wouldn't be anywhere else.

She stepped into the living room. Something moved at the far end, over by the wall. Something bigger than a rat. Dee fought the urge to turn, to run away. Stood her ground.

'So.' A cracked voice came out of the darkness. 'The second wife meets the first wife. At last.'

A light went on. Sharp, blinding after such darkness. Dee screwed her eyes tight shut. Opened them again slowly. The figure before her was holding a gun on her. She looked at that, felt fear. Then looked at the figure itself.

And her stomach churned.

103

'DI May.' The handshake was firm, strong. Balding, grey-haired and bearded, DI May seemed like an old-school copper. His accent was rough, working-class Essex tempered by learning and experience.

Mickey gave his own name. Anni did likewise. 'Right,' Mickey said. 'What have we got?'

'We believe DS James and DC Shah were working the same street as you two,' May said.

'Yeah,' confirmed Mickey. 'Couple of murders, missing person, kidnapped child and the Sloane family involved somehow.'

'Ah,' said May, smiling, 'Suffolk's Howard Hughes. Local royalty. The untouchables.'

'So we believe,' said Anni.

They were standing at the gates to the freight port at Harwich. The mist had returned, and with it the cold. Mickey and Anni were shivering. The parking bays were virtually empty, the lorries and trucks all loaded and left. Ahead of them stood berthed cargo ships and tankers. The floodlights ringing the walls shone down hard, making the scene look bleak and desolate.

May was bundled up inside a quilted jacket, but he still looked cold. 'And you . . . what?' he said to Mickey. 'What happened exactly?'

Mickey told him about the phone call. The message. May nodded.

'Well we've pinpointed DC Shah's GPS signal. That's a bonus. Weak. So we'd better get a move on.'

'Whereabouts is it?' asked Mickey.

May pointed at one of the cargo ships. 'Over there, apparently.'

'The ship?' asked Anni. 'That one there?'

May nodded. 'Far as we can make out. Had our experts in analysing it. Wanted to get it checked as quickly as possible before his battery went.'

'Who's the ship registered to?' asked Mickey.

May smiled. 'Good question. Sloane Holdings.'

'I think that confirms it, then. Do we need a warrant?'

'Acting on information received, DS Philips.' May looked round. There were another three officers with him. Both looking as thrilled as Mickey and Anni to have been dragged out of bed in the middle of the night.

'You ready?' he said.

They were.

'Let's go, then.'

104

'Where is he, then?'

The woman was speaking, but Dee wasn't hearing her. She was staring, open-mouthed. The woman before her, the one who used to be Dee Sloane, was completely naked.

'Where is he?' Screaming now.

Dee managed to recover enough from the sight in front of her to force some words out. 'He's . . . busy. He sent me.'

'Busy? Busy?' Body vibrating in anger. 'Too busy to see me? Bastard . . .' The words were spat out. She moved closer to Dee. 'Too busy.' She smiled. 'Like what you see? Do you?'

Dee was trying not to look, wanted to turn her head away, close her eyes. Anything. But she kept on staring, eyes drawn to the sight before her as to a car crash. Wanting to see the mutilation, the destruction. Wanting to say, thank God that's not me there.

'This is what it looks like. When you've been brought back from the dead . . .'

Her body had once been female. There was only one breast, and even that looked mangled. In place of the other one was a collection of grafted skin and scar tissue, by turns smooth and ridged, in varying shades of red. The scars stretched down the side of her body, creating a swirling vortex of flesh on her side.

But it was her face that was the worst. Her face and her head.

She was bald but for a few odd tufts of hair sprouting in between healed scars and grafts. Her skull was uneven, misshapen, covered in crests and craters, like a shattered egg that had been put together again without the instruction manual. Without make-up, the lines on her patchwork skin were vivid and throbbing. She had taken out the partial palate that held her false teeth, letting her mouth collapse in on itself on one side. One ear was just a curled stub.

And her hand, clawed and gnarled, was shaking as it held the gun on Dee.

'This is what he did to me . . . Take a good look, go on. Stare. This is his creation. This is what he made of me.'

Dee's mouth worked furiously but no sound emerged. No words seemed adequate.

'And he's not coming . . .' Amy shook her head. 'Not coming . . .' She dropped her head and with it the light.

Dee thought she would be thankful that the beam had been taken away from the deformed body, but the shadows it cast made the sight even worse.

Amy looked up once more. 'Why you? I don't want to see you. Why you and not him?'

Dee felt she had to answer this time. 'Because I . . . I wanted to see you.'

'You wanted to see me?' Her voice was getting louder. 'You wanted to see me?' She stepped closer. 'Well now you've seen me. Look. Go on, look.' She swung the torch over her body again. 'And don't stop looking.' Her voice reduced down to a hiss now. 'This will be you. Oh yes . . . this will be you.'

'What . . . what d'you mean?'

'When he gets bored of you. When he wants rid of you.'

Amy stepped closer. Reached out a hand.

'I want to touch you . . .'

Dee tried hard not to scream.

105

'Here.' Sloane held out his hand. A thick pile of notes in it.

The money was taken without even a smile.

'Enough?' Sloane knew the answer already. He wouldn't have asked the question otherwise.

The other man nodded, as expected. 'Quite sufficient, thank you.'

'Good.'

Sloane looked round. Listened. He could hear nothing but the low hum of the ship's motors as they turned over. The slap of water against the side of the hull. Nothing unusual or out of the ordinary.

Good.

The ship's captain was a man used to asking no questions. He had as many blind eyes to turn as Sloane had notes to give him. Working for the Sloanes, he had discovered it a useful commodity.

Sloane watched the money disappear inside the man's coat. 'You know what to do?'

The captain nodded. 'Same as usual. I know.'

'Yes, I know you know.' Sloane's eyes lit up with annoyance. 'Humour me. Imagine I'm the man paying you and I want to make sure you know what's happening. Go over it one more time.'

If the captain was angry at Sloane's words, he didn't show it. His employer could be difficult at times, but there were compensations. 'When we get out to sea, jettison one of the containers.'

'The one that doesn't appear in the ship's manifest. The one that isn't here.'

The captain nodded.

'Good.' Sloane looked round once more. Listened. Nothing. 'One more thing. You've got an extra passenger.'

The captain frowned. This was a deviation from the script. 'Who?'

Sloane smiled. 'Me.'

The captain's eyes widened. 'But . . . this is unexpected. I'll have to—'

'You don't have to do anything. I'm not here officially. I'm not crew, I'm not a passenger. I'm a paying stowaway. And there's only you and me to know about it, OK?'

The captain nodded, knowing how much another blind eye would pay.

'Good. How soon before we set sail?'

The captain checked his watch. 'Couple of hours. First light. Wait for the tide.'

Sloane nodded. Smiled. 'Plenty of time for you to find me a cabin, make myself comfortable.'

'Will there be just you on the voyage, Mr Sloane? Or will anyone else be joining us?'

Sloane thought for a moment.

'Just me,' he said.

106

'Dee Sloane? Pretending to be your sister?' Franks was confused.

Stuart just nodded as if it was perfectly obvious.

'Yes,' said Marina. 'Yes.' Understanding hit her like a sudden flash of electricity through her synapses. 'The woman on the phone. To me. Is that who you mean?'

Stuart nodded patiently, as if he was the only intelligent person in the room, explaining a simple point to a couple of thickos.

'She's Dee Sloane.'

He nodded again.

'The real Dee Sloane, is that what you mean?'

Franks looked between the two of them, not understanding what was going on.

'What gave her away, Stuart? How did you know?'

'The eyes,' he said. 'She looked different. Less . . . nice. Than before. But she couldn't hide her eyes . . .'

Franks turned to Marina. 'What's he talking about?'

'The woman who's been phoning me, the woman who's got my daughter, is Dee Sloane.'

'But . . . who's the woman with Michael Sloane? The one who's claiming to be his sister?'

'No idea,' said Marina. 'But she's not Dee Sloane.'

'Why not?'

Marina turned to Stuart. 'Why not, Stuart?'

He looked confused.

'You said she looked less nice. What did you mean?'

'Less nice. Less . . . pretty. Not like before. She was pretty before. She's not now.'

He shivered.

Marina turned to Franks once more. 'Dee Sloane was hit with a shotgun blast. When her father and Stuart's mother were killed. She almost died, but she and her brother survived. She took a lot of patching up, though. Maybe it was . . . I don't know. Too much work?'

'You mean replace her with another model?' asked Franks.

'Stuart says he didn't kill his mother and stepfather and attempt to kill his stepsister and brother. He says Michael Sloane did. Now if Sloane is the kind of person who would engineer a shooting like that, it's not beyond the bounds of possibility that he would replace his sister, wouldn't you say?'

'But . . . shoot his own sister?'

'Why not? He shot his own father and stepmother. If this hypothesis is right.'

'Still . . .'

'Gary.' Marina lowered her voice, tried to keep the conversation as private as possible in front of Stuart. Stuart showed no signs of listening. 'Someone shot that family. I worked the original case and I never for one minute believed it was this gentleman here.'

Franks said nothing.

Marina leaned forward once more, trying to engage Stuart before he drifted off to sleep again. 'You said she'd gone home, Stuart.'

Stuart looked confused. 'What?'

'The real Dee,' said Marina, as patiently as she could manage. 'Your pretend sister. You said she'd gone home.'

Stuart thought for a few seconds, eyelids drooping.

'Stuart . . .'

He jumped. 'Yes. Home. Yes.'

'Good.' Marina nodded. 'Good. Where is home, Stuart?'

Stuart looked puzzled once more.

'Home,' she persisted. 'Where is it?'

'Home?' he said. 'Well it's . . . home.' His eyelids closed once more.

Franks sighed. Marina kept staring at Stuart.

'We could look it up,' said Franks. 'Check some records.'

Marina stood up. 'No need. I know where she is.'

107

Dee stepped backwards, tried to stay out of the woman's reach. 'Don't.' Her voice was small, trembling.

Amy stopped moving. Put her head on one side, like a dog listening. The torch lit up her eyes. It wasn't pleasant. 'Why not? Afraid it'll rub off on you? Afraid if I touch you, you'll end up like me?'

'I . . .' Backing away. 'I . . .'

'I just want to touch you. Where's the harm in that? Feel what I used to feel like . . .'

Amy advanced once more. This time Dee stayed where she was. It was better, her mind quickly and reluctantly rationalised, to let a madwoman with a gun touch you rather than shoot you. The Golem must be around somewhere, she thought, but even he wouldn't be quick enough to stop a bullet from close range.

Amy moved in close to her. Her breath smelled like the rotting house around them. She reached out a hand, stroked Dee's cheek. Her fingers were rough, callused. Like being touched by tree bark. Dee tried not to move.

'It's . . . it's like looking in a mirror, one that takes you back in time . . .' Her voice was low, calm. Almost a whisper. 'How much?'

'What?'

'How much did it cost? To make . . . whoever you were . . . look like me?'

'I . . . I don't know. Lots.'

'Lots.' Amy nodded as if she had given the correct answer. 'Lots.'

'He . . . he said he wanted me to, to look more beautiful. Said I would, I could, if I would let him do it.'

'And you did.' Still stroking her cheek. Eyes travelling all over her features, appraising her. Her expression changeable; sometimes like she was looking at old love letters, sometimes like a farmer at a livestock market. 'You did . . .'

Encouraged by Amy's tone, Dee continued to talk. 'I didn't mind,' she said. 'What he wanted to do. It hurt, but . . .'

'Yes.' Still stroking. Still the same quiet voice. 'My operations hurt too.'

'More beautiful. That's what he said. And that's what I am. Beautiful.' Dee looked at Amy. Found strength in her words. Her position. Because she was the winner. She was young, beautiful. And she had Michael. This mad old woman had nothing. She smiled. 'He recognised something in me. We connected. Like no one I've ever met before. We're soulmates.'

Amy drew back, her hand falling to her side. She stared Dee in the eye. 'Pathetic. Soulmates. You know nothing.'

'I know everything.'

'You know nothing.' Her voice rising, starting to shake once more. 'About him. About me. Nothing.' She stood where she was, still staring at Dee. 'Soulmates. That's what we were. He wanted me. And I wanted him. We had each other. All that we needed. We were our world.' Her face twisted. 'And then the boy arrived . . .'

'I know all this,' said Dee. 'He's told me. How the two of you hated Stuart. How your father wanted to make him part of the family, marry his mother. How he wrote a new will with him in it, threatened to write you out if you complained.'

'He told you all this, did he?'

'He did. How he faked the shotgun attack, made it look like Stuart had done it. And he told me how sad he was about what happened to you.'

'You were doing so well up until the last part. The last part's a lie.'

'He said he went all over Europe, taking you to specialists to fix you up.'

Amy was beginning to shake with anger. 'That was what he told you, was it? Even he couldn't bear to be seen as a bastard. Even he . . .'

'What d'you mean?'

'You think it was an accident? What happened to me? Do you? He shot me . . .'

'He said he had to make it look real.'

'Bullshit. I looked in his eyes and I saw it. It just . . . went wrong, that's all.' She shook her head. Eyes fluttering, miles away. 'Do you know . . . do you know what it feels like to watch the man you love . . . the absolute, total love of your life, the only person you're ever going to feel like that about, pick up a gun, point it at you and . . .' Amy stared at Dee with renewed hatred. 'He's gone, you know.'

'What d'you mean?'

'Left you. Dumped you.'

'No, no, he hasn't . . .'

'Yes he has.' The words spat out. 'I know what he's like. He wouldn't have sent you here if he hadn't left you. He's gone off without you.'

'He wouldn't do that . . .'

Amy laughed. It sounded like something was being dislodged inside her. 'Yeah . . . that's what I said. He wouldn't do anything to me. Wouldn't hurt me . . . But he did, didn't he? Tried to kill me. Thought it would be easier to find a new one, make her the way he wanted, rather than make me well again . . .'

She swung the gun on Dee. Started squeezing the trigger.

Dee looked round, desperately trying to signal to the Golem.

But he was nowhere to be found.

108

'Where?' asked Franks, looking puzzled. 'Where is she?'

Marina looked at him, didn't answer. She leant over the desk, brought her face right up against Stuart's. 'Home,' she said, her voice loud enough to make him open his eyes. 'Home.'

He nodded, closed his eyes again.

'It's the house, isn't it? The one in Wrabness? The one the Sloanes wanted to let crumble away?'

He didn't answer. She reached over, shook him by the shoulders.

'Isn't it?'

'Leave me alone . . .'

She pulled him up close to her. Franks made to stop her, but she gestured at him to leave her alone. He dropped back. Stuart's eyes were wide and staring, like he had been woken from a particularly deep sleep.

'No, Stuart, I won't leave you alone. Amy has taken my daughter, Josephina, the little girl you said you wanted to protect, to the house in Wrabness, hasn't she?'

Stuart nodded.

Marina let him go. She looked at Franks.

'Wrabness,' she said, eyes lit by triumph. 'Let's go.'

109

Mickey had never liked ships. And containers at Harwich held equally bad, violent memories for him. But he put that all aside. He had work to do.

Harbour security was minimal as May and his team had driven up to the main gate. May had shown his warrant card and explained that two senior officers had gone missing, believed to have been abducted and placed on board the waiting cargo ship. The two rent-a-cops on the gate had jumped to attention. This was the most action they had ever seen on duty. They allowed the car through with no fuss. May asked them not to contact the ship and, thrilled at being in the presence of real coppers, they agreed.

They had embarked from the cars, stood on the pier. Mist and fog settled on them, dampening their clothes and hair, belabouring their breathing. May turned to his second in command, DS Terry.

'What's it say, Philip?'

DS Terry scrutinised a hand-held device, looked around. Converted what he saw on screen to what was in front of him.

'That ship,' he said pointing to the one in front of them. 'Somewhere near the back.'

May nodded. 'Come on then.'

The walkway was long, raked. The ship, one of several, looked huge against the pier, the cars, the people. A vast metal town. But Mickey was sure it would look tiny once it was out to sea, dwarfed against the waves.

The containers were piled high in the centre of the ship. Multicoloured, uniform and battered, they looked like enormous grubby bricks in some oversized, rusted Lego set.

The six officers arrived onboard and were met by a crew member. Bleary-eyed and unshaven, his eyes darting warily, guiltily about, he looked to Mickey not like a ship's crewman but more like the kind of guy who operated fairground rides. Mickey never felt comfortable on fairground rides.

May flashed his warrant card once more. 'The captain around?'

'Got a warrant?'

'Don't need one.' May pushed past him, made his way to the bridge.

The captain was waiting for them. Face calm but looking warmer than the night air would have suggested.

May explained who he was, why he was there. 'We have reason to believe two of my officers have been kidnapped and are being held on this ship. We'd like your permission to search.'

'You need a warrant for that.'

'Or your co-operation. Probable cause.'

The captain shrugged. 'We're preparing to sail on the morning tide. Get a warrant.' His voice displaying studied disinterest.

May was about to speak, but Mickey stepped in. 'Listen, mate,' he said, 'it's the middle of the night and we can't get a warrant until morning, as well you know. During which time you'll have sailed away and left us to it. Well, we can't let you do that. We'll make sure you're delayed here for as long as necessary. Could take us days to get a warrant. And all the while you're going nowhere. And losing money. You want that?'

That got his attention. 'You don't know who owns this ship.'

'I do know who owns this ship. And we're not leaving until we've searched it.'

The police officers stood their ground. The captain had no choice but to allow them access. He gave a small, defeated wave.

'Thank you,' said May. 'Now let me see the ship's manifest.'

The captain reluctantly handed it over.

'Right.' May looked at Mickey. 'You and DC Hepburn take the stern.'

'That's the back, right?' said Anni.

'Correct.' He divided up the rest of his team into port and starboard.

'All the terms,' said Anni, impressed.

'Grew up on a narrowboat outside Harlow,' said May. 'Right. I'll take the pointy end. Let's go.'

Mickey and Anni made their way towards the back of the ship. It was quite bright due to the overhead pier lights, but Mickey still swung a torch left and right. They stood before a stack of containers and looked up. He held the torch on them. They were piled so high, the beam died.

'Great,' said Anni. She put her hand on the first one. 'Let's start here, shall we?'

She worked the handle, swung the door open. Mickey shone the torch inside. The beam picked out stacked cardboard boxes.

'Something going outbound,' he said, then turned to her. 'Hey, that's a thought.'

'What?'

'Well, it might be worth checking that list—'

'The manifest,' said Anni.

'Yeah,' said Mickey. 'I'm betting most of these are going out empty.'

'Why?'

'Because we hardly make anything any more. We import. So we check the empty ones first.'

'Good idea.'

'Right, let's—'

A noise from the other side of the container stack. Like someone had been listening, was trying to get away.

Mickey and Anni shared a glance. Mickey gestured with his eyes; Anni nodded. They divided up either side of the container, began to creep round.

Another sound before they had got halfway. Someone moving away quickly.

Mickey sprinted to the corner. A figure was running towards the middle of the ship. Male, tall, well dressed. Suede jacket. He turned back to face them. Mickey recognised him. He had last seen him sitting in the back of a police car in Aldeburgh.

Calling himself Stuart Milton.

'Come on,' he shouted to Anni, and gave chase.

110

'No. Definitely not.'

Marina stopped walking, not believing what she had just heard. 'No? What d'you mean, no?'

Franks stopped walking also, turned, came back to her. 'I mean no.'

They were in the corridor outside the interview room. Stuart Milton had been left to sleep while they went about putting the circus together to ride on Wrabness. Or at least Marina had thought that was what they were doing.

'But that's not fair. After what I've just done . . . Gary, that's my daughter out there. I've got to come. No question.'

'I'm sorry, Marina, but you're not. It's my decision. I listened to your arguments and let you in there and you did a damned good job. But you're a psychologist. Your presence on a police field operation could be detrimental to its success. So I'm sorry, but no.'

Marina didn't know what to say, how to reply.

Franks's features softened. 'I'm sorry, Marina, I really am. If there was a way you could be there, I would let you.'

She said nothing.

'You can stay here. Or you can go home. But you can't come with us. I'm sorry. We'll call you as soon as we can.' He gave a tight smile. 'With good news, I hope.'

She felt like she was about to explode. 'I'm not some fucking grieving relative, Gary. I'm one of the team. A valued member. Or I thought I was.'

Franks's eyes widened. Clearly unhappy with women swearing. 'You are,' he said. 'Of course you are.'

'Yeah,' said Marina. 'Right.' She turned away from him, strode off down the corridor towards the reception area. Keyed in the pass code, slammed through the door. To find her brother sitting in reception. She stopped walking, looked at him.

'What are you doing here?' she asked.

'Waiting for you,' he said. 'Fuckers let me go. Couldn't hold me.'

She looked at him. He looked like she felt. Dirty, dishevelled. His sweats and trainers filthy.

'What's happened?' he asked.

Marina opened her mouth to tell him, closed it again. She looked round. Checked no one was in earshot.

'Where's your car?'

'Outside. They brought it here. Why?'

She thought. 'Got anything planned for the rest of the night?'

Sandro, his face lined and tired, gave her a suspicious look. 'I have a feelin' the right answer isn't "Goin' home to bed".'

'Dead right,' she said. 'We're going to Wrabness. To get my daughter back.'

111

Amy kept trying to squeeze the trigger, but her hand was shaking too much to complete the action. Dee could see how unhinged she was, so she tried to play for time until the Golem arrived. Kept talking. 'What exactly did you think you were going to achieve?' she said. 'With all this.'

'You know what I was going to achieve,' said Amy. 'Get what was mine. What's owed to me. It's what I deserve.'

'So why haven't you tried to do it before? Why now?'

She lowered the gun slightly, concentrating on her words, focusing her anger. 'I did try. A few times. But it costs money, doesn't it? And when you're a non-person, when you don't exist, you don't have any, do you? Not that you would know.'

Dee said nothing. Her previous life flashed through her mind. She ignored it.

'Who would believe a madwoman? No one. That's who.'

'But a madwoman with a convicted murderer — that'd work . . .' Dee almost smiled at her own words, knowing they would just enrage Amy further.

'Shut up! Shut up! You know that's not true . . . And we could have proved it. Graham and me. That was the plan. That's why he fell out with Michael. Over me. Graham hated what Michael had done to me. Hated it. Oh, he was all for it at first. He was with us. One of us. He helped put the blame on Stuart, get him sent down for the killings. But he hated what Michael had done to me. And then when you came along . . .'

'He left.'

Amy smiled. 'Yes. He hated you as much as he hated Michael. And when Michael wouldn't give him or me any money, we came up with the plan.'

'This plan.'

'Yes. Graham had kept a copy of the will, after all these years. The one my father made just before he died. The one that included Stuart. All we had to do was wait until Stuart was released, have him declared sane, show that he didn't do the killings and him and me could be cut in. Michael wouldn't let that happen, of course. Came after us.'

'And did a pretty good job.'

Amy didn't reply with words. She just growled.

'It was foolproof. Get that psychologist back, the one who said the right things about him at the time. Because she's made quite a name for herself. She's high profile now.' Amy sighed. 'Foolproof. That's what Graham said.' Her eyes became wet.

'How wrong he was.' Dee could sense Amy weakening. When the Golem appeared, that would be the end of it. Then she could join Michael and say hello to a new life. But she couldn't resist one last gloat. 'You failed,' she said. 'Failed.'

'Shut up! Shut up!'

'Failed.'

Amy brought the gun up once more, levelled it. Dee stopped talking, thought she had actually gone too far this time. But then she felt rather than saw movement at her side. A shadow flowed, became corporeal. The Golem appeared.

Dee smiled. Her confidence returned. 'As I said. You failed.'

Amy stared at the two of them.

And laughed.

112

Mickey ran. The other man ran faster. He seemed to know his way around better too, weaving in and out of the container stacks and negotiating on-deck obstacles that Mickey had difficulty seeing until he was on them. Coils of rope. Storage chests. The man jumped and dodged, avoiding them. Or deliberately taking a route that would slow Mickey down.

Mickey began to see where his quarry was headed. The ramp. The pier. Then off and away.

He couldn't let that happen, had to stop him from reaching it.

The figure broke cover, came running out from behind another container stack, heading away from Mickey. Mickey gave chase, jumping over a coil of rope in his path.

The fleeing man looked backwards, checked that Mickey was still with him. Mickey ran harder, gaining on him. The man turned, ducked behind another container stack. Mickey, still running, followed him.

And felt an immediate pain in his chest.

He dropped to the deck, sore and winded. When he opened his eyes, the well-dressed man was standing over him, a length of metal in his hand. Mickey's hand went to his chest. He gave a practice breath. It hurt. A lot.

The man gave a quick look round, then brought the metal bar down once more.

Mickey managed to roll out of the way, letting his shoulder take most of the blow that had been intended for his torso. He felt something crack as he did so. Pain shot down the length of his arm. He tried to pick his arm up, move it. Couldn't.

He was out of it.

He could only watch as the man dropped the bar, looked round quickly to see if any other police officers were in sight. There weren't. He looked down at Mickey again. Smiled.

'Terribly sorry, old chum. Must dash.'

Mickey tried to rise, grab him, stop him from leaving. Felt a web of pain anchor him to the deck, pull him back down again.

He gasped, groaned. Tried to get his two-way radio out of his pocket, tell May what was happening. But it hurt too much. Couldn't even manage that. His arm dropped down again. He sighed. He could only watch as the well-spoken, well-dressed man turned, walked away.

And immediately crashed face forward on to the deck.

Anni emerged from behind a stack of containers swinging a length of wood in her hand. She dropped it, bent over the man, brought his arm sharply round, cuffed him.

'Gotcha,' she said. 'You're nicked, mate.'

'Oh, very good . . .' The man was wriggling, trying to get up. Hurting himself even more in the process, but not stopping. 'Just you wait, bitch . . . Do you know who I am?'

'No sir, I don't,' said Anni. 'But we'll find out soon enough.'

'I own this ship . . . and when I get up . . . I'll take out your fucking eyeballs with my fingers . . .'

'Whatever.'

'Bite your tongue out . . .' He wriggled some more. 'Let . . . me . . . go . . .'

Anni looked over at Mickey. 'Give DI May a call, will you?'

'You are in so much fucking trouble . . .' Fire burned in the man's eyes. An ugly, twisted rage. 'I'll have your fucking jobs . . . I'll take your fucking life . . .'

'That's all well and good, sir,' said Anni, tightening her grip on him. 'Now can you tell us why two police officers have been kidnapped, brought on board and detained against their will?'

The man fell silent. Stopped moving.

'I want my lawyer.'

Damn, thought Anni. The magic words. The custody clock had started ticking. She looked over at Mickey, who was still lying on the ground. 'You OK?'

Mickey tried to sit up. Couldn't. Flopped back down again. Winced from the pain. 'What . . . d'you think?'

'Chuck me your radio.'

It took a great deal of painful effort, but Mickey managed to send his radio sliding along the deck towards Anni. She picked it up and spoke into it without loosening her grip on Michael Sloane.

'DI May, DC Hepburn here. We've apprehended a suspect who's attacked DS Philips. He needs medical attention.'

DI May's voice crackled back. 'Good work, DC Hepburn. We'll get that to him. And I was just about to call you,' he said. 'We've found them. Jessie and Deepak plus Helen Hibbert.'

'They OK?'

'They'll need looking over by the paramedics too. They say it was the Sloanes who did this to them. Michael and Dee Sloane.'

Anni looked at the prone man, who had reacted to the name. 'I think we've got Mr Sloane here.'

'Don't let him get away, DC Hepburn.'

She gave an extra squeeze. He wasn't happy about it. 'He's not going anywhere, don't worry.'

She cut the connection, looked over at Mickey. Smiled. 'We make a good team, don't we?'

Mickey managed to return the smile. 'Yeah . . .'

113

'That it?' Sandro peered through the windscreen. 'Looks like it's falling into the river.'

'Looks like the river's sucking it down,' said Marina.

They had driven along the narrow road Marina had walked two days earlier. She found it hard to believe that it was only two days ago. So much had happened in such a small space of time. She parked in front of the house, turning her lights off as she made the approach. There were two cars there already. One that matched the kind of clunker Sandro would buy; the other a small, expensive sports car.

No police. They had managed to get there first. But they wouldn't be far behind, so every second had to count.

Marina killed the engine, made to get out. Sandro placed a restraining hand on her arm. She looked at him, irritated to be held up. His eyes showed nothing but concern.

'You sure about this? You don't want to wait for your lot to arrive? There's people there already. Might get a bit hairy.'

Marina closed her eyes tight, shook her head. 'No, I can't. Can't wait. Josephina's in there. We can't wait any longer. We have to get her out straight away.'

Sandro nodded. 'Fair enough. I'm coming with you.'

Marina didn't answer. She just wanted to close her eyes, go to sleep. Make it all go away. Have a normal life again. She didn't want to walk into a haunted-looking house to get her daughter back from a psychopath. She felt tears squeezing their way out of the corners of her eyes. Put her fists there to stop them.

'Hey . . .' Sandro made to hug her.

'Don't,' she said, pulling away. 'If you do that, I'll crumble. And if I crumble, I won't want to go in there . . .'

Sandro nodded, moved away from her. 'OK. But don't worry. I've got you, sis. We're good.'

She squeezed his hand. Gave another nod.

They got out of the car. Made their way cautiously but quickly towards the house.

114

'What's so funny?' asked Dee.

Amy shook her head. 'Nothing. Nothing.' She laughed again, as if she had just heard a great joke and was savouring the punchline.

Despite the reassuring presence of the Golem at her side, the laughter was starting to unnerve Dee. 'I said, what's so funny?' she asked again, her voice louder, higher this time.

Amy straightened up. Retrained the gun on Dee. 'You are.'

'Me.'

'Yes. You. You're so sure of yourself, aren't you? Always right. And even if you're not, you've got enough money to convince everyone that you are. *My* money.'

Dee said nothing. Just waited. Let her say her piece, she thought. Then the Golem can deal with her and we can be gone.

'So,' said Amy, circling the gun, looking down the sights, smiling still, 'what d'you think you're going to do now?'

'Me?' said Dee. 'Nothing. Not a thing.' She gestured with her thumb towards the Golem, who had moved close beside her. Almost behind her. 'He is.'

Amy kept the smile on her face, the gun pointed. She looked like she was struggling not to laugh.

Mad bitch, thought Dee. Time to finish this. 'We can't have you around any longer. Making accusations. Planning and plotting against us. Getting in the way . . . We've had enough. Time for it to stop.'

Amy giggled. It infuriated Dee.

'You played a long game this time. And it failed. There's no prize for second place.'

'Oh,' said Amy, 'you're so right. So right.' She moved her attention from Dee to the Golem. Addressed him directly. 'Remember our agreement?' she said, her eyes suddenly unclouded by madness, just vicious, businesslike. 'The money? The shares?'

The Golem nodded.

'Good. Get on with it.'

Dee felt the Golem's hand encircle her throat. She had no time to shout out, to plead for mercy. She had no time to prepare herself for death.

He snapped.

She only had time to die.

115

Marina and Sandro walked towards the house, the mist parting with their footsteps. Whatever front door had once been there had fallen off and was rotting away. Marina stepped over the threshold, stopped. Listened. Heard creaking, groaning. Heard the river water sloshing round the foundations of the house, lapping away at it.

And something else. Faint and muffled. Small screams. Small hands hitting something.

Marina gasped. 'Josie . . .'

She made to run inside the house. Sandro stopped her. Marina glared at him, tried to shake off his grip.

'Wait,' he said, voice a hissed whisper. 'The cars outside, remember? We don't know who's here. Let's go carefully.'

The words didn't penetrate. All she could hear was her daughter's screams. She shook Sandro off and ran into the house.

She found herself in a central hall, huge, tall, a rotting staircase in the centre. She looked round, tried to get her eyes accustomed to the change in darkness. Saw movement, a light coming from a room off to her left. Ran towards it.

And found herself in what must have once been the living room. There was a woman lying on the floor, unmoving.

Standing over her was one of the biggest men she had ever seen. And standing opposite, a naked, bald woman holding a gun.

The woman looked up from the body on the floor, stared at her. Marina took her in. She was like a female version of Frankenstein's monster. A patchwork person. Marina flinched at the sight of her, but didn't stop moving forward.

'Where's my daughter, bitch?' She moved right up to the ruined woman.

The woman looked at her. Smiled. 'Dr Esposito, I presume?'

Marina stopped. Looked at her. 'You're the one, aren't you? You took my daughter . . .'

The woman looked over Marina's shoulder. 'Golem . . .'

Marina felt movement behind her. Smelt something rank, Decomposition and corruption to match the smell of the house itself. She turned. The man mountain was moving towards her. She had time to notice him. His skin was grey. Like a dead person. Filthy, bloodied bandages were hanging off his arms. She saw glistening wounds beneath. He smiled.

And stopped moving. Turned.

'Hey, mate . . .'

Sandro had tapped him on the shoulder. He took advantage of the Golem not moving. Swung a punch at him.

The Golem, eyes full of surprise, tottered, slipped. Sandro followed up with another punch. The Golem went down on one knee, a look of surprise on his face.

Sandro looked at Marina. 'I've got this. Go on.'

Marina turned back to the woman before her. Made her hand into a fist. Put everything she could behind it. All the pain, anguish, heartache of the past few days. And the rage, the silent screams she had wanted to release but had been unable to. Everything. And let it fly.

Her knuckles stung, her arm shook from the reverberation of the impact. She might have done serious damage to her hand, but she didn't care.

The punch had connected with the woman's jaw, spun her head backwards, her body following. She had let go of the gun in her hand, sending it flying across the room, and stumbled to her knees. Marina bent down, picked her up by her chin. There was blood all round her mouth. She made a kind of strangled growl as Marina pulled at her.

'Where . . . is . . . my . . . daughter?'

The woman smiled. Blood glistening on her teeth. 'Feel better for that? Won't help you . . . because it . . . it doesn't matter any more . . .'

Marina pulled back her hand to slap her face but stopped. The woman was staring up at her, madness dancing in her eyes. 'Where is she? Tell me . . .'

The woman laughed. You can't talk to me like that. I'm . . . I'm Dee Sloane . . .'

Marina knew she would get nothing more from the woman. She was enjoying Marina's pain. Instead she turned round, scanned the room, tried to tune out what was before her, listened for sounds of her daughter.

She heard them. Faint but unmistakable. Screams. Pounding. 'Josie . . .'

She dropped the woman who called herself Dee Sloane. Let her crumple to the floor.

116

Sandro was aware of Marina leaving the room. But he didn't let his concentration slip, didn't take his eyes off his opponent. Golem? Was that what the insane woman had called him? Whatever or whoever he was, he was there to be beaten. But it wouldn't be easy.

The Golem looked at him, smiled. Advanced. He looked like he was going to relish the fight. Sandro hated those kinds of opponents. He always just wanted to get it over with. Put the other guy down as hard and as fast as possible. Win. And that was what he planned to do here.

'You not hurt me,' said the Golem. 'I Superman . . .'

Oh God, thought Sandro. Chatty and mental. Just what I need.

He squared up to the man mountain before him. The lack of sleep, the exhaustion of the previous few hours slipped away from him. The adrenalin high he had been on when he stepped into the ring hours ago kicked in once more. He brought his fists up, his system pumping. Felt that familiar bodily engine revving. It always kicked in. Like he was a car, speedy and powerful, one that couldn't wait for the brake to be slipped so he could see how far he could get and how fast he could go.

And something else. Something that was always there. In every fight, in every aspect of every day of his life.

The rage. The familiar rage.

The Golem came towards him. Sandro saw his father's features imprinted on his opponent's face.

'I feel no pain,' said the Golem. 'But you will.'

Sandro was ready.

He swung the first blow.

117

Marina ran. In and out of rooms, trying to make out shapes, objects in the dark, trying to find her daughter. Calling all the time, letting Josephina know she was coming for her. That it was all right. Her mother was here.

'Josie, keep shouting, keep shouting . . .'

She did. Calling for her, pounding too. But the calls, the pounding were starting to weaken.

'Josie . . . Josie . . . keep going, keep going . . .'

Marina ran into a room at the back of the house. The sound, the smell of the river was strong in there. She could hear it lapping at the foundations, curling underneath her, the wood beneath the floorboards creaking as it did so.

'Josie . . .'

The pounding had been coming from this room. Marina listened, tried to hear it. Couldn't.

'Josie . . . I'm here, Mummy's here . . . Tell me, tell me where you are . . .'

A thump. Small. Weak.

Marina looked round, scanned the room, eyes now accustomed to the darkness. Checking the rotting furniture, looking for cupboards, anything.

'Again, darling, do it again . . .'

Another thump, even weaker this time.

Another desperate scan of the room. The walls held nothing. Marina looked down, scanned the floor.

And then she saw it.

The trapdoor.

She knelt down, found the metal ring, recessed in the wood. Pulled. It wouldn't budge. The wood damp and warped.

She pulled harder. Nothing.

Marina felt tears well up within her. Anger, rage and sorrow all built to an emotional crescendo. She wasn't going to let this happen, she wasn't . . .

She pulled again. Put everything she had behind it, every last piece of herself. If she never moved again, it would be worth it to get the trapdoor opened.

It moved. A small amount, but definite movement.

Encouraged, she pulled again, harder this time.

More movement.

She pulled harder, screaming at the top of her lungs.

The trapdoor gave, opened fully.

Marina fell backwards as it did so, letting the heavy wood drop to the floor, the noise echoing round the house, reverberating away to nothing. She got quickly to her knees, looked down into dark space.

And there was her daughter.

Pushed up against the top of the steps, her eyes wide with terror, soaking wet. Marina leaned in and Josie came straight into her arms.

'It's OK, it's OK, Mummy's here now . . .'

She stood up, holding her daughter close to her, tighter than she ever had before, never wanting to let go. Josephina did the same, clinging on for her life. She smoothed her daughter's matted hair away from her face, wet from the cellar, from tears. She could barely see her through her own tears. There were times she had doubted that she would ever see her again, ever feel her, hear her. But there she was.

'It's OK, Mummy's here, I've got you, don't worry . . .' The words came out in a cascade of relief. She rocked her daughter backwards and forwards as she spoke.

'Have they hurt you, darling, have they . . .'

Muffled against her, Marina felt Josephina shake her head.

'I wanted you, Mummy . . .'

'I know you did, darling, and I wanted you too.' She clutched her tighter. 'I'm here now. And I won't let anyone take you away again. Ever.'

Josephina didn't move. Just clung on to her.

Marina dug into her pocket, brought out the tattered, dirty soft toy. 'Look,' she said. 'Lady. I kept her for you . . .'

Josephina took it, hugged it to herself.

'Ah, how sweet.'

Marina turned. Amy had entered the room. Still naked, face a bloodied mask.

And holding the gun.

118

Sandro's blow connected. The Golem reeled backwards.

'Gotcha,' said Sandro, huffing out breaths.

The Golem quickly recovered, looked back at him. Smiled again.

'You can't hurt me,' he said. 'You can't kill me.'

Sandro moved round the floor, fists at the ready. Trying to find the right next move, the right combination of blows, the best attack. 'Is that so? You look like you're in a bit of a state to me. Like some other fella's already had a go at you.'

The Golem moved too. Not as light or nimble as Sandro, not a distance fighter like him, just used to relying on his size and the power that came with it for his advantage.

'Not a state.' Another laugh. 'Invulnerable. Invincible. Unbeatable.'

'Yeah, right, pal.'

Sandro had to admit that there was something behind those words. The dead woman on the floor was testament to that. And the size of him . . . Sandro had fought some big guys before. And they had been hard fights. The big fellas could throw a punch and get behind it. Make it hurt. He'd had to use every trick he knew just to avoid a beating. And they hadn't been as big as this one.

He had to win this fight. Because if he didn't, he would be dead.

The Golem made a move. Faster than Sandro would have expected. He just had time to duck out of the way as the big man's fist came towards him.

He kept the momentum going, dodged round the side of his opponent, let loose a couple of punches to his ribs. His fingers hurt, it was like hitting a wall, but when he looked at where he had made contact, he noticed blood starting to seep through the other man's T-shirt.

Result, thought Sandro. Like his arms, he's got a wound there. A target. Something to aim for.

He swung again. But the Golem was waiting for him. He brought his arm backwards, smacked Sandro in the face, sent him flying. He stumbled backwards, tripped over the body lying on the floor, crashing into the rotted curtain hanging over a window. He tried to grab hold of it to stop his fall, but went down with it in his hands, the curtain pole following.

The Golem, again faster than Sandro would have expected, was on him.

Sandro was trying to wriggle free from the curtain as the Golem brought back his booted foot ready for a kick that would have shattered Sandro's ribs and taken out at least one of his kidneys. Sandro thought fast. Grabbed the foot as it came towards him. Twisted. Hard.

He heard the terminal creak and snap as cartilage and bone were forced in directions never intended for them. The Golem dropped to one knee. But his features registered no pain. In fact it just seemed to make him angrier.

'You think that would hurt me? I told you. You cannot hurt me.'

Sandro was momentarily shocked into inactivity. He had expected his move to work. Expected the big man to collapse in agony. Instead, the Golem was back on his feet, his leg twisted, pulling back his fist, readying it to fly.

Sandro turned, scrambled along the floor on his hands and knees to get out of the way. He grabbed the fallen curtain pole to help lever himself to his feet, but the pole snapped in two. He had just got to his feet when the Golem came up behind him, smashed him in the back.

The blow caught him between the shoulder blades, knocked the air from him. He went down again.

The Golem moved in. Turned him over. Knelt over him.

'You put up a good fight. And I respect that. But now, you die.'

Sandro felt the Golem's fingers tighten around his throat. Knew he had to do something. Thought fast. He knew the Golem didn't respond to pain, so there was no point in trying to hurt him. Instead he had to do something physically incapacitating.

The Golem's fingers were on his neck. Sandro grabbed a thumb with each hand. Bent them back as far as he could. The Golem released his grip slightly, tried to fight him off. Sandro kept on pulling. Felt them snap.

The Golem looked confused, wondering why his hands didn't have the same grip, why he couldn't squeeze hard any more. He tried. But it was no use. Without his thumbs, he couldn't snap anyone's neck.

Sandro knew he couldn't rest, that his opponent was still dangerous. He felt around on the floor, found the broken curtain pole. Yes. That would do.

With the Golem still on top of him, he gripped the pole in his left hand, brought it into the Golem's side, right into the bleeding wound he had discovered earlier.

The Golem didn't flinch. So Sandro did it again. And again.

The third time he left it there and pushed. Hard as he could. Something changed in the Golem's eyes. A light dimming.

Sandro stared into his opponent's face. Saw not the Golem, but his own father. Bearing down on him, hurting him. Ruining him. He had never been able to fight back when he was younger. Used to lie awake at nights planning all the things he was going to do to get even. Never having the nerve to put any of them into practice. Just letting the rage build inside him. Taking it out on anyone else, finding surrogates for his anger.

And here he was again.

Sandro let go of the pole, flattened out both of his hands and smacked the Golem over the ears.

It was one of the most dangerous moves he could make. Not even allowed in the bare-knuckle ring. The mildest thing the blow could do was disorientate, hit an opponent's centre of balance. It could also burst the eardrums. But the worst thing, if enough force was applied, was unconsciousness and even brain damage.

And Sandro hoped he had applied enough force.

He saw his father disappear, saw the Golem once more.

He looked into the Golem's eyes again. The light was going out. Blood began to trickle out of his ears. His mouth went slack.

And he collapsed on top of Sandro.

'Brilliant . . .' Sandro could barely breathe.

He managed to push himself out from under, let the Golem's broken body slump to the floor. He climbed slowly to his feet. Legs unsteady, head and body sore. Breathing ragged.

But alive.

119

'And it was all going so well . . .' Amy held the gun on Marina and Josephina. Her bloodied features filled with regret.

'So well?' said Marina, clutching her daughter tightly to her chest.

'Yes. Everything was planned, everything was ready.'

'Everything planned? You killed . . . killed someone I loved. You tried to kill everyone I love.'

'No, not me. Michael Sloane. He did that. I'm not responsible for what happened to your family.'

'Michael Sloane did that?' Marina clearly didn't believe her.

'Graham and I were going to approach you. Ask you to help us with Stuart. We were going to do it properly, formally. But Michael found out. We didn't plan it well enough. He found out we were going to approach you when you were in that cottage in Aldeburgh. So he got there before us. Fire-bombed the place. Only I managed to get you and your daughter out of there. And then . . . we had to improvise.'

'I don't believe you.'

Amy sighed. 'I don't care.'

'You blame Michael Sloane for everything.'

Her eyes flashed. 'And why do you think that is?'

'You used me. You kidnapped my daughter.'

'I panicked. After the blast. Had to do something. I'd come to speak to you, ask you nicely, but then there was the blast. And Michael was there. You were unconscious, I pulled you out of its range so he couldn't grab you, throw you back in. Then the car went up. And the only thing I could do was take your daughter. And run.'

'But . . . you tortured us — me and my daughter . . . you enjoyed it.'

'So melodramatic. We had to see that you weren't being followed, hadn't told anyone. So we set a test for you. In the bar in Southend. Told you which motel to sleep at. I even came into the hospital, put the book of maps and the phone in your bag.'

'You were spying on me.'

'We already had the equipment. The Sloanes knew what we were up to. Were trying to stop it. Even if it meant killing us. So we were monitoring their calls, checking that they weren't getting too near us.' She sighed. Readjusted the gun. 'Still, it doesn't matter. Not now. Not any more.'

Marina stared at her, unable to move.

Amy's finger tightened on the trigger.

There was nowhere for Marina to run, nowhere she could hide that would take her out of range of the gun. And she couldn't make a grab for it, not with Josephina in her arms. As she closed her eyes to accept was about to happen to her, Sandro stepped out of the shadows and came up silently behind Amy.

He reached round, grabbed the hand that was holding the gun, hooked his other arm round her neck.

Marina put Josephina down. The girl didn't wanted to be parted from her mother, complained. 'Just for a second, darling. Mummy's got something to do.'

Josephina did as she was told.

Marina stepped forward. Sandro twisted Amy's hand, making her drop the gun. His other arm gripped her even tighter round the neck.

'What do we do with her?' he asked.

'Franks should be here soon. We'll leave her for him.'

Amy squirmed and wriggled against Sandro's grip. Marina stared at her.

'I'm a mother. A very angry mother. You stole my daughter. You tried to kill me and my family. You killed someone I loved.'

'Not me,' said Amy, gasping and struggling. 'Michael . . .'

'But you stole my daughter.'

Amy managed to get free of Sandro's grip. She looked to the door, thinking of making a run for it, but Marina and Sandro were blocking her way. Instead she backed away from them, tripped and lost her footing.

Marina put out an arm to catch her but missed. Amy fell backwards through the trapdoor into the water below. She tried to reach the side, pull herself out, but Marina stood over her. Looked down at her.

Then slammed the trapdoor shut.

120

'You can't leave her like that,' said Sandro.

'Why not?'

'Because she'll die. You'll kill her.'

Hammering came from the trapdoor behind them. Marina seemed to be ignoring it. Sandro couldn't.

Marina shrugged, picked up Josephina once more. 'So?'

Sandro looked from the trapdoor to his sister. 'You'll have the law down on you. You'll be done for murder. Is that what you want for your daughter? A criminal for a mother? You're not your father's daughter, Marina. You're better than that.'

Something changed in Marina's features. The anger, the rage drained out of her. She sighed. 'I'm too tired to open it. I'm taking my daughter home. You do it if you want to.' She turned and left the room.

Sandro stared at the trapdoor.

121

Dawn was breaking. The room was getting lighter. Phil Brennan opened his eyes. It took him a few seconds to orientate himself, remember where he was. Hospital. Then he remembered what had happened. And his heart became heavy as lead.

He tried to move his arms, his legs. Flex them, test that they still worked. They did.

His door opened. Light from the corridor flooded in, making silhouettes of the figures in the doorway.

He squinted at them, wondered who it was.

Then realised.

Marina was walking towards the bed, their daughter in her arms. The lead in his heart began to dissipate. He smiled. Marina came nearer. She looked terrible. Hair all over the place, clothing dirtied and torn. Josephina the same.

But to Phil, they had never looked more beautiful.

Marina sat on the side of the bed. Leaned in, stroked his face. Josephina hugged him.

'Hey,' Marina said.

'Hey yourself.'

Up close, Marina looked like she was on the verge of breaking down. He placed his wired and tubed hand on top of hers.

'We're here,' she said. 'Sorry it took so long . . .'

Then the tears started.

From all three of them.

EPILOGUE: ASCENSION

122

There was Don, in uniform. Alone. Young, unbending, standing stiffly for the camera, unsmiling for fear of not being taken seriously. A man on a mission, with something to prove.

Then out of uniform, with his mates. All wearing the same ensemble of wide-lapelled jackets in shades of brown or oversized checks, huge-collared shirts and kipper ties, sporting the same overlong hair and Elvis sideburns, showing the same cocky smiles and glinting eyes. Thief takers and dandies, gods among men. Plenty of laughter at that.

Then him and Eileen. In a garden, at a barbecue, eating chicken legs, drinking beer. Looking happy. With everything ahead of them.

Eileen choked at that one. Recovered quickly.

Then the two of them with Phil as a small child. Hard to decide which of them looked happiest.

Then others, all variations on the same theme, all showing different aspects of the same man. Admirable aspects, strong, lovable. Over and over in a continuous loop.

A celebration of Don Brennan. His life in pictures.

And words. All around the room, sitting at tables, standing at the bar, stories were being told and retold, anecdotes shared. People laughing together, fighting off the darkness.

Marina looked round. Her heart heavy with grief but lightened by the fact that she had known the man, that he had been an important part of her life.

The service had been at the crematorium. Humanist. The speaker had come to see them days ago, asked about Don, his character, his likes and dislikes, any stories they wanted her to tell, any they wanted to avoid. Marina and Phil had done most of the talking, Eileen still too emotional.

The speaker had been excellent. Others had been asked to contribute. One of Don's old colleagues had got up to say something. A big ex-copper, broken-nosed and red-faced, heavier than when he was in the job but still carrying himself with authority, had made his way to the podium, started to tell an anecdote about Don, stumbled over his words, burst into tears. Had to be led away.

Then it was Phil's turn.

Marina had told him he didn't have to do it if he didn't want to. If he didn't feel up to it. Or if he needed help getting to the lectern and back, she would assist. He refused all offers. He felt it was something he had to do alone and unaided.

It was over a week since Easter, since she had walked into his hospital room and held him and held him and held him. And never wanted to let him go.

He had been discharged from the hospital and was at home convalescing, on sick leave from work. His injuries hadn't been as severe as had first been thought. He would be up and about, walking more or less unaided, in a few days. He had turned down the offer of a wheelchair and only reluctantly accepted a crutch. He was determined to get better. And he had been determined to speak at Don's funeral.

He had squeezed Marina's hand before getting up and she had looked into his eyes. Haunted and damaged, almost mirrors of her own. But eyes she loved. Eyes she never tired of looking into, where she found everything she hoped for being returned to her.

He had smiled, got slowly to his feet and, the crutch in his left hand, made his way to the lectern.

He spoke without notes. From his heart, his soul. He told everyone there that, in case they didn't know, he had been adopted by Don and Eileen. He wasn't their biological son. And they weren't his biological parents. They were more than that. So much more.

He had gone on to talk of what Don had meant to him. How he owed his career, his attitude, everything he had to him. And how he would miss him. God, how he would miss him.

There was more. But Marina couldn't remember it. She had been crying too much.

When he had finished, Phil had walked back to her side. Alone. Unaided.

And in that moment, she knew everything was going to be all right.

123

Marina had barely let Josephina out of her sight. Even in the hospital when they wanted to check her over she had insisted on being with her. She wouldn't be parted for one second. And Josephina, clinging to her, felt exactly that same way.

Once they had returned home, there had been a week of sleepless nights. Josephina not wanting to close her eyes in case the scary woman was there. Marina had done everything she could to reassure the child, and she had gradually started to sleep. But the nights then became punctuated by nightmares, with Josephina waking up crying and screaming. They had moved her bed into their bedroom to have her near to them. Eventually they had just let her into their bed.

She hadn't let go of Lady. Marina had tried to take the toy off her, wash it at least, but Josephina wouldn't let her. So there it had stayed. Filthy dirty, ragged, but loved.

And that was OK.

One night after getting Josephina into bed, Marina and Phil had sat in their living room, trying to lead normal lives once more. Pretend they were ordinary again. Sharing a bottle of wine.

'Only to be expected,' Phil had said, 'after what she's been through.'

'Oh, absolutely,' Marina had replied.

'Is she going to be . . . you know. Scarred by this for life.'

Marina had shrugged. 'I hope not. You and I had much more traumatic childhoods and we did all right.'

'We were lucky, though,' said Phil. 'We found ways out.'

'True. We'll just have to make sure that Josephina doesn't need luck. Children are resilient and they can forget things. But trauma like this can do massive damage. Massive. Even if she buries it deep in her subconscious, under all the other layers of memory she'll acquire. There'll be some trace memory of it, some emotional unease.'

'Should we be worried about that?'

'I don't know. We'll have to wait and see. All we can do is be there for her. Make her feel safe. Loved. Yes, take her to a specialist if we need to, if things get worse and she needs professional help. But for now, let's just see how it goes. Let's help her to get over it.'

Phil said nothing.

'We're here,' said Marina. 'We're alive. That's the main thing. If we're alive there's always hope.'

'And human beings forget things,' said Phil. 'Memories fade. Pain fades. It's how we can carry on. All of us.'

She looked across at him. Wondered if the words hadn't just been about their daughter but his father as well.

They had sat in silence.

124

In the upstairs room of the King's Head, amidst the noise of the mourners and celebrants, with Don's pictures on the wall behind them, Phil and Marina stood like a small island. The calm at the eye of the storm.

Franks looked over at them, nodded. But didn't come any closer. Marina wasn't surprised.

Franks had been furious with Marina for what she had done that night in Wrabness. He had called her into his office the next day, didn't invite her to sit. He clearly wanted to stay sitting himself but was too angry so stood up, faced her over the desk top.

'What the bloody hell did you think you were playing at? That was a police operation and you are one of this team. You were given a direct instruction and you ignored it.'

Marina stood up to him. 'And it was a good job I did. If I'd waited for you to get there, my daughter might well have been dead.'

Franks's mouth had twisted but he hadn't given her a reply. 'We were right behind you. And not only did you interfere with a police operation, you left a murder scene. One dead, two seriously injured.'

'I had my daughter to take care of. And as you said, you and the team were on the way.'

Franks didn't seem to have been spoken to like this before. He didn't know quite how to respond. Anger and sympathy vied for prominence in his features. He sighed. 'Yes. I understand. I realise you were under a lot of strain, with what you've had to go through in the last few days. But it doesn't alter the fact that you're part of this team. And there's a chain of command. This is the Major Incident Squad, not some cowboy outfit. If you can't understand that and be part of it, then perhaps it's best you're not here.'

'Fine,' she said.

'What?' He stopped talking, stared at her, surprised at her answer. 'You mean that?'

'Yes, I do. I've been thinking about it a lot in the last couple of days. Maybe it's time I had a change.'

Franks fell silent for a few seconds, then nodded. 'Right. Spend some time at home. With your daughter.'

'Yes. And go back into private practice. Or consultancy. Or academia. Somewhere where my talents will be more appreciated.'

Franks reddened, tried to say something consoling, but she was no longer listening.

And that had been the end of that.

125

Sandro had visited Marina and Phil a few nights earlier. Gone to their home and been welcomed in. Well that makes a change, he had thought. Hell of a change. He had even sat with Phil, drank a beer. Talked. He wasn't a bad bloke, Sandro had decided. For a copper.

But when Marina pulled him aside into the kitchen to have a word in private, he knew what she was about to say.

'You OK?' he asked.

She nodded. 'Well as can be expected. You?'

'Yeah.' He sighed. Ran his hand over his head. 'Mental.'

'I'm sorry,' Marina said.

Sandro nodded. He knew what she was talking about.

'I shouldn't have left you to make that choice. Open the trapdoor or not. It should never have happened.'

Sandro shrugged, aimed for nonchalance. Missed. 'I couldn't leave her,' he said. 'Just walk out of that house and leave her to die.' He sighed. 'I couldn't.'

Marina nodded.

'It was a crazy night.' Sandro thought for a while, head down. Then looked up, directly at Marina. 'I've been thinkin' about this, though. A lot. What happened with the Golem, that was a fight, yeah? Proper kill-or-be-killed fight.'

'What you did was self-defence.'

'Yeah. But leaving that madwoman there, even after everything she'd done, that would have made you just as bad. And me.'

'I've been thinking about Mum again,' said Marina. 'What she did for us. A mother will do anything, Sandro, anything — everything — to protect her children. Our mother put herself, her own body, in the way of blows meant for us. All I could see was Josephina. All I wanted to do was . . . neutralise the threat to her as best I could.'

'And I let her out.'

'She was no threat then. Not really. But you were the one with compassion.'

'Yeah.' He nodded. 'Maybe I don't take after Dad after all.'

'Maybe you don't.'

He smiled. 'Maybe there's hope for me yet.'

Marina returned the smile. 'Maybe.'

They fell into a resigned silence. Still, like a ceasefire after a war.

'He's not a bad bloke either,' said Sandro, gesturing to the living room. 'For a copper.'

'What about your other trouble?' said Marina. 'The money you owed?'

A smile crept across Sandro's features. He kept his eyes averted from his sister. 'Fine. Everything's fine there. No worries.'

'Sandro . . .'

'It's fine, I said. Fine.'

Marina knew she would get nothing more from him, let it drop. 'Look after yourself. You know where I am if you need me.'

He knew.

'And Sandro . . . thank you. Really. Thank you. I couldn't have . . .'

He hugged her. They didn't speak.

Both choked.

126

'You ready to go?' said Mickey.

Anni picked up her glass. 'Just finish this.'

'If we don't get out now, we'll be here all night.' He looked round the room. Officers and ex-officers were settling in for the duration. Lubricated by alcohol and camaraderie, old war stories were being trotted out again, anecdotes given a polish and put on display once more.

She looked up at him. Smiled.

He loved that smile. Hoped he never tired of seeing it. Or that she never tired of directing it at him.

They had spent the last few days dealing with the paperwork fallout from the case. Wrapping it up as tight as they could for the CPS. Michael Sloane was looking at serious prison time. He had his allies, his supporters, all wealthy, putting money before morality. And he could afford the best legal defence, but even with all that, it was looking like he would go down for a long time. There was too much against him. Mickey and Anni doubted he would have as many allies if that happened.

Mickey had heard that Sloane had contemplated entering a plea of insanity. If he did that, he might end up with no prison time but he would probably be looking at life in a secure hospital. And he would probably lose access to his fortune. Either way, he would die behind bars.

His sister was definitely insane. Her fate would be relatively straightforward.

'And the half-brother gets the lot,' Anni had said.

'Could be,' Mickey had replied. 'He'd better get himself some good advisers, though. Otherwise he'll be picked dry.'

The Golem, as they had found out he was called, had been taken to hospital. A combination of severe wounds and a lethal drug cocktail had left him near death. They sincerely hoped he pulled through. There were a lot of murders to pin on him.

'Who is he?' asked Anni.

Mickey had shrugged. 'Just some East European hired muscle. Nobody special.'

And that had been that. Apart from a call Mickey had received from Jessie James.

'How are you?' he had asked.

'Oh, you know,' she had replied. 'Arm's in a cast, itches like hell. But other than that, not too bad.'

'Snap,' Mickey had said. 'That iron bar to the shoulder left me with my arm strapped up.'

'Twins,' she said.

'How's everything there?'

'OK.' Her voice guarded when she said it. 'Having a bit of time off. Taking long walks along the beach at Aldeburgh. Doing a lot of thinking.'

'Yeah,' said Mickey. 'Near-death experiences do that to people.'

'You sound like you know what you're talking about.'

He gave a small laugh. 'Dangerous profession, this.'

'Yeah.' She told him about Helen Hibbert, the other woman in the container. 'Put in a claim against the police. Suing for negligence, mental anguish and anything else this ambulance chaser she's employed can think of.'

Mickey laughed. 'Good luck to her.' He paused. Felt there was something she wanted to say but wasn't able to. 'So you're OK.'

'Yeah. I've . . . got a lot of decisions to make. Trying to stay off the booze.'

'Well I hope you make the right ones.'

'Me too. I think I know what I don't want. It's just finding out what I do want that's the hard bit.'

Anni put her glass down, bringing Mickey out of his reverie.

'You ready?' he said.

'Yeah.'

'Let's go home, then.'

127

Talking. Talking. Always talking. That was what Stuart's life seemed to have become. People wanting to talk to him. All the time. On and on and on. Never leaving him alone. And he was tired of it.

At least they had all gone, left him alone for now. In his room. In silence. That was something.

He sat back in his easy chair. Tried to relax.

The room was small. He liked that. But comfortable. Relaxing. And that was good too.

He closed his eyes. Tried to think. Put everything together. Make a timeline.

The police had let him go. He hadn't done anything wrong, they said. But they did think he needed someone to look after him. So he had been placed in a special hostel. Sheltered accommodation, they said it was called. For people with learning difficulties. He hadn't spoken to the others yet, but they looked friendly enough.

But for now he just wanted to spend some time on his own. In his own head.

They said he was going to be rich. And that was nice. Rich was nice. They sent him a solicitor. He seemed very pleased to see Stuart. Told him Jack Sloane's final will had been verified and he could see no reason why he shouldn't get his share of the Sloane money. He was also in line for a lot of compensation. Said that he could be Stuart's new best friend. But his probation worker had told him to be careful. Not to sign anything without checking with her first. So he would. Definitely.

He opened his eyes, got up. Crossed to the window, looked out. He smiled. Saw the same things he had seen from his prison cell. Birds. Trees. The sky. Other people, but far away. That was good. Reassuring.

And he was sleeping better too. No more nightmares about being trapped inside his body. At least not yet. Some about the last few days. Of being stuck with Amy/Dee again. Of having to hold a gun to Josephina's head. Horrible things. But nothing too bad. Nothing about his childhood again. Or his body. Just . . . nothing. And nothing was better than something when the something had been horrible.

He turned from the window, sat back down again.

Josephina. She was a lovely girl. Really lovely. And he was so happy she had gone back home and was with her mother again. He had spoken to her mother, asked her if he could come and see Josephina. Maybe take her out, play with her. Her mother said she didn't think that was a good idea. She didn't want anyone or anything that would remind the little girl of what she had been through. Stuart had understood. It had made him sad. But if it helped Josephina, that was OK. That was fine. It was what being an adult was all about.

He closed his eyes once more. He thought there were things he should probably be doing but couldn't remember any. People looked after him. Helped him. It was strange living here, but he would get used to it.

He smiled.

He didn't have to do anything. All he had to do was wait.

128

Phil had to sit down. His legs were aching. Marina got him a drink. Non-alcoholic. The party continued all around them. He watched. She studied him.

Already the bruises were beginning to fade. The cuts and abrasions starting to heal. There wasn't anything on his face that was expected to leave a lasting scar. The stitches along his hairline and over his scalp were still vivid-looking and would be for some time. But his hair was starting to grow back and the stitches would dissolve away eventually. There would be a few lines, a few scars, but his hair would mostly hide those. Most importantly, they didn't think there would be any long-term damage.

He had been lucky, she thought. Very lucky. She looked over at Eileen. Felt a pang of guilt at how lucky.

Mickey came towards them, Anni not far behind.

'How you feeling, boss?' asked Mickey.

Phil managed a smile. 'Not too bad. I'll be well again soon. And back at work.'

Mickey smiled. 'Don't make it too soon, yeah?'

Phil laughed. It seemed to quickly exhaust him.

Anni appeared alongside Mickey. Stood close to him.

'We're off now,' she said.

'Going anywhere nice?' asked Marina.

'Just . . .' Mickey searched for the right words. 'Early start tomorrow. Could do without a late one.'

'Well I'm not in charge at the moment,' said Phil, 'so I can't tell you what to do.'

Anni smiled. 'Won't be too long, though. The old team back together again.' She looked between Phil and Marina.

Phil nodded. 'Something like that,' he said.

Mickey tried to shake hands, but the cast on his arm made it difficult. Anni kissed cheeks.

'It was a great send-off,' said Anni. 'Don would've been proud.'

Phil nodded, said nothing.

Mickey and Anni moved away. Phil and Marina watched them go.

'Do you think they're . . . ?' Phil frowned.

'If they're not, it's about time they did.'

They both managed a laugh, then fell into silence. Eventually Phil shook his head, sighed. Marina turned to him.

'You OK?'

He nodded. 'Yeah. I was just . . . that speech. About Don. That I made. Was it all right?'

'It was wonderful. You said everything you should have said. Incredibly moving.'

'Good.' But Phil didn't look convinced. 'It just felt . . . like there was more to say.'

'There's always more to say.'

'No, but . . . you know what it's been like recently. Everything that's gone on. Before all this. Family stuff. My . . . biological parents. All that.'

Marina said nothing. She knew.

'Well it's just . . . I don't know. It's like . . . we'd just bonded. Recently. Properly. Don and me. Fully acknowledged father and son. And now . . . he's gone.'

'At least you had that. Some sons never even get that much.'

He nodded. 'Suppose you're right.'

She said nothing.

'Enjoy every sandwich,' he said.

'What?'

'Something Warren Zevon said. Just before he died of cancer. He was asked if he'd learned anything about life. Enjoy every sandwich, he said. Because one day it'll be your last.'

Marina just stared into her drink. 'Maybe it's time we went home too.'

Phil looked round. Don's old friends were fully engaged in their war stories. Even Eileen was talking to friends. The party had moved on from him and Marina. 'Yeah,' he said. 'Let's.'

They left the pub and walked down the street arm in arm.

THE END

THE JOFFE BOOKS STORY

We began in 2014 when Jasper agreed to publish his mum's much-rejected romance novel and it became a bestseller.

Since then we've grown into the largest independent publisher in the UK. We're extremely proud to publish some of the very best writers in the world, including Joy Ellis, Faith Martin, Caro Ramsay, Helen Forrester, Simon Brett and Robert Goddard. Everyone at Joffe Books loves reading and we never forget that it all begins with the magic of an author telling a story.

We are proud to publish talented first-time authors, as well as established writers whose books we love introducing to a new generation of readers.

We won Trade Publisher of the Year at the Independent Publishing Awards in 2023 and Best Publisher Award in 2024 at the People's Book Prize. We have been shortlisted for Independent Publisher of the Year at the British Book Awards for the last five years, and were shortlisted for the Diversity and Inclusivity Award at the 2022 Independent Publishing Awards. In 2023 we were shortlisted for Publisher of the Year at the RNA Industry Awards, and in 2024 we were shortlisted at the CWA Daggers for the Best Crime and Mystery Publisher.

We built this company with your help, and we love to hear from you, so please email us about absolutely anything bookish at feedback@joffebooks.com.

If you want to receive free books every Friday and hear about all our new releases, join our mailing list here: www.joffebooks.com/freebooks.

And when you tell your friends about us, just remember: it's pronounced Joffe as in coffee or toffee!

Printed in Dunstable, United Kingdom

66641979R00256